A LITTLE LOWER THAN THE ANGELS

a novel

by

Marty Gallanter

Christine Mrazovich and John P. Rutledge, Editors

Dedication

in memory of

Rabbi Oscar Groner, teacher and friend.

THIRD EDITION
2004

ISBN 1-929429-51-7

THIS LITERARY WORK WAS CREATED IN THE UNITED STATES OF AMERICA, IS COPYRIGHT © 1999, 2002 BY MARTY GALLANTER (DEAD END STREET, LLC, EXCLUSIVE LICENSEE) AND IS REGISTERED WITH THE UNITED STATES COPYRIGHT OFFICE. ALL RIGHTS RESERVED. ALL COVER ART WAS CREATED BY HOLLY SMITH AND IS COPYRIGHT © 2002 BY DEAD END STREET, LLC. THIS WORK HAS BEEN FORMATTED BY DEAD END STREET® WITH THE AUTHOR'S EXPRESS PERMISSION.

THIS LITERARY WORK IS ENTIRELY FICTION. NO SIMILARITY TO ACTUAL PERSONS, LIVING OR DEAD, IS INTENDED OR SHOULD BE INFERRED, UNLESS SUCH PERSON(S) IS/ARE EXPRESSLY IDENTIFIED BY NAME. NO ONE IS INTENTIONALLY DEFAMED OR EXPLOITED IN THIS WORK IN VIOLATION OF ANY RIGHT OF PUBLICITY LAW. LIKEWISE, NO INTELLECTUAL PROPERTY RIGHT OF ANY PARTY WAS INTENTIONALY VIOLATED IN THIS WORK. THE AUTHOR AND PUBLISHER ARE WILLING TO CONSIDER AMENDING THIS TEXT TO ERADICATE ANY UNLAWFUL LANGUAGE, DESCRIPTION OR CONTENT.

ALL RIGHTS RESERVED. NO PART OF THIS LITERARY WORK (AND/OR ANY ACCOMPANYING ARTWORK) MAY BE REPRODUCED IN ANY MANNER WITHOUT THE EXPRESS, WRITTEN CONSENT OF DEAD END STREET, LLC (EXCEPT IN THE CASE OF BRIEF QUOTATIONS EMBODIED IN CRITICAL ARTICLES AND REVIEWS). FOR INFORMATION OR CONSENT, PLEASE CONTACT US THROUGH DEADENDSTREET.COM.

DEAD END STREET® is a registered service mark of Dead End Street, LLC. An intent-to-use trademark application for A LITTLE LOWER THAN THE ANGELS™ is pending with the United States Patent & Trademark Office.

For you have made him a little lower than the angels
and crowned him with glory and honor.

Psalm 8 of the Holy Scriptures

CHAPTER ONE

In this place there is no need for the illusion of power, no need for the indulgence of vast, empty spaces that lesser corporations create as temples to the concept of an imagined self-importance. Not here, where illusions are worse than unnecessary. They denigrate the real power. Here decisions are measured by the proportions of history, not by the rise and fall of stock prices, or by polls, focus groups or consumer surveys. What they do in this room can always, and often does, impact hundreds of millions and direct the path of civilizations. When one considers the magnitude of the might that gathers within its walls, this is a very small room.

In its center rests a fourteen-foot, deep mahogany conference table, surface waxed to a flawless finish more reflective than even the smoked mirror behind the room's corner bar. A half-dozen chairs are neatly set around it, three on each side, large and red-leather, like those in the best London men's clubs, with stiff, carved wooden legs buried into deep pile, earth-tone carpet. Before each chair lies a fresh, green blotter, fulfilling its mission to protect the surface from fingerprints or lines traced to a carelessly used ballpoint. A Tiffany-shaded lamp guards each spot, projecting a gentle ring of light onto the green blotters.

There is a seventh chair, taller, wider, more imposing than its mates, placed at the head of the table – set back because that's the way its exclusive occupant likes it. He has no need to lean on the shined surface, and insists on the extra space to stretch his legs. No blotter or lamp decorates the spot in front of his chair. For this is the Chairman's place. And the Chairman doesn't take notes, ever.

When the Chairman enters, the room is still empty and dark,

protected from the sun by tapestry-like curtains. As usual, he is the first to arrive for the meeting. He enjoys a few minutes alone in the understated, mighty room before the others arrive. It is his time to think and ponder, completely alone, on the problems they are about to discuss, and the actions they might take.

The rest of the Management Team knows the Chairman's solitary nature. Out of respect, they always arrive for a meeting with him exactly at the scheduled time – never late, never early. They would rather stand in the hallway if necessary and wait for the ancient but accurate grandfather clock to reach the appointed hour than disturb the Chairman's moment of introspection.

And on this day in particular, he needs some time alone. He appears unusually tired. His eyes stare out black and angry from what are normally gentle, warm circles. His starched white shirt is limp with sweat and the jacket of the high-fashioned, hand-tailored gray pinstripe is less than carefully draped over his chair. He brushes the fabric thoughtlessly as though his hand will cause the wrinkles to flee, and sits down, falling into the soft, loving arms of the familiar red leather. The Chairman sighs, filling the room's corners with the sound of his pain.

If this was a regular day, he would have opened the heavy, dark curtains himself. He enjoys the act of bathing the room in light, enjoys it so much, in fact, that the maintenance crew intentionally close the curtains to allow him the pleasure. On a regular day, for a normal gathering, he would stand for a while in front of the glass wall and rest his eyes on the green, rolling hills that seem to reach out forever. Not today, though. Today he relishes the very lack of light, retreating inward and using the quiet, dark room to envelop and shield him for a moment from the weight of the day's concerns.

The Tiffany lamps glow gently, broadcasting circles of warm incandescent light softly onto the six empty places. The bright colors, pieced together by the shades' artist become an eternal jigsaw puzzle, projecting silently against the ceiling, offering an alternative to the friendly, yet unfriendly, darkness of the room. The Chairman seems oblivious to his environment.

He leaves his trance for a moment and notices that all six places are lit. The full Management Team will not be meeting today, not on this topic. Only the Executive Committee, the Chairman and his two key assistants, will gather. He has already decided to keep the matter quiet until a solution is reached, and if not a solution, then at least a conclusion.

The Chairman brushes back his thick white hair and with the same hand reaches down to touch a hidden control panel on the side of his chair. Four of the lights go dark leaving illuminated only the ones on his immediate right and left. Then, resting his chin on his hand, eyes staring at the far dark corner of the Board Room, the Chairman returns to his fierce concentration.

This was the very pose, the Chairman chose for his official portrait. The painting hung on the wall beside him, a neater, more relaxed image. In the picture, there are no circles under his dark brown, steel-hard eyes. His long, thick gray hair is neat and the artist had suppressed every wrinkle in the severe suit that covers the physique of a much younger man. The broad chin is hairless and the mustache perfectly trimmed while the real image would benefit from a barber's aggressive touch.

The Chairman actually seems more alive and vital in the frame. But that isn't surprising. Like the lamps, the absolute best artist available had created the painting. And with the Corporation's resources, every artist was available.

This wasn't his first portrait, only the latest in a line of masterpieces. He had been the head of the Corporation for a long time, a very long time. Every so often the picture needed to be redone to show a leader who had lived the Corporation's history, but who still knew the meaning of being a modern business executive. Clearly, the Chairman fit that billing.

The clock in the tower outside chimes in perfect synchronization with the grandfather clock in the hallway and the Chairman brings his eyes and focus back into the room. The rest of the Executive Committee was waiting for that impartial signal and would now enter. He takes a deep breath and throws his shoulders back. It would not be appropriate for them to see his actual level of distress.

"Good morning, Boss," says a cheery voice cast by the tall, thin black man with a modified Afro, Brooks Brothers suit and a smile that spread from his sparkling black eyes to the tips of his polished Florsheims. He's younger than the chairman, but it's hard to tell by how much. In his right hand he carries a small leather attaché, the kind too compact to hold anything of substance. The man notes the unusual closed atmosphere of the room and is troubled, though he says nothing.

A woman, whose age is not revealed by her appearance, immediately follows him. At first glance, she appears younger than the Chairman, but older than the man preceding her. A trained eye would likely expand the observation by saying that, while just as well-dressed as either of the two men, in manner and style she can only be considered the black man's opposite.

The gender difference only highlights the contrast. His skin is bittersweet chocolate, hers a paste-white. His deep black eyes and her pale blue ones are as far apart as the two ends of a traffic signal. His tight, curly, dark hair absorbs the light, making his soft features even brighter, while her light blond, shoulder length tresses punctuate the sharp lines of her hard-set face. His suit, tie and shirt combination says "sophisticated yet carefree." If her clothes were a shade darker she'd be properly dressed for a funeral – though, granted, a very fashionable funeral.

She enters the Board Room without comment or expression and

gently brushes back her blond hair, making sure each strand is in place as she stares ahead through moist, unreadable eyes. Beyond the neutrality of expression, her thin lips are bent with the hint of a smile.

"Only the three of us Boss?" The black man asks, as he settles into the red chair on the Chairman's right, placing his leather case on the floor beside him.

"That's correct Eli," the Chairman answers. "This is Executive Committee stuff. I don't want anyone else internal involved until it's taken care of."

The Chairman's hand returns to the control panel under his chair and the Board Room door locks.

"This sounds serious Boss," the black man responds, his tone shifting to one of definite concern, his eyes drifting again to the closed curtains.

"Yes, very serious. Lucky caught the oversight, so she ought to make the presentation." The Chairman turns toward the blond woman who is sitting stiffly upright, her hands folded in front of her.

Invisibly, internally, the woman winces at the Chairman's use of the hated nickname. No one else calls her "Lucky." No one else dares. Only a few of her closest associates are permitted to call her Elizabeth. Most simply refer to her as "Ma'am." And the masses get no closer than "Ms. Luckholt."

Elizabeth Luckholt is aware that the Chairman knows everything about her particular brand of protocol. No one has better information. The Chairman seems to know everything. That's because he's the Chairman, or maybe that's why he's the Chairman. But once he discovered Luckholt's fastidious insistence that other business executives address her formally, the Chairman instantly dubbed her "Lucky" (just to annoy her, she was sure).

Though a minor humiliation, it is one that always reminds Luckholt who and where she is, of her failed attempt, some years before, to depose the Chairman and take control. Despite that singular, major act of disloyalty, she still sits on the Executive Committee because no one else can, or will, do what she does. Next to the Chairman himself, she is the Corporation's most indispensable executive. So let him have fun with his silly nickname. She knows where she stands in the order.

Without a further thought, Elizabeth Luckholt presents the problem.

CHAPTER TWO

For nearly an hour, Suzanne Rosewell had been resisting the urge to downshift. Her right hand has drifted toward the stick every time her concentration weakened. And that was often. It was as if her fingers were acting on their own. She knew why, but the knowledge didn't stop the motion. Subconsciously, she was trying to do something, anything, to break the monotony. The motion of her arm, the change in the relentless hum of the engine, those things would achieve the goal, but she continued to resist. Even a prime condition, brand new BMW would not have appreciated being downshifted at seventy-five miles an hour. Yet there had to be some way to relieve the boredom.

Mile after mile, hour after hour, the speedometer holding steady at well over a mile a minute, and the South Dakota landscape still looked the same. It was as if the car were frozen in place, the scenery painted on some huge circular Hollywood backdrop, repeating the same pattern over and over, like standing in the center of a carousel.

Maybe that was it. Maybe she was stuck on some cosmic treadmill, car tires spinning, no progress made, in a dream, a nightmare. Would that be a rational explanation for all the irrational things that have happened these last few days? No, a dream ends.

The clock radio clicks, soft music breaks the silence. She opens her eyes, concentrates on the sunlight squeezing around the dark curtains in her Manhattan bedroom, runs her fingers through her curly red hair, forces herself out of the warm, loving bed and resumes her life.

No alarm this time. Just the same rolling plains, the same thin brown grass, nothing to break the monotony but an occasional truck stop or a lonely tractor standing in an otherwise empty field. An unending, monotonous view.

Still, there was a magnificence to this scenery, an expansive sky, flatland grandeur that said clearly "The Great American West." The land spoke of countless unrecorded cowboys buried in history, of a thousand Western movies resting in studio archives and in the back corners of video stores. Suzanne felt she should be looking at this broad prairie while sitting in a darkened room. Yes, this was magnificent, for about an hour.

The fascination had worn off a hundred miles west of Sioux Falls. Another hundred miles of highway were in her rear view mirror and a couple hundred remained before Rapid City.

For the twentieth time, Suzanne wondered why she drove in the first place. Why wasn't she comfortably settled in a jet plane thirty thousand feet over these dried-out fields? For the twentieth time the absurdity of her own question made her laugh.

"The honest question," she said, speaking aloud to the empty landscape and to her large, green eyes framed in the rear view mirror, "is not my choice of conveyance, but what in Heaven's name am I doing here in the first place?"

To that inquiry she had no real answer. There wasn't one when she crossed the Delaware Water Gap into Pennsylvania and still none as the country flattened out through Ohio, Indiana, and Illinois. She began to tire of the self-interrogation by the time she reached the Wisconsin Dells and then didn't repeat the question until she'd crossed the Mississippi and gone half way through Minnesota on Interstate 90. That's when the query came up again. Still she couldn't formulate even the beginning of an answer. Not unless she was willing to admit that there was some reality, some specific meaning to the strange series of events that had led her to this lonely highway. So far, Suzanne was only willing to concede that her experiences qualified as a very unusual string of seemingly unrelated coincidences. She was also willing to admit that those coincidences were powerful enough to put her on the road and sufficiently disturbing that she had decided to take the BMW. The car was a conscious choice, a purposeful move to isolate herself inside the steel frame and surround herself with music from the all-too-sensitive sound system, an expensive distraction that, once put to the test, had worn thin before reaching Toledo.

The weird, mystical coincidences that had motivated the journey were still unacceptable in Suzanne's legally trained mind. Her upbringing, considerable intelligence and the special mental discipline she'd learned in law school had joined to resist passive acceptance.

A good lawyer, she felt, would divide every problem into two parts – the facts on one side, theory on the other. Weigh everything and reclassify theory into fact only when proven or when one could convince a judge or jury that it had been proven. That was her approach.

In this case, the facts were thin, and the only theory that could justify this journey was so hard to accept that her attorney brain continued to reject it as nothing more than illusion, an illusion that had carried her through nine states. She forced herself to concentrate on the tiny pieces of reality.

That reality was very basic. Suzanne had driven more than a thousand miles to visit with Professor Herman W. Fields, an instructor who taught the strange, almost contradictory combination of Ethics and Government at St. Olive's College in rural South Dakota.

Only two years prior, Fields had been an obscure teacher on the faculty of an institution better known for sports than great minds. Then he submitted an article on the lofty topic of "World Peace" to the New York Times' Op Ed page. The *Times* editors, normally more impressed by big names than by the content of submissions, were captivated by the professor's powerful style and his clear, direct answers to complex problems. They published the article in the largely ignored Saturday edition. This particular piece was anything but ignored.

The *Times* article led to more publications and to appearances on radio and television. A frustrated, tired diplomat, moved by the Field's articles and a resulting interview with Diane Sawyer, extended an invitation to the professor to help mediate a stubborn civil war in the Horn of Africa.

To everyone's surprise, the attempt was wildly successful and Professor Fields' journey to notoriety was launched, moving faster and higher than the Minute Man missiles once hidden under the prairie just outside his classroom window. His articles began to appear in international publications. Shockingly to most, he declined a solicitation to join the State Department as a roving ambassador. The immediate fallout came in the form of more invitations to solve other international disputes.

With a style nothing short of brilliant, Professor Fields chalked up small, but significant victories in the impossible muck of the Middle East and again in Northern Ireland. He became an instant legend, garnering simultaneous cover stories on Time and Newsweek. He was even credited with fathering six separate anti-war movements. A few months later he won the Nobel Peace Prize. Now his name was everywhere and, thanks to television, his face became familiar.

Because of the professor's new fame, he'd hired a very professional secretary to keep him from being pestered to death. Despite Suzanne Rosewell's attachment to Markam, Wilber, Kent & Todd, one of Wall Street's most important firms, neither she nor her employer were prestigious enough to get past his guardian.

"Put your problem in a letter," she was told, "and Professor Fields will respond, though an answer will likely take several months." The stupid bitch, Suzanne thought.

Funny though, she reflected, only a short time ago no one could get past her own "stupid bitch" of a secretary. That was one of the reasons Margaret was paid so much – to keep away the riff-raff and allow through only those who were clients, or potential clients, with big money.

This was all Suzanne was willing to concede to that so-called logical side of the equation. Was it enough to have brought her to South Dakota? Not likely. Just meeting Professor Fields, as unusual and important as he may be, would, alone, not justify this impulsive act. Suzanne had simply ordered her high-priced secretary to clear her calendar. Then, without even the slightest idea of what clothes were proper for South Dakota in July, she packed a bag and departed. She didn't even bother to leave a return date, much to the distress of the firm's managing partner.

How he'd fumed and sputtered as she informed him of her unplanned leave, less than convinced by her vague promise to return quickly, and simultaneously service her caseload. He mumbled something about how partnerships given could be taken back. But that made no difference. She simply had to see Professor Fields and, as his damn secretary wouldn't arrange a meeting, she was going to find him on her own. The best information she could find placed him outside of Rapid City, hiding in his Black Hills summer cabin.

Blessed relief. The topography changed. As suddenly as if someone had switched a slide in the projector, the road dipped and the Missouri River valley spread out in front of her. In the quiet July haze, the scene was two-dimensional, more like a painting than a photograph. The car accelerated as the straight flat highway fell into the valley and stretched its set of double-laned fingers across the bridge. The sense of lost dimension remained. Suzanne felt like she was driving right through the painting.

As the road reached up, seeking the level plain, the tired attorney spotted a restaurant and decided to take advantage of the pastoral setting to unwind. Suzanne turned the BMW sharply, drove down the exit ramp and pulled into the parking lot of a large, low, log cabin-like tourist structure marked by a huge plaster buffalo. The sign advertised burgers made from the meat of the same animal enshrined by the twelve-foot-high statue. The interior of the restaurant offered no surprises, souvenirs, candy, cigarettes, or any food offering even remotely light.

"When in Rome," she muttered to herself and ordered a buffalo burger and a coke to go. She wondered if part of the price for saving the world was her own good nutrition.

Carrying the food in a brown paper bag, she walked to a picnic bench at the top of a long slope that ended at the shore of the Missouri River. The scenery generated images from history, movies and even songs. Suzanne was in a place she'd never been before, physically or emotionally.

The tables around her were filled with families, their mini-vans and RVs parked in the lot, enhancing the geographic contrast made by her BMW and its New York plates. She studied them, observed children, listened to noises and noticed, between bites of meat with a surprisingly pleasant flavor, that she was hardly the object of attention she had expected. More. It was as if she were not really there. The thought was distressing. Was she trapped in some fancy, high-powered hallucination? Maybe these people in fact didn't see her. Strangely enough, no one even stole a glance, despite her Eastern clothing, her out-of-place automobile, and her rather striking, in a New York way, good looks. Just as she approached paranoia, one very blond little girl, about seven years old, on the way to the trash can, deposited a friendly smile in Suzanne's direction.

"You're pretty," the child paused and observed.

"Thank you," answered Suzanne. "So are you." The little girl was pleased by the compliment from this strange grown-up. She giggled and ran on. Suzanne had also been flattered, even though the observation came from one so small.

As a teenager she had not been attractive. Her looks blossomed with adulthood. Unlike other women who found beauty to be a detriment when dealing with a man's opinion of her intelligence, Suzanne's good looks had not hurt her career one bit.

The child had raised her spirits and provided a small connection back to the earth. But Suzanne found that she involuntarily wondered if even this little person had not been an emissary, someone sent specifically to make her feel better. Her absurd thoughts were reaching an extreme and were no longer funny. She paused and concentrated, blaming all her wild reasoning on the strange New York encounters with the man who called himself Elias Garner.

Who was this Elias Garner anyway, some being with mystical powers? He never claimed such a lofty status, but there were insinuations. The man only admitted to being an amateur musician and to working for the eccentric chairman of an unnamed corporation. He never said anything about saving the world. That conclusion was her own, drawn from stories provided by an old Jewish academician, who, by the way, never claimed that his information was anything more than legend. And then there was that woman. Why would she be involved if this wasn't important? The memory made Suzanne shiver. For a moment she knew what her grandfather must have felt when he stepped off the boat from Ellis Island, a stranger in a strange land. She longed to be back in New York. Maybe it wasn't too late to turn around and go home.

CHAPTER THREE

"Ms. Rosewell," the secretary interrupted through the intercom, "Mr. Blake is still waiting on line three."

"Thank you Margaret," Suzanne Rosewell responded, not sounding in the least like she really meant the courtesy.

Though her own polite phrases were automatic, Suzanne always enjoyed hearing her secretary address her by her last name. In fact, Suzanne insisted on it. These days, most of the other lawyers, except for the older partners who retained a link to the traditional propriety of Markam, Wilber, Kent & Todd, allowed a first name relationship with their secretaries. Not Suzanne Rosewell. She took pleasure in the idea that this serious, efficient woman, ten years her senior, was forced to use the formal mode of address, while the person the secretary served spoke to her as if she were a child. They both knew the name thing was nothing more than an amusement of power, but exercising power, with amusement or otherwise, was something Suzanne Rosewell enjoyed. Exercising power had a purpose unto itself. The game went with the territory and was one of the rewards of success.

"Arthur, what's up?" she said to the speaker box with impatience. "I'm busy right now."

"You're always busy," the voice responded, not the least bit intimidated by her manner, "especially since you made partner."

"That's how I got to be a partner," she snapped back, catching herself just before she reminded him that she was also the youngest woman ever awarded a partnership. Suzanne's hands rolled into fists, her eyes scanning the desk for a document, only a small part of her attention remaining on the call. "Now what do you want?" She tried to cover her distraction by coating her voice with syrup.

"Well, if you are not above socializing with lowly associates, there's a group of us going to the Wood Horn Case tonight for drinks and music. Maybe you'd like to come along?"

"Wood Horn Case?" she responded, providing even a more minor portion of her brain to the conversation. "What the hell is that?"

"Oh, come on," Arthur whined, the impatience now full in his voice. "Don't you pay attention to anything besides your case load? The new jazz joint that just opened up in the next building."

The realization that he was discussing a social occasion finally penetrated and Suzanne's first impulse was to decline, but she knew that a good lawyer never reacts impulsively. Instead she pondered the request, finally focusing her full attention on the conversation. If Arthur Blake had been in the room, he would have known that she was giving his idea serious thought. He would have watched her go through her habitual and unconscious routine of leaning back in her chair and using both hands to brush the loose falls of red hair that framed her large green eyes. But Suzanne was alone in her office, with no one to observe her habits or admire her physical appearance. And that was fine. Lately, Suzanne preferred to be alone.

This invitation was unusual. Even when she was a "lowly associate" she barely socialized with her coworkers. They were too frivolous, not as ambitious as they should be. Besides, they didn't seem to like her very much.

Suzanne Rosewell, third in her class at NYU Law, was the one who worked while the Harvard and Yale graduates played. And Suzanne Rosewell was the one first elected to partnership. Now they were calling her for a social event even though she knew they generally didn't enjoy her company. Certainly, she didn't care to be with very many of them.

Arthur Blake was the exception. Oh, he was as lazy as the rest, but so very smart that he almost didn't need to work at all. Good looking besides. They'd been, as the office gossip termed their relationship, an "item," for a short while. But Suzanne had decided that there was no room in her life for career and romance. She broke off the relationship before she and Arthur became anything more than a minor office rumor.

The invitation made Suzanne suspicious. Was Arthur trying to get something started again? Not likely. Maybe he represented a group of associates trying to kiss up to a new partner and get on her good side, which was a place they certainly knew they didn't currently occupy. Whatever the reason, Suzanne quickly decided that alienating the associates would not strengthen her position in the firm. They were the legal labor force and could make a junior partner look very good or very stupid based entirely on their enthusiasm for a task. Lately, the projects she'd assigned to several of the associates were taking longer than they should. This was an opportunity for Suzanne to show she was "one of the guys" despite her success. Especially since there were still some partners around who felt that her elevation was premature. She dropped the impatient tone and substituted the voice used with important clients – confident, firm, but very friendly.

"Arthur, is this your invitation, or do the others want me to come as well?"

"Everyone wants you to come. I'm only the messenger."

She didn't believe him, heard the hesitation in his voice and, despite the lie, decided to go anyway. Maybe because of it.

"I think it's a great idea," she responded, "but I am buried with work. I could join you guys a bit later."

"Sure," Arthur answered, recognizing the change in speech and aware of her real motivation. He didn't care why she came. "We'll keep a seat for you. Music starts at nine and I understand the place gets crowded, so come as soon as you can. See you later."

"Later," she replied, but her finger was already on the cutoff button, her mind on the next file. At nine-thirty Suzanne was still at her desk, the rest of the floor dark, her secretary gone and the Wood Horn Case forgotten. She leaned back, lit a cigarette and noticed that the ashtray was overflowing.

"Damn," Suzanne said out loud as if discussing the issue with someone else in the office. "I must have smoked almost a whole pack since five." The burn of too much tobacco filled her throat and the late hour was responsible for her stomach growling.

"Time to go home," she said to the missing audience as she stood to leave. With her eyes rapidly providing the data, her brain automatically inventoried the desk. Everything could just be left as it was. She could lock the door, go out, grab a quick bite to eat, shower, sleep and come back early in the morning, before anyone else arrived to disturb the flow of her work. She would have to empty her own ashtray, though. The cleaning people had come and gone hours ago, skipping her office, as they often were forced to do.

So as not to have to face the entire mess in daylight, Suzanne dumped the ashes onto the pile of papers filling her trash basket. Without looking back, she went to the elevator, nodding a brief "good night" to the unnamed black man who served as security guard.

The number of cars parked along the curb was what surprised her. Markam, Wilber, Kent & Todd was located on Wall Street. No one lived here. At least no one with a car. After a certain hour, the Street was always deserted save for a few wandering businessmen staying at local hotels and a couple of prostitutes plying their trade on the wanderers. For the block to be full of cars was definitely abnormal.

Noise to her left drew her attention. Suzanne turned in time to see the front door of the Wood Horn Case slam shut, blocking the sounds and smells, music, applause, and cigarette smoke that had momentarily escaped into the warm night air. She remembered her commitment.

Suzanne reconsiders, convinced that her colleagues have forgotten that she was expected. Several, she is sure, are relieved she hasn't shown. She turns away and moves toward the subway but finds herself unable to take the first step. Something compels her toward the door, some force much stronger than a fleeting promise made in a phone conversation. All her senses are directed to the wooden door. The muted colors of the night brighten, the red sign draws her like a moth toward a bare bulb. Everything, the street lights, the New York humidity, the traffic sounds, become momentarily intense. The feeling is powerful but brief, so short that she takes a half step in the direction this internal electricity desires and the compulsion goes, disappearing before she can get a grip on it, before she is even sure that something has happened. Still, once propelled in its direction, she can not bring herself to turn and walk away.

Suzanne pulls back her shoulders and marches through the door. The statue of George Washington, on the steps of the Exchange, watches her go. Had someone been staring at the statue, someone observant and sober, that person would have sworn Washington seemed to smile. But statues can't change their expressions and, no matter, there was no one watching.

On the other side of the door, Suzanne becomes convinced that she has entered an alien dimension. So great is the contrast between the club's interior and the city outside that a moment passes before she finds the courage to press forward. An image invades her mind. She is back in undergraduate literature class and Dante's vision of the Underworld is right before her eyes. Suzanne feels her stomach fill with fear and indecision, two emotions that have been virtual strangers in her adult life (but old companions from her childhood). With very little grown-up experience with the dark side of her heart, the only thing Suzanne can think to do is respond like an eight-year-old and run.

But the reflection of Hades, like the feeling on the street, is fleeting, as if the frightening intrusion in her brain has been blocked by something more powerful. The threat of the room flees, strangely replaced by an opposing sense of calm and fascination. Suzanne focuses on how the building space is filled with colors, muted and moving from the spotlights, reds, blues, yellows, greens, drifting in imperfect circles. At their center, a stage, empty but for a single microphone and a single musician playing a huge brass trumpet, whose gold color reflects each of the traveling hues back toward her in flashes with no particular pattern.

Before she hears the music, she's aware of the crowd. The room is filled with people, standing around circular tables, chairs pushed back, swaying in time with the sound. And such a sound! Music that suddenly becomes everything, completely dominating her awareness ... a single clear trumpet filling every cube of space, reaching every corner, coating every crack in the wall, surrounding Suzanne with a mournful, and, at the same time, inexplicably joyous sound, the likes of which she's never heard before. The tones envelop her, wrap her like a cloak passed by a lover for protection against a chilly breeze. She is not listening to the music. She is part of it.

This incredible sound that seems to be from somewhere beyond her reality, lasts only seconds. The musician has arrived at the end of the solo. Suzanne gasps as the final note echoes through her dazzled brain.

For an incredibly long moment the whole room is silent. Suddenly the crowd erupts in a thunder of cheering. The tall, not-so-young, black musician bows deeply and remains bent like a hairpin while the audience goes wild. A touch on Suzanne's arm makes her jump a foot off the floor. The hand belongs to Arthur Blake.

"Suzanne," he said with genuine joy, "I'm glad you made it before Elias Garner finished his set. This guy is unbelievable. Come. We have a table in the corner."

He took her arm and led her unresisting body through the crowd. For a moment she felt overcome, once again, by fear, but as the crowd quieted in anticipation of more music, as people began to sit and the room looked more normal, the fear left. Suzanne easily decides that her strange reaction is credited to not having eaten all day and to the effects of too much coffee and too many cigarettes.

No one else at the table matched Arthur's enthusiasm for her arrival. Their greetings were perfunctory. Some offered none at all, but the lack of courtesy seemed to come more from undivided attention toward the stage rather than anything they may have felt about Suzanne. The musician, still in his hairpin bow, straightened up and faced the audience, a broad smile decorating his dark face.

"Thank you, thank you," he said softly, the room quieting even further to allow his hushed voice to be heard. "I will now play something special, a piece I wrote very recently. I would like to dedicate this to someone in the room."

"Must be for you," Arthur said, joking into Suzanne's ear.

"I call it *Suzanne's Blues*," the musician said, raising the horn to his lips. Arthur Blake swallowed his laughter while Suzanne suddenly inhaled.

"Do you know Elias Garner?" Arthur asked before the music reached them.

"Elias who?" she answered.

"The musician... Elias Garner. He dedicated the song to you. Don't you know him?"

There was no time for response. The clear, low, long notes of blues rolled over and between the tables, drowning Suzanne in the music. For a split second, she couldn't breath at all. And then, just as suddenly, the ability to fill her lungs returned. For another moment she felt the identical fear that had greeted her in the entrance way. Once again, the feeling fled, leaving behind that same heightened intensity that she'd experienced during his first piece.

His music seemed to flow from the horn by itself, music like she'd never heard before. Blues so acute, so touching that her eyes filled with tears. She could feel salt water running down her cheeks and the emotions nourished by the sound increased almost to the point where they could not be contained. For the first time in her life, Suzanne understood why teenagers scream at rock concerts.

But before her own need to shriek went beyond control, Garner's music retreated. The tune became mellow, the notes relaxing. Suzanne snuggled into the sound. The piece became a huge feather comforter on a cold winter night. She felt warm... contented... safe, as though she were a little girl and the song was her father wrapping his long arms around her and rocking her in front of the fireplace. Suzanne's body swayed with the long-ago memory. The tears were still rolling from her eyes, but she was no longer conscious of them. Nor was she conscious of anyone in the room except the tall black musician on stage.

That was when she became aware, or seemed to become aware, that the golden horn was pointed directly at her and had been through the entire piece. She rationalized that this sense of focus was her unique perception and came only because she was enjoying his performance so much. Most of the people in the room probably felt the same way she did. Every good performer has the ability to make members of the audience feel like the show is directed specifically at each of them, or so she rationalized.

She'd never been a particular fan of jazz before. But this man's music was so personal. The bright spots lifted her, the sad passages tapped her pain. Each section, each phrase, touched some old and forgotten spot deep in the hidden, protected parts of her spirit. The music moved around her barriers and penetrated her walls. Even when the notes reached her sore spots, Suzanne consumed the sounds as if they were cleansing and healing old wounds. And then, cruelly and too soon, the music stopped. Elias Garner was finished. He lowered his horn and seemed to stare directly into Suzanne's eyes, all the way across the room. It made her terribly uncomfortable.

"Well, do you know him?" Arthur said to her over the applause.

"No, of course not," Suzanne snapped back, annoyed at having her reverie disturbed. "I've never seen him before."

"Then why did he dedicate a song to you?"

"Don't be silly. That's coincidence. It's for another Suzanne."

"Maybe," Arthur said with a grin, "but he looks like he's on his way over here."

Suzanne glanced toward the stage. Sure enough, the musician was heading in her direction. His progress was slowed by the adoration he received and politely acknowledged at each gathering, but all the while he seemed focused on Suzanne's table. Each time he thanked another fan, his eyes would return to Suzanne, and his smile would broaden.

Though she didn't know why, Susanne was frightened by the thought of speaking with this man. The bite of fear returned like a tidal wave and, without a word, she ran from the table, rushed out the door and fled into the street.

> *As Suzanne runs toward the subway, the smile on George Washington's face fades.*

CHAPTER FOUR

Suzanne's memory of her trip home simply didn't exist. She had no distinct image of entering the subway, even though a mental picture of the train roaring into the station was still sharp. She remembered clearly how her mind filled with relief as the silver cars behind the double headlights came into view, but she did not recall boarding the train.

Nor would the stations between Wall Street and home return to her. It was as if the subway stopped only once, at 86th Street, where she stepped through the open doors and into familiar surroundings. Even the usually threatening figures of shabby people in the shadows and the oppressive aroma of heat, smoke and urine were comforting. Suzanne knew these particular stimuli. They weren't pleasant, but she understood them. They had a place in her life, not at all like the strange and unknown feelings she'd experienced in the Wooden Horn Case.

As she walked down Madison Avenue, reducing the distance to the steel and glass tower she called home, Suzanne began to justify, explain, in rational terms, the events of the past few hours. She retreated deep into familiar excuses – lack of nourishment, excess nicotine and caffeine, wine on an empty stomach, these all could have contributed to the phenomenon.

Or did she even have a glass of wine? She didn't remember ordering any, but the sour after-flavor of the beverage hung on her tongue, or was that something else? Maybe there was no taste in her mouth after all. This was all too strange, too confusing. Nothing seemed to be in its proper place.

As though only for the purpose of continuing the disruption, the local Chinese restaurant, usually long closed by this hour, was full of people. In one last attempt to take charge of her evening, Suzanne decided to at least settle her nutrition problem before going home to bed.

"One hot and sour soup and a pint of vegetable lo mein, to go, please," she said to the distracted young woman behind the register.

"Yes, Miss," came the response, the cashier's eyes marking a spot in a textbook that she was studying between customers. Suzanne noticed that the book was protected with that familiar New York University cover. The young woman disappeared to fill the order.

Suzanne was astounded by the number of people eating full meals at eleven o'clock on a weekday night. There wasn't a vacant seat in the establishment. She knew the restaurant, a popular place for lunch and early in the evening, but this was the first time she'd ever seen the eatery open at this hour. She was certain – almost certain – that the store was always shuttered, locked and dark whenever she passed late at night.

Now her mind questioned her own powers of observation. The standard memories that existed as background to her conscious life, like a closed Chinese restaurant, came under scrutiny. Maybe everything she saw, or thought she saw, should also be questioned. Maybe she was working too hard. The student returned with her order.

"Tell me," Suzanne asked, deciding to check the accuracy of her memories, "Are you always open at this time of the night?"

"No Miss," came the response. "Very funny evening. The customers just kept coming. We've been full all the time. My father runs the restaurant. He was born and raised in China, where you work until the work is done. He says as long as people are hungry, we'll keep feeding them. Truth is, I can't remember another night like this."

Suzanne was comforted by the reply. Her recollection had been accurate. She felt herself relax a bit as she scanned the crowd, waiting for change from the twenty-dollar bill. For the first time in hours, Suzanne felt like she was catching her breath.

The restaurant was not well lit, hard to see the faces of people in the back, but almost every seat was occupied. Suzanne's eyes passed over the place twice before her gaze touched on a twosome in the back corner, deeply involved in food and conversation – a blonde woman and a black man, who, from the back, looked remarkably like Elias Garner.

"Not possible," she said aloud in a near panic, words that were drowned by a bus coming around the corner. For a brief moment the beam of the halogen headlights touched the mirrored back wall and illuminated the black man's reflection. She only caught his smile, a broad and friendly grin, like the one she'd seen on the face of the musician. Her heart jumped to her throat. She froze, her hand halfway toward the register.

"Your change, Miss," the cashier said, impatient to return to her studies. She placed the money in Suzanne's hand and her touch brought the lawyer back to the restaurant.

"Not possible," she said again as she crumpled the bills together and shoved them into her pocket.

"I beg your pardon?" the woman behind the register asked. Her inquiry went unanswered. For the second time in one evening, Suzanne Rosewell escaped into the night.

High heeled shoes and skirt not withstanding, Suzanne ran to her building, her labored breathing lessening only after she had ascended in the elevator and double locked her apartment door behind her. Almost an hour passed before she could bring herself to reheat and consume the food, then shower and prepare for bed.

Sleep? Ridiculous!

Suzanne lay awake, staring at the ceiling, the evening's events racing through her brain, a 1960s psychedelic movie being run over and over again.

"The song was not for you," she told herself a hundred times. "A coincidence. He was just touring the crowd, not coming to see you. It wasn't him in the restaurant. Not possible. You are exaggerating this in your head, taking everything out of proportion. You're just too tired, working too hard."

Rationalization did not bring rest. She surrendered, took a sleeping medication, shed her nightgown, settled under the sheet and turned on the television. The pill took hold and she dozed to the drone of the Cable News Network, drifting into a dreamless drug sleep that lasted until four a.m.

> *Suddenly Suzanne is awake with the impression of music fading away from her ears. The sounds linger in her mind, as if the piece had ended only at the moment she regained consciousness. While she could not remember a single note, her strong sense is that she had just heard* Suzanne's Blues *played as it had been played hours before by Elias Garner in that crowded downtown club.*
>
> *But this time there is no fear, as she might have expected. Nor is she groggy as she should have been when awakened prematurely from a drug sleep. Suzanne feels strangely calm and well rested.*
>
> *CNN is still reporting, a profile on the latest peace effort in some African nation, the project of Professor Herman W. Fields, a Nobel laureate from someplace called Saint Olive's College in South Dakota. The program barely registers in Suzanne's consciousness as she presses the remote to black out the screen. Quietly she lifts herself from the bed. Drawn to the window, she carries her bare body to the closed glass and stares down twenty-two floors toward the street.*
>
> *The view of 85th street seems normal, parked cars, streetlights, no one around. A few moments go by before Suzanne convinces herself that the source of the music had either been the television or her dreams. She suspects the latter. Still, she remains watching the*

street, her narrow figure bathed in moonlight, her dark eyes focused on the far away sidewalk. She watches him as he walks out of the shadows.

He is strolling along the north side of the street, Madison Avenue behind him, Central Park his seeming destination. Suzanne's mind fills with the image of a tall, thin black man, carrying an old fashioned wooden case under his arm. The figure stops, pauses and seems to look up, seems to look directly at her. He holds that posture for perhaps thirty seconds. Suzanne's mental impression is completely dominated by the likeness of Elias Garner.

From twenty-two stories up there is no possibility of recognizing anyone on a dark street, hard enough to tell man from woman. Suzanne's legally trained mind tells her that these pictures in her brain are not physical images, but only internal impressions of reality and probably not accurate ones. Even if the solitary figure is Elias Garner, she can not know for sure, not from her apartment window. The impression had to be, simply had to be produced by her imagination.

Yet the impressions are so real... the images clear as though her eyes are taking on superhuman powers or that the aura of the person on the street is so powerful that a picture is being projected, a holographic image, raised to her window.

That particular, peculiar thought came so easily to her that Suzanne immediately considered a vacation or a psychiatrist.

What bothered Suzanne, what actually produced her contemplation of treatment, was not that she saw the image of a lone man projected twenty-two stories in the air. She wasn't even disturbed by the notes of a phantom trumpet or the belief that a strange musician was treating her like an old friend and apparently sending his apparition to follow her all over town. What frightened Suzanne Rosewell, Attorney-at-Law, was her reaction to these events. Every part of the delusion seemed perfectly normal, at least while it was going on.

A few hours earlier, as she went through those events, those coincidences, she'd been driven to near panic. A song that seemed to be named and played for her had filled her with dread. A performer heading in her direction had driven her out of a club. These minor events had propelled her into a state of uncontrolled fear, weirdly alternating with moments of total confidence and calm. Not the same confidence she felt when dealing with a client, but a genuine sense of deep relaxation, a feeling that could almost be called serenity.

Each of her individual emotions seemed to last only a moment, as if they were the direct result of opposite forces battling for control, one side bright and calm, one cold and frightening. But when the *really* strange things happened, images projected from the street, music coming from nowhere, none of it upset her. The bright, calm force prevailed.

With one totally intellectual thought, Suzanne concluded that she'd gone completely mad, crossed the line between sane and insane. Her rational part told her that this calm acceptance of the unreal as real was the very definition of insanity. She was behaving not too differently from the stereotypical madman, confined to an asylum, believing himself to be Bonaparte. In imitation of the image, she tried to hide her right hand under her shirt, remembered she was naked and laughed out loud at the absurdity. Isn't that exactly what a mad man would have done? Uninterested in the answer to her own question, Suzanne crawled back into bed, covered her eyes with her long warm hair, pulled the sheet tightly against her cool skin and fell instantly into a deep, dreamless sleep.

She awoke, her room drenched in sunlight and the clock on the nightstand reading nine a.m. Suzanne normally was out of the house by seven-thirty. Disrupted by the change in routine, her adrenaline level rose, pushing the prior day's events into that part of her mind reserved for barely remembered dreams. She jumped out of bed, skipped her morning shower and was on the street by nine-twenty. For a change, the subway connections worked to her advantage and she was in front of the office building by a quarter to ten.

In Suzanne's rush to reach the revolving doors, she almost missed the red and white banner draped over the Wooden Horn Case. Something flashed in the corner of her eye and she stopped and stared.

STARTING TONIGHT:

DIXIELAND JAZZ WITH
THE DIXIE KINGS

The banner rested on the large, heavy wooden door that the night before had opened and, for Suzanne, ended the separation of the jazz club from the rest of New York. The entrance was now sealed with a huge padlock that she presumed would be removed in time for the evening show, a show apparently without Elias Garner. Somewhere in her mental recesses she had already decided to return and see Garner one more time, but the opportunity had apparently vanished.

The red neon sign still swayed gently and silently in the summer breeze as it had the night before. The wooden door and the brick wall still looked the same, but the building itself seemed different. Suzanne lost all desire to go back inside. Unless, maybe the manager could tell her where Elias Garner was performing. She took one step in the direction of the entrance, remembered the padlock and turned away.

Suzanne shook her head and resumed the journey toward her office, her pace less rapid now, some of the energy gone from her blood. Arthur Blake was standing near the elevator as she stepped off the car.

"Arthur," she said speaking slowly, "what happened to the trumpet player?"

"And good morning to you too," Arthur answered. "Fine start to a conversation, especially after the way you ran out last night."

"Oh, come on Arthur. I don't have time for this," she barked back, adrenaline rising once more. "Just tell me what happened to Elias Garner."

"I haven't the slightest idea what you're talking about."

"There's a new act in there, starting tonight."

"Where?"

"In the Wooden Horn Case." She was shouting.

"How do you know?"

"Because I've got eyes. There's a huge banner announcing the arrival of something called the Dixie Kings."

"I hadn't noticed." Arthur seemed uninterested in the entire topic.

"How could you not notice?" Suzanne's volume level elevated further. "There's a twenty foot red-and-white banner draped across the front."

"I simply hadn't noticed."

"A lot of help you are." She waved her arm in frustration and brushed by him.

"Well, I'm sure glad to see that you are your same old sweet, lovable self," he shouted, as she paced down the hall.

"He's right," she thought. "He didn't mean that remark as a compliment, but I am back to normal. I didn't go crazy. Last night was just a fluke."

Not real! Not real!

The place in her brain where barely remembered dreams rested was shouting back, permitting her no comfort in thoughts of restored sanity. The adrenaline took another leap and for one second Suzanne longed for the quiet serenity of her short retreat to insanity.

"Ms. Rosewell!" The secretary was shouting. "I've been calling you since eight-thirty. You missed an appointment with Mr. Roberts from SellWell Corporation."

"I know, I know, Margaret," the lawyer snapped back. "I slept through my alarm. But you called the wrong number. I was home and in bed at eight-thirty."

"No, Ms. Rosewell," Margaret answered defensively. "I got your machine every time. I left three messages."

"That's not possible. I sleep right next to the machine and I never turn off the phone or lower the volume on the tape. I would have heard it."

"I'm sorry, Ms. Rosewell. All I know is I left messages on a machine that answered with your voice."

Suzanne felt herself grow dizzy. Margaret wouldn't lie. There was no point. The evidence would be on the tape. The whole thing didn't compute, but now was not the time to figure out why.

"Forget it. What about the guy from SellWell?"

"Oh, Mr. Roberts," the secretary said with pride. "He was really very nice about the mix-up. I gave him coffee and told him that you must be stuck in the subway. We rescheduled for two this afternoon."

"Thank God," Suzanne mumbled too softly for Margaret to hear, relieved that oversleeping had not cost the firm a client.

"I'm sorry, Ms. Rosewell. I didn't hear you," Margaret said invading Suzanne's moment of comfort.

"Nothing, Margaret, not important," Suzanne disappeared into her office.

The office was the same. Somehow she'd expected it to be different, but the desk was still covered with papers, the wastebasket still full. The only contrast to the night before was the sunlight streaming through the window.

Suzanne sat down, lit her premier cigarette of the day and turned to admire the panorama of lower New York beyond the tinted glass. This was the first occasion she remembered just looking out the window since they'd given her this office. A hundred times she had stood and stared in that direction, her mind concentrating on some business problem, her vision never going beyond her own dull reflection. She wondered why she didn't spend some time each day simply watching through the glass. It was a nice view, very peaceful, part of the harbor, overlooking the smaller, older buildings. New York looked much calmer from here. The intercom buzzer demanded her attention.

"Yes, Margaret," she said, more sad than angry at being disturbed.

"There are messages, Ms. Rosewell," the tentative voice responded.

"Bring them in, please." Another first. She hadn't remembered saying *please* to Margaret in a very long time.

Suzanne turned her back to the city, crushed out the cigarette and actually smiled as her secretary came through the door. Margaret, somewhat disarmed by her superior's unexpected pleasant expression, moved slowly toward the desk, walking with the deliberateness of a soldier crossing a minefield. She handed the thick pile of slips to Suzanne.

Suzanne reviewed them quickly and returned them one at a time to Margaret who recorded the rapid fire instructions in efficient little notes made on every page. When Suzanne reached the sixth message slip, her hand trembled. The paper had only a name written on it: Elias Garner.

"What's this?" Suzanne demanded.

"I'm sorry, Ms. Rosewell," Margaret responded quickly. "That's not supposed to be there. I thought I threw that one in the garbage. I was just doodling. Just some kind of crank call." She reached forward for the paper but Suzanne pulled the message away.

"What kind of crank call?" Suzanne asked with a strange calm in her voice.

"I'm not sure I remember," Margaret said, flustered. "This man called for an appointment and said his name was Elias Garner. He... he refused to give me any more information. Said he was sort of General

Counsel for a very large corporation. He wanted you to handle something for his company."

"Sort of General Counsel?"

"That's all he would say, Ms. Rosewell, I swear. He wouldn't give me the name of his company or what kind of business he wanted you to handle. I told him I could not make an appointment without more information, but he refused. I figured he was just a nut and I threw the note away, or thought I threw it away."

"Well, I'll throw it away," Suzanne said. Instead she placed the paper on top of another pile of older messages. She finished reviewing the remaining calls and Margaret left.

Suzanne was alone again, the room quiet except for the background hum of the air conditioning system. She lit another cigarette and started to turn back toward the window when the phone rang.

The lawyer immediately knew which phone was summoning her by its distinctive sound, the private line, an unlisted number given only to select clients and her closest friends... well, to select clients. During the first two rings, she stayed her hand. The call was probably about something important, something that would require her immediate attention, intense action. This line was never used for anything else. She decided that a business disaster, a broken deal ready for repair, was just what she needed to put herself back on track. Suzanne lifted the receiver.

"Suzanne Rosewell," she said with her best business expression.

"Hello, Suzanne," the soft words flowed after a moment of quiet. "Do you know who this is?"

There was no doubt. She knew the sound of that voice. She'd heard it the night before and she'd heard it specifically speak her name. The voice was only a sound, a sound absorbed for just a moment, but one that remained in her head for hours. There was a gentle, comforting lilt in the very way this voice said the word "Suzanne." The sound was a cradle and she wanted to snuggle deep inside the cover. Still, the internal lawyer was stubborn. No one was going to pull her strings.

"I have no idea," she snapped with a nasty, sharp edge added to her expression. "This is a private line. How did you get the number?"

"Then you *do* know who I am," he answered, ignoring her tone and the question. "It's very important that we talk. May I come and see you? I am near your building."

"No, I'm busy," she said, the nastiness tone turning frightened. "Call my secretary and make an appointment." Suzanne slammed down the receiver, leaped to her feet and backed away from the desk, distancing herself as if the telephone were an armed nuclear bomb.

She stood in frozen silence – one minute... two minutes... three minutes, and the phone remained quiet. At the moment she first felt herself able to take a deep breath, the electronic instrument spoke again. Suzanne wanted to scream, opened her mouth to scream, but held the sound in her throat. On the fifth ring, the answering machine would pick up the call. All she had to do was remain in control a little while longer.

That little while took forever, each ring seemed to be ten times longer than normal. After a millennium, the reassuring click of the recording device echoed through the office. A few moments for her message and then the familiar tone.

"Suzanne," a different voice was coming through the speaker. "This is Harry. We've got a problem. Call me back at…."

"Hello, Harry," she lifted the receiver, stopping the machine. "I'm sorry. I was coming back into my office when I heard your voice." Not a total lie.

"Good, good," the client said through the wire. "I'm glad you're there. You know that merger problem. Well, it just got out of control. Sam called and…."

Suzanne disappeared into her comfortable lawyer's world where she knew all the rules of navigation. She pushed the earlier call away, and everything that went with it, and concentrated on Harry's troubles. Soon her brain and time were filled with this crisis of commerce.

The project occupied several hours and used a dozen phone calls, to the party of the first part, the party of the second part, back and around again. Finally, she'd resolved her client's problem. At a little before two, she was on the line with Harry again.

"You are a genius and I love you," the grateful client said. "Today you earned your fee. Thanks for getting things straightened out so fast."

"That's what I'm here for," the lawyer said in her patented manner. "You remember what you said, and how much you love me, when the bill arrives. Talk to you soon."

The legal mental exercise was followed by her delayed meeting with Roberts of the huge SellWell Corporation. Though her apology for the morning reminded her of those strange experiences, the memory was brief. She discovered that Roberts had not eaten lunch and convinced him to continue business over a meal. As they left the building, Suzanne took another long look at the banner covering the facade of the jazz club.

Dan Roberts of SellWell turned out to be charming and he carried a briefcase full of potential business. By the time lunch was over, Suzanne Rosewell had added another client to her portfolio. The senior partners would be happy.

Markam, Wilber, Kent & Todd's youngest female partner returned to her office in an excellent mood, radiating power and basking in her ability to take charge of own her life. She walked on a golden highway she'd constructed all by herself. Her disposition was destroyed by the vision of her office door open wide and an unmistakable sense that someone was waiting inside.

She crept closer to the unblocked portal, stepping gently in the thick carpet, moving a few inches at a time, straining her eyes until she reached a spot where she could see his reflection looking back from the glass picture window, a tall black man in a suit. Her heart stopped beating. She retreated to Margaret's desk.

"Who is in my office?" Suzanne murmured.

"There's no one in your office, Ms. Rosewell," Margaret answered with almost a question mark in her tone.

"Yes there is." Suzanne choked on her own whisper.

"I'm sorry, Ms. Rosewell," Margaret said annoyed, even angered that her ability to guard the doorway had been questioned. "I have not left this desk since you went out with Mr. Roberts. There is no one in your office." She was standing, walking around her desk and moving aggressively toward the open door. Suzanne followed meekly behind her, using the older woman as her shield.

"Let me just reassure you," the secretary was saying as she walked through the door ahead of Suzanne, "that no one could get by without my seeing them and... Oh, my God. Who are you? How did you get in here?" The last sentence ended in a near shout. Margaret had stopped short and Suzanne almost collided with her.

The tall black man turned toward the door. His suit was dark, dignified, expensive. His tie sported bright colors that reflected in the high shine of his shoes. He smiled gently. A thin, leather portfolio was tucked in the chair beside him and an old-fashioned wooden box with an ivory handle lay on the floor next to him.

"Sorry to have surprised you," the man said softly. "I'm here to see Suzanne. My name is Elias Garner."

CHAPTER FIVE

"I am terribly sorry sir," Margaret snapped, her professional secretarial instincts managing to overcome the surprise. "I personally keep Ms. Rosewell's calendar and you do not have an appointment. I must ask that you leave, now, or I will be forced to call a security guard."

Suzanne stayed hidden behind her subordinate's protective body. Margaret seemed to be doing just fine and the normally in-control lawyer was quite content to let her secretary solve this problem. Despite the woman's bluster, Elias Garner was entirely unruffled by the protective manner of the guardian of Suzanne's gate.

"You must be Margaret," he said in a calming voice, the vibrations virtually enveloping the two women. Suzanne sighed audibly, remembering how, last night *(Was that only last night?)* his tones had filled her when he simply said her name in the jazz club. Suzanne noticed how Margaret released the tension in her back and relaxed her shoulders at the sound of Elias Garner's voice. She concluded that there probably wasn't anything that this man could not sell to a woman. If that was not his profession, then he was in the wrong business.

"I spoke to you this morning and made an appointment," the intruder continued. "Maybe I'm not here at the right hour, but if you check your book, I'm sure you will find that I did reserve some time."

"No sir," Margaret said with conviction, recovering her professional demeanor. The tension returned to her frame. "I remember your phone call well, but I did not give you an appointment. You must leave, right now!"

"Very well," Garner said somewhat sadly. He stood but made no attempt to collect his portfolio or the ancient wooden box. “Please, why don’t you just check your book once more, Margaret? I’m sure you said that you were writing the time down. If there’s no appointment there, I will leave, I promise, without any more trouble.”

“Well, that’s simple enough,” Margaret responded, turning on her heels and moving quickly toward her desk where the sacrosanct appointment book rested. The sooner she could prove this man wrong, the sooner he would abandon his delusions and leave. And that couldn’t be soon enough for Margaret. The secretary’s departure left Suzanne unshielded with nothing between her and the visitor but an open doorway.

Garner smiled and Suzanne felt like she was six years old, the object of attention from a loved and affectionate uncle. They stared at each other for one long moment, the smiling stranger and the little girl who earlier had thought she was a grown-up attorney.

“I don’t understand,” Margaret’s voice of panic floated over from her desk, drawing both their gazes toward her. “Ms. Rosewell, look!” She held the appointment book open, a finger glued to a spot on the page. Suzanne’s eyes drifted to where the chewed, once-manicured nail rested. In the four o’clock slot, written boldly, and in a familiar hand, there was an entry.

Elias Garner

“I’m sorry, Ms. Rosewell. I am dreadfully sorry,” Margaret stammered, shaken by her discovery. “I don’t remember writing that entry. I distinctly recall refusing him an appointment. In fact, I checked your book before you went out with Mr. Roberts. Your afternoon was clear. I know it was. Isn’t that what I always do, Ms. Rosewell? There’s something wrong with my mind….”

“It’s all right Margaret. I think we’ve all been working too hard,”

Suzanne said, placing her hand gently on her secretary's shoulder, surprising herself both with her sympathy for the distraught woman and her sudden ability to express it. "Since there is an appointment written in the book, we will honor our commitment." And turning to the still standing visitor. "Sit down please. Mr. Garner."

"Just call me Eli. Everyone else does."

Suzanne gave Margaret one more reassuring pat, gently guiding her with a touch toward her desk. The secretary traveled in a trance while the lawyer watched the defeated woman shuffle away. She'd never known Margaret to make such a mistake. Suzanne was worried.

Trying to look confident, knowing she wasn't succeeding, the lawyer tentatively entered her own office, closed the door, paused to gain some composure and traversed the terribly long distance over the carpet to her desk. Suzanne could feel Garner's eyes locked on her, following her journey, turning in his chair ever so slightly to parallel her progress. His charming, gentle, relaxing smile never faded and never appeared forced. Suzanne steeled herself and looked directly into his eyes. She found him exceptionally handsome with bittersweet chocolate skin and deep, sparkling, dark eyes. From the top of his modified Afro, to his Brooks Brothers pinstripe suit, to the tips of his polished Florsheims, he was the perfect "Gentlemen's Quarterly" cover model. She couldn't tell his age, though he was definitely her senior, but she did notice how his tight, curly dark hair absorbed the light coming through the windows, making his features glow and hiding any aging his face might otherwise have revealed. It took all her self-control just to keep herself from reaching across the desk to touch him.

"Are you a lawyer, Mr. Garner?" she asked him as she caught her breath. Ignoring his request for familiarity was intentional. He didn't seem to notice.

"Oh, heavens no," he laughed. "Not that there's anything wrong in being a lawyer. After all, I am here… seeing you, a lawyer, for help.

But, no, I'm only a musician."

"And a very good one," Suzanne found herself saying without really meaning to. The thought was in her mind but she had no intention of speaking it. Yet, the words came out anyway. He nodded his thanks and let her continue.

"You don't dress like a musician," she proceeded after recovering. "Margaret said something about your being General Counsel for some corporation."

"No," he said slowly, "she misunderstood. Let me explain. It's hard to make a living as a jazz musician. So, in 'real life' as we say, I am the personal counselor to the Chairman of the Board of a very large international corporation...."

"What corporation?" Suzanne interrupted.

"We'll get to that," Garner replied. "I am one of his two primary counselors. The Chairman hardly makes a single move without consulting me and my opposite."

"Your opposite?" she interrupted again.

"Ms. Rosewell," a hint of impatience entered his tone and Suzanne realized that maybe the man was not perfect after all.

"How can I explain everything if you won't let me talk?" Suzanne was six years old again and muttered an apology.

"My Chairman is a very important and powerful man," Garner continued, as if the interruptions had never happened. "For the purposes of this conversation, at least for now, he must remain anonymous." Suzanne prepared to break in again. Garner noticed her move and raised his hand. She fell back in her chair, silent.

"In your circles, my Chairman would be called, well, eccentric," he said, choosing his words carefully, "but believe me, he knows what he's doing. He's run the Corporation for a very long time. And he keeps extensive records on all sorts of things. These records, these lists are very important to him. A few weeks ago, our central computer crashed and when the data was restored, part of one list was missing. The inventory, as he calls it, was short. Coming directly to the point, we need some very discreet help, here in the United States to locate the missing inventory. That's why I'm here."

Elias Garner fell silent and Suzanne suddenly realized it was her turn to speak. Despite the multitude of questions in her head, she had difficulty forming a sentence.

"What... what type of inventory?" was all she found herself able to say.

"Well, in reality, we're talking about people," Garner continued so quickly that he had to have anticipated the question. "Are you familiar with the Jewish legend of the Thirty-Six Righteous Ones? You are Jewish, aren't you?"

"My parents were born Jewish," Suzanne answered, wondering why she was responding to a personal question posed by a stranger. "I was raised without any religion. I don't think of myself as Jewish, or anything else for that matter. And I am not familiar with much Jewish culture…." Catching herself, she continued, "no, I haven't heard of that legend."

"The story is part of a very ancient tradition. This tale contends that the Supreme Being has arranged that there are always, at all times throughout history, thirty-six truly righteous people on the earth. Thirty-six, who know the Divine Will. Through these people, and because of them, the human race has the resources for its own salvation. Right now five of these people are missing from the Chairman's list. I need your help to find them."

"Your Chairman keeps a list of righteous people out of some old Jewish legend?" she said with astonishment.

"Accept that my Chairman has his reasons, or chalk it up to his being eccentric, whatever you like. I have learned not to question what he does, simply to help him to do what he wants. The list contains no names in the United States and, while that's possible, it's highly unlikely that there are no righteous people here at all. The Chairman has sent me here to find the missing ones, and I have come to recruit you into this effort."

"This is more than a little crazy," Suzanne answered. "Read the New York Times, put the President on your list."

"Would you consider the President to be a righteous person?" he asked simply.

"No, I guess not," she answered after thinking for a moment. Then she realized what she was doing, her very participation in the conversation was drifting her toward acceptance. She corrected the deviation immediately. "This is nuts. I can't sit here and listen to this fantasy. You may be a fine musician, a great dresser and a good looking, well spoken man, but I think you're crazy." The last sentence was the expression of another thought that she had not intended to relate. Suzanne seemed to have very little control over her vocal cords.

"I would be surprised if you didn't consider me as such," he answered, unoffended. "I ask only that you hear the rest of my story before requesting me to leave." She nodded, not trusting her own speech, afraid to open her mouth and free the thoughts she had locked in her head.

"My opposite... oh yes, I said I would explain that to you. My opposite is a woman named Elizabeth Luckholt. I call her my opposite because she usually takes the opposite position to me when advising the Chairman. She is very bright and very determined. Many years ago she led a proxy fight and tried to unseat the Chairman. She lost, but he still keeps her at his left hand because her advice is important and because it allows him to watch her closely."

"The politics in your office are really wicked," she said with sarcasm, as Garner paused to take a breath.

"Yes, that's right, wicked is a good word," he said. "I believe

Elizabeth took advantage of the computer failure. I think she has intentionally hidden the names of five missing Righteous Ones. If they're not found, the Chairman will... well, make certain decisions that I'd rather he not make."

"And your opposite would like the chairman to make these decisions, I presume." Sarcasm still there, and not in small doses.

"She does have a vested interest in certain possible scenarios. Additionally, she has been known to behave in less a than scrupulous manner." His smile broadened. "Can you help me?"

"Let me be honest, Mr. Garner," she said, leaning forward in her chair.

"Please, can't you just call me Eli?"

"No, I don't think so, Mr. Garner," she retorted, emphasizing his last name. Her rejection did not seem to affect his comfortable expression one way or another.

Suzanne realized that although Elias Garner was strange, maybe even a little crazy, he was a man of immense confidence and high personal power. If she was to continue to resist his charms, she dare not make eye contact with the man across her desk. Each time she looked at his face she wanted to believe his preposterous story. He didn't appear or sound like a madman, but his tale was not one for a sane person to take seriously.

"Frankly, sir," she continued, "this sounds like a job for a private detective, not a lawyer. Even if I did think myself appropriate, you won't tell me the name of your company, or your chairman, or, for that matter, anything about you. I only work with clients who trust me. Besides, I don't come cheap."

"Yes, I know," he said. Behind his measured tones, she was sure he was laughing at her. "I have told you all I can without breaking my vow of secrecy. You were not chosen because you are an excellent lawyer, which, counselor, is *what* you are. You, Suzanne Rosewell, were chosen because of *who* you are. Had you become a doctor or a housewife or a waitress, we would still be having this conversation. In fact, I must say that if you had not been trained in the logic of law, you might be more willing to shut down your mind and open your heart. This is a very important assignment. Your fee is not a consideration. It is imperative that you accept this task as a volunteer."

"I beg your pardon?"

"I said… it is imperative..."

"I know what you said. I just don't believe that you said it." Suddenly she was back in control, her patience at an end. "You waste my time with this... this story, and then tell me you want me to waste more on a wild goose chase *and* to do it for free. Well, Mr. Elias Garner, I don't know where you come from, but I think you ought to go back there. Things just don't work that way in my world. This meeting is over."

She stood to emphasize her position. Garner remained seated. His smile never dimmed. The gentle look in his dark eyes did not harden. He stared intensely at Suzanne, his eyelids half closed, white teeth in contrast to dark lips. Suzanne's legs began to quiver. A comment buried in her mind was trying to force its way through her vocal cords. She could only resist for a small moment.

"You're a fine musician Mr. Garner," she said, only in partial control of her words. "I was moved by your performance." She wanted to add that he should stick to music, that he should not have come on this fool's fantasy. The rest of the thought – all the critical phrases – would simply not come out.

"Thank you," he finally said. "You know that the piece in the club was written for you."

Suddenly the wall that held back all her words was breached. His gentle voice was the tool that seemed to open and close the blockage. Yet everything she wanted to say would still not come and some of what she wanted to keep back flowed freely. There were holes in the wall and some of her thoughts were able to flow randomly through the small openings.

"Now cut that out," she snapped in anger, embarrassed at the memories of the emotions evoked by the music. "You never saw me before last night and certainly did not expect that I would be in that club. That was a coincidence you are trying to take advantage of for your own purposes."

"Many wise people, throughout the centuries, have believed that there is no such thing as a coincidence," Garner rebutted. "You were chosen, Suzanne. But I see that I will not convince you on this day. I will leave now. Please, think about my proposal. If you change your mind, you can tell me when we next meet." He stood, gathering his portfolio and his strange wooden box as he rose. Suzanne's mobility was abruptly restored.

"We will not meet again," she said, moving around her desk, taking his arm and guiding him toward the door. "Don't call and don't come to see me. I have no time for you."

"I hope that you will soon come to understand that you have no time for anyone else," he answered, while being directed by Suzanne's touch toward the door. "We will meet again. I say this so that you know *that* occasion will not be coincidence." He looked into her eyes and another question appeared in her brain.

"What do you carry in the wooden box?" she inquired, knowing that it was useless to resist the impulse.

"Let me show you," he said, turning free of her grasp and setting the wooden case on her desk.

Slowly, as if performing a ceremony, Elias Garner loosens the brass clasps. Carefully he lifts the lid. Resting on a bed of deep, black velvet, is the most beautiful horn Suzanne has ever seen.

The instrument appears to be a trumpet, but without the usual valves to control tones. The horn is the color of pure gold and glows as if creating its own light rather than simply reflecting the afternoon sun. Of course, that's impossible. The trumpet can not generate its own illumination. What she sees has to be a reflection. Yet the room seems to grow brighter the moment the lid is lifted. Suzanne gasps out loud at its beauty.

"It gleams like gold," she said.

"It is gold," Garner answered. "As pure as possible… while still holding its shape."

"The engraving," she said, pointing with her index finger but afraid to bring her hand close for fear that her fingers may be absorbed by the strange light. "Is that Hebrew?"

"They are Hebrew letters," he explained, "and the language is very ancient, reflecting how the average person living in Jerusalem spoke in the days when the instrument was believed to have been made. Would you like to know what the words say?"

Suzanne can only nod.

"For you have made him a little lower than the angels and crowned him with glory and honor," the musician recited without bothering to read. "The quote comes from the Book of Psalms, psalm eight in particular, written by the poet King David. It is said that he wrote the psalm in honor of the chief musician of the court.

"How old is this trumpet?" she asked.

"That's not really known. Maybe only a few hundred years. There is a legend connected to the trumpet that says King David himself commissioned its construction and personally approved the final product, but that may only be a tale."

"Like the story of the Thirty-Six Righteous Ones?" she asked, finally able to turn away from the glowing horn and toward the musician's face.

"That could be," Elias Garner answered, the golden light alive and dancing in his dark eyes. "But the horn itself is real, Suzanne. You see it here in front of you. And in my portfolio I have a page with the names of thirty-one righteous people. That same page has five blank spaces." He closed the lid and the room was dark and gray. She tried to ignore the remark and change the topic.

"Why do you carry the horn with you? It seems much too valuable to be carted all over New York. You should have all that gold locked in a vault."

"I wanted you to see the instrument, close up. I thought you might enjoy the display."

"Have you ever played it?"

"Of course. You heard the music last night. Pretty impressive instrument, don't you think?"

"The music was stunning," she responded only half voluntarily. "But why did you play that club for only one night?"

"Oh yes, the life of an unknown jazz musician. The number of my fans is limited. One night is enough."

"I don't agree," Suzanne answered, pleased to be able to argue with him about a different topic. "There were many people at the Wooden Horn Case who would've come back for more."

"That's what they always say," Garner answered, "but when the second night comes, they always have something more important to do. I know. I've been playing for years. That's all right. I don't mind one-night stands. In fact, I somewhat like them. And I want to continue to play them, but that may be impossible if you don't help me."

"Please, let's not start that again," she was able to snap back, with the spell of the horn gone. "I don't know what you are talking about and I don't want to know. Just leave."

Garner collected his things and this time stepped toward the door when one more unstoppable question filled Suzanne's mind.

"Will you leave a copy of the list?" she asked before she knew what she was saying.

"I brought this just for you," he said as his smile returned. Elias Garner reached into his portfolio and removed a single sheet of paper that he laid carefully on Suzanne's desk. "Until next time." He opened the office door himself and strolled purposefully down the corridor, past the still pale Margaret and toward the elevators.

Suzanne watched him as he walked. She could feel the mix of emotions inside her, strange feelings, confusion and contentment blended together, tension and relaxation merged in her belly, the same buffet of feelings she experienced in the jazz club and again in her bedroom. Concern for her own sanity once more filled her brain.

The lawyer's eyes remained on the departing musician, stayed with him as he pressed the button to call the elevator. She waited while he waited and maintained her vigil as the door opened, allowing a thin, blond woman dressed all in black to step out. The figure stopped directly in front of the tall strange man. They were talking. They knew each other.

From Suzanne's vantage point, the woman seemed older than Garner. Her hair was light blond and fell gently over her shoulders. Even from down the corridor, Suzanne could see that the woman's eyes were deep blue, to go along with her hair and very pale skin. Though certainly beautiful, the lines around her face seemed hard and sharp, blunting the otherwise pleasant impact of her clear, cream skin as it contrasted with her dark clothing. In every way, from gender to accessories, the blond woman appeared to be the black man's opposite. The thought made Suzanne shiver. She wished she could hear their conversation, but the distance was too far and they spoke in whispers.

"Elizabeth," Elias Garner said without surprise, "what are you doing here?"

"As if you didn't know," Elizabeth Luckholt responded. There was no humor in her voice.

"Tell me anyway."

"I am here to make sure your recount of the inventory is honest," she said without averting her gaze.

"Everyone doesn't do business the way you do, Ms. Luckholt," he answered with what sounded like pity in his voice.

"Oh yes they do, Eli," she replied with a smile that could never be described as warm. "Most simply do not have the courage to act out what they think. Everyone has a piece of me inside them, even you Elias Garner." She did not allow him to answer. Instead she moved her eyes down the corridor and focused on the lawyer standing in her doorway. "Is that the one you chose?"

"You already know Suzanne is my choice."

"How would I know such a thing?"

"Because you were in the club when I played for her."

"You saw me?"

"No, but I knew you were there anyway." His smile was completely gone. "You tried to interfere."

"Now how could I do that?" she said with her mouth turned to sly grin. "But you made a poor choice Eli, a poor choice. She does business closer to my style than to yours."

The subject of their conversation could not hear them, but when the blond woman turned her eyes, Suzanne could feel the piercing gaze penetrate her body, filling her with an oppressive sense of fear. This too she'd felt before, on the street and in the club, but now the cold grip of fright refused to yield, driving away all of her other feelings. The grasp of dread stayed with her until the two figures at the end of the hallway finally stepped into an elevator and disappeared.

CHAPTER SIX

The office was like a war zone after a major battle and the soldiers, Suzanne and Margaret, were perfectly exhausted and severely shaken.

Initially powerless to move, they watched each other silently, the lawyer and boss standing in the open doorway of her office, leaning against the frame; the secretary and subordinate fortressed behind her desk, slumped into a deep curve, face drooping, expression glazed and frightened. If she'd tried to lift her hands from the desktop, they would have been shaking. Each avoided looking directly at the other until some inner need forced their eyes to meet. Then neither was willing let go of the gaze.

These two women, who had felt little fondness for each other, whose relationship was based on mutual professional need merged with stubborn law firm pride, had, for the first time, shared something significant and personal, and it had frightened them both. As their eyes locked, they understood what each other felt for the first time.

In truth, their experiences were fundamentally different. Margaret thought she'd simply gone crazy and was suffering from delusions and mental lapses. She knew that there was something strange, maybe even mystical about the appearance of an appointment, penned in her own handwriting, that she would have sworn, even in a court of law, had not been put in the book by her. She looked at the entry with no recollection of having made it. Worse, she had the distinct memory of having written *nothing* there. Yet the evidence was in front of her. No matter how many times she stared, the lines of the black pen would not go away. She suspected something was seriously awry and not through any fault of her own. An entry in ink did not fit her habit. She kept the book in pencil so appointments could be easily adjusted. But this was definitely her handwriting and the book had hardly been out of her sight all day. She had little choice but to admit that the evidence pointed toward her.

Margaret alternated between feeling like a victim and like the perpetrator of a major mess. She knew nothing of the conversation that had gone on behind the closed door. For all Margaret knew, Suzanne's appointment with the mysterious Elias Garner had been about some routine issue. Though after seeing the look in her boss's eyes, she doubted it.

Suzanne knew all the events, from both sides of the door, and having that knowledge frightened her far more than she would've believed possible. Still, the lawyer part of her was almost persuaded she'd spent twenty minutes with a madman; a convincing, credible and very unusual lunatic, but a lunatic nonetheless. For the moment, she decided to ignore the strangeness of her own reactions. She dismissed her periodic inability to ask, or to keep from asking, certain questions. And she gave no credibility to that nagging feeling inside that she really wanted to believe the insane man's story.

The one thing she couldn't ignore, try as she might, was the deep, paralyzing fear now associated with the blond woman in the black suit. This person had to be the one Elias Garner called his "opposite," Elizabeth Luckholt. The logical part of Suzanne's mind focused on the concern that there were now two escaped mental patients wandering in the halls of her building. But her subconscious, the part of her willing to accept unacceptable explanations, dwelt on issues far more serious.

If the form of their experiences had differed, these two women had shared the substance of a frightening half-hour and this was the first time they'd ever shared anything. Work, instructions, directions had always been imposed, hardly shared. Victories belonged to Suzanne alone and Margaret's pride in working for the youngest female partner, something she enjoyed bragging about to her colleagues, was carefully hidden from her boss as part of the game that each played in pretending they had no real need for the other.

"Margaret," the lawyer finally said, "if there are no more appointments, I think I'm going home and you should do the same."

"But it's not even four-thirty, Ms. Rosewell," she responded.

"I know. For once, let's break the rules, both of us. This has been a rough day." She paused for a moment. Maintaining a consistent train of thought was difficult.

While Suzanne's mind drifted, Margaret waited, wondering if there were more instructions to come. With great effort, the lawyer centered her focus on her secretary and asked a question that startled them both.

"I would like a cup of coffee. Would you join me?"

Under the weight of all that had already happened, the invitation became the final act, too heavy for Margaret to handle. She became flustered.

"Well... I... I'd be happy to get coffee for you, Ms. Rosewell." There were tears in Margaret's eyes as she spoke. For a moment Suzanne thought to tell the secretary that she could address her superior by her first name, but she dismissed the idea.

"No, you just go on home. I can get the coffee myself. I'm sure tomorrow will be a better day. And Margaret... maybe we'd better keep all this to ourselves, not share it around the office."

"Oh, I agree completely. I wouldn't even know how to tell anyone about *this*." She paused and looked back at Suzanne who nodded and waved her hand toward the elevator doors.

"Good night Ms. Rosewell." Margaret wanted to leave that office more than anything in the world. She did not have to be encouraged further. Suzanne leaned on the door post and watched her go, efficiently gathering her things, then speeding up the corridor with only a brief glance back to see if Suzanne was still standing there.

As Margaret entered the elevator, a feeling of intolerable

loneliness remained behind with Suzanne. Her office was no retreat, nor could she envision moving to the solitude of her apartment. Under the circumstances, coffee in the law firm's cafeteria sounded appealing.

At four-thirty in the afternoon, the cafeteria was nearly empty. The steam tables were cleaned and cold, chairs were stacked high while a man in a dirty white uniform mopped the tiles. One coffee bar and a soft drink station remained open near a bank of vending machines that dispensed candy and tobacco.

It made Suzanne realize that she'd left her own smokes on the cluttered desk in her office. She ordered a cup of coffee, got change from the bored woman at the register, made a cigarette purchase and looked for a place to sit. The smoking room, a glassed-off, sealed section of the room, was empty, a reflection of both the hour and the thinning ranks of people who still indulged in the unhealthy habit. It reminded Suzanne of her often-repeated promise to join those who sit at tables without ashtrays.

Among the few sitting in the area reserved for the healthy, drinking a cup of tea and concentrating on a book, was Arthur Blake. Suzanne decided that company was more important than smoking. She stuffed the cigarettes in her pocket and walked to his table.

"Hello, Arthur," she said, her voice hushed. She realized she was disturbing him but tried to keep the intrusion from being too abrupt. He looked up from the book slowly, his motion stage-like. She had the impression he knew she was in the room and was only pretending to be absorbed. The pretense annoyed her and she regretted her attempt at being gentle.

"Hello, Suzanne," Arthur said. He spoke cautiously, remembering that their earlier encounter had not been congenial. "I am surprised to see you in the cafeteria so late."

"Oh, I just needed some... some coffee before I went out to fight with the subway," she responded. There was something else she had intended to say. His knowledge of her was acute enough to notice the omission. He also knew that she would speak her mind only when she wanted to. Right now she didn't want to.

"You're not usually here at this time either, are you?" was all she managed to say.

"No, just taking a break… gotta work late," he answered with a somewhat condescending smile.

"Working late tonight. You?" she said very quickly. He mistook her disappointment for surprise.

"I do work late from time to time," he shot back defensively.

"I didn't mean anything Arthur," she was uncharacteristically flustered. "I... I was just going to ask if you were free for dinner tonight." Now *he* was the one surprised.

"Really?" In a much softer tone. "You're asking me to dinner? That's certainly unexpected." He paused. "I would love to join you. I would very much like that, but not tonight. I'm in court in the morning and I've gotta do some last minute research. Can I take a rain check?"

"Sure, I guess... but I'll have to check my book," she said, because she didn't know what else to say. This time he heard the disappointment.

"Is there something wrong, Suzanne?"

"No... yes... no. I'm extremely tired, that's all." There was no point in pressing the matter. Arthur sat without speaking and watched her, waiting to hear if she would say more.

Suzanne, on the other hand, was experiencing a rare moment in her adult life when she had something to say but did not know where or if to begin. One option was to share the entire bizarre ordeal from start to finish. Unless Arthur could feel what she had felt, was still feeling, he would never understand. He would dismiss Elias Garner as just another nut. They met lots of them in their business. So she returned only his silence until the stress of no conversation reached a point where not talking was more painful than breaking the quiet.

"What are you reading?" She asked, unable to continue to breathe through the lack of talk, but intent on moving the topic in another direction. Her eyes pointed at the book under his hand. "Is this part of your research for the case?" He looked down at the pages as if he'd forgotten they were there.

"No, this book was here when I arrived. Someone must have left it on the table. Very strange text to find in a law firm cafeteria." He closed the cover and turned the volume around so Suzanne could read the title. The color drained from her face. The blue cover with bold white letters burned its imprint through her now tightly closed eyelids, forcing itself deep into her brain...

JEWISH LEGENDS AND FOLK TALES
a collection by Elias Abromowitz

It would have been hard to miss the book's impact on Suzanne.

"You look like you just saw Jacob Marley's ghost, and it's the wrong season," he said, trying to mask his concern with a joke. "Is this your book?"

"No," she snapped, leaning back and away from the offending publication. "I've never seen it before!"

The violence of her response shocked Arthur. He was unused to seeing Suzanne express raw emotion and he was at a complete loss as to how to react. More as a nervous gesture than a real concern for time, he glanced at his watch.

"Oh boy," he said, torn between worry, curiosity and the information his timepiece provided, "I got so interested in this thing that I lost track of the hour. There's a research team waiting for me in the library. I'm sorry Suzanne, I must go. Are you all right?"

"Of course, of course," she answered with the shaking still in her voice. "Go ahead. I understand. I'm fine." Arthur rose and moved to depart. He made no attempt to collect the book.

"Take this with you," Suzanne nearly shouted.

"Not mine," Arthur answered even as he was moving away. "Leave it on the table. The person who forgot the silly thing might come back." And he was gone. Suzanne and the book remained.

She fingered the cover gently, touching it as one does when testing an iron for heat. After her hand came away unburned, she reached out again and turned the book over, looking for the traditional author's photo. There was none. She opened the jacket, checking the publisher and copyright date. The volume had been printed by the Jewish Theological Seminary and was recently released. She closed the cover and flipped the book again, still in search of the author's biography.

Despite the first-name coincidence, Suzanne could not imagine that the tall, thin black man in her office was connected to the family Abromowitz. Still, anything was possible. Maybe the entire meeting was some sort of strange promotional stunt for this very book. This small straw of logic, a possible, though admittedly remote, answer to the puzzle gave her courage and she turned one more page. There, finally, was the author's biography, photo and all.

Displayed in front of her was a picture of an elderly Jewish scholar with a traditional, gray beard, white hair topped by a skullcap and photographed with the expected wall of books as a backdrop.

The text described Professor Dr. Elias Abromowitz as an instructor at the Jewish Theological Seminary, probably the largest rabbinical training school in the country. His biography offered a standard religious and academic background that wasn't even particularly interesting, except for the last line. An unconnected sentence told the reader that Dr. Abromowitz, in his youth, had been a well-respected jazz trumpeter.

Suzanne slammed the cover shut. Again she was fleeing,

abandoning her coffee and the book, retreating to her office as quickly as she could, attempting not to broadcast the panic that gripped her.

The law firm was almost empty as Suzanne raced down the internal spiral staircase, past the elevator doors and through the corridor toward her office. So intent was her journey, so directly had she focused on the retreat to the sanctuary of her workspace that she completely missed the figure seated behind a desk in one of the empty offices. From her vantage point, the blonde woman did not miss seeing Suzanne.

As the lawyer rushed passed, Elizabeth Luckholt stepped silently into the empty corridor and stared at Suzanne's back, watched her as she bounded into her office and slammed the door shut. Then, with a twist of her mouth that someone else might have taken as a smile, Luckholt turned around and headed into a waiting elevator.

> *To draw her curtains and hide in the dark is Suzanne's sole preoccupation when she finds her office blazing with hot light. The intense, red afternoon sun, hours away from its resting place behind the hills of New Jersey, angrily glows outside her window. The fireball is huge, three, four, five times its normal size, filling the sky as though someone, or something, had moved Sol closer for the single purpose of overheating Suzanne's office.*
>
> *The rays of the July sun are penetrating the tinted glass, filling the room and overpowering the air conditioning. The office, behaving like a glass-walled sauna, refuses to offer the slightest respite of cool darkness.*
>
> *Suzanne tries to lower the shade but the latch will not release. With sweat pouring down her back, she pulls on the cord, but the shade is impossibly stuck. The hellish heat has turned her own office, her personal sanctuary, into a hostile tropical greenhouse. There is nowhere to hide.*

But even as she stands helpless in the heat, a cool thought registers in a corner of Suzanne's mind. Something recorded by a tiny section of her eye, implanted in her brain sometime during her flight, is penetrating her consciousness, a sense more than a thought, a feeling more than an image. She opens the door, backs away from the attacking sun and retreats up the corridor to the same empty office recently appropriated by the blonde stranger.

Suzanne peeked around the corner and was almost astonished to see the space vacant. There was no real reason for her surprise. The associate who had once used the room left the firm a month earlier. The place had been cleaned, repainted and prepared for its next occupant. Something in Suzanne's subconscious saw the room's emptiness as being unusual, but she was still willing to take advantage of the vacancy.

While the sun's rays tore into the other side of the building, this office was dark and cool. Suzanne went inside, closed the door, settled behind the desk, loosened her collar and bathed in the frigid air that filled the space. She was finally able to draw a deep breath.

Suzanne Rosewell, Markam, Wilber, Kent & Todd's youngest female partner, sat in the tiny office and waited for her heart to slow down to a normal pace, waiting while the terror ebbed from her system, until she felt whole again. The process took nearly two hours.

When she finally emerged from her cave, everyone was gone. The sun had dropped below the next row of buildings and the air conditioning was in control once more, even in her office. The cleaning people had been through and, except for her desk, which they never touched, the office was neat and smelled of fresh lemon oil polish.

The aroma lifted her spirits and, realizing she still had the capacity to feel good, Suzanne plunged into the relief. Surrendering to a lost sense of well being was just what she needed. She felt better and the better she felt, the more she enjoyed feeling better. To increase the high still further, she gathered her briefcase and purse and headed out the door. So relieved was she to be unburdened from the fear, that she actually said "good night" to the nameless security guard seated in the hallway. This was a first.

"Have a nice evening, Ms. Rosewell," he responded. Suzanne wondered how the man knew her name.

The good feelings remained with her all the way home, though tempered by the usual hassles of the subway.

"I'm like a yo-yo," she thought to herself, climbing the stairs at 86th Street. "One moment I'm up, one moment I'm down." A yo-yo, with some stranger pulling the string. She worried about her health, wondering if she might be suffering through PMS or a summer cold. But as she was riding on the high end of the string, her concerns did not linger long. Suppressing a strong desire to whistle, Suzanne strode confidently to the front door of her home.

"Good evening Ms. Rosewell," the doorman greeted her. "Some lady dropped off a box for you." He handed her a wrapped package and waited for his tip. She puzzled over the parcel as she passed him a dollar, shrugged her shoulders and took the elevator to the 22nd floor. Inside her apartment, the answering machine winked for her attention.

The first three messages were from Margaret. The morning's confusion returned as she heard her secretary remind her, thrice, of the meeting that she'd missed, the same messages Margaret had sworn she'd left and Suzanne had sworn never arrived. Yet the machine's time stamp confirmed Margaret's claim.

"I must have been in the shower when she called," Suzanne thought, forgetting that she had skipped her morning shower. The fourth call had come later in the day.

"Hello dear," the recorded voice said. "This is Mother. In case that doorman of yours didn't tell you, I left a package, a book I just finished. I know you're going to think it's strange but I have found this topic rather interesting lately. Maybe I'm getting older... oh well, I hope you like what you read. Call me soon." Suzanne wondered why her mother hadn't left the message and book at the office. Bothering her daughter at work had never constrained her before.

Ripping the paper away, Suzanne knew just what book she held in her hand long before the package was unwrapped. Her fingers were only able to grip the copy of *JEWISH LEGENDS AND FOLK TALES* by Elias Abromowitz for a split second. She dropped the volume as though it were diseased. The thing fell on the still unmade bed and bounced to the floor just as she walked out of the room.

Finding the mental switch, Suzanne turned off her brain and turned on the stereo, filling her apartment, and likely all her neighbors' apartments, with Mozart's 39th Symphony. She set the CD player on indefinite repeat and turned the volume so high that the windows began to vibrate. With the music loud enough to forbid independent thinking, she went about changing her clothes, making a light dinner and cleaning the rooms while avoiding the bedroom and the abandoned book. At eleven o'clock, she shut off the music, watched the news and prepared for bed. The clock showed nearly midnight when she settled under the covers with the light out, intent on going right to sleep.

From the floor beneath the bed, the book called to her. She could hear its silent summons no matter which way she turned, and she knew that she would not sleep as long as the pages remained untouched. Suzanne turned on the light and picked up the book. Her finger reached randomly for a spot. Before opening the page, she knew how the chapter title would read.

LAMED VAV ZADDIKIM
THIRTY-SIX RIGHTEOUS ONES

"According to the Encyclopedia Judaica, they are the minimal number of anonymous righteous people living in the world in every generation. They are privileged to see the Divine Presence and the world exists on their merit."

The text went on for several pages describing the origins of the legend in Jewish culture, including commentaries of scholars and rabbis, and the use of the tale in Jewish literature. The writing was dry and academic, almost dull. But Suzanne consumed every word and was disappointed when the chapter ended a few pages later. She tossed the book back on the floor, uninterested in what else might be within the covers. A phrase continued to repeat in her mind.

"The world exists on their merit," she said out loud. "What does that mean? Why does that seem to be so important?" At nearly two a.m., Suzanne rose from bed, went into the kitchen, pulled out the telephone directory and thumbed through the pages until the listing jumped out at her, just as she expected it would. She was beginning to depend on these strange coincidences. She dialed and a sleepy voice picked up after five rings.

"Hello?" said the sleepy voice.

"Dr. Elias Abromowitz?" she asked with her best professional tone.

"Yes, who is this please?" the voice had a gentle European accent.

"My name is Suzanne Rosewell. I am an attorney with the firm of Markam, Wilber, Kent & Todd on Wall Street. I need to speak with you about your book... *Jewish Legends and Folktales*?"

"You need to talk with me about my book *at two o'clock in the morning*?"

"I am sorry to call you so late, but I need to meet with you first thing tomorrow. This is a matter of some urgency."

"I assume so. It must be urgent to wake an old man from his sleep,"

Abromowitz said without a hint of annoyance. "What time would you like to meet young lady? You are *a young* lady, yes?"

"Yes," she responded, softening to his friendly manner. "How did you know?"

"An old man envies the intensity of the young. If you were my age, this call would have waited until the morning. Besides, no man is ever so old that he forgets the special sound of a young woman's voice. What time would you like to meet?"

"Is eight o'clock too early?"

"No, I rise early, providing you let me get back to sleep. Do you drink coffee?"

"Yes, I do," she said hesitantly.

"Good, then I will have a pot brewing in my office at the Seminary at eight o'clock. The security guard will direct you. Tell me your name once again." The old man spoke with the authority of one who had controlled generations of young people in his classroom.

"Suzanne Rosewell," she answered, feeling somewhat like a college student.

"Very well, Suzanne. Eight o'clock." The line went dead. Suzanne slept soundly until the alarm went off at six. She felt refreshed and energized.

CHAPTER SEVEN

To Suzanne, the streets around the Jewish Theological Seminary appeared much too busy for eight a.m. on a lazy, warm summer's morning. With strength that seemingly belonged to the crisp, energetic fall, knots of students moved up and down the sidewalk, all heading, at their own various paces, for the entrance.

Some were dressed in professional attire – men in suits and ties, women in simple, severe outfits with full sleeves and long skirts. These people moved quickly, carrying briefcases and book bags, walking alone or in small groups, focused straight ahead, expressions intent. There was little conversation between them, as they greeted familiar faces with only a blink of their eyes or, at most, a slight nod of their heads.

There were others clad in blue jeans and printed t-shirts with messages ranging from Jewish camp experiences to rock concerts. Most of these people carried backpacks and were involved in deep, animated conversations, debating issues of the world or at least of the classroom. They walked in crowds, less fast, but hardly slow, all speaking and gesturing at the same time, oblivious to anything outside their own tightly packed universe.

Scattered here and there she spotted people who appeared, by their age and demeanor, to be faculty members. They progressed singly, or in pairs, greeting the large groups of young people with a nod. With the exception of those wearing skullcaps, *yarmulkas* she remembered they were called, the Gothic building and its inhabitants seemed, to Suzanne's surprise, as if they could have been a part of any American college campus. She wasn't sure what she had expected, but this certainly wasn't it. Maybe she'd thought they would all resemble, in varying ages, the bookplate photo of Dr. Abromowitz. She had certainly not anticipated that so many of the students, and the faculty for that matter, would be women.

Suzanne's childhood memories were all she knew of Judaism. They centered exclusively on her mother's Eastern European immigrant father; an old fashioned, devoted, devout grandfather. He had passed away around her eighth birthday and had been the only religious influence in her life. Grandmother Molly lit candles on Friday night, maybe. But if she did that much, she certainly didn't do anything more. Grandpa Morris' funeral was the last Jewish ritual Suzanne remembered.

Evelyn and Eliot Rosewell, Suzanne's parents, barely acknowledged their Jewish roots and their only child grew up sharing Christmas trees and Easter egg hunts with her Christian playmates. Once she had asked to attend church Sunday school with her friends, but her father had drawn the line at that.

That particular memory succeeded in completely stopping Suzanne's progress toward the entrance. She didn't think much about her father anymore. It had been a long time since his sudden and premature death, two weeks before her high school graduation when she had planned to make the valedictory speech in his honor. Instead she delivered the address in his memory. The audience was crying with her by the time she reached the last page of the text.

Suzanne had always found her father's Sunday school decision out of character. Though he'd married a Jewish woman, there was absolutely nothing religious or culturally Jewish in his life, not even his wedding ceremony, she'd been told. Nor did the Jewish religion seem to exist in the lives of her paternal grandparents who joined the Unitarian Church when her father, their only child, was born.

Yet he had been more than adamant in his opposition to the Sunday school idea. Suzanne knew, even as a very young child, that it was useless to resist him when his mind was made up. Most of the time he would listen and could often be reasoned into a change of heart. But every so often an issue came to mind that caused him to plant his feet and close his thoughts. Sunday school had been one of those issues. Maybe there was some truth to the family whispers about Zionist activity in his youth.

He had left Suzanne and her mother very suddenly and, by doing so, very wealthy. His insurance policies made the family far richer than they would have been had his heart not stopped beating. Though the money bought her a law school education, the bank accounts did not fill the empty place. His absence left a hurt so great that she tried not to think of him. But from time to time she missed him terribly. The pain came mostly on major life occasions, her graduations from college and law school, her selection as partner and, for some strange reason, this beautiful July morning.

Suzanne shook away the memory and strode to the security guard at the main gate. Her immediate need was for directions to Dr. Abromowitz's office.

"Good morning, Ms. Rosewell," the security guard said before she could introduce herself. "How may I help you?"

"I beg your pardon? How do you know my name?" Suzanne responded, shocked by the greeting.

"I'm sorry," the guard said with a slight smile. "I thought you recognized me. I work nights at your office. You often see me when you leave late. I'm Burt."

"Yes, of course," she said, covering over the reality that she did not recognize him in the slightest.

"He works in my office?" she thought to herself. Suzanne doubted that she'd ever looked him in the face. He was simply a body in a uniform, seated at the desk when she left after a certain hour. But then again, so were many of the other lawyers. Suzanne quickly realized how few of her coworkers she knew by name.

"I'm sorry I didn't recognize you at first," she continued. "You work two jobs?"

"I have to Ms. Rosewell. Need the money to raise my family." The man seemed a little embarrassed, maybe humbled, by his answer. She allowed him to change the topic.

"Isn't this is a small world to have seen you last night in the office and now here this morning?" he commented more comfortably.

"Yes, Burt, it's an incredible coincidence," she started to say, but the last word stuck in her throat. He noticed.

"Is something wrong?" Burt asked.

"No, no," she said, regaining her composure. "It's just that I had a conversation yesterday about coincidences and... well, never mind. Can you direct me to Dr. Abromowitz's office please?"

"Of course. Go through the double glass doors, take the elevator to the fourth floor, turn left and go to room 410. You should find him there."

"You arrive here early Burt?" For some reason Suzanne was not yet ready to end the conversation.

"I leave our building at five and start my day shift at seven. I have a little while to go home, take a quick breakfast with the wife and kids, change uniforms and come over here. I don't live far from the Seminary."

"When do you really get to see your family?" she asked, surprised by her own interest.

"I get off at three, about when the kids come home from school. Course, this time of year they're already home. Wife comes in about six. We spend a few hours together and I go to Wall Street for the eight o'clock shift. On my days off we have lots more time."

"That doesn't leave you many hours for sleep," she said with concern.

"Oh, I don't sleep much, Ms. Rosewell. A couple hours here and a couple there. Plenty of time for that after the kids grow up."

There was not a hint of resentment in the man's voice. That surprised Suzanne. She knew that if her life had been like his, working days and nights for nearly minimum wage, she would have been filled with anger. She stored the information in the back of her mind and wondered if there was something she might do to make his life a little easier. The very thought concerned her. Didn't she have enough on her mind without worrying about the problems of others? Now was the time to end the conversation!

"Thank you Burt," she said as she moved toward the double glass doors. "I'm sure we'll talk again."

"I hope so, Ms. Rosewell," she heard him say as she crossed into the building.

The elevator was waiting as she entered the empty hallway and the ride to the fourth floor took only a few moments. Her mind remained occupied with the "coincidence" of meeting her firm's security guard at the front gate. So intent was this thought that she made the instructed left turn without any conscious effort. The smell of fresh brewing coffee drifting through the open door of room 410 was the only thing that brought her back to her original purpose.

"Are you Suzanne?" the voice from the room asked before she entered.

"Yes, I am. Professor Abromowitz I presume."

Suzanne passed through the door and was startled by how much the man and his surroundings looked just like the picture she'd seen in the book. The windowless office was covered, on all four walls, with an endless collection of volumes, of all sizes, colors and topics. Books filled every available space. They were stacked in the corners, on the floor, on the tops of the bookcases, over the doorway and on every chair except the one behind the desk occupied by the smiling, bearded old Jew.

"Please sit down, Ms. Rosewell. Just move that pile to the floor." He pointed at a chair but when she stretched her hands toward the half-dozen volumes, he seemed to change his mind.

"Wait, wait, let me look first." He stood up and glared over his half-glasses at the titles. Then he took a deep breath and sat back down. "It's all right," he said, smiling once again. "I wanted to make sure that there were no holy books there. It's not right to put them on the floor, you know."

"No, I'm afraid that I don't know, Professor," she said as she moved the books to the carpet and settled into the battered old chair. "I don't know very much about Jewish things and that's part of why I came to see you."

"Then the first Jewish thing I will teach you is that before we get down to business, we have coffee. How do you take yours?"

"Uh, just black please. Is that really a Jewish thing?" she asked as he passed her the steaming cup.

"Well, for this Jew. I am sorry I can't offer you some cakes. The bakery I use is closed for vacation. My apologies."

"Please, that's unnecessary," she responded, feeling more comfortable in the company of this aged scholar with each passing moment. "I am most grateful for your time. And I am very sorry for waking you up so late last night."

"Early this morning, but who's watching the clock?" he answered, the smile broadening through the beard. "I was, I must admit, a bit annoyed, but now that I see how pretty you are, I have lost any annoyance that may have been left. Oh, I guess that's a sexist remark. My female students are always telling me that I have to change my attitudes. But I am an old man and for many years there were no women in any of my classes. I think I like this new system better. The women are a refreshing challenge, so intent, so demanding of knowledge. But I haven't yet been able to change the way I think. My reactions are often just the habits of many years. I hope I didn't offend you."

"No," Suzanne answered, aware that the remark would have been offensive coming from almost any other man. "I'm flattered. But I did come here to speak with you about a very specific matter and if we may...."

"Please." The professor's expression grew serious. "A moment more. I am a man who has spent his whole life devoted to learning and to teaching. Most of my world is in these books." He gestured as if presenting his family to Suzanne. "And these books have taught me that no piece of knowledge exists in a void. Tell me a little more about you before you tell me what you want from me."

Apparently, a conversation was the price Suzanne would have to pay for the information she sought. At first the question annoyed her. But from the moment she began to talk, the irritation fled. She found herself relaxing and telling the gentle bearded man her entire life story. Her tale ended just short of the string of strange coincidences that had brought her to this office. Professor Abromowitz sighed and leaned back in his chair, hands wrapped around the coffee mug, a half smile peeking through the gray beard.

"Ah, that is sad, Suzanne," he said simply.

"I'm sorry?" She had no idea what he meant.

"The sadness comes from knowing so little about your heritage," he explained. "I would feel that way if you were Irish or Spanish or American Indian. But since I am one of the Children of Israel, and since there are so few of us in this large world, I am especially saddened to see a smart, lovely young Jewish girl so separated from her people and the blood that flows in her veins. Being part of something greater than ourselves is such a beautiful thing. I urge you to learn about your past, about yourself. I would be happy to give you a reading list and...." He noticed the expression on her face. "But, forgive me. That's the teacher in me talking. You have not come for that reason and I did not mean to trespass. Please tell me what you want from me."

"Thank you Professor. Maybe someday I will take you up on your offer, but for now, I would like to discuss something you wrote."

She reached into her bag and pulled out the volume, putting the book on the desk in front of him and opening it. The page she sought was not set apart by a bookmark, but she found the proper place on the first try, just as she expected. Some of the "coincidences" were becoming routine.

"Ah, the legend of the Thirty-Six Righteous Ones. A marvelous folktale used often in literature, but not a particularly important part of Jewish culture. Unlike some Jewish legends, the tale is not universal to our people. The story was only known to those whose families lived in Eastern Europe. What can I tell you about it?" His eyes riveted on her over his wire rim glasses. Suzanne suddenly became very nervous.

"Specifically, Professor..." she stammered, "tell me about the concept that these people are privileged to see the Divine Presence and that the world exists on their merit. What does that mean?"

"Those are two separate issues. The first part means that while the rest of us spend our lives wondering what God wants us to do, the Righteous Ones know. The Divine Presence is within them." There was no hint of frivolity in his tone.

"Do you mean they speak with God?" she asked.

"No, not in the sense that Moses spoke with God. They simply know what God wants of them and they do it, probably without even being aware they are carrying out God's will every day. They do what God wants because it's the right thing to do."

"And what about the part where the world exists on their merit. I don't understand that at all." He could hear the frustration in her voice and responded by speaking even more slowly.

"As long as there are thirty-six people on this earth who know the Divine, the rest of us have the resources for our own salvation. By tapping into the spiritual power of the thirty-six, mankind... uh, *humankind* has the ability to create God's kingdom on earth and to save ourselves from the horrors that we've created. We have never, in all our history, used the riches God has provided, but as long as the thirty-six exist it is always possible for us to do so. God is the original eternal optimist and will continue to wait for us to find and use what he has put on earth for our benefit. Therefore, the world exists on their merit, for without the divine guidance and morality represented by the thirty-six, there would be no reason for the world to exist."

"You speak with tremendous conviction Professor," she said carefully.

"Suzanne, I do not accept all of the legends I have put down in this book," tapping the volume with a long, bony finger. "But I do believe this particular story. I have had faith in this tale since my grandmother taught it to me. This was the first chapter I wrote for this book because I believe in God and I believe that we are all God's children. Presuming those things, I found it inconceivable that God would not invest his presence with some of us. The persistence of this legend, and its simple logic makes me convinced that it is true."

"If we did choose to use these people as resources, how would we know who they are?"

"There is no answer to that question in the literature. Probably because we've never tried to seek them out. But I think that when and if we make a true decision to find them, they will become known to us."

"And Professor," he could hear the hesitation in her voice. "What would happen if there were not thirty-six Righteous Ones but only, say, thirty-one?"

"The world exists on their merit. As I said, without them there would be no reason for the world to exist at all. If such a tragedy were to happen... if, for example, we humans in our madness murdered too many of the Zaddikim, and we killed them faster than God could or was willing to create new ones, then I believe God would destroy the world, or simply let us destroy ourselves."

Silence, only the sounds of two people breathing, the coffeepot steaming and the ticking of a clock, one that Suzanne had not noticed before. The hallway outside the office was completely vacant and totally quiet. The two of them stared at each other for a minute and a half before Suzanne found the courage to speak.

"And you truly believe this legend?" she asked, desperately hoping he'd say no.

"I truly believe," he answered without hesitation. "And I sense that something has happened to prompt you to ask these questions. If you would like to tell me a story, I am a very good listener." His soft and gentle nature rekindled the thoughts of her father again.

The story came spilling out. She told him everything, relating the entire experience without excluding a single detail. Suzanne felt as if she had no control over her words. Unlike the conversation she had with Elias Garner in her office, when things she only thought suddenly burst into words, there was no attempt, or even desire, on her part to stop the flood of information flowing from her lips.

Suzanne did manage to retreat into an unemotional, lawyer-like explanation as she related the incident in the night club, the unscheduled, yet scheduled appointment, the strange meeting with Eli Garner, his golden horn, the mystical appearances of the professor's book and even the dreamy visions of the man from her apartment window as well as the blazing sun in her overheated office. The only thing she neglected was the brief encounter between the jazz musician-messenger and the woman dressed in black. Somehow, she'd forgotten about it. When the lawyer finished her unlawyer-like tale, an eerie silence enveloped the room again.

Professor Abromowitz's expression was troubled as he leaned back in his chair pondering the events placed before him. Suzanne thought of how relaxed the old man might look smoking a pipe, as her father did. For a moment she could almost smell the sweetness of burning tobacco. The silence became overbearing.

"What do you think, Professor? Am I crazy?" she finally said, for no other reason than to hear the sound of her own voice.

"I am not qualified to answer such a question," Abromowitz said with more than a touch of sadness. "Everything you told me could be explained by joining a few every-day coincidences with the normal stresses of an overworked attorney. I might brush off the entire thing and suggest you seek professional help, someone to help you work everything through. There is part of me that says I should do just that."

He paused, reading her face, sharing a worried expression with her. Then, as if the mask of habit had fallen away, his features brightened and a broad grin appeared behind the white beard.

"But I'm not going to," he continued. "A larger part of me wants to believe that something very important has happened to you. Suzanne, the story you tell does not perfectly match the legend. The fit is not quite right. Somehow there has been an alteration. But your version still feels good, sort of like a comfortable old suit. Who knows if the story in my book is quite right. The legend was passed down verbally for generations, told over and over again, before someone finally put it to paper. Maybe what you're living is the reality and what I wrote is the fantasy. And then again, maybe this man Garner is an accomplished con artist who seeks something as of yet unknown. Or the whole thing could be the product of a very tired mind. If so, I wouldn't trust it. The mind can play tricks. Perhaps it's the product of your spirit, in which case I would trust myself to follow that feeling to the ends of the universe."

"I don't understand," Suzanne said, her confusion obvious.

"I don't either," said the professor, "and that's why I've outlined more choices than you want to hear. If your mind has created this fantasy, you need professional help. But if what you feel comes from your soul, you may have been inspired, even touched."

"But why me?" The response was soaked in terror.

"Moses asked God that question when he was chosen to lead the people. Jesus may have asked the same before he was nailed to the cross. Every human being who has suffered a tragedy has screamed or thought those words. Oh yes, and many who have been blessed have used that phrase because they didn't feel deserving. The answer to you, and to all of them, is the same. Why not you? If there is a certain store of joy and tragedies in this world, someone has to get them. And if there are a certain number of tasks to be done, someone has to do them. This may be your task, or," the professor hesitated, "this may be your personal dose of madness."

"How do I know?"

The professor was silent for a long moment. While he was comfortable answering most questions quickly, drawing from his decades of study, this query was more important than all the others put together, and he needed more time to consider it. Those few seconds were an eternity to Suzanne.

"You don't know, not for sure," he finally said. "You may never know, not in this life. There are many questions to which we never learn the answers. That factor is the center, the essential element of faith, the concept we theologians retreat to when the logical thinkers of the world ask us questions we cannot answer. But faith is not an excuse, Suzanne. It's a reason. You must touch your own spirit and decide for yourself if it's reason enough to take on this task. Whether your quandary comes out of madness or a supernatural reality, this may be the most important choice of your life. You may even be choosing between sanity and salvation. Like all decisions of such magnitude, you will have to make the choice yourself. I'm sorry I cannot help you more."

Suzanne was already standing before the last words had left the professor's throat. Her body was numb, her ears ringing like a drunk's, her mind incapable of functioning. She might have muttered a polite phrase of thanks as she shuffled out the professor's door and into the hall. If she did, he didn't respond or make any attempt to stop her from leaving.

Suzanne Rosewell has no memory of returning to the street. She recalls touching Burt's shoulder as she passed through the security checkpoint. She knows that he said something in farewell, but just what it was escapes her.

The journey to the subway was also gone from her mind, the walk to the station, going through the turnstile, even boarding the train was lost. When the switch in her brain finally engaged again, she was standing in the center of a car on the Broadway local. The sign on the platform read "66 Street - Lincoln Center," a long way and many stops from the Jewish Theological Seminary. The world that had been dark and foggy from the time she left Abromowitz' office, was suddenly very bright and clear, a place of high contrast in illuminated colors suited better to an Ektachrome slide than to the usual atmosphere of the New York City transit system. The intensity demanded her attention.

Suddenly Suzanne was frightened. With a New Yorker's instinct, the fear came before the observation of any specific danger. She looked around quickly, scanning the car for the trouble that she sensed only internally. At the back end, standing near the door, stood the blond, pale woman still dressed in black, glaring at Suzanne. The young lawyer's terror grew exponentially. With a smile that was not a smile, the white-skinned figure moved slowly toward the frightened young attorney. Suzanne watched as this source of terror drew closer, the blonde woman gently rocking in time with the motion of the train. Suzanne's mind screamed for help. She turned away from the threat and moved toward the opposite exit of the otherwise empty car, seeking sanctuary.

Then the car was no longer empty. There at the door stood Elias Garner. He was dressed in the same stylish suit, now sharply pressed, still carrying the incongruous wooden box under his arm. Suzanne froze, unable to move toward him or away from the advancing danger in black. Garner smiled and strode to Suzanne's side, the distance between them covered in seconds.

Elias was standing next to Suzanne when the blond woman arrived. Though she couldn't bring herself to look, Suzanne knew the woman was there. She sensed her presence, felt her steady breathing on the back of her neck, but could not turn her head to check if she was correct. Her eyes locked on Elias and she allowed herself to be captured by his stare. She could not look away, and then Suzanne realized that she was also no longer afraid.

"Ms. Rosewell," he said easily, "it's so good to see you again. You may not believe this, but I was just on my way to your office."

"I do believe you," Suzanne responded, "But I will be in conference most of the day." She surprised herself with how calm and businesslike she spoke.

"Then my good fortune that I found you here," he answered easily. "I am sure my business can be concluded before we reach your stop. Allow me to introduce my colleague, the one I spoke about, Ms. Elizabeth Luckholt."

The lock on Suzanne's eyes snapped loose. She turned to find the pale woman's face only inches from her own. Resisting both the impulse to scream and to protectively grab Garner's arm, Suzanne maintained her calm exterior.

"A pleasure, I'm sure," her voice on automatic pilot.

"Don't be so sure," Luckholt shot back, her anger sending a chill right through Suzanne's body. "Not if Eli has described me as he usually does."

"Now, now Elizabeth," Garner answered before Suzanne could say a word. "I simply told Ms. Rosewell that we are on opposite sides of every issue, as we are on this one."

"It's a fool's errand," Luckholt said sharply, drawing the younger woman's attention back. "And I'm sure Ms. Rosewell is no fool." Suzanne remembered that she'd used the very same words herself in describing the task presented by Elias Garner in her office.

"That's not how I would depict something the Chairman wants accomplished," Garner shot back with an uncharacteristic hint of his own anger.

"This entire task is your interpretation of the Chairman's order," Luckholt answered, her eyes still locked on Suzanne, "not what he told you to do."

"Let's save our arguments to hold in private," Garner answered, returning to his normal voice. "Ms. Rosewell is capable of making her own decisions."

Now they were both quiet, waiting for Suzanne to respond. She remained passive, concentrating on the sound of the metal wheels against the steel track, hoping her answer might come from some nurturing presence deep inside the tunnel. She felt the two pairs of eyes focus exclusively on her.

"I will take the assignment," she said turning toward Garner. She had no idea where her voice had come from, but she knew the decision had been hers alone.

"Damn!" she heard the woman's voice behind her shout and her fear returned as the train came to a sudden, screeching halt. Suzanne almost fell, but the tall man held her upright. The strength in his arm was magnificent.

The doors opened and a noisy flood of little ones, day-camp children in shorts and t-shirts, filled the car, followed by several distraught adults frantically trying to maintain order. The doors closed and the train lurched forward. Suzanne turned. Elizabeth Luckholt was gone.

"She left," Eli said to the unasked question, raising his voice above the youthful din. "You gave her an answer that she didn't like. Besides she's not fond of children."

"And you?"

"I love children, but I too will be gone at the next stop. I have completed my task. The job belongs to you now Suzanne. It is important that you succeed."

"Where can I reach you for... for progress reports?"

"I will stay in touch, don't worry. Do you have the list?"

"Yes."

"Then you probably don't need me any more. But keep watch for Elizabeth. She doesn't want you to succeed, and I don't know how far she'll go to interfere."

"What can... what will she do to stop me?" Garner heard the panic rise. He placed his hand gently on Suzanne's shoulder. Her tension drained.

"Nothing. No matter how threatening she gets, Elizabeth can't do anything as long as your desire to succeed is stronger than your tolerance of failure. If you lose faith, Elizabeth can become very powerful. So, keep the faith!"

There was that word again. Faith. Faith in what? Dr. Abromowitz had said faith was not an excuse but a reason. Suzanne did not understand and she wanted Elias Garner to explain, but without realizing the train had stopped and started again, she looked out the window and saw the tall black man with the wooden horn case under his arm standing on the platform watching her train disappear into the dark tunnel.

CHAPTER EIGHT

"Excuse me, miss," the bearded man with the wide shoulders twisted his baseball cap to the side of his head in a gesture of impatience. He behaved as though he had been speaking to Suzanne for quite sometime. Maybe he had. The memories had transfixed her mind and so focused her in the events of the past few days, that she had been impervious to the present. But the annoyed man in the Peterbilt hat was definitely part of the present.

"Yes, I'm sorry. Are you speaking to me?" she answered as she finally turned her face toward him.

There was something in her expression, or maybe in her dress, or manner, or just her general good looks that quickly diffused the man's anger. His impatience disappeared and he suddenly seemed embarrassed. With a boyish gesture that Suzanne thought belonged in an old movie, he snatched the cap from his head and twisted it in his hands, holding it directly in front of a perfectly flat, muscular stomach. He looked like an over-aged Mickey Rooney playing a scene in black and white. The almost comic formality drew a warm smile from Suzanne and that made the trucker more uncomfortable.

"Yes, ma'am. I was... I was wondering if... if that was your BMW?" he gestured with his chin, pointing toward the plaster buffalo. Her eyes, following the direction indicated by the tip of his gray beard, found her vehicle, now the only one in the shadow of the statue. A long, silver, oversized eighteen wheeler, was parked next to the dusty, black BMW, the bumper of the cab almost against her car while the back of the long trailer crossed the entrance driveway, a mechanized mouse barring the path of an elephant.

"If you could just move the car over to the other lot," he continued, "I could get my truck all the way in and not block up the place. Do you mind?"

"No, I don't mind at all," she answered, the smile still intact and sincere, though Suzanne knew she'd have been annoyed had the same favor been requested of her in New York. "It's time I got on the road anyway."

She tossed the remnants of her lunch wrappings into the trash can, gathered her purse under her arm in the manner used by all city dwellers to discourage those who might snatch the bag away, and started to walk across the patch of prairie grass that separated her from the plaster guardian of her expensive automobile. The trucker walked along beside her until her less than friendly glance made him realize that his closeness was being perceived as a threat. He arranged himself about a half step behind.

"You're from New York, huh?" he asked.

"Yes." Dumb question. All he had to do was read the license plate.

"From New York City?" Not much better since the dealer's sticker on the back said "Manhattan Imports."

"Yes, that's where I live." She responded, her speech still chilled though she realized that he was only trying to be friendly. Suzanne wondered why she couldn't have met a strong, silent (emphasis on silent) type of trucker portrayed on TV.

"Never been there," he mumbled, "What brings you way out here?"

Suzanne had known the question was coming. She'd hoped they might reach the truck before the query was voiced. She'd prepared several possible, some not-so-friendly, responses. One of her scripted answers even told him that the information was none of his business. But when the actual question came, the reason she gave had not been included among those that she'd prepared.

"You wouldn't believe me if I told you," was all she said.

"Try me," came the unexpected reply as they reached the parking lot. Something in his voice had changed. An inflection of confidence, and possibly of concern, came clear in those two simple words and Suzanne stopped walking. She turned to face him. The man was easily in his forties. The gray beard and the line of gray around the edges of his thick hair along with some serious creases in his sunburned expression allowed for no fewer years. His body though, was as lean and trim as any younger man's, and better than most.

"OK, I will," she said, as she looked him in the eyes. He was standing upright, shoulders pulled back, feet set comfortably apart. He took one reverse step as Suzanne moved toward him, but she wouldn't permit the distance between them to widen. If he was going to get nosey, she decided, then let him satisfy his curiosity eyeball to eyeball.

Suzanne was sure the man had, maybe not too long ago, been in the military. She could almost see him younger and in uniform. So she spoke to him as she imagined a senior officer might have addressed him.

"I am a lawyer on a mission of some urgency, looking for Professor Herman W. Fields of St. Olive's College, the man who recently won the Nobel Peace Prize. His secretary would not tell me how to find him. All I know is that he's vacationing in his cabin in the Black Hills. Now you know my mission and since I doubt that you are acquainted with Professor Fields, I will just move my car so you can park your truck." Her hand reached into her purse for her keys while her eyes remained locked on the trucker.

"That doesn't sound so hard to believe," he responded.

"Well," Suzanne answered, without hesitation, "I decided not to tell you the whole story."

"I might be able to help anyway," he said simply.

"I beg your pardon?"

"I said that I might be able to help anyway. I'm not from South Dakota. I'm a Montana fellow myself. But, if there had been a Nobel Prize winner in Montana, we'd be so proud that everyone would know something about him, maybe even where he has a summer cabin. If you want to wait few minutes, I may be able to get someone on the radio who knows what you need to know."

Suzanne backed down. He had her attention, and the look on her face exposed her interest. In turn, the Montana truck driver was more than a little pleased that he'd been able to impress this tough New York attorney. He was not making a pass. The thought had never crossed his mind. Though Suzanne's beauty and sophistication had not gone unnoticed, the opportunity to show this educated Easterner that there were resourceful people west of the Mississippi, hell, west of the Hudson, was accomplishment enough. The truck driver grinned, climbed into his cab and switched on the CB radio.

"Breaker, breaker," he said into the microphone, "this is Montana Monty looking for a South Dakota man. Someone from around Rapid City."

Several voices seemed to respond at the same time and Montana Monty's smile broadened as he reached out and closed the door. Suzanne understood that he didn't want her to hear his conversation. Probably, at least in part, because he intended to talk about her and not likely in a flattering way.

She was already embarrassed about her behavior. Though she doubted that his plan was going to work, it had been a kind gesture on Monty's part. Since she had no other solution at the moment, why not let this stranger try to be her hero? Besides, so many weird things had already happened.

She opened the BMW, took out her cigarettes and lit one. Leaning back against the car, smoking in long, slow puffs, Suzanne waited. The discussion on the radio was taking a long time. The cigarette finished, she nearly threw the filter on the ground, and though hers would not have been the only one, another glance along the lonely, endless prairie made her hesitate. She put the butt into the car's ashtray.

Montana Monty was still on the radio. Suzanne thought about lighting another. She thought about leaving. She thought how empty the land around her looked, how hot and strong the sun was, how the rays soaked into her pale skin, and how the sweltering breeze was so steady, so regular, so part of every moment that one almost forgot there was a wind at all. She thought about these things without moving a step from the fender of her high priced automobile. Only when she finally reached for a second cigarette, did Montana Monty come down from his cab. His beaming face proclaimed his success.

"You shouldn't touch those things," he said, pointing to the pack and effectively destroying her desire to smoke. "They'll kill you eventually. I quit. So can you."

"Yes, you're right. I've been planning to." She stumbled over her words as she stuffed the pack into her pocket. "Did you get any information?"

"Oh, sure. Almost everything you need. One guy knew another who knew a third. All of them were familiar with the general area where the Professor summers, but the third guy was able to get specific. He runs a moving van and he took a load of furniture to a Black Hills encampment in June. He says there are about a dozen cabins around a small lake. His customer told him that a neighbor had won the Nobel Prize. In New York I guess that could be any one of a bunch of people, but in South Dakota he's got to be your man."

"There aren't that many in New York either," Suzanne said genuinely excited. "This is wonderful news. Tell me how to find this place." She reached for the pad that she kept on the front seat.

"The guy's writing out the directions and drawing a map. He'll fax the stuff to me in a couple of minutes."

"Fax it to you?"

"Sure, lady." The truck driver was laughing. "These are the nineties and I run a business here. I have to stay in touch with my customers. There's a cellular telephone and a fax machine in the cabin behind the driver's seat. A man's got to keep up." He could see that Suzanne was flustered by her assumption that modern technology stopped somewhere east of her current longitude. He didn't intend to make her suffer for too long, but the opportunity to rub some arrogance out of a New Yorker was too good to ignore.

"Yes ma'am," he continued. "We have cable television, radio, health clubs, DVDs, computers and, occasionally, good Chinese food in this part of the world." The blush in her cheeks was more embarrassing to him than the teasing was to her. "Let me check and see if that fax has arrived," he said in the kind of whisper that was also an apology.

Montana Monty opened the door behind the driver's cab and briefly revealed a surprisingly substantial space complete with sleeping cot, stereo and the already-mentioned phone and fax. He took a sheet of paper from the small machine and delivered it to Suzanne.

"Just like the man promised," he said.

Suzanne studied the single sheet of curled, coated paper. The handwritten directions were printed clearly with a bold, thick felt pen. They began at the Mt. Rushmore monument, a place the other trucker assumed Suzanne would have no trouble finding. Each road and turn was clearly delineated and a small map showed her how to find the lakeside encampment. At the bottom there was a brief message from the document's author and his "handle" as signature.

The large J marks the place where I delivered the furniture, the Millerson household. Mrs. Millerson might know where the professor lives. Good luck.
Indian Joe.

She wondered if "Indian Joe" was really Indian. The picture of a dark-skinned, high cheek-boned man with long, straight, black hair, standing by the fax machine in his own truck flashed through her mind. The image disappeared quickly.

"Thank you very much Mister..." Suzanne started to say.

"Oh, just call me Monty," he said, "and no need to thank me. There's lots of flat, straight roads in this part of the world and not many of us traveling them. We've got to help each other out, us long-haul drivers, right?"

"Right. I'm Suzanne and I'm grateful to you Monty." She put out her hand. He took it gingerly. Their touch lasted only a second.

"Good luck, Suzanne," he shouted as he climbed back into the big silver cab. "I hope you find your professor."

She started to reply, wanted to ask him for his cell phone number, reluctant to end their contact, but the huge diesel engine roared alive and she knew that her voice could never rise above the noisy motor. But he was only moving the truck. She could have waited and continued their dialogue, but there was nothing left to say.

Carrying a new sensation, a stomach knot that had to be described as loneliness, Suzanne climbed inside the car, started the engine and pointed the dark machine back toward the highway.

Truck stop, river, bridge and Monty's silver rig suddenly shrunk in her rear view mirror as though they all belonged to *Alice Through the Looking Glass*. The landscape regained its Hollywood backdrop sameness and before long the steady drone of her engine became the ruling sound. Suzanne was alone again. She took comfort by touching the single sheet of fax paper from Indian Joe.

Miles disappeared. She passed the exit for the Badlands National Park and marveled at the moonscape erosion that touched the edges of Interstate 90. She even skipped the tourist stop at Wall Drug, the Western shopping Mecca advertised by strange, old-fashioned, Burma

Shave-like billboards for a thousand miles in every direction. Like the prospectors long ago who invaded sacred Indian land in search of gold, Suzanne's uncompromising destination was the Black Hills and the quest for treasure.

The sun dipped below the horizon, replaced by a far-away, thunderless lightening storm that silently lit the Western sky with multiple white flashes. Suzanne drove toward the turbulence as the dark clouds simultaneously moved quickly across the plains toward her. Before too long the lightening was finally accompanied by distant thunder as the BMW and the storm grew closer together. The natural light show was breathtakingly beautiful and frightening at the same time. Several times during the display of nature's rawest power, Suzanne found herself thinking about the woman in black and the encounter on the subway.

The storm and the lawyer reached Rapid City at the same time and greeted each other in the parking lot of a Super 8 Motel whose flashing sign indicated available rooms. As she reached the front desk, the squall was in full fury, illuminating the city in flashes, shaking the motel with thunder and washing the streets clean of summer dust. The elderly clerk, ignoring the activity outside, directed Suzanne to her lodgings.

The room was new, fairly large and rather pleasant, but the motel was without a restaurant or bar and the driving rain was a significant deterrent to exploration. Suzanne accepted a paper cup of scotch from the desk clerk's private stock along with his simple directions to the Rushmore Monument.

"Go straight down this road," he said, "and follow the big green signs. Take a blind person to miss the monument."

She thanked the man and retired to her bedroom, where she kicked off her shoes, turned on the TV and rested on the queen size bed, the scotch, her cigarettes, a few snacks purchased from a vending machine and an ash tray lined up on the nightstand. The television was still on and the whiskey untouched when the sun woke her a little past nine in the morning. She had slept for nearly twelve hours straight.

Suzanne Rosewell was refreshed and energized. She reached for the phone to have room service send up breakfast before she realized that the call would be a waste of time. Still wearing the same clothes she'd worn since Wisconsin, Suzanne slipped down the stairs and was well onto the black top of the parking lot before she became aware that she hadn't bothered with shoes. Undeterred, even finding her memory lapse to be comical, the New York lawyer entered a diner that shared the asphalt lot with the motel. She was the object of attention from the moment she passed through the door.

The mirror behind the counter told Suzanne that her bare feet were not the only reason everyone stared. Her clothes were wrinkled and road-dusty; red hair flew in every direction and her makeup needed major repair. She looked as though she'd crossed the prairie on foot.

"You OK, honey?" the Western-stereotype counter-girl asked as Suzanne sat down.

"Oh, yes, yes," she answered. "I drove all day yesterday and I fell asleep before I could even undress, never looked in the mirror when I got up. Never occurred to me to look. Now that I think about it, I don't ever look in the mirror until I have coffee, not even at home." Suzanne smiled and the waitress laughed.

"I know just what you mean, honey. I need at least three cups before I can handle myself over the bathroom sink." She turned and glared down toward the line of male faces at the counter. "What are you guys gawking at?" she shouted. The heads turned away in unison. "Didn't your wives ever tell you that it's not nice to stare at a lady in the morning, not until she puts herself in order?"

The waitress packed several large containers of coffee and a hearty breakfast that Suzanne carried back across the parking lot to the motel. She could feel a dozen pairs of male eyes at her back as she walked.

Despite her disheveled appearance, the attention was strangely flattering.

Less than an hour later, washed, fed, redressed and ready, Suzanne aimed the BMW toward the main road. For a moment she considered a brief stop at the diner just to show the crowd how good she could look, but vanity would just have to wait until later.

As promised, the trip to the monument was easy, the road crowded with buses, campers and other vehicles displaying a continent-wide selection of license plates. She felt almost unpatriotic driving by without stopping as the huge stone faces lingered in her rear view mirror until the curve of the highway obscured their permanently dignified expressions. Suzanne focused on the map.

The balance of this first journey filled only an additional hour and took the lawyer far into the Black Hills, following narrow winding roads, that carried her past peaceful streams, by small lakes and through patches of tall pine trees sheltering assorted wildlife that magically appeared at the edge of the forest as if to specifically watch her drive by. In contrast to the unending sameness of the prairie, Suzanne's senses were continuously stimulated by the raw beauty of the scenery. She felt that she could almost touch the ancient spirits Indians believe still dwell between the colonies of cabins and the patches of aging neon-signed motels. She understood why the Lakota consider the Black Hills sacred.

Her attention to mystic surroundings was so intense that the arrival at the end of the fax-paper map came as an abrupt surprise. Suddenly she was facing the artificial log walls of a tiny cottage whose front path was adorned with a green mailbox decorated in yellow-paint letters that read "Millerson."

Suzanne was unsure of her next step. The cabin seemed empty. Laundry on the clothesline attested to its occupancy, but there were no signs of residents. The windows were all invitingly opened to the morning breezes and the sunlight off the lake reflected back through the rooms, confirming the lack of human presence.

She pondered her next move and considered walking down to the water. Maybe they were swimming, or doing whatever people do when they're on summer vacation. But the ability to make a decision eluded her. She sat behind the wheel of the BMW and stared at the empty house, watching as the sheets tried to ride the gentle wind in a weak attempt to escape their clothespin imprisonment.

"Can I help you?" Suzanne jumped at the unexpected sound of the woman's voice next to her ear. She had been so intent at staring across the front seat and through the passenger's window at the house, that the woman, dressed in a blue jogging suit and bright-white running shoes, had been able to approach unnoticed.

"Oh, you startled me," Suzanne said, as she tried to catch her breath. She concentrated on the face, about forty, natural blond, blue eyes, nice features, a wanting-to-please smile. Did everybody in South Dakota smile all the time? she wondered. Weren't there just a few grumpy people? Suzanne was tempted to be intentionally rude just to see if there might be a little New York-like temper somewhere deep inside the pleasant looking woman. Her practical side prevailed. The mission was first priority.

"I'm looking for Mrs. Millerson," Suzanne said, after a few moment's hesitation.

"Well you found her," was the still-cheery reply. "What can I do for you?"

"Well, actually I am really looking for Professor Fields. I was led to believe you might know where to find him." The woman's face shifted like a television changing channels. Without a moment of transition, the smile was replaced by a scowl.

"Are you a reporter?" she asked curtly.

"No, I'm an attorney and I must see him on a matter of some urgency."

Judging from the expression on the woman's face, Suzanne's

revelation of her profession was not well received.

"Do you have an appointment?" she asked harshly.

"No," came the almost shy response.

"Then I think you should leave. It isn't polite to interrupt people during their vacation."

"To be completely honest, I tried to make an appointment with the professor when I was in New York, but his secretary wasn't very cooperative. So I got in my car and just drove out here on a chance."

"You drove all the way from New York without an appointment?" Mrs. Millerson asked. Her surprised voice seemed to have some sympathy behind it.

"Yes, my mission is quite important."

"I guess," she replied, her body language confirmed the edge of compassion now apparent.

"Forgive me for being curt. Why don't you come inside and I'll see what I can do." The woman turned and walked toward the porch. After a moment's hesitation, Suzanne followed.

The cabin's interior was homey, that was the only word Suzanne could think of to describe it. Though very different in decor, the place had a feeling that took her back to her childhood and the small house in the Catskills that her father rented every summer. How he used to love escaping to that quiet spot surrounded by the tall pines. The recollection helped her to relax. Mrs. Millerson gestured toward a wicker couch and Suzanne sat down to wait.

Her ears followed the woman's footsteps as she walked across the uncarpeted wooden floor and into the kitchen out of Suzanne's sight. A moment later she heard the phone dialing, an old rotary type with a clicking sound familiar now only in memories. A few more seconds passed and Suzanne could hear Mrs. Millerson speaking, just a whisper, allowing only a few words to drift back to the wicker sofa.

"Yes," Suzanne heard, "drove all the way from New York. Her car is right outside." Then she could hear no more.

She didn't hear the phone being returned to its cradle or the woman walking back into the living room. But, before she knew it, Mrs. Millerson was standing over her and projecting that South Dakota smile.

"I'll make some coffee," she said, the hospitality part of her completely in charge. "The professor will be here in a few minutes. I told him that you two could use our place to chat. He would rather you not know where he lives, at least not yet. I'm sure you understand."

Suzanne nodded in response and the woman continued.

"When he arrives, well, I'll just disappear."

"Thank you, Mrs. Millerson," Suzanne said to her back as she returned to the kitchen.

"Oh you're very welcome," she answered, already banging the coffeepot against the sink. "But call me Alice, please, just Alice."

"Thank you Alice," Suzanne responded so softly that she barely heard herself speak. Her eyes were already locked on the front door while her heart rate increased steadily.

The coffee was not quite ready when she heard the sound of footsteps on the front porch. The screen door opened and a small man, about fifty years old, with shoulder length gray hair, bare feet, wearing brown shorts and a St. Olive's College t-shirt came through the door.

"Good morning," the man said pausing in the doorway. "I am Herman Fields. What can I do for you?"

For a moment Suzanne was speechless. The man had the deepest, burning blue eyes she'd ever seen. Besides, this was the first time she'd ever met a Nobel Prize winner and Suzanne didn't know quite how to behave. He waited patiently until she regained her composure.

"I'm Suzanne Rosewell," she said, standing and extending her hand, "and I've come a long way to see you."

CHAPTER NINE

Professor Fields was only reluctantly friendly. An embarrassingly long moment passed between the time Suzanne extended her hand and the professor responded. His hesitation to accept her greeting seemed, to Suzanne, very unusual behavior for an internationally renowned mediator. The man's conversational manner was even less diplomatic.

"If you've come, Miss Rosewell," he said just before releasing her handshake, "to engage me as a mediator for one of your big corporate clients, forget it. I don't do that kind of work."

"No Professor," she started to say as he loosened his unexpectedly weak grip, "my purpose is to…."

"Well, if you represent a publisher," he interrupted, "I have an agent in Los Angeles who is marketing my new book."

"No, Professor," she said again, a little more slowly, wondering how she should present her mission. "My objective is a little more unusual."

For some reason he seemed suddenly ready to listen, and abruptly and silently sat down on one end of the wicker couch. Suzanne followed by gently placing herself at the furniture's other extreme. She still hadn't the slightest idea how to approach her subject, but her growing need to speak was frustrated again by Professor Field's rejuvenated desire to keep talking.

"I don't know what your objective is, but frankly I can't think of a single thing that I'm prepared to discuss with you," his challenging tone was more ominous than his words.

"Then why were you willing to see me at all?" she asked, more as a way of delaying the start of her own topic than any real interest in the answer. The query seemed to relax him. The professor smiled and focused his burning blue eyes directly on the already uncomfortable New York lawyer. His gaze provided the first real hint as to why this man was so successful in difficult negotiations. Fields' eyes seemed to project a blue light of calm confidence. Instead of his stare making Suzanne more edgy, she settled comfortably in her seat, suddenly interested in his response and slightly annoyed when his answer was delayed by the entrance of Alice Millerson carrying a tray of coffee. She set her burden gently on the table in front of them.

"Here we are," the woman whispered almost too quietly to be heard. She was obviously a great fan of her celebrity guest. "I'm going into town to shop. Just leave the dishes when you're finished."

"Thank you Alice," Fields responded, turning his gaze toward his hostess and smiling even more broadly. The woman physically shuttered with adoration, much like a teenager basking in the light of her favorite rock star. She moved in the direction of the door, turned to leave, then, remembering her manners, focused back toward Suzanne.

"In case you are not here when I return," she said to her female guest with her eyes darting back to the professor every few seconds. "It was a pleasure meeting you Miss Rosewell."

"The pleasure was all mine," Suzanne muttered, truthfully a bit jealous of the special glances the other two shared. "Thank you for all your help." Alice Millerson nodded and retreated backwards into the sunshine.

"A very pleasant woman," the Nobel laureate said as he lifted his cup. "She acts as my protector out here, sees that I eat properly and manage to get my laundry done. She's probably just lonely. Her husband only comes out on the weekends, but I guess I should be grateful for his schedule."

Suzanne had the sense that Professor Fields wanted her to ask more about his relationship with Alice Millerson. She intentionally chose to ignore the implication and continued on her own quest.

"You were going to tell me why you were willing to see me, Professor," Suzanne inquired again.

"Oh yes," he said with the blue eyes back in her direction, "I will. Part of the reason was because Alice told me you drove here all the way from New York. That's unusual. Most business people would have flown to Rapid City and rented a car. The other reason was that Alice also said you were very pretty. Her appraisal was quite accurate."

"Thank you, Professor. I'm flattered. I don't really know why I decided to drive. That was rather an impulsive decision, one that I regretted a number of times when the road seemed never to end. But since driving helped me to get to see you, I'm glad that I made the right choice."

"You're a partner in a major New York law firm?" he asked.

"Yes, how did you know? I'm with..."

"No matter. I wouldn't know one from another. And I guessed. I'm good at that. The fancy car, the fine clothes, the way you carry yourself, they are all indicators of a very successful, very driven person. I am surprised that a young woman like yourself has achieved such a position in this male dominated world, but I am more surprised that you are willing to spend so much time away from the office. This must be a very important mission."

"I am sorry. I don't understand your point."

"It has taken you three or four days to drive this far and will take you just as long to drive back. That's a whole week of work missed on just one errand. A lot of, what do you call them, billable hours lost. More important, you have left the field of battle, so to speak, and those who resent you, for your youth or your gender, or just because they're jealous, can use this absence against you. I do not believe that anyone of your age can achieve a partnership in an important New York law firm without understanding the rules of engagement. Therefore, I must assume that you set out on this quest with your eyes open as to the risks and that the prize must be well worth its potential cost. Tell me, how does one professor of political science from a small western college rate such attention?"

"You are too modest," she said, shaken by his insights and playing for time as she tried to organize her thoughts. "Winning the Nobel Peace Prize does put you in a very special fraternity."

"Oh, I am very honored, even humbled," he said, as he set down his cup so he could use both hands to emphasize his point, "to even be on the same list with people like Martin Luther King. And I feel that way despite knowing that I truly deserved to win the prize."

He noticed her reaction to the sudden display of arrogance.

"Oh, please," he continued, "we can get down to the real business at hand if we dispense with the usual foolish procedures, like false modesty. I know that the prize, and its winners, have considerable commercial value, but the pattern of your visit does not speak to traditional commerce. Something special is going on. So, shall we put our cards on the table right now or would you rather play your game a little while longer?"

"This is a bit difficult for me," Suzanne answered, staring into her cup of coffee. She raised her eyes to find the gentle blue fires focused directly at her. It seemed easier to say even the most ridiculous things when he looked at her that way.

"I recently met a man," she continued, "who engaged me in a search to find five particular and very special people. You are correct when you concluded that this was not a normal commercial venture. I'm doing this work outside the firm and for no fee. It's very hard to explain, but I am convinced that either I am doing the most important thing I've ever done, or I'm participating in the most singular foolish act I could ever imagine."

"This has become intriguing," Fields said with a hint of laughter as he settled back against the old flowered cushion that protected the even older wicker. "Is my name on your friend's list of five?"

"No sir," she said, becoming more anxious as she approached the central aim of her journey. "We don't know their names. I am seeking five anonymous individuals. I am on a search for five people who can be defined as... well, truly righteous."

There. She'd finally told him, said the words out loud and his reaction was totally unexpected. The amusement disappeared from his face and the warmth shut down in his eyes, replaced by a cold, blue light, more like neon than sunshine. He remained silent, forcing her to continue.

She told him the story from the beginning, including the coincidences, the visions, the pursuit of knowledge with Professor Abromowitz and the final meeting with the protagonists in the unlikely setting of a New York City subway car. The longer she talked the more visible the discomfort her listener displayed. By the time she finished, Suzanne was convinced the professor had decided he was sharing coffee with a mad woman.

Suddenly he stood and walked toward the large picture window that framed Suzanne's road-dusty BMW resting on the blacktop. He spoke with his back toward her.

"A rational person, Miss Rosewell," he said hesitatingly, the arrogance and confidence gone from his voice, "might have concluded that you are quite insane. And part of me agrees with that assessment. Yet there is another part that wants to take you seriously. That part will answer you. But when we're finished I request that you leave immediately. I take that precaution should you be someone who only imagines herself to be a female Jewish Diogenes traveling the back roads of America when you should really be searching for a good psychiatrist."

Professor Herman W. Fields turned to face Suzanne. She was not surprised to see the pomposity gone from his expression. This was evident by the tone of his voice even though the actual text of his words failed to reflect any retreat from his position of intellectual superiority. But she was shocked to see the vanity replaced by what she could only describe as pain, terrible pain.

"I would like to think of myself as a righteous man. But since your definition includes, what were your words... people who know the Divine Will, I am not a person whose name belongs on your list," he said, his anguish amplified in his near wail.

She started to protest, but he raised his hand to silence her.

"I'll speak to you honestly because I think that you believe in the reality of your search. I think I feel this way because you have, shall we say coincidentally, touched on a sensitivity of mine. Really I should be calling the authorities. But you did leave your life behind to seek me out. You left a vacancy in that place where you live and work and should your employers find out why, they would probably take away your job. If you were a famous television personality, or a Nobel Prize winner, and you chose to run away to the Black Hills and find the wisdom of the ages, your career would be enhanced. The news teams would follow you, as they did me for a while, and your eccentricities would make you a greater personality, more valuable on the public stage. But someone like you has risked everything and you do all of that while presenting a very normal outward image. And, as I said, you tread on a tender topic, a wound on my soul. So, on the slight chance, the very slight chance that you are not completely insane, I will answer your question, though probably not in the way you'd like."

Once more she tried to interrupt and again he silenced her with a wave of his hand.

"I came here to see you because I was told that you were pretty and because I thought you might make an interesting sexual diversion. Yes, that's true. It's something that comes with celebrity status. Until I became famous, I had very little success with women. Now they are everywhere I go and I enjoy it. Further, our liaison was, in fact, encouraged by a woman who sometimes shares my bed, but only when the mood strikes me and when her husband is not around. And she asked me to see you because she knows that the only way I will continue to pay that kind of attention to her is if I have a periodic supply of younger, prettier women to satisfy my insatiable ego."

"But Professor Fields," she was finally able to interject, "your work has saved the lives of tens of thousands, people who would have been innocent victims of the wars you prevented. Surely sexual indiscretions are outweighed by the good you do."

"Yes, my dear," he responded as some of the warmth returned to his eyes. "The work of the peacemaker is righteous work, but not often done by righteous men. Nations, causes, even good causes, are usually led by egotists and fanatics, or by the power-hungry. That's the kind of person required to even consider using the horrible tool of war to advance a political agenda.

"Righteousness among peace makers is a rare asset and one we usually can't afford. Look what happened to Woodrow Wilson. He negotiated a righteous peace and his own Congress destroyed him while the so-called peacemakers of Europe seeded the rise of Hitler and another war far more horrible than the one they'd just ended.

"I succeed because I understand these people better than they understand themselves, and that makes me more like them than I usually admit. In this world, doing what I do, no one dares to be righteous. We bury the righteous alongside the same roads that are choked with fleeing refugees, outside the gates of Wilson's graveyard. Though I would like to be remembered in history with the affection given the great Princeton professor, I would prefer to sacrifice whatever ethics I might have in order to succeed. And, maybe save a few lives. Now, I would request that you leave immediately."

"But Professor," she continued her attempt at dissent, "I am certain you didn't start out..."

"It doesn't matter how I started," he shouted. "You simply don't understand. When I first got an opportunity to enter the international arena and work for peace, to have a chance to save more lives than a hundred doctors do in their combined careers, I thought I was blessed by God himself and I was a grateful man. Then I learned about the cost of success. Surrender the lives of a few to save the lives of many. Don't ask about the political prisoners. Give up the human rights of a minority to assure the political, sometimes-inhuman rights of the majority. Allow truly evil men to hold some power so that they're less likely to undermine the power of the few good ones that still remain. Ms. Rosewell, it's only a short distance from that constant compromise of values to seducing lonely women for some company on a long empty night. And seduction seems like a much more minor crime. Know the Divine Will? Don't be ridiculous. Don't you dare put my name on your list and please get the hell out of my sight!"

Suzanne had driven almost ten miles before her hands stopped shaking. The professor's tirade had not only frightened her, but had brought to the surface a pair of emotions that were now in charge of her psyche, confusion and doubt.

"It was going to be simple," she thought as the BMW, moving seemingly under its own power, approached Mt. Rushmore. "All I had to do was meet him, put his name on the list and then I would only have four more to find."

She barely noticed as the car turned into the parking lot of the national monument. She also observed that she didn't personally make the decision. Not that the BMW had turned itself, but more like Suzanne had a partner in the navigation of her vehicle.

Suzanne and her unseen, unfelt companion place the

car carefully between an RV and a station wagon. But Suzanne doesn't care. Her mind is elsewhere, too far away to even be concerned as to why she's climbing the steps to the observation platform. Her ears, listening instead to the sounds in her brain, filtering out the conversations of hundreds of tourist families as they pass each other. Suzanne could not ignore them with any more efficiency were she completely alone, drifting across a broad, empty patio instead of in the company of thousands.

The people move aside as she walks, stepping away, creating an unimpeded path for her progress and then stepping back to continue their initial routes as she passes, filling the briefly constructed void with an ocean of bodies the way the waves smooth the sand on the beach. They aren't clearing out of her way out of courtesy, nor are they motivated by any fear of the blank, almost demented, expression she wears. Though she's dressed in her New York finery, in stark contrast to their summer vacation outfits, the tourists are not retreating because she looks so different. They simply move.

Everywhere she steps, even when she approaches them from the rear, they create the space she needs. Suzanne walks as though following an invisible figure whose outstretched hands guide the people into motion, so gently that each and every one of them shifts as if of their own volition and by their own free and uninfluenced will. When Suzanne's mind moves from the state of half-attention to becoming once again fully aware of her surroundings, she is standing at the edge of the observation platform in the spot generally acknowledged by most as having the singular best view of the monument.

"Four great presidents," she thought to herself. "Were they righteous men? Washington and Jefferson both owned slaves. Lincoln waged a bloody war to preserve a political entity. Teddy Roosevelt rose to political power on his theatrical participation in an imperialistic war where the enemy surrendered even before the first shot was fired, but they fought the war anyway. Would they have considered themselves to be righteous men? What does it mean to know the Divine Will? And what if someone knows it and follows his own path instead? Is righteousness also perfection? What in God's name does Elias Garner want me to do?" It was rare for Suzanne to invoke a deity, even in the privacy of her own brain.

"Keep the faith," his distinct, gentle voice in her mind said, repeating his last words to her in the subway car. "Want to succeed more than you want to fail."

Suzanne was certain that she was hearing these words vibrate in her ears, not only in her thoughts. It was almost as if Elias Garner was standing somewhere in the crowd around her. The echo faded and then, for a fleeting moment, out of the corner of her eye, the New York lawyer was certain that she'd seen a blond woman, all in black, like herself, standing out as overdressed in the July tourist crowd. The sighting was only momentary, but long enough for the image to fill Suzanne with dread, the same sort of fear that she'd felt for a few moments in the club and again in her office when the place was filled with hellish sunshine. Almost the same, but not quite. This time she felt, along with the apprehension, an undercurrent of anger, her own anger, not projected from some outside entity, but generated from inside her belly and rising furiously into her throat.

Stating the case plainly, Suzanne was pissed off. She turned hard on her heels and threaded her way through the still-thick crowd. This time she had to turn, stop, push and apologize, just like everyone else. Her invisible guide and guardian was apparently left behind in her backwash of fury. She found the BMW, started the engine, and irritably punished the machine by slamming the car into reverse.

CHAPTER TEN

The road back from Rapid City appeared to consume much less time than the same highway had devoured in the other direction. Suzanne's anger, first felt at the Mt. Rushmore Monument, and still burning brightly in her gut was solely responsible for her perceptional shift of the passing hours. The furious sensation had stayed, grew inside her and ate up the clock as efficiently as the imported German tires gobbled the miles of poured concrete. Plain, ordinary outrage was keeping her nerves sharp, her attention tightly focused on the highway ahead. The feeling made her muscles taut, drove her brain faster even than she was pushing the BMW, so rapid that her mind rarely gave her the opportunity to ask herself why she was feeling so angry. Part of the reason she already knew. Suzanne was mad at Elias Garner.

"If he's who he's supposed to be," she thought, "then he would've known that the professor wasn't qualified. He should have told me."

"But, then again," her own voice in the back of her head seemed to say, speaking to her from somewhere else, "he never claimed to be anyone special. You were the one who vested him with supernatural powers. Maybe his uncommon persona was all in your imagination."

And if that was the case, Suzanne decided she was even madder at Elias Garner for prodding her fancy to create such a complex illusion.

In part, Suzanne also knew that she was mad at Elizabeth Luckholt. But that was something she was understandably reluctant to admit. The woman had been there, at the monument, had tried to scare Suzanne, had tried to make her too afraid to continue.

"That's doesn't make sense either," her own voice in the back of her brain continued. "If Garner is not from some other planet, then neither is Luckholt and not even two lunatics working together have the power to magically put ideas in your head."

Intellectually, Suzanne agreed with herself. To think, for as little as a moment, that these two might be more than they appeared was far more frightening than the idea that she might have been fooled by a couple of escaped mental patients. So if the second scenario is true, if all they are is a couple of very convincing nuts, what was she angry about in the first place?

Emotion was still in charge. She told herself to ignore reason and just keep moving. She did not know what she should be looking for when she finally reached the end of the long highway. She did know, however, that she had to get back to the city as quickly as possible.

Anger is a poor motivator, and worse still when used also as fuel. The emotion can make a captive rise to action, but the action has no direction and the very act itself becomes exhausting. Suzanne tired quickly. The sameness of the scenery and the tension combined to cause a deep weariness that reached her about the same time she reached the Minnesota line.

She'd been looking forward to the border, expecting the demarcation to bring a new look to the land. The only thing that changed as she crossed the long awaited line, marked by a large steel sign, was the name of the state she was traveling through. The empty prairie, the almost vacant highway, the widely separated towns, the road here was just like South Dakota except the fields that lined the route were filled with slightly more corn and a little less buffalo grass. "Damn, got to go slower," she thought, as the speed limit changed from seventy-five to sixty-five, and Suzanne adjusted the cruise control to the corresponding spot on the speedometer.

She simply had to break the monotony. She felt like she'd been trapped in her European iron chariot for months while the same carousel of movie backdrop scenery flowed by the windows. As she passed her very last possible mile of toleration, and then drove a mile more, there was, mercifully, a highway exit ramp. Without a second thought, in a conscious act of defiance, she stepped on the brake, turned the wheel and directed the BMW north, forcing the car to follow a circular ramp under the arrow that pointed toward:

MN 23
PIPESTONE

As the car settled on the concrete of the straight, flat thoroughfare that pointed north, Suzanne re-engaged the cruise and settled back in her seat, steering the almost independently propelled vehicle. At least, she reasoned, she would soon be someplace she'd never been before.

In the less rebellious part of her mind, Suzanne Rosewell planned only to find a simple little diner, a place to avoid the fast food culture of the Interstate, have a pleasant country lunch and then return to the highway and her properly ordered journey. But underneath that portion of responsibility, Suzanne longed to escape, guide the expensive automobile straight north, all the way to the North Pole, where even her cellular phone wouldn't work, and just desert this crazy crusade.

And when she tired of the ice and snow, the deadly silence of permanent winter, she would continue the drive. Since she would now be as far north as the planet permitted, any forward motion would automatically bring her south again, but this time on the other side of the world. Suzanne would push forward until she found someplace warm, safe and very far away from Nobel Prize winning professors and horn blowing jazz musicians.

She thought not at all about open oceans or glaciers or impassible jungles or even gasoline for the car. Her mind, her will, her desire, for that matter, her anger, would solve all those problems and more.

Suzanne's reverie was broken, shattered rather, by the sound of a police siren. Her eyes automatically went to the rear view mirror. There, perfectly framed and centered in her reflected vision, was a state trooper's car, large and dark, with headlights blinking on and off, red flashing lamps on the roof, and emitting a long, low electronic moan that sounded more like an ancient mythical monster in torment than a police siren. At the same moment as her mind absorbed all these images, she spied the sign along the side of Route 23 to Pipestone plainly announcing a speed limit of fifty-five miles per hour. The cruise control was still set for the Interstate.

"Damn," Suzanne muttered as she pulled off onto the shoulder.

The trooper stopped behind her and she watched him, again in the rear view mirror, as he pulled the brown, growling automobile so close that she thought his grill was about to ingest her rear bumper. Her eyes darted to the side view mirror when the policeman left his hungry-looking transport and walked, swaggered, to Suzanne's car.

The Minnesota State Trooper looked just like a cop in the movies, or maybe more like the way a law enforcement officer in the movies was expected to look, with mirrored sunglasses, thick mustache, hard, square jaw, totally neutral expression, showing no emotion at all. A cop from central casting.

For a moment Suzanne felt afraid, but the feeling passed. She knew the man would be polite. They always are. And he'd caution her not to go so fast. Maybe give her a written warning, or, at worst, a ticket. The encounter might be annoying, might even cost a little money, but there was nothing to fear. So why did the fear refuse to disappear?

"License and registration," he snarled the moment he reached the driver's window. Suzanne noticed that he failed to fulfill her courteous stereotype reserved for those who protect and serve by not bothering to say "please." She handed the documents without a word and he accepted them by returning equal silence. Then he examined the papers closely, not removing or even adjusting the steel-rimmed mirrors that covered much of his face. For a moment Suzanne imagined the trooper to be a person without sight, two empty holes behind the opaque coverings, hiding a void where his eyes belonged. She shuttered outwardly at the thought of the face behind the disguise projected in her mind. The trooper noticed her reaction.

"Is there something wrong, Miss?" he said. His words did not reflect any concern for Suzanne's condition. They were unquestionably a challenge, accusing her of laughing at him, or possibly of something more sinister.

"No sir," she said, very distressed by his hostile manner. Suzanne realized that not a single other vehicle had passed since she responded to the trooper's strange siren and pulled onto the shoulder. The road was far too deserted for her taste. "I was just thinking how stupid I was to have forgotten to reset the cruise control when I left the Interstate."

"That was stupid," he agreed, in continued violation of the model of politeness he was supposed to represent. "Driving a hot foreign car with New York plates... that attracts a lot of attention. A *lot* of attention. You Easterners think we're just a bunch of dumb farmers anyway... certainly too dumb to stop a fancy BMW, which obviously is being driven by someone very rich and important. Much too rich and important to pay attention to any of our dumb hick laws."

"No officer," Suzanne answered, quickly, maybe too quickly. She was confused by the hostility of the man and more than a little intimidated by his manner. And still, no other automobile had yet passed. "I certainly don't feel that I'm above the law. It's just that I had my cruise control set for the Interstate and I forgot to change it. I know I deserve a ticket and I wouldn't think of criticizing you for giving me one. As a lawyer…." She knew immediately that she'd said the wrong thing.

"Oh, a lawyer besides," he growled back. She could almost see his non-eyes glow with anger right through the mirrored glass. For a long second he didn't even look human. With his face distorted by rage, his chin thrust forward, his ears standing out from his close cropped hair and the imagined fire where his eyes belonged, he appeared to Suzanne as if he were a demon in a police uniform. She became very frightened.

The trooper sensed her fear and did everything he could to heighten her discomfort.

"A New York lawyer," now he was almost shouting. "We know all about you people out here. All your kind does is make trouble for folks like us. Why there are so many of you Jew lawyers in New York that they probably wouldn't even miss one if you never get back. And you'd better be careful if you're planning to get home. You drive this fast around here you might just run off the road. You and your car could end up buried in a cornfield. They wouldn't find you until harvest. Maybe you had a bit too much to drink, or maybe you're snorting drugs. In fact, I kind of remember that there's a warrant out for somebody who fits your description… exactly. Armed and dangerous the notice said. Handcuff the subject as a precaution... that's what I remember, yeah. I think you'd better get out of that car and get into the cruiser. I think I ought to take you down to the station."

The last thing that Suzanne could ever imagine doing was to voluntarily abandon the relative safety of her car and go anywhere with the erratic policeman. Her body was telling her to raise the electric windows, duck down under the steering wheel, grab the car phone and call the Minnesota equivalent of 911. But she didn't know what number they used in this part of the world and the demon-cop was beginning to finger his gun as he raged. She was fearful that if she moved suddenly, he would draw the large revolver and shoot.

Just as the terror in her rose toward panic, just before she reached the moment where a loss of control was a real possibility, a noise in the distance refocused her anxiety, an engine far away and moving rapidly toward them. She centered on the sound and the hum of the motor kept her from screaming.

The cop too heard the clatter. His hand dropped away from his gun and he stopped speaking. He turned his face south, the direction of the oncoming vehicle, and stood perfectly still. From Suzanne's point of view, he was not even breathing.

The engine came closer and Suzanne recognized the distinctive growl of a large truck, the diesel motor straining to haul a heavy load. She couldn't see anything, but the tone was unmistakable, as a huge truck was certainly roaring nearer and nearer. The trooper stood like a stone statue.

Now she imagines, the big rig finally arrives and she leaps out the door of her car and waves in panic to the driver. He stops and helps her. But if he doesn't stop, and she allows this thought to remain for only a split second, she is alone again with the trooper, separated from what little protection is provided by the BMW and listening to the truck's motor disappear in the distance.

The sound of the engine is almost upon them. The trooper still stands stiffly. Suzanne wonders if he is really even a living creature. She has never seen someone stand so still for quite so long. But there are more important things on her mind. Her hand is on the door handle, her muscles tense to prepare for the sudden motion that is only seconds away when the engine slows and strains further as the truck downshifts.

Suzanne turns, looks out the back window and recognizes the silver machine pulling up on the shoulder directly behind the police cruiser. It's Monty's truck, Montana license plates and too much shiny chrome. Suzanne nearly cries with relief and joy.

The small, wiry man in the Peterbilt cap climbs down from his cab and walks, without hesitation, directly up to the trooper. The policeman stands about a head taller than Monty and is at least fifteen years his junior but there is nothing in the smaller man's tone or manner to indicate that he might be afraid.

"Is there a problem officer?" he asks with a friendly lilt.

"None where you need involve yourself," the trooper growls back. Somehow, this time, the policeman's voice is different. His Minnesota accent seems to have disappeared, replaced by something beyond identity. The phrases he chooses are strangely formal. Monty is not aware of the sudden metamorphosis, but Suzanne notices the change immediately.

"Well," he says, letting the words roll off his tongue in an especially slow, deliberate manner, "the lady is sort of a friend and I thought maybe her car broke down or something and I could give her a lift. But if she's violated the law, you go right ahead and write your ticket."

"Monty," Suzanne shouts, deciding to take the risk, "he's been threatening to arrest me, put me in handcuffs and take me to the station."

"For speeding?" Monty asks. The question is directed to the officer.

"The woman has misunderstood my intent," the trooper says firmly. "I merely stopped to issue her a warning regarding excessive speed."

"Not true," cries out Suzanne, "he is intentionally intimating me." The trooper has already started to move toward his own car. For a moment Monty considers blocking his path but at the last second thinks better of the idea. If the large, potentially dangerous man wants to retreat, let him do so. Even in his withdrawal, the trooper protests his innocence.

"Nothing of the sort ever happened," he continues with his back toward Monty. The words sound almost as if they had been uttered by someone to whom English is a foreign language. "The woman is fantasizing. She needs professional care." The final phrase is spoken as he closes the door of the cruiser. Without even a glance back at the stunned pair, the policeman starts the engine and begins to manipulate the huge car from his tight space between the BMW and the eighteen wheeler.

"Hold it," Monty shouts, "I want to talk to you. What's your name? I think we should settle this in front of your commander."

The trooper ignores the challenge, frees his car from the grip of the other vehicles and makes a sharp u-turn on the concrete of Route 23. Monty reaches into his shirt pocket, withdraws a pad and pen and scribbles the identification numbers displayed on the rear of the rapidly escaping patrol car. He then turns his attention back to Suzanne who finally feels secure enough to leave the security of her locked BMW.

"Are you OK? You look terribly pale, like you've just seen a ghost."

"Not exactly a ghost," she said, leaning against the auto for support, "but that was an awfully strange experience. I am so glad you came along. What are you doing on this desolate stretch of highway anyway?"

"I should be asking you that question. I'm making a delivery to Pipestone," he answered, "thirty miles or so up the road. But why are you here? I thought you would be with your Nobel Prize winner. Couldn't you find him?"

"Oh yes, thank you, I found him. But things... well, they didn't work out. I was on my way home and impulsively got off here to find some lunch when that trooper stopped me."

"That trooper? Oh yeah, *that* trooper," Monty said remembering the confrontation with the officer. "I'm going to call his commander and file a complaint. That man doesn't know how to behave."

"Why don't we just forget it? He's gone now."

"No, can't do that," Monty answered with conviction. "When you live on the road like I do, you get used to taking punishment when you do wrong. But when the police are the offenders, they have to take responsibility for their actions. I will make the call, file my complaint and then, if you'll let me, I'll show you the best place to have lunch in the whole of Pipestone County."

"Great," said Suzanne, the color slowly returning to her cheeks, "but you must let me buy. I feel like I owe you my life."

"I'm a modern man. I can live with that," he said as he flashed a broad, warm grin. Suzanne felt safe and finally somewhat relaxed.

Monty climbed into the back portion of his cab where he kept his fax machine and cellular phone. Suzanne decided to stand back and let him handle the problem in his own style. She was not close enough to clearly hear the words he spoke, but there was something in the tone of his voice that disturbed her. A few minutes later he emerged wearing a hard frown over a puzzled countenance.

"What's wrong?" Suzanne asked.

"I'm not sure," Monty answered. "I talked to a shift commander and he said that the numbers I wrote down don't match any police car in his district. He ran them through the state computer and told me that not one Minnesota trooper's car came up, not even close. Then I described the cop and he said that the man doesn't sound at all familiar. So he broadcast a bulletin to all his units and asked if anyone had just stopped a black BMW with New York plates. No one responded."

"That is strange," Suzanne said, feeling more uncomfortable than Monty could ever imagine.

"Yeah, well, could be the captain was covering for one of his men and was plain lying, hoping that I wouldn't hang around and make a big issue out of it. Or maybe I copied the numbers down wrong." Monty didn't sound satisfied with either answer.

"But I don't think so," Monty continued. "The captain certainly sounded sincere and just as confused as I was. And I think I got the right numbers. But if the man is some sort of an imposter, at least the state police know about him. There's nothing else we can do. Let's go have lunch."

Suzanne's hands shook as she got behind the wheel of her car. She was still remembering the brief moment when the policeman seemed to reveal almost demon-like qualities and she couldn't help but wonder about Elizabeth Luckholt. Was there some connection between the possible imposter cop and the woman in black? The very insanity of the concept made her shake her head as if the motion could throw the absurd thoughts away. For the moment, Suzanne was happy that Monty's oversize rig was moving so slowly as he led her further north on Route 23. The extended ride gave her the time she needed to gather her damaged composure.

They drove by open fields of waving corn and other crops that were beyond Suzanne's ability to identify, rolled through a few very small towns and on into an area somewhat more densely settled. They passed a green sign that announced the Pipestone city limits, weaved through town until Monty pulled his truck into the parking lot of a rather old, very brightly painted diner with a huge replica of an Indian teepee dominating the facade. Suzanne wondered if every encounter with Monty was destined to be associated with some tacky Western symbol. She put the BMW next to the silver rig and watched as the trucker climbed down from his cab. Monty talked steadily from the moment his feet touched the ground. He sounded like a nervous teenager on his first date with a popular cheerleader.

"Everybody thinks that truckers know the best places to eat," he said as he walked over to Suzanne. "But the truth is we only know the places that have parking lots big enough for an eighteen wheeler. I hope you like the food here. The menu is simple, but everything's pretty tasty."

"Don't worry," she said as she walked with him past the teepee and into the front door. "I'm sure lunch will be fine."

As promised, the menu was unpretentious and the service was friendly. They each ordered soup and a sandwich. Coffee was served without their asking. For a long moment they looked at each other in silence. When Suzanne realized that Monty did not know how to begin a conversation with a pretty stranger from New York, she took the lead, but in a gentle way.

"Why the teepee?" she asked. "What has this place got to with Indians?"

While her opening line might have sounded normal enough to a stranger, if any of Suzanne's professional colleagues had heard it, they would have been shocked. Small talk was something very unusual in Suzanne's regular life. To the young, aggressive lawyer, a lull in the conversation had always been an opportunity to take over, control the subject and dominate the discourse. A pause gave her an advantage in negotiations and she carried the technique into her personal life simply out of habit. Suzanne took only brief note of her uncharacteristic behavior as she turned the topic back to Monty.

"This is Pipestone," he answered. "In this place, long before the white man came, the Indians quarried a special stone that is found only here. They used the red soft rock to make ceremonial pipes. All the tribes in the entire region shared this site. Some would travel for months just to take a small quantity of the holy stone from the earth. Their traditions forbid them to make war while in the sacred quarry. Out on the plains they would kill each other, but if they met here, violence was forbidden. The site is a national park now, but only Indians are allowed to take stone from the quarry and only if they use the same kind of ancient hand tools their people have used for generations. You should visit the place before you leave. It's a very, well, spiritual spot."

"I will," she responded, sending the nervous, middle-aged man her sweetest smile. Suzanne's tenderness made him more anxious and he launched into an extended history of the Plains Indians, covering, in some detail, all of the regions where he regularly drove his truck.

Suzanne listened to the man closely enough to be impressed by the scope of his knowledge, but her mind had quickly wandered back to the confrontation with the professor, so she only heard bits and pieces of Monty's monologue. Eventually Monty noticed that he was doing all of the talking. Without realizing it, he asked the one question that could yank Suzanne back to her table in the diner.

"What happened between you and the Nobel Prize professor? You said that things didn't work out."

Suzanne's mind snapped into gear. In the high-speed microprocessor of her brain she quickly decided how to answer his question. She would tell Monty that she had been seeking the professor to hire him as a negotiator for one of her clients, but he flatly refused. Her mind had the whole story worked out. She could hear the words in her thoughts. But her mouth insisted on telling Monty at least the basic outline of the truth.

Unlike the incident in her office where she couldn't prevent herself from asking Elias Garner certain questions, there seemed to be no outside power that controlled her. Suzanne knew that she was perfectly capable of physically stopping herself from speaking. She merely could not dredge up the desire to do so. The real story was simpler and easier to tell.

Monty listened carefully and at every spot where he could have chosen to judge her crazy, as she expected he would, he stepped into the story as effortlessly as if he'd witnessed the whole drama himself.

"Not an easy task," he commented as he shook his head. "I'll bet finding righteous people on this unrighteous planet is a very difficult chore."

"Why," Suzanne asked, "should that be so? Why would so many people be unrighteous? Most people just live normal, regular lives. What the hell is so unrighteous about that? What about you? You seem like a pretty decent guy to me. Wouldn't you qualify?"

A dark cloud passed over Monty's face. Suzanne's question

touched something inside the truck driver. A melancholy seemed to settle in his eyes and he had genuine difficulty speaking.

"I'm sorry," Suzanne added quickly, trying to relieve his discomfort. "I've gotten personal and I have no right to do that."

"No, it's OK," Monty said, choking a bit on his words. "I haven't told anybody about this for a long time and maybe hearing the story will help you on your search, or maybe it won't. For some strange reason I feel like I can trust you. Do you mind hearing a very sad tale?"

"Please," she answered, keeping her voice carefully soft and gentle. "Tell me."

The truck driver's story carried them back more than a quarter of a century in time and ten thousand miles in distance to Viet Nam where a much younger Monty, barely twenty, carried a large automatic weapon and moved slowly through the jungle with his comrades on a search and destroy mission seeking the Viet Cong. A veteran, combat-experienced corporal commanded the squad of still naive youngsters in a platoon of men whose idealism had long ago been buried in the jungle mud. Normally the group would have been led by a sergeant but their regular three-striper was disabled and in the infirmary after losing a battle with some exotic tropical fever.

Second in command was Monty himself, one fresh stripe sewn on the sleeve of his army uniform and only his third combat trip into the jungle. Though not awarded until he arrived in Viet Nam, the first, and proudly worn stripe had been earned stateside in far less dangerous duty.

The veteran corporal, distressed with the fact that most of the men in the squad were new replacements who'd never fired their weapons in defense of their own lives, was violating good military practice by personally taking the point position and leading the rest of his men into the bush. He was angry about the disproportionate number of new recruits assigned to his squad and the anger was clouding his judgement. The corporal resented being placed in command of such a poorly prepared squad where only the PFC from Montana had any prior combat experience.

He had protested to the lieutenant before being sent out, but the West Point wise guy just quoted orders and dispatched the soldiers without heeding any of the corporal's concerns. Monty, who knew nothing of the conversation held with the officer, accidentally rubbed salt in the corporal's ego wounds.

"Corporal," he shouted from the rear position that his rank required, "do you think you should be taking the point? I didn't think the person in command was supposed to do that."

"Shut up, Montana," the corporal shouted back. "After you learn more, then you can talk. Trying to tell Charlie we're coming?"

"Yeah," said one of the other soldiers, "when Charlie hears us, he can run away and we won't be able to find him. I like that idea."

"The whole reason you're here is to find Charlie and kill him," the corporal snapped back, "and Charlie ain't gonna run till he's done some damage. Don't you ever forget that."

Assumedly the corporal never forgot his own warning since that was the last thing he ever spoke about. A single gunshot shattered the jungle noises and the skull of the corporal at the very same moment. Monty heard the shot, saw a flash of blood and, without sound or protest, the corporal died. His body collapsed like a scarecrow released from his nail.

"He should have screamed or something," Monty thought. "A man should not have to die like that without even having the chance to yell out and let God know that he didn't wanna leave."

The soldiers dropped to their stomachs in the grass, their rifles pointing around them, creating a circle of defense as their discipline had taught, looking for some movement in the bush, waiting for the attack to continue. Monty realized that each and every one of the other men was looking to him for guidance.

His mind raced back through his training. Desperately, he recalled his two other brief trips into the bush seeking the enemy and remembered one veteran commander who said the VC like to get the bulk of their force behind a patrol while leaving only one sniper up front. When the sniper fired, the American patrol would either retreat directly into the trap set by the main VC force or concentrate their return fire so heavily toward the forward position that they could easily be attacked from the rear.

"Forward," he shouted, "crawl forward, quickly. Don't stand and don't shoot unless you have a real target." The soldiers immediately followed his instructions.

"Henderson," Monty shouted to the man now in the front, "you're on point. Keep your eyes open."

"Right," the newcomer Henderson acknowledged. Monty hoped the fear he heard in the soldier's voice would not deteriorate into panic. The PFC from Montana felt enough panic in himself to supply the entire squad.

"Monty, there!" Henderson shouted, pointing while still crawling on his belly. He had just reached the spot in the trail where the corporal had taken his fatal wound. The squad stopped and Monty crawled forward to see what Henderson had found. Just around the curve was a cluster of very crude thatch and grass huts.

"The one on the left," Henderson whispered loudly to Monty. "I saw the flash of a rifle barrel in the opening just as I spotted the place."

"Are you sure?" Monty asked. Henderson was about to answer but was preempted as another shot was fired, this one missing them all by at least ten feet.

"You and you," Monty instructed to the two soldiers at the back. "Cover the rear. Everyone else open fire on that hut."

He barely got the words out when the bullets began to fly, ripping through the thatch and disappearing into the now silent interior. Monty shouldered his automatic weapon and joined the barrage. A rain of smoke-surrounded grass fell and after only a few moments the raging bullets destroyed the simple construction. The roof of the hut caved into the center in one piece, pushing the walls outward and collapsing the structure as if the whole thing had been built from playing cards. Monty did not have to give the order. Everyone stopped shooting.

They remained very still in the high grass at the edge of the trail. The corporal's body continued to bleed only a few feet away, but the huts were now silent. Monty held the squad in position for what seemed to be an extra long time making sure that no one was planning to attack from behind. Then he moved the soldiers slowly forward, keeping them covered in the grass and behind the trees.

Monty's silent signal told them to skip the hut they'd devastated and attack the other two. With bravery and skill far beyond their experience, the young men did as their equally young PFC commanded. They found both of the other huts empty. Now the entire squad was pretty much out in the open and still no further shots had been fired. If Charlie had been there at all, he was gone now, except for whatever might be left of him in the destroyed hut.

"OK," Monty ordered, his heart still beating at many times its normal rate, "let's check it out." He pointed to the hut with the fallen walls. Two men shouldered their rifles and each took a side of the still almost whole thatched roof. The others spread out and pointed their weapons in case the original assailant might still be alive and ready to fight. On Monty's signal, the roof was flung aside and the squad tensed.

Five dead bodies were under their burden, each of them shot several times. One was a black-clad Viet Cong soldier, still gripping the rifle he had used to kill the corporal. There was a very old man and an equally old woman lying side by side. Each of them clutched a young child, a boy under the age of ten in the old man's arms, a teenage girl still holding the old woman. All four had been huddled in what had been the back corner of the structure. Apparently the Viet Cong soldier had taken shelter with grandparents and their grandchildren. None of them would ever need shelter again. Monty fainted.

That scene was the last thing he remembered. The other soldiers carried him and the body of the corporal back to the fire base. When Monty became conscious again, he was under the care of a medic. Seated next to the medic was an officer who wore a cross in each of the lapels of his shirt collar.

"I'm Father Martin," the chaplain said quietly, "are you a Catholic?"

"No Father, I'm not," Monty answered. "I was born a Methodist, but now I'm just a murderer."

"The others told me what happened," the priest said as he put his hand on Monty's shoulder. "It's too bad you're not a Catholic. A Catholic would take comfort in the confession. All I can say is that the death of the innocents was not your fault. You were fired on. You returned the fire. You had to protect your comrades. You had no way of knowing that the VC had hostages. This is a lousy war. Things like that happen here. The death of those innocents was not your fault."

"But I always felt that family died because of me," Monty said to Suzanne over what was now cold soup. "I think the chaplain felt that way too. He kept calling them 'innocents,' like the lambs in the Bible." Monty took a deep breath. "I spent a year there and earned two more stripes because I did my job, went out on lots of search and destroy missions, worked hard to keep my buddies alive. But I was always more afraid of shooting my gun than being shot. I kept trying to help the locals, the orphans, the homeless, the injured, especially the children. You know, sort of making up to them for what I did, but not a single night went by that I didn't dream about that moment when the roof was lifted. So you see, lots of us have horrible secrets. Those secrets make finding a righteous man among us very hard."

"Monty, I'm sorry," Suzanne said, obviously not only moved by the story also but by the way it was told. Though more than twenty-five years had passed since that bloody day, Monty's eyes still filled with tears as he described, in detail, the five bodies. He saw them for only a moment and then he fainted. Yet their images were permanently impressed in his memory, undulled by over two and a half decades. And the detail he could recall, how their hands were folded, the expressions on the dead faces, the colors of the clothing under the blood. This had certainly been the singular defining moment of the man's life.

Suzanne wanted to say something of comfort but nothing seemed to fit the suffering of a man whose personal horror took place when she was only a small child. Still, the few words she had already chosen without thinking emerged as just what Monty needed.

"Thank you," he said, "thank you for only saying that you were sorry and nothing more. I don't tell this story very often and one of the reasons I don't is that people are always trying to make me feel better. For so many years I have heard that none of the killing was my fault. They make political speeches about a war that placed young soldiers in an impossible situation, or they spout racist garbage and say that the people I killed were less than people. Most everyone has tried to convince me that the responsibility was not mine. I've learned to live with that horror because I accept what I did... because I allow myself to feel the pain. In all these years, I don't remember anyone simply saying that they were sorry and then being smart enough not to say anything more."

"They were the first words that came to mind," she responded, after a long silence. "I hope I didn't sound like I was offering pity."

"Oh, no," Monty answered, "I didn't think you were saying that you felt sorry for me. I took what you said to mean that you were sorry the whole thing happened."

"Yes, that's just what I meant." Suzanne was starting to feel uncomfortable. She looked at her watch. "I really have to get back on the road. I've been away from my office long enough."

"Oh, yes, certainly," he answered, with a nervousness that hadn't been there before. Suzanne understood that her sudden mention of departure had made Monty think that she was really leaving because she did not want to sit at a table with a murderer. Time became less important than the need to change that impression.

"Wait," she said to Monty as he started to rise. "Tell me more about the Indian quarry. You know a lot about Indians, don't you?"

"Yes," he said, sitting back down somewhat hesitantly, "I know a lot about the Indians. I spend a lot of time with them."

"Do you have Indian blood?"

"No, no," he answered, slightly more relaxed, "mostly Scotch and Irish with a little bit of Swede thrown in. It's not blood. It's guilt. When I came back from Viet Nam I realized that the Indians were the most neglected, brutalized people in the United States. I killed a whole bunch of native Vietnamese, so I thought I might make up for it by helping a few Native Americans. Somehow I decided that's what God wanted me to do. So I sort of adopted a family. The father had been a drunk and he was gone and the mother was trying to raise three sons. I gave them money, spent time with the boys, watched them grow up and eventually helped one of them get through college. All three are adults now, taking good care of their mom and their own families, busy being useful, productive people. They send me Christmas cards and visit when they're home in Montana.

"I enjoyed the first family so much, I adopted a few others, from a few other tribes, learned a lot about their history and their culture. I'm a white grandpa to a whole bunch of little red kids. Maybe that puts a bit on the other side of the scale too."

"You are an awfully good man, Montana Monty," she said to him very sweetly. "I think you balanced that scale a long time ago."

"No," he said sadly, "more than that is needed for forgiveness. Nothing I ever do can bring back those people, children who had their whole lives in front of them and never got to live any of it. And the worse part is that they must have been so frightened in their final moments. When my judgement day comes, I'm afraid God and I will still have some business left open on that subject."

"Tell me," Suzanne said with a special softness in her voice, "if you did believe you were forgiven. If... if an angel of God came down from heaven and told you that you were absolved, would you stop doing the things you're doing? Would you stop being a white grandpa to all those little red kids?"

The truck driver paused and thought for a moment. He wiped a drop of water from his eye but a fresh one quickly replaced it.

"No, I don't think so," he answered slowly. "I like what I'm doing. My trips into the reservations, the small, little things I do for those families, make me feel good... make me feel right. Even if I didn't have sins to make up."

"I don't know much about these things," Suzanne responded, "but I can't imagine that you've not been forgiven a long time ago and that now you do these things because you're simply a good man, Montana Monty."

The truck driver shook his head as though to say no, but he spoke not a single word.

"Well you may not know it," she continued, "but I do."

Suzanne felt unusually content as she backed the BMW from behind the truck and past the teepee. One last wave to Monty, who was standing beside his rig still holding her business card in his hand. On the card, hand-written, in another break with old habits, Suzanne had added her home number. She pulled out onto the highway pointing the BMW south. When the lawyer finally separated from Monty in the parking lot, she was having a hard time keeping her own eyes from moistening over.

Tears and all, Suzanne felt strangely content. She was just refocusing her mind on the drive home, glancing at the different signs, some directing her back toward the Interstate, others to the Pipestone National Monument, when the phone in her car rang. Completely startled, she immediately pulled onto the shoulder and just listened to the instrument ring.

The last time she'd heard this particular phone produce its electronic chirp was when the technician first installed the damn thing. She had bought a cellular to make calls, not to receive them. Only a very few people even had the number and they wouldn't call unless it was an emergency. Hesitantly she reached for the telephone, brought the receiver slowly to her ear, pressed the answer button and remained silent.

"Hello Suzanne," came the clear unmistakable voice of Elias Garner. "I wanted to call and say congratulations. One down and four to go."

"You mean... Monty?" she asked, surprised.

"Who else?" Garner answered.

"Despite what happened to him in Viet Nam?"

"I don't know what happened to him in Viet Nam," Garner responded. "I don't know what happened between the two of you. All I know is that there is an additional name on the computer screen. But knowing what you know about him, do you think he belongs on the list?"

"I do," she answered, without a second's hesitation, "but since when does my opinion mean anything?"

"You're not the only judge," the voice through the phone said, "but your judgment carries weight, lots of weight actually."

"I have to go and tell Monty," she said, just then realizing the magnitude of what she was hearing. "The truth will relieve the burden he's been carrying for so long."

"Wait, Suzanne," Elias Garner said, "do you think he'll believe you? That a stranger called you on your cellular phone and identified him a righteous man? Or, maybe he'll think you're claiming to be an angel from God." Suzanne was silent for a long moment. She wondered at the coincidence of Garner using almost exactly the same phrase she had used when speaking with Monty.

"No, I guess not," she finally said.

"Maybe it's better for your man to remain anonymous, even with himself."

"Well, maybe..." she said into the phone, "maybe I can succeed at this after all."

"I hope so," the gentle voice responded.

"I will keep trying," she answered, "but first I have to visit a quarry."

"A quarry?"

"Yes, a stone quarry. A righteous man, who doesn't know that he's a righteous man, told me I should not leave this town without visiting the quarry. He said it was a very spiritual place. Who am I to question a righteous man?"

"Who indeed? Enjoy your visit Suzanne," Elias Garner laughed. "I hope we talk again soon."

CHAPTER ELEVEN

Even when compared to the crowded Northeast, where public space is stolen in bits and pieces and hidden from commercial development, the Pipestone National Monument was still a very small place. If the park appeared large at all, it was because of the surrounding prairie that stretched, perfectly flat, to the horizon in all directions, an endless view broken only by acres of crops and a few low farm buildings. The openness managed to give the place a false sense of space. In reality, the national shrine occupied a stingy amount of land set just outside of town with the boundaries seeming almost reluctant to infringe on the neighboring ground, acreage used year in and year out to produce food and fiber. Even the little territory set aside was dominated by the parking lot and one single-story, rambling brick building whose design spoke loudly of the federal government, Department of the Interior, model 1A, right down to the flagpole that rose a hundred feet above the black Minnesota soil. This white spire was topped with a huge Stars and Stripes in perpetual motion thanks to the constant Great Plains wind. This was a place, mused Suzanne, completely lacking in architectural form or imagination and Monty had called it "spiritual."

The parking lot hosted only a couple of passenger cars and two similar but still distinct species of the vehicle that had become Suzanne's representation of the Midwest in July, the opulent rolling motor homes known by their understated initials – RVs. Each was from an entirely different part of the nation. One wore Florida plates while the other was licensed in Oregon. Probably as a direct result of her good mood, Suzanne saw them as the source of wonderful stories. She wondered what had brought these rolling homes from so far away to this tiny curiosity hidden on the edge of the Minnesota map.

She parked the BMW near the other passenger cars and, with a New Yorker's unbreakable habit, snapped shut the electric locks without the slightest thought about what she was bothering to secure the car against.

Suzanne shivered as the brief, automatic action brought the unfocused thought of potential enemies to the front of her mind. For a second she remembered the state trooper who became a phantom and for more than a second, she was afraid. But the logic of the lawyer's brain drove the thoughts away. She was almost certain that one of Monty's several theories adequately explained why the cop seemed to just disappear.

Maybe that's why Elias Garner came seeking an attorney, someone whose logically trained mind would not allow for the possibility, no matter how remote, of supernatural events. For a moment Suzanne wondered if her background was an asset or a shield of delusion that allowed a fool to walk in a place that all the angels knew how to avoid.

Suzanne proceeded through the glass door entrance of the federal brick building into a circular, air-conditioned foyer, leaving her doubts on the prairie outside. They could always be retrieved when she left. For the moment, she was seeking to touch the "very spiritual place" Monty had described.

A young woman in a park ranger's uniform offered Suzanne a silent smile greeting. The gesture was accepted and returned. A sign advised that an admission fee was required. The New Yorker, finding the price reasonable, paid the tariff and received some brochures including a self-guided tour map of something called the "nature trail." There were also a few words offered by the green clad woman, but these failed to register in Suzanne's consciousness.

The lawyer's attention had been drawn by an orchestra of strange noise drifting toward her from the other end of a short corridor. She clearly heard the clatter of hammers, saws and sandpaper but the sounds seemed to be working together in a most unfamiliar rhythm. The clamor had a special quality, tool vibrations that reverberated as though they were tuned together, like musical instruments, cutting, scraping, striking, all in the appropriate octave, at the same pitch, each following a line of preplanned cadence contrived to blend them into a specific primitive symphony of work.

Suzanne is drawn by the strange music. Almost without the power to resist, she follows the vibrations to find where the concert is being performed. The allure is familiar. Just as had happened before, she knows she has the power to resist but she does not have the desire to exercise that particular part of her will. Suzanne is compelled to find the source of the bizarre song.

The corridor opens into a much wider area of the structure, a large room at the back of the building, separated by partitions into a number of booths, every one bordered by a railing to define precisely how close a visitor can approach. Each of these three sided rooms, display cages without bars, is inhabited by a single individual, some men, some women, every one intent on a specific task. As Suzanne draws still nearer, she realizes that these people are artisans, hard at work in the hand manufacture of various items. Their tools are producing the vibrations that blend together into the symphony. As her eyes drift from face to face, and she notices their distinctive features, Suzanne realizes that all of the work-musicians are American Indians.

For a moment she feels she is in a living museum, with each booth a separate exhibit of a nearly extinct culture. Then the thought crosses her mind that maybe this room is sort of a zoo, with these dark-skinned, strong-featured people forced to be on display while their hands are required to produce the magnificent music.

Suzanne stands back, leaning on the wall, where she can observe all of the booths at once. She turns her head to the far left and watches as a middle-aged woman works with a rose colored stone. The woman stops and lifts her head. The symphony seems suddenly diminished by one instrument portion. The Indian woman is scrutinizing Suzanne while staring at her through unreadable eyes. The gaze makes Suzanne nervous and she turns to her right, focusing on the next booth where a young man, working with the same kind of stone, responds in exactly the same manner.

One more instrument is removed from the orchestra and one more pair of eyes is directed at Suzanne. Her nervousness increases and she repeats the process, moving her own gaze again to the right. Again she repeats the experience. The same reaction comes from the old man with the shoulder length gray hair who occupies the next booth. The music is further reduced and darker eyes watch. Again and again, over and over, with every artisan that Suzanne watches, watching her until the entire room is mute, the music gone, and all eyes on Suzanne. She wants to scream but now knows that she dare not break the silence of the concert hall.

Then, like that first patron who clears his throat at the end of performance, just before the audience breaks into applause, she can stand the silent tension no longer and turns sharply to her right, walking rapidly to the far corner where a long, glass counter is watched over by a young Indian woman heavily laden with silver and rose-stone jewelry, unaware of the pause in the performance. The craft people start their work again and the symphony proceeds as if the interruption were something expected, written into the score.

The corner of the room, protected from the dark staring eyes by a rack of books, belongs to the souvenir counter and the souvenir counter belongs to the Native American Craft Cooperative. Here they sell ritual pipes, jewelry, arrow heads and other trinkets made from the rose-colored material that Suzanne finally learns is called "pipestone," just like the town. The soft rock comes from the ancient quarry directly outside the door of the building. From here, even the work symphony sounds different, less musical, more like normal work and far less disquieting.

Suzanne was able to relax, just a little, and lose herself in asking the jewelry-decked youngster a hundred questions, all of which had been asked by a thousand tourists before her. And the counter girl answered them with the enthusiasm of one who repeats the same responses over and over, day after day.

Like a tourist, she bought a few small articles, put them in her purse and went rapidly back down the corridor, afraid to allow her eyes to rest on the workers for even a moment. Not far from the sometimes concert hall, was the entrance to the "nature trail." She stepped through these glass doors and out into the July sunshine hoping that unlike Alice, these doors would take her away from Wonderland.

Outside, the mystic sounds and smells and sights that had almost overwhelmed her in the building were gone, completely gone, as though the aura had never existed at all. The unrelenting wind moving grass and branches, the cries of small birds, the noise of a car in the parking lot, all helped Suzanne to focus on the normal. In a few moments, she touched her world just as if she'd never attended the concert.

Once again a faithful tourist, the young New Yorker turned her high heels down the trail, steadfast to the course outlined in the government brochure. Directly on the path, blocking her progress, were two families, adults dressed in tourist clothes, each patriarch carrying a video camera, each matriarch a bag of souvenirs and a pile of brochures, children being children, bored and restless. They were the owners of the long fancy recreational vehicles ruling the parking lot. The human caravan had paused for the express purpose of allowing the fathers to engage in conversation on their favorite topic. One rested his older, outsized camcorder on his shoulder. The other allowed his more compact model to hang from a strap at his side. Suzanne stepped onto the grass and off the blacktop path as she went around them.

"That's right," she heard from the man with the large belly hanging over his shorts, "we've had trouble with the hot water heater since Orlando. I found a dealer in Ohio who knew just what was wrong and he fixed the thing... cheap."

"Really," said the other, "mine has been acting up too. Can you give me the name of that dealer, 'cause we'll...." The voices disappeared as Suzanne progressed further down the trail. In passing the families, she had walked through a curtain that became the final separation between the strange, sort of metaphysical place where Suzanne had been wandering, the place where work tools make music and Indian eyes focus on her for no reason, and the so-called real world where Suzanne usually felt more comfortable. This time she just wasn't sure. There wasn't much comfort on this side of the border either.

Seated on a bench under the broad open sky studying a segment of ground that the guide book described as one of the few remaining sections of never-touched-by-a-plow virgin prairie, Suzanne found her lost logic. The skepticism endemic in her lawyer's training, and in her natural inclination, finally surfaced.

"What the hell's the matter with me?" she said out loud to the prairie and to herself, "why have I been impressed with all this crap? Every single event is easily explained. First Garner got the number to my cell phone. Not so hard. He snooped around my desk while he waited in my office, or even the parking lot to read the number right off the phone. When he called, he never specifically named the 'righteous' person he congratulated me on finding. I guess I mentioned that I was coming out to see Professor Fields. I must have... I don't remember, but

I must have. Or he found out from Margaret. Simple enough. He knew Fields was in South Dakota, so he tried the car phone. As soon as he connected, he assumes I'm on my way back, so he plays his little game and I'm impressed, convinced he has supernatural powers. That damn con man! I feel really stupid."

The two RV families caught up with her and strolled by the bench where she contemplated how a smart, NYU educated lawyer could have been so easily duped. In their presence, she ceased the monologue and even turned off her thoughts, as though she was hiding her brain waves. Suzanne filled her mind with the sounds of nature. Only when the two families had safely passed did she allow herself to return to her mental soliloquy.

"The only thing I still can't figure out," she said to the grass, "is his motive. Why does he want me to do all these strange things? What's in it for him? Is he really just some sort of ingenious nut? And then there's Elizabeth Luckholt. Sure, I've heard about shared fantasies, but a shared obsession? How did I get so lucky to meet these people?"

Now the open prairie no longer seemed peaceful. The songs of the birds quickly moved to the edge of irritation. Suzanne had, once more, become convinced that the great quest was a sham, some sort of complex con game whose real ending had not yet been revealed. And that goal would never be known because she was no longer going to play. Enough was enough. Time to get back to New York and get on with her life.

That settled the issue. Suzanne stood and tugged at her blouse to flatten the wrinkles. It was the same gesture she always made before entering an important meeting. Then she walked, marched really, down the pathway, determined to complete only the distance of the nature trail, a tiny remnant of her commitment to Monty, get in her car and drive to New York as fast as the roads would permit.

The enigma was gone, the puzzle solved. Suzanne's intellect had prevailed. She would no longer allow herself to be distracted by foolish games. She would tell her friends, and her partners, that the trip was in reality a small, and very impulsive vacation. Now she had her rest and was just fine. She'd work twice as hard, dazzle her clients and her colleagues, as only she could, and they would quickly forget. The South Dakota adventure would fade in their minds until the deviation became a minor aberration in her behavior pattern. From this moment on, Suzanne Rosewell was back on the fast track to success.

These decisions did not make her feel better. The joyful contentment that filled her after parting company with Monty was eclipsed, replaced by nothing. The sense of mystery, both stimulating and frightening, that surrounded the craft symphony and when the Indians stopped working and stared, that too had disappeared. And those lost feelings had not been supplanted by the old familiar thrill of adrenaline that had once been her delight when she prepared to do battle in the Wall Street wars. All she could feel, hiding carefully behind the barrier of intellectual determination, was a vague sense of free floating anxiety, the same emotion she used to experience as a child when she thought she'd done something wrong and was waiting for some adult to dispense discipline. Suzanne increased the tempo of her pace.

The trail carried her finally along an open, rock-lined trench, the very reason this park existed in the first place. It wasn't much of a quarry by modern standards, just a long scar in the earth, only ten or twelve feet at the deepest point. Suzanne's legs slowed as her eyes were drawn into the pit. She couldn't help but think about the ancient temperament of this hole in the ground, the generations of natives who crawled here, drawing the rose stone from out of the earth with only their fingers or with simple, primitive tools, widening and deepening the hole, one small pebble at a time, painfully slowly.

Her eyes followed the color of the pipestone vein as she permitted her vision to feast on the jagged edges of human cut rock and the angled patterns jointly created by man and earth. To savor fully the banquet of light and shadow, she slowed her steps until her gait was no more than a lingering stroll.

The figure of the man in the pit took her completely by surprise. Suzanne swallowed a gasp when his image appeared suddenly from nowhere. Half of the almost sound was surprise and the other half was rising from the fear that, after logically explaining all these strange events, she was now being visited by yet another spirit. But she held the audible part of her astonishment when she realized that her concentration on the rock patterns had been so intense that she simply hadn't seen him until he was directly in her line of sight.

Nor did he seemingly see her. His deliberation was total and focused entirely on a particular section of the pipestone vein. The man, who appeared from the rear to be somewhere between 50 and 60, with broad, bare, bronze shoulders, muscular arms and mostly gray hair that fell loosely on the back of his neck, was certainly an Indian. At his side rested a black steel hammer and a shining metal chisel. While his right hand stroked the tools, as if warning them of their imminent need, he seemed to be doing very little more than watching the stone. Every so often he would lift his left hand apparently to measure a section of rock between his thumb and forefinger. He repeated the gesture several times, raising his fingers to the same portion of the vein while his lips moved silently as though he were talking to himself, or the stone.

Suzanne felt like she had rudely and invisibly entered his private world. Though she was embarrassed and uncomfortable in the role of uninvited observer, she was also captivated by his ritual and could not bring herself to leave or even to turn away. Eventually she recognized him as being one of those she saw working in the craft area.

After a few additional minutes of diligence, he picked up the tools, passing the chisel to his left hand. Without taking his eyes from the rock, he raised the hammer over his shoulder and held it there as he set the sharp steel against the vein. Gently he brought the hammer down to meet the metal, moving carefully as if he expected the vein to bleed. The sound of metal hammer against metal chisel rang clear and was softly echoed back by the canopy of protective trees. Suzanne presumed there would be more noise. She braced herself for the shock of the impact, but judging by the sound, the Indian was trying to urge the stone loose, convince the rose-rock to leave its prehistoric protected world and voluntarily enter the one inhabited by the dark-skinned digger.

The process was repeated over and over, hammer against chisel, each time so unexpectedly tender that even the birds in the neighboring branches were undisturbed by the work. Finally, after a very long time, he set down the tools and, with his eyes still locked on the same spot, lowered both his hands to the stone and, with kindness in his touch, extracted a large, flat piece of the rock. He turned around and displayed the section to Suzanne, smiling at her, two soft lights of late afternoon sun reflected in his dark eyes. He behaved as if Suzanne's presence was perfectly normal and known to him all along.

"It's a beauty, isn't it?" said the Indian.

"I'm afraid I wouldn't know one piece of rock from another, but this one has a very pretty color," Suzanne responded.

The Indian climbed out of the pit, meticulously placed the section of stone on the grass, pushed the hammer and chisel into the back pocket of his overalls and reached out to a nearby bench where he retrieved a gray New York Yankees t-shirt that he proceeded to pull over his hardened torso. Then he placed a battered black cowboy hat on his head. Suzanne had not previously noticed the bench, the shirt or the hat. After dressing, the Indian put out his hand in greeting.

"I am Red Cloud," he said. "Who are you?"

"I'm Suzanne," she responded while tentatively shaking his large hand. "I'm here visiting... from New York."

"Why?"

"I beg your pardon?"

"Why are you visiting? Obviously, from the way you're dressed, you're not one of our usual sightseers. And this place is more than a bit off the regular tourist track. Is there some reason you've come here?"

Suzanne was more than a bit taken back by the directness of the man. She did not know how or even whether to answer his question. All she could do was stand in the same spot, shifting her weight from one foot to the other, wrapping her hands together in front of her, and twisting her fingers in the same manner used by a child when she doesn't know the answer to a school question. How much notice Red Cloud took of the smaller words in Suzanne's body language was not apparent, but he felt her discomfort and tried to put her at ease.

"I'm sorry," he said, keeping his eyes locked on hers, "I'm just a nosey old man and I should learn to mind my own business. I just had this feeling you were in pain and I thought maybe I could help. You focused so hard on me while I was removing the stone, the idea came to me that maybe you were watching me so you didn't have to look at yourself."

"You knew I was watching?"

"Certainly," the Indian said with a smile, "I heard your footsteps coming and I heard them stop. I could even hear the sound of your breathing as you waited."

"And you felt no need to turn around? No need to know who was behind you and why?"

"Spoken like a New Yorker," he laughed. "Keep an eye over your shoulder all the time. Can't blame you. I lived there for a while in the sixties. But out here... well, let's just say that here in this quarry, where even my most savage forbearers renounced violence, surrounded by the spirits of my ancestors, protected by the birds and breezes and the trees, I don't feel at all threatened. The important thing, at that moment, was to cut the rock correctly, not to know who was watching me."

"You certainly were intent," she replied, feeling more comfortable, "Why did you stare at the rock for so long and were you singing or praying while you waited?"

"Both," he said, now looking a bit embarrassed. "This is going to sound corny, but... well, the earth and the pipestone have been together for all eternity. I am just a simple man and I have been in this world for only fifty-five years. Before I have the audacity to separate a relationship that has gone on for millions of years, I must pay homage. I pray, I sing and I ask the forgiveness of the earth for taking away the pipestone. Then I wrest the stone, gently as possible, from the only home it has ever known. All of this has to be done correctly if the spirits are going to give me a piece that I can make into a good pipe. That's how I earn my living. I am an artist in the craft cooperative."

"I know," Suzanne said, "I saw you a little earlier, working inside."

"Oh really?" he said, as he turned his attention back to the stone. "I didn't notice and I should be ashamed of myself for not noticing you." He looked up at her and smiled. "I'm really not making a pass at you. I'm a happily married man. But after so many years of chasing after beautiful women, noticing has sort of become a habit. I mean only to compliment."

"Thank you," Suzanne said, feeling sincerely flattered, "may I ask you another question?"

"Sure."

"Those things you said about the earth and the stone and the spirits... is that part of your religion? I'm interested in learning." Red Cloud grinned broadly. He was trying to suppress a laugh.

"You're not one of these New Age people are you Miss?" he said. "I really have a hard time with these folks who think everything that's done by every Indian is always spiritual and in perfect tune with nature."

"No, I'm not a New Age person. I don't even own a crystal. I'm just interested, that's all." She spoke to him sternly, in defense of her dignity, but with appropriate humor. He respected the mixture.

"I'm not talking about religion, not in the usual sense," he said. "The words are a hazy reflection of the things I feel, things I learned over these past few years as I allowed the spirits to touch me. I don't use the right words because the concepts are all very new to me. While it is true that I have always been blessed with skilled hands and my hands were always there to earn me a living, until recently, I used them primarily to get money for alcohol and drugs. For many years I lived the bigoted white stereotype of an Indian, a drunken no good thief. A few years ago, pretty defeated by your world, I came home, to the Pine Ridge reservation in South Dakota where I found plenty of other defeated men. They became my drinking companions. That went on for quite some time until an old medicine man turned me on to making pipes. He taught me to use my hands for something different. And he taught me that if I looked beyond my foolish, drunken friends, I'd find my people and my past right there on the reservation. Suddenly, I didn't want to be drunk or stoned anymore. But here I was, fifty-one years old and starting my life all over. With the help of some new friends, I stayed away from the drugs and booze. When my hands stopped shaking, I learned the craft of making beautiful things from pipestone.

"A while later, I came here, to the quarry, where I work every day with the earth and the rock that the earth gives me. And every day I get better. For the last three years, I have lived here from Spring through Fall and then I leave the quarry so the site can have a winter rest. Even for those few months I miss this spot. This is really a very spiritual place."

"A man I met earlier told me that very same thing, in those exact same words," Suzanne said, "And that's why I came here."

"So you do have a reason for being here after all. I guess that's why I told you my story."

"I've lost you."

"Well, do you think I tell my life story to every pretty young woman I meet in the quarry? I didn't really mean to bore you with all that stuff, but you listened so intently that I allowed my ego to believe you needed to hear what I had to say. Tell me I'm right so I won't be embarrassed."

"Yes, yes… you're right, and the story was far from boring. I am… sort of on a quest. And I think I came here looking for you." Red Cloud's expression grew curious.

"Looking for me?" he said, "I doubt it. We don't even know each other."

"You're going to find this a little strange," Suzanne said with hesitation, "but I am out looking for righteous people."

"You are one of those New Age people," he laughed.

"No, I promise you," she laughed back, pleased to find herself, for once, not taking the topic quite so seriously. "I am a Wall Street lawyer, that's about as far away from being spiritual as one can get. Please don't ask me to explain. It's too hard." Her voice had become quite serious. "I don't know if I am doing something crazy or noble, and, right now, I don't want to know. I just have a feeling that you are one of the people I am seeking."

"No Suzanne," he said, "I don't know who you're looking for, but I can't allow it to be me. I'm still in the process of finding myself after a long time of being lost. I cannot permit anyone else to need my energy until I have finished my own search." He reached out to comfort her, to touch her shoulder, but he hesitated. Suzanne took his hand in hers.

"You wouldn't happen to know a man named Elias Garner would you?" She said, not quite willing to surrender, but with the touch, humor came back into her voice, easing the moment of tension. "He's a tall black man who plays a mean trumpet."

"No, can't say I do," Red Cloud responded, his own smile returning, "but if he comes this way, I'll tell him you were looking for him."

"Thank you Red Cloud. I appreciate that." Suzanne turned to continue the rest of the way down the nature trail.

"Suzanne, wait a moment," the Indian shouted. She paused and turned back. "Did you buy souvenirs in the shop?"

"Yes, I did," she answered, puzzled by the question.

"May I see them?" he asked. She reached into her shoulder bag and removed the paper sack with the rose colored, pipestone trinkets. One of them was a small turtle attached to long strip of leather. It was designed to be worn as a necklace.

"I made this one," Red Cloud said pointing to the turtle. He turned the carving over. "See, here is my mark." He picked up his art and held it at arm's length in front of him. "This is a symbol of family. I know the color doesn't go with your outfit, but wear the turtle anyway Suzanne. It's better than a crystal. Maybe the magic will work for you."

Suzanne didn't answer but stood unresisting as the Indian tied the amulet around her neck. The leather was short and the turtle hung close to the base of Suzanne's throat. She reached up and stroked the smooth stone.

"Thank you," she said, "thank you very much." Suzanne turned again. With her hand still on the carving, she backed away, eyes fixed on Red Cloud, then turned abruptly and walked rapidly down the path, passing through yet another set of glass doors, down the corridor and out the front entrance into the parking lot.

Her hand was still on the turtle when she saw the police car parked at the curb. Behind the wheel was that same state trooper and next to him, in the passenger's seat, sat a stern-faced Elizabeth Luckholt.

"Ms. Rosewell," Luckholt said with an unbroken expression, "What a strange coincidence meeting you here. But it is good to see you again."

The very presence of the woman frightened Suzanne. More than fright. In reality, she stood directly on the edge of terror. Still, at the same moment, an opposite force, whatever one calls that internal thing that stands against fear, resting dormant inside her and activated by Luckholt's presence, seemed to offer her power. When tapped, the power grew into strength and the strength into courage, not a lot, but just enough to hide her fright. Suzanne gratefully accepted the offer.

"I doubt if either of those statements is true, Ms. Luckholt," Suzanne snapped back as though she was trying to convince a jury. "This is not a coincidence and you're not overjoyed to see me. But don't worry about it. I'm not too thrilled to see you either. Is there something I can do for you? If not, I suggest you tell your driver to move his car. A state trooper should know better than to park in a handicapped zone."

Suzanne knew she was bluffing and that if Luckholt called her bluff, threatened her in any way, she would likely fall completely apart. But she was determined that the woman should not see the terror behind the thin veneer.

Actually, the pale woman was impressed by the New York lawyer's tenacious response. Luckholt stepped out of the car and stood on the sidewalk, blocking Suzanne's path but seemingly reluctant to move too close. As always, dressed all in very stylish black, Elizabeth looked even more out of place on the sun-soaked July prairie than did Suzanne. The two of them must have been a very strange sight for the few tourists in the neighborhood.

Luckholt gestured gently, moving just a finger, and the trooper engaged the cruiser, taking the car to the other side of the parking lot.

"That's a demonstration of my good will," she said. "I don't want you to feel intimidated. My friend can be very frightening when he wants to be. But I understand that you two have already met."

"Yes, we have, but I didn't know he was a buddy of yours. I probably should have guessed." The observation elicited a sort of smile from Luckholt, an expression so cold that Suzanne was relieved when the look disappeared from the blonde woman's face.

"Oh, yes, we're very old friends. That's why he allows me to ride in the patrol car in violation of all the rules. I called on him first when I was trying to find you and was delighted by the happenstance that he knew precisely where you were."

"That's the second time you've referred to this meeting as almost accidental," Suzanne responded, trying hard to sound as serene as her adversary. Despite her dark clothing, and the sun's burning heat, Elizabeth Luckholt failed to show even a drop of sweat. Her attitude appeared as cool as her skin while Suzanne was occupied with trying to ignore the perspiration running down her back. "Your friend Elias Garner has said that he doesn't believe in coincidences."

"Eli is very naive and rather impractical. You, on the other hand, Ms. Rosewell, are a very pragmatic person. I judge you as one who knows the advantages of a good business deal, which is precisely what I'd like to discuss. And, unlike the agreement you made with Eli, mine can offer you considerable profit."

"I'm listening."

"Is there somewhere more private we can talk?"

"I know a very nice spot, a bench in the shade, just inside the park, quiet, shady and very secluded, down this path, in through the first set of double glass doors and out through the second."

Luckholt nodded and moved toward the building. She had taken only one step forward, just far enough to leave the sidewalk and rest her foot on the first stone of the pathway when she paused, froze, and stared straight ahead. Just on the other side of the glass stood Red Cloud, quietly standing and watching them.

"Please, continue Ms. Luckholt," Suzanne said. "Don't be concerned about that man. He's a friendly Indian. Go right ahead. This is a very spiritual place."

"So I've heard," said Luckholt. "But I think not. I really don't like trees, forests and all of those natural things. Let's just stay here in the parking lot. I think we can conclude our discussions quickly. Why don't we just go over by your expensive German car? Let's use the BMW as a reminder of life's finer things." Suddenly Suzanne regretted having purchased the high-priced automobile.

Still unwilling to show any hesitation, Suzanne shrugged her shoulders and silently led Luckholt across the steaming blacktop to her car. The lawyer intentionally moved quickly so that the woman in black would have to struggle just to walk at Suzanne's side.

Luckholt didn't even try. She seemed quite content to trail behind and when Suzanne took her position on the driver's side, the woman comfortably settled by the passenger's door. The broad black hood spread out between them like a polished steel conference table.

"Let's get right to business, Ms. Luckholt," Suzanne barked across the BMW. "I plan to get back on the road and go home."

"Fine, I too have a busy schedule. We will get directly to the point, Suzanne. Do you mind if I call you Suzanne?"

"I do, but if it will speed things up, you may call me anything you like." Suzanne spoke quickly while focusing her eyes directly into Luckholt's cold blue orbs. She sensed the blonde woman was beginning to grow uncomfortable under the lawyer's stare. Suzanne couldn't imagine why Luckholt should feel discomforted, but if the tactic worked, Suzanne wouldn't question it.

"Very well, Ms. Rosewell. I do not desire to offend, at least not yet." The threat was very plain. "I am here to offer you the opportunity to represent a corporation that can provide more work to your firm than the rest of your other clients combined."

"Do you mean the corporation that employs both you and Garner?"

"I do. And as you have probably surmised, Eli and I are rivals. This quest you undertook, at no fee, may seem silly, even a fool's errand, but the task is most important to Elias Garner."

"And to your Chairman," Suzanne interjected.

"Oh, not really. The Chairman is interested in the results, vitally interested, but only because he wants all the facts in proper order to make some very major decisions. But he doesn't have a particular preference for how they turn out, one way or another."

"Your chairman will make business decisions based on whether or not I find a few righteous people? What makes you think I would want to represent a corporation run by a bunch of nuts?"

"Don't underestimate the seriousness of the business in which you have involved yourself Ms. Rosewell," Luckholt snapped back, her eyes flaring with anger. "That would be a critical mistake, even a fatal one." A chill followed the sweat down Suzanne's spine, but she forced herself to continue staring directly into Luckholt's eyes. The blond woman continued. "Our chairman may sound strange, but he rarely makes a mistake. If Eli succeeds, or should I say, if you succeed on his behalf, the victory will enhance my rival's influence. Mr. Garner will send you his thanks and you will never hear from him again. But if you fail, my star will rise in the corporation and I, on the other hand, can be very generous. What do you think, Ms. Rosewell?"

"I think you offer a lot of words, Ms. Luckholt, but neither you nor Garner will even tell me the name of this mythical corporation, so why should I believe either of you?"

"Your skepticism is very healthy and was to be expected," Luckholt answered, "so I brought you some proof of my good intentions. This retainer is far more than you will ever see from my opposite and only the beginning of what I can do for you." Luckholt fingered an envelope that seemed to appear from nowhere and slid it across the hood to Suzanne. "Open this, my dear, and see which of us offers the better deal in this game."

Suzanne took the envelope hesitantly and allowing her eyes to finally move away from Luckholt's face for even a moment, she tore the thing open. Her fingers could feel what her eyes confirmed, a cashier's check in the amount of $100,000 made out to Suzanne Rosewell. The lawyer's eyes shot back to Luckholt and found her face decorated with that same frightening smile.

"I am sorry that I still have to keep the name of the company secret. When you have cashed the check and are committed to our cause, I can tell you more. You will notice that the bank draft made out to you personally. Share it with the firm you'd like, or keep it for yourself. It makes no difference to me."

That's when Suzanne felt the anger rise. The outrage started below her belly, entered a main artery and rapidly flowed through her veins. When the fury reached her right hand, she crumpled the check into a tight little paper ball. Luckholt's smile vanished.

"Damn you," Suzanne shouted, throwing the check at Luckholt, who flinched as though the target of a rock. "An hour ago I was ready to go home and forget the entire trip, you would have won and the victory wouldn't have cost a cent. But I learned something here. I learned that I don't like you. I don't like you one bit, and if this search is all that important to you, if you're willing to pay me to fail, I am going to try very hard to succeed." With the most threatening body language she could project, Suzanne advanced around the front of the car toward Luckholt. Much to the lawyer's surprise, the woman in black retreated.

"She's afraid of me," Suzanne thought to herself, "this bitch is really afraid of me." She grew heady with the power and advanced further. Luckholt continued to retreat. There was no fear in the blonde woman's face, but she refused to allow the distance between them to close, backing away only just as far as Suzanne moved forward.

"Do not approach me. That's an action you will regret," Luckholt hissed.

"Prove it," answered Suzanne and took another step. Luckholt waved her hand and from across the parking lot the trooper car responded. Suzanne stopped moving.

"To hell with you," the lawyer shouted. "You and your cop friend can do whatever you like. I'm leaving." Suzanne returned to the driver's door, unlocked the car and climbed in behind the wheel. Through the rear view mirror she saw the police cruiser on the move while Luckholt stood in the parking space next to the BMW and glared.

"Don't make me your enemy Ms. Rosewell," she said. "It's very bad to have me as your enemy."

"I don't need to listen to you," Suzanne muttered. She started the engine and switched on the radio, turning the volume as high as possible. Jim Morrison and the Doors came blasting out of the speakers, filling the interior with sound, and covering every other noise.

"Come on baby light my fire," Morrison sang, in the long version of the song rarely played on the radio, and Suzanne heard Luckholt's voice no more. She put the car in reverse, backed out, and then moved forward as rapidly as the road would permit. The image of Elizabeth Luckholt in the rear view mirror, standing next to the police car grew smaller and smaller. Morrison continued to sing.

"Try to set the night on fire!"

Without warning, without a crackle from the radio to prepare her for the coming silence, the music simply stopped. From the car radio, or maybe from inside her head, Suzanne heard, or thought she heard, the clear, sharp, crisp voice of Elizabeth Luckholt.

"You will regret this beyond your dying day. Do you hear me? Beyond your dying day," Suzanne thought she heard the voice say. But the moment passed, and the Doors were back. Only the rock and roll guitar filled her ears.

"She's a spooky lady," Suzanne said out loud, her own voice drowned by Jim Morrison's. "She's got me hearing things."

Then she turned the car back onto the highway and headed for the Interstate and home.

CHAPTER TWELVE

A drive across half the country is a great excuse for some deep thinking. Minnesota, the whole state, passed outside of Suzanne's windshield before she even reached out to turn on the radio, and that was only to help slow the speeding freight train that had taken over her brain. Her mental absorption was so complete that crossing the Mississippi River into Wisconsin was a surprise. So she consciously used all of that state and some of Illinois to reexamine, in great detail, the confrontation with Elizabeth Luckholt.

No doubt about it, this was a battle… with a clear winner and an equally evident loser. The victory belonged to Suzanne. Not only had Luckholt failed to intimidate, she'd blundered by attempting a bribe. As a result of her own errors, the woman in black was reduced to shouting empty threats. Yes. Victory.

That part was simple. But there was, resting on Suzanne's shoulders, a burden of unanswered questions that no amount of Interstate seemed to diminish. Key among them was the mystery of Luckholt's, and for that matter Garner's, real agenda in this strange search.

The miles of highway had not brought Suzanne any closer to accepting that the Chairman of a major corporation would be basing business decisions on the outcome of an ancient Jewish legend. Yet, Elias Garner and Luckholt certainly pursued their particular sides of the issue with unrestrained passion. They each took this exercise very seriously. And while all of the spiritual stuff was very hard to accept in a corporate context, was this really any stranger, Suzanne thought, than the stories of an astrologer in the White House? Then there was always Professor Abromowitz and his trust in the value of blind faith. The New

York lawyer found herself wishing she could believe… in anything, as easily and as thoroughly as the old professor.

Suzanne's skepticism ran deep, her disbelief of anything supernatural was so strong that she was still trying to reason out how Luckholt had managed to pull that cute trick with the radio back in Pipestone. She was certainly a skeptic, one who trusted that there were always rational, reasonable answers to mysteries. Yet the thought of that particular strange moment still made Suzanne shiver.

That is, until Suzanne found the answer to one of her questions at a truck stop near the Illinois border. In a left-on-the-table electronics magazine, she read that police departments were experimenting, though not too successfully, with a short range broadcast device designed to address drivers directly through their FM radios. The technology was still extremely unreliable.

So that's how she pulled her trick. Still, Suzanne took pleasure in picturing Luckholt, her pale skin red with anger, grabbing the microphone in the police cruiser and shouting her threats, lacking even the satisfaction of knowing if they were really heard.

The revelation that electronics might have been behind one of the more frightening riddles provided Suzanne with, at best, mixed satisfaction. While finding a logical solution fed the rational portion of her mind with solid theory, the reason also diminished a new ability that she was beginning to develop: the capacity to believe in the impossible. Strangely, she found this loss to be disappointing.

Suzanne had already realized that she could consider the parking lot encounter to have been a victory only if she were to cast Garner in the role of the good guy and Luckholt as his evil opposite. And that would happen only if Eli's story was basically true. In order to believe him, Suzanne had to believe things she'd previously considered impossible. Otherwise, Elias Garner was nothing more than a liar, or both of them were simply crazy. If this were the truth, then Suzanne had thrown away one hundred thousand dollars.

Oh, the check was real. Of that much, Suzanne was sure. She'd seen enough cashier's checks in her time to know one when it was waved in front of her nose. Apparently Luckholt would have gladly let her keep all the money if the New York lawyer would have only gone home and done nothing, which was just what she had intended to do before running into Luckholt.

No, that's not entirely accurate. The truth was that Suzanne had intended to abandon the quest, right up until the moment she ran into Red Cloud. In that short time between the end of the encounter with the Indian craftsman and the beginning of the one with Luckholt, her resolve had wavered. The clarity of the decision to simply go home and resume her life had been muddied by Red Cloud's uncomplicated story, and Suzanne didn't have the slightest idea why.

Red Cloud himself was another of the questions she carried. Even if she was to believe the unbelievable, why wasn't he among the Righteous Ones? He seemed to fit, but when she approached the idea, he slammed the door in her face, as though he knew just what she wanted and would have no part of it. Sure, Monty rejected the concept too, but not with the same conviction and not before the notion was even presented. But there was something still more important. With Red Cloud, things just didn't feel right. This was not an impression she could articulate, or even clarify in her thoughts. With Monty there had been a certain sense of satisfaction, a feeling of completion that just wasn't there with Red Cloud. Suzanne felt the difference the moment she turned away from the Indian and continued down the trail.

And, of course, there was no phone call from Garner. But the telephone didn't prove anything one way or another. If he had called, if the phone had rung and the voice had said "nice try but no luck," now that would have been mystical. But apparently things were not going to work that way. Elias Garner, and for that matter Elizabeth Luckholt, were not going to cooperate by making miracles, or pulling rabbits out of hats. They weren't about to offer the kind of proof she would need were she putting the case before a court. No, and her mind drifted back to her conversations with Professor Abromowitz. The decision would have to be hers, all hers and only hers.

The internal battle continued. Her intellect rejected the concept, demanded that she extract herself from this insanity before she too became insane, while a slowly awakening internal sense that defied label or identity, was telling her to continue. Ride the wave and just let the tide carry you to shore. And always, the one nagging question that remained, what would happen if the Righteous Ones were never found? What decisions would Garner's chairman make?

The entire exercise was just too tiring and there was only an hour or so of daylight remaining. Suzanne hated to drive tired. Even worse, she hated a dark highway. The idea, briefly considered, of pushing the BMW beyond both the setting sun and her stock of energy was completely unacceptable. As much as she wanted to get back to the Madison Avenue apartment, to sit behind her Wall Street desk, Suzanne pulled off the Interstate and settled for the first decent motel she found.

The Red Carpet Motor Inn was a state-of-the-art tourist accommodation... in 1955. It was a long, U-shaped, single level structure, with a restaurant on one end and what appeared to be a bar on the other. Despite the building's advanced age, the paint was fresh, the flowers around the tiny swimming pool and those displayed in window boxes by the office were bright and healthy. There appeared to be an air conditioner built into the wall of each unit. The indicators all translated to clean, basic overnight housing.

Suzanne parked the BMW directly in front of the office and stepped out into the rapidly fading July sunshine, long shadows and an orange red sky. The acres of surrounding fields, corn and soy beans, seemed the same as they had for the past 500 miles, as if there were one very long field of each crop that constantly followed her journey. The vegetation stood quietly absorbing the sun and rocking gently in the almost constant but barely perceptible breeze.

Suzanne envied the plants. Their entire purpose on this planet, their only task was to grow and wait patiently for harvest. They seemed to be accomplishing their work very well.

Suzanne left her automobile and went directly into the office. For the first time on the trip, the automatic conditioning that was part of a New Yorker's life failed to function. The car doors were left unlocked. Had she been aware of her lapse, she'd probably have thought the omission was no big deal. The large picture window in the office provided her a constant view of the car, and there was certainly no one hanging out in the parking lot who appeared at all threatening. In fact, there was no one else in the parking lot.

"Good afternoon," said the more than middle-aged woman behind the counter. "Can I help you?"

The desk clerk was tall and thin and anywhere between 50 and 70 years old. Her makeup was carefully, if not too skillfully, applied. And her hair, which had probably been gray before the chemical treatment, was very precisely tended. The friendly demeanor seemed genuine.

"I'm looking for a room."

"That's what I'm here for. Do you have a reservation?"

"No, I'm afraid not. I saw the vacancy sign."

"No problem. I do have one unreserved room left. But it's the one right next to the office, has a water bed and costs fifty-five dollars." She rattled off the description as if she were listing disadvantages. Suzanne considered neither the price nor the location to be a negative. She would have preferred to sleep on something less exotic, but that was unimportant. Now that Suzanne recognized how tired she'd become, a wooden plank with a pillow and light blanket would have been acceptable.

"I'll take the room."

The woman slid a registration card across the counter, trading the form for Suzanne's gold American Express card. Then she turned and with an exaggerated gesture, flicked a switch on the wall. Suzanne noticed that the neon sign in front now read "no vacancy."

"May I leave my car right where it is?"

"Sure," said the woman. "No problem. You're right next door anyway." She gave the traveler back her credit card along with a key, both in exchange for the completed registration. Suzanne went directly to the room for an inspection.

As promised, an oversize waterbed took up most of the available space. There was a TV bolted to a platform on the wall, a desk, a telephone, several large mirrors, an orange carpet that matched the bedspread, and an ample, very clean bathroom. The room was dark with the only inlet for natural light a picture window at the front, now covered by drawn orange drapes that completed the single-color scheme. Opening the curtains called for a trade between her privacy and the rapidly fading sunlight, so Suzanne accepted living entirely by the glow of the lamps. She propped open the door with the desk chair and went back to the trunk of the BMW for her suitcase.

The desk clerk was now seated outdoors in a lawn chair, drinking a Diet Coke and apparently enjoying the sunset. The two women nodded silently toward each other. Suzanne closed the trunk, which locked automatically, and returned to the orange carpet with the suitcase, double locking the room door behind her. She still did not realize that the doors to the BMW remained open and the electronic alarm disengaged.

Exhausted by the drive, Suzanne kicked off her shoes, fell on top of the orange spread and with the bed gently rocking her in its aquatic arms, quickly dozed off. She slept for nearly two hours before the emptiness in her stomach forced her awake. The glowing orange face of the alarm clock on the nightstand reported the time to be nearly nine o'clock. There wasn't a sound outside the window.

Suzanne pulled herself out of bed and peeked through the curtains. The stillness was eerie. Even the highway was empty as though closed to traffic. Suzanne briefly wondered if Luckholt also had friends in the Illinois State Police Department. She splashed water on her face and poked her hair in a half-hearted but habitual effort at repair before she went out in search of food.

The evening was pleasant, warm and very empty. The motel office, locked and dark, was decorated with a sign instructing patrons to ring the bell if service was desired. Bare yellow bulbs, spaced about every ten feet and attached to a narrow overhang, lit the pathway in front of the rooms. Another light next to each doorway added somewhat to the illumination, but apparently few, if any, of the guests were at home. The parking lot hosted hardly an automobile.

Suzanne drifted to the end where she'd seen the restaurant only to find the place closed for the night. She walked back to the door of her room. Though she had traversed a full half of the building, she'd observed not one other person, heard not a sound from any of the rooms nor seen a single car go by on the road. The only noises were the buzzing of the insects against the bulbs, the crickets singing in the fields and what sounded like several motorcycles far in the distance. The void was more than a little spooky.

Hoping that she might find a meal, and now, more importantly, some sign of continued human existence, Suzanne traveled to the tavern at other end of the motel. Here her luck was better. Bar sights, sounds and smells washed over her as she opened the heavy, soundproof door. Suzanne breathed a sigh of relief. Civilization had not fled and left her alone in the middle of an Illinois cornfield.

To the contrary, the drinking establishment was fairly busy. About two-dozen people, most of them young, were clustered at one end of the large oval bar, the side that was farthest from the door. This group was both presided over and served by a tall, bronzed woman of no more than thirty who was mixing drinks with both hands. The vast majority of these patrons, along with the bartender, were dressed in shorts and t-shirts. Some wore bathing suits. Suzanne in her wrinkled, though very New York outfit, immediately stood out from the crowd.

The young men paused, attracted to her direction by the entrance of a stranger. They looked at her and smiled. The women looked as well, hesitated and scowled, interpreting Suzanne's reason for being there to be the same as their own, and fearing the exotic and apparently sophisticated competitor. Suzanne's thoughts were so far away from the gender tournament taking place in the tavern that she couldn't understand why the people were watching her. Their eyes made her nervous.

The end of the bar nearest the door was the territory of the older folks. A few were seated there, including the woman who had rented Suzanne her room. They watched the young ones perform their mating rituals, whispered quiet jokes and laughed at them while their hands remained tightly gripped around wet glasses and aluminum beer cans.

Suzanne chose to sit in the territory of the elders on an open stool next to the desk clerk. The interest of the young men faded and was directed back to the women around them who seemed universally relieved at Suzanne's choice of seating.

"Miss Rosewell, right?" said the woman, as the lawyer settled onto the bar stool.

"Yes, but Suzanne would be more appropriate."

"Hi, Suzanne. I'm Harriet. Welcome to the hottest evening spot in Stone Lake. If you want a drink, we might be able to get you one, but I don't know why you want to sit at this end of the bar with us old folks. The action is down there. Over here, we're just memories." She laughed out loud at her own witticism, and the woman sitting to her other side automatically joined in the howl, even though she hadn't heard the joke.

"I don't think so," Suzanne responded. "I just came in to see if I could get something to eat. That scene isn't quite my style."

"Well, you're certainly not too old," Harriet answered without a moment's hesitation. "Do you have a husband or a boyfriend back east? Is that what made you sit here with us?"

"No, there's no one back east. I just never cared much for the kind of romances that start in a bar."

"Oh, come on, Suzanne," Harriet teased, "you're just passing through. You go down to that end of the bar. Give some of our boys a thrill with your attention, a New York girl and all, and then, when you go back to your room alone, you'll make our local ladies feel better."

"Thank you Harriet, but I'm just too tired."

"Such crap. You got plenty of time to be tired when you're my age. I'm 68, my dear, and I fight my age every day. I've done a lot of livin' during my years and the only things I regret are those I didn't do ... like the nights I was too tired to flirt with the fellas. Now, even when I'm not too tired, they don't want to flirt with me." She laughed out loud again and this time Suzanne joined her.

"Harriet," Suzanne asked when the hilarity ended, "why are you pushing me so hard? You don't even know me. What's the real story? Why do you want me to go to that end of the bar?"

"Oh, you are a smart one, Suzanne," Harriet answered, after a brief pull on her gin and tonic. "Ain't she a smart one, Doris?" she said, nudging the woman on her other side, who promptly agreed, though she hadn't the slightest idea as to the thought she was confirming. Nor did it matter.

"OK," Harriet continued, with a light in her eyes that made Suzanne think a much younger person was really behind that wrinkled face. "I'll tell you the truth. Every night we sit here and watch the young folks. They start to come in just after the sun goes down, and by eleven they've all coupled off and gone to the beach."

"The beach?" Suzanne asked.

"Sure, Stone Lake, just up that road about a quarter mile. Big lake with a nice sand beach, state park, real pretty. Anyway, like I said, we like to watch 'em... I mean us older folk, but after a while, the show gets boring. Same kids, night after night, usually end up in the same couples. They need a little variety."

"You mean you need a little variety," Suzanne said chuckling. She was surprised that she found the situation quite so amusing. A few weeks ago, back in New York, this Wall Street attorney would have been offended by Harriet's suggestion.

"Yeah, that's true. But so what? We've been talkin' about you for a good part of the evening. I didn't really think you would come into the bar, but my friends and me been guessin' how everyone would react if you did. Now, how about it?"

"I don't know," Suzanne answered, somewhat flattered by the suggestion. "This is not how I was taught a modern woman should behave."

"Now, now," Harriet spoke almost in a scolding tone, "We're not just a bunch of farm folks here. We know all about liberated women and such. We read the papers, watch cable TV. But there are some things about being young that just don't change, no matter what label you want to put on. Besides, Carol, the bartender, don't hardly ever come up to this end. So if you want a drink anytime soon, you're just going to have to go down to that end and find out if a New York woman can stand up to our tough little farm girls."

Suzanne lifted herself off the bar stool, brushed her red hair back with her hands, tried to flatten the wrinkles on her blouse, smiled at Harriet and marched down the length of the long bar. By the time she reached the crowd of young people, she was the center of attention. All conversation stopped and the room was filled with only the jukebox's persistent whine.

Rather than plunge into the center, Suzanne took a seat at the edge of the crowd, next to a tall thin young man in a baseball cap who seemed completely engrossed in studying the top of the beer can gripped tightly between his long fingers. The crowd of men shifted, not too subtly, in her direction while the women moved around to take up defensive positions. The result was that Suzanne found herself, through no effort of her own, virtually in the center of the action. She noticed that Harriet and her companions were roaring with glee at the latest steps in the dance.

"Can I help you miss?" The bronze bartender was standing directly in front of Suzanne. She leaned forward in an aggressive stance while wearing an expression that clearly communicated her displeasure with Suzanne's presence. Obviously she was much more a part of the party than just an employee. With her lawyer's training to support her, Suzanne ignored the posture and the presentation.

"I'd like a draught beer and something to eat please."

"Nothing on tap. Only cans and only hamburgers or pizza. The pizza's frozen. We heat it in the microwave."

"I'll have a can of beer, any kind, and a hamburger."

Suzanne laid a twenty on the bar and Carol set down a wet beer can with an unfamiliar logo.

"You want a glass?"

"Yes, thank you." Suzanne was working hard at staying polite but she really wanted to tell the barmaid precisely where to go, and that wasn't into the kitchen to get the food. But that's where the woman went and her absence gave Suzanne the time to regain a sense of humor.

The bar sharks had been circling since the moment she crossed into their territory, but so far none of them had tried an attack. She had assumed the man next to her would've been the first, but he was still studying the top of his beer can and seemed not to notice her arrival.

Suzanne wondered, and then worried… maybe he was drunk.

The attack began with one young man who offered a trite line about her being a stranger to these parts. Suzanne responded politely, refused his offer of a drink and smiled at him as he retreated in defeat. Two more came and left, using almost the same approach, before the arrival of the burger seemed to signal a truce. They probably didn't think disturbing her meal would be productive. The man next to her still seemed not to notice her presence.

The assault resumed the moment she swallowed the last bite of what turned out to be a very tasty sandwich. The level of aggression increased dramatically. Still, she successfully fended them off.

Then a large man with a black beard, a significant tattoo, and ample beer belly, only partially covered by his leather vest, pressed his way from the back of the room to the bar and ended up right where he wanted to be – next to Suzanne.

"You a tourist?" he asked, half growling his words. There was no doubt that this one was intoxicated.

"No," Suzanne said, "just driving through and got off the highway to find a place for the night.

"Where you from?"

"New York."

"Oh, and that's what makes you too good for us."

"I beg your pardon?" Suzanne asked, taken back by the statement and somewhat frightened by his tone.

"A whole bunch of nice fellows have asked you to let them buy you a drink and you just brush 'em off. And that's after you come strutting down to this end of the room like God's gift to the boys."

"I don't want to drink anything more, that's all."

"You could have a coke or somethin', just to be polite. Or maybe us country boys are only some kind of dirt to this big city girl."

Suzanne was torn between anger and fear. The man was certainly rude and presumptuous. In New York she would have told him off quickly, verbally ripping him apart for the crime of thinking that she owed even courtesy to a bunch of carnivores trying to pick her up in a public bar. In New York she would not have felt afraid. But here, in this strange territory, she was frightened. He appeared dangerous and his voice, the tone of his voice, reminded her of Luckholt's State Trooper friend.

Also, he was at least partially right. She had taken up Harriet's challenge and strutted down into the middle of the pack and then refused to consider playing by their rules. Suzanne was struggling to figure out what to say, contemplating an apology, when a voice from over her shoulder cut through the tension.

"Leave the lady alone John. If she don't wanna' drink, she don't have to." The announcement came from the man who had been studying his beer can. He now sat up straight, the baseball hat pushed back and his eyes directly on the bearded man.

"Oh, Harvey speaks," John said loudly. "Wispy Harvey who sits here all night and never talks to the girls, but he'll defend the honor of a snob from New York."

"Listen John," Harvey continued, apparently both angry and sober, "you spend hours dressing up to look like a Hell's Angels biker, but can you fight like one? That's just what you're gonna have to do if you keep talkin' to this lady that way. She's a guest in our town and we don't treat guests that way."

John appeared shocked. He was struggling for an answer when the barmaid interrupted.

"There'll be no fighting in here," Carol said. "You guys know the rules. Any fighting and you'll be out of here for the rest of the summer."

The two men stared at each other for a long moment until Suzanne decided to make her own move. She picked up her change and turned to her unrecruited defender.

"I'm leaving. Would you be good enough to see me to the door of my room?"

"Sure," Harvey said. There was almost the sound of relief in his voice.

"I'll deal with you later, Harvey," John shouted, as the two of them moved toward the door.

"I told you," yelled the barmaid, "any trouble, and I'll kick you out for the rest of the summer."

As Suzanne passed the group of older people, Harriet looked up, her wrinkled face covered with distress. The show had not worked out the way she'd planned. Suzanne just shrugged her shoulders and walked out into the night with Harvey at her side.

"Jesus, what the hell come over Harvey," said one of the other men. "I never heard him talk like that before. He's not a tough guy."

"No," said another, "but you gotta watch them quiet ones. I hear they're the most dangerous." Some of the women continued to stare at the closed door, adjusting their image of the man who prior to tonight had always sat only on the edge of the action.

"Thank you for your help," Suzanne said, as they walked into the night breeze. "I hope you're not going to be in trouble with your friends."

"No, no," Harvey said without concern, "John will rant and rave a while, but he'll pretend that getting kicked out of the bar is what keeps him from kicking my butt. He's got to save face. Next week I'll buy him a beer and we'll be friends again. He's a jerk, but I've known him since I was a kid. Let me take you to your room."

"I heard there was a beach nearby. Can we walk?"

"Are you sure you want me to take you to the beach? You don't have to be nice to me just because I did you a favor."

"Doing favors is not in my nature... Harvey, that's your name, right?" He nodded.

They walked a short stretch of dark dirt road and came out on a sand bar alongside a large lake. A few small lanterns illuminated the shore and out on the water were the red and green running lights of several motor boats. Suzanne realized that they were the source of the sound she'd heard earlier and had mistaken for far away motorcycles.

Though short, the walk was distant enough for introductions and brief biographies. Harvey was just a little older than Suzanne and had gone to Chicago for two years of college before dropping out and returning to Stone Lake, where he'd been born and raised. The time in the big city had convinced him that he'd never be comfortable among the miles of asphalt and concrete streets. At the same time, the stimulation of Chicago had changed him and he'd never quite gotten used to the quiet of Stone Lake. Now, past thirty, he worked as a tractor mechanic, adding extra income by fixing outboards during the season, reading a lot, thinking about leaving, and hanging out on the edge of the crowd in the local bar.

"I've never been particularly known for my courage," he said, as he watched Suzanne smoke a cigarette while sitting on a bench overlooking the lake. "If I were brave, I'd have left Stone Lake a long time ago."

"You were pretty brave tonight."

"That wasn't brave," he laughed. "That was opportunistic."

"What?"

"Passing up the chance to rescue you would've been stupid. I just made the move before someone else did."

"Am I that desirable?" Suzanne said lightly.

"No... I mean yes... no, that's not what I mean."

Harvey was really flustered and they both laughed for a moment before he regained his composure.

"Sure Suzanne, you're a pretty girl. And everyone knew you were from New York, thanks to Harriet's big mouth. So you're unspoken competition. And if a guy made time with you… the rest of the women will be eyeing him after you're gone tomorrow. My stock has been so low that uhh… I needed to do it!"

"Oh, you used me?" Suzanne asked but with the lightness still in her voice.

"Yeah, as a matter of fact. Do you mind?"

"I should," she said, "but I don't." That was when he leaned over and kissed her, gently and softly on the lips.

"Why are you here, Suzanne?" he asked with the expectation that she'd reveal something profound.

"I'm on a search, Harvey, a quest. I'm looking for something and I'm not sure it exists. I don't even know what it is."

"Who isn't looking for something? But most of us don't drive across the country in a BMW to search for it."

"You know what kind of car I'm driving?"

"It's a small town. We don't see many super expensive cars. And like I said, Harriet's got a big mouth."

"Then you know I'm on my way home and I'm leaving in the morning."

"No, I didn't, but I do now. So let me take you back to your room," he said in an almost whisper.

"Fine, but I'm not going to invite you in."

"That's alright. I didn't think you would. How much luck can a guy expect in one evening?" They were so comfortable as they walked back down the dirt road that Suzanne almost regretted her inability to stay in Stone Lake a few days longer.

The waterbed gently embraced the New York lawyer and she slept peacefully, while quiet dreams of slow walks on beaches and through cornfields carried her until morning.

The alarm clock she thought she set failed to rouse her and Suzanne slept until the heat of the morning sun against the curtained window finally made the room too warm for sleeping. The hour was well past nine and she'd hoped to be on the road much earlier.

Suzanne showered and dressed quickly. The restaurant was open and she enjoyed a hearty country breakfast with several cups of strong black coffee. Refreshed and rejuvenated, she went back to her room, packed her bag and put the suitcase in the trunk of the BMW. Then she went into the office to return her key. Harriet was behind the desk.

"Suzanne, I am so glad you stopped by. I really wanted to apologize for last night. I never thought there would be any trouble."

"Oh, that was hardly what I'd call trouble, Harriet. I just hope that Harvey doesn't have any problems after I'm gone."

"I don't think so. You know men. They just like to toot their horns every so often. The hot air usually passes, one way or another. This is a small town. Folks can't afford to have feuds that last more than a day or two. I hope the rest of your trip goes well."

"Thank you Harriet. Take care."

Suzanne felt renewed and unconfined, ready for a comfortable ride across America's heartland and back to New York. That is, right until she realized that her car was not locked. The revelation tied a small knot in her stomach. She peered carefully into the back seat wondering what monster was hidden there preparing to leap on her when she settled into the driver's seat. Only when she was sure that the auto was empty, did she open the door. There on the front seat was a manila envelope with her first name written boldly across the front. Suzanne was afraid to touch the package.

After a few moments, paranoia gave way enough to reason. She reached out and moved the envelope a few inches. When the package didn't explode, she lifted the bundle gingerly and set it on the roof of the car. Then, slowly and carefully, she opened the clasp and withdrew a book. In the lower corner of the cover was a sticker from the Northwestern University bookstore. Suzanne was more than startled when she read the title:

MESSENGERS OF GOD
Biblical Portraits & Legends
by Elie Wiesel

Stuck in the pages of the book was a red envelope, the kind that usually contains a greeting card. Her hand shook as she extracted the red rectangle and opened the flap, unconsciously preserving the page from where the envelope had rested by inserting the flap of the book jacket. The card was a humorous "bon voyage" Hallmark with a handwritten inscription on the interior panel.

> Sorry, this was the only card in the house that even came close to being appropriate. It was wonderful meeting you and I hope you have a good trip home. Please accept this book as a present from me. Elie Wiesel meant a lot to me when I was in college and I thought you might enjoy his work. Besides, this will give you something to do in the motel rooms and keep you out of trouble in the bars. I hope we see each other again.
>
> Harvey

The card made Suzanne smile, but the title of the book continued to knot her gut. Slowly she opened the volume to the page where the card had been placed. Was this random or did Harvey pick the spot to send a message? Her finger was on page 139, the beginning of a chapter entitled *"Joseph, or the Education of a Tzaddik."*

Suzanne dropped the book on the pebbled ground of the parking lot. At least three full minutes passed before she could bring herself to pick it up again. She went back to page 139 and began to read.

> *This is a story of dreams and dreamers. It brings into play every facet of human passion: love and hate, ambition and jealousy, glory and spite. A strange story it is, filled with spectacular turns of fortune. Its heroes are warriors and prisoners, beggars and princes who know but do not recognize one another: characters in search of a destiny.*

Characters in search of a destiny! The line echoed in her head. "If some are searching," she thought, "then others must have completed their search. They must be the ones Elias Garner wants me to find."

Suzanne now felt she knew why Monty could be added to the list and Red Cloud could not, why righteous people were so hard to find and why the search to find them was so important.

Suzanne kept the book at her side for the balance of her uneventful drive to New York. She read at every rest stop and over every meal. It was the last thing she did at night and the first thing in the morning. She finished the final chapter while ascending in the elevator of her Madison Avenue apartment building.

CHAPTER THIRTEEN

Eli paced nervously. His long legs carried him up and down the length of the room while his feet kept trying to flatten the deep pile carpet in the empty corporate conference area. He had passed in front of the huge picture window twenty times without once looking through the spotless glass. The thick drapes, pulled back by the steward when he brought the coffee, framed the flood of warm late-day sunlight that filled the room with a light touch of magnificent amber. The landscape, painted by the same light, presented a peaceful, pastoral scene that, on a normal day, would have drawn Garner's full attention and appreciation. But this was not a normal day and pacing was the only way the tall black man could deal with his uncharacteristic and almost never displayed tension.

Just this morning, as he considered requesting an audience with the Chairman, a summons arrived in the form of phone call from the Chief's secretary.

"Coffee at three in the conference room. Are you available?" she said without emotion in her normal efficient, even demanding manner.

He knew this was not in fact a question but a request for confirmation. He also knew that the space on his calendar was vacant and had the spot not been available, he would have cleared the time. The Chairman rarely called a special meeting and then always for matters of a most serious nature. Even as he confirmed his availability, he wondered who else might be in attendance. But asking questions about a beckon from the Boss was not considered good form.

Eli showed up ten minutes early just to see how many places were set at the big table. His curiosity was so intense that he risked disturbing the Chairman's tradition of spending a few minutes in pre-meeting solitude alone in the conference room. He secretly hoped that the Man would be there so he could steal a moment with him. It came as a complete surprise when Eli found the steward opening the drapes and setting the table with coffeepots, cups and spoons for two.

"Are you sure that there'll be only two," he asked, knowing the answer. The steward never made a mistake and resented the implication.

"Yes, sir," he answered, setting out the Chairman's special espresso pot. "Those were my orders."

Though Eli wanted to speak to the Chairman privately, he wondered, and then worried, about what was so important that it deserved a face-to-face meeting. That thought started him pacing the moment the steward left the room. At two minutes before the hour, the Chairman entered, suit-jacket draped across his arm and wearing a fresh, starched white shirt. Without a word of greeting, he tossed the jacket over a vacant chair, took his place at the big table, and gestured for Garner to do the same.

"How is that inventory going?" he asked without hesitation. While the Chairman was not known for small talk, especially when he had something important on his mind, he usually at least commented on the coffee before getting directly to the topic at hand.

"Try the coffee Eli," the Chairman said as an afterthought while loosening his silk tie, filling his cup from the silver pot and taking a sip. "It's excellent today." The courtesy sounded forced.

Garner, jacket and tie still in place, poured from his own pot and took a swallow. Jamaican Blue Mountain brewed in the espresso fashion. A refreshing change from the usual Italian Roast. The steward, who had absolute authority over the food served in the main conference room, took pride in pleasantly surprising the Chairman. The thick rich liquid helped Eli's courage.

"My emissary has located one person and added him to the list."

"Yes, I saw that on the central computer. But only one? Twelve days have passed. We need five."

"I know," Elias Garner answered after sipping more caffeinated liquid courage. He wished the steward had set out the bottle of anisette, though unheard of at any gathering held before five p.m. "But Boss, the discovery of even one proves that Luckholt's inventory list is inaccurate. I'm sure that, given sufficient time, Ms. Rosewell will find the other four."

"Just because she found one does not invalidate Elizabeth's inventory. She must find four more." He hesitated as though steeling himself for the next sentence. "And I've decided that this issue must be resolved before the next Management Team meeting. If not, a discussion on our withdrawing from the whole operation will be the first item on the agenda. And you know that our mutual friend Elizabeth Luckholt is capable of having everything dismantled before another dawn touches New York's Central Park. In fact, Luckholt is very much involved already. She recently tried and failed to bribe your Ms. Rosewell with a substantial amount of money. But she will try again and she may even get rough. Eli, I don't want this to happen any more than you do, so if the missing four exist, find them and find them quickly."

"Is there even the slightest chance of delaying the Management Team meeting and extending the deadline?" Garner asked sadly.

"None," the Chairman snapped back as he rose from the table. "You can tell Ms. Rosewell that if she does not accomplish her task in the next nine days... well, you can decide what to tell her." He started to leave, but paused at the conference room door and turned back toward Garner with his finger pointed at Eli in a way that sent chills through the black man's body.

"Let me tell you Elias Garner, things run smoothly here, in part because everyone knows that my word is good. I always keep my promises, and always fulfill my threats. As much as I hate having made this one, I won't go back on the commitment. A full count of thirty-six or a complete shutdown. All or nothing. Now it's up to you and Ms. Rosewell to get me out of this mess. Don't let me down."

The Chairman turned and left the room, slamming the door behind him. Garner sat before his half-empty coffee cup for a long moment. Now he was grateful for the lack of alcohol on the table. He had a lot of work to do. Slowly, as though he was an old man troubled by joint pain, Eli rose from the table and left the room.

The steward, seeing the two unfinished cups of coffee in the empty conference room, would draw the wrong the conclusion. To the unspoken disappointment of the Chairman, the man would never again serve Jamaican Blue Mountain in the special espresso pots.

Two floors below, Elizabeth Luckholt sat by herself in her office. She knew the Chairman and Elias Garner had met in the conference room. For a brief time she'd even considered placing a microphone under the table, but she was certain the Chairman would discover it. He always did. In reality, hearing what went on between them was unnecessary. There was only one subject they'd be discussing and she could easily guess the direction of the meeting. A deadline would be imposed. Eli would ask for more time and the Chairman would refuse. She smiled to herself and privately vowed that Garner's efforts would be in vain. She would see to it herself, personally if needed.

CHAPTER FOURTEEN

The phone rang stubbornly. No, more accurately, it chirped… repeatedly. And with each intonation of the computer chip substitute for a bell, the machine expressed a determination well beyond that of a simple mindless communications instrument. The short, sharp, electronic tones demanded attention, speaking to Suzanne with a completely independent will, or at least that's what she believed in that brief yet endless moment between sleep and awake.

The long drive had left her bodily exhausted and the growing concern over her mission depleted her mentally. If she could have chosen between the disabilities, she would've accepted physical collapse without a second thought. Instead she wore the mantle of both as she stumbled through her apartment door. From the moment she finally settled into her own bed late Wednesday night, the first time in more than a week, Suzanne decided she wasn't going to be in the office tomorrow, at least not at her usual morning hour, no matter what the senior partners thought.

It had been her intention to put the phone switch on the silent position where the answering machine would intercept the calls and she would sleep undisturbed. Suzanne was certain that she'd pressed all the correct buttons, moved all the appropriate switches just before dozing off. The screaming telephone was evidence to the contrary. Even as her brain was raised slowly to consciousness, the exhausted sleeper knew whose voice would be at the other end of the line. He spoke before she could acknowledge the call.

"Suzanne, is that you? Are you there?" The voice was only familiar. She thought it was him, but this sound lacked his usual quiet calm.

"Garner?" Her mind came rapidly to attention as she finally recognized the tension that was effecting his tone. The very concept of anxiety and Elias Garner should have been a contradiction. That they might be compatible was a frightening thought.

"Yes," he said simply, taking a long, deep breath that echoed over the wire. "We need to meet. What time shall I come to your office?"

"I wasn't planning to go in today. Is this important?"

"Very. We could meet at your apartment."

"When?"

"Now."

"I'm still in bed," she answered though she was already moving out from under the covers. "Give me half an hour. Do you know where I live?"

"Yes," he said without elaboration.

"Of course, I should have expected. Half-an-hour then. I'll make coffee. You do drink coffee?"

"Oh yes," he answered with a little, but very little, of his usual humor returning to the voice in her ear. "I'll see you in thirty-minutes."

The phone went silent and Suzanne shifted into high gear. She was showered and dressed in fifteen minutes. Brewing a pot of coffee took another seven. She'd just poured her second cup when the doorbell rang, exactly thirty minutes after the phone conversation had ended.

Suzanne started to reach for the intercom switch, planning to tell the doorman to let Mr. Garner pass when she realized that the sound now invading the morning calm of her home was from the bell mounted on the outside of her apartment door.

"Sure," she said out loud to herself, "why would he concern himself with a doorman?" Without bothering to look through the peephole, the lawyer disengaged the three security locks and swung open the heavy steel door. As she expected, Eli stood alone in the hallway.

He was dressed as fashionably as he had been the day she met him in her office, but the sharp freshness was gone from the suit as though he'd been a passenger on a crowded subway when the temperature and humidity both topped ninety. Her subconscious image of him had been that he was somehow immune to such mundane human discomforts. His appearance increased her concern.

"Good morning," he said, his voice distant, almost distracted. "Welcome home."

She silently stepped back and he entered the apartment, moving toward the kitchen with more ease than her most frequent visitor. "The coffee smells good."

Suzanne followed her guest and watched him as he opened a cabinet door and, finding them on the first try, removed a mug, filled the cup with thick black liquid and sat down at her table, placing himself in the chair opposite Suzanne's normal seat. She joined him, still silent. He seemed not to notice that Suzanne had yet to speak a single word.

"The security in your building is not so good," he said, the firmness in his voice telling her that he considered this an important issue. But was safety the only reason for his visit? "The doorman was not on duty and the front door was unlocked. I came in the lobby and up the elevator completely unchallenged. That's not good, Suzanne. You need to be more careful, especially now."

"That's very unusual," she responded, ignoring his implied warning for the moment. "They pride themselves on the security here."

"I suggest you call downstairs and ask."

"I will." She stood and walked to the intercom. After a brief look back at Garner, she pressed the buzzer.

"Can I help you?" a voice answered instantly. Suzanne smiled smugly at her guest whose expression told her to proceed further with her investigation.

"Carlos," she said to the speaker, "this is Suzanne Rosewell on twenty-two."

"Yes, Miss Rosewell? What can I do for you?"

"I have a visitor here who says that you were not on duty when he came through a few minutes ago. He says he was able to come in unchallenged."

"I did step away to the bathroom for a moment, but the front door was securely locked."

"My friend says that the door was unlocked."

"I'm sure he's wrong. Just a second while I check." There was a moment of silence before Carlos' voice came back on the speaker. Suzanne easily heard the added strain.

"Oh, I am so sorry, Miss Rosewell. Your friend is right. I must have turned the latch the wrong way. Please don't tell the building management. I'll be in a lot of trouble."

"Don't worry Carlos. Just be more careful, OK?"

"Thank you Miss Rosewell. It won't happen again." Suzanne turned off the intercom and turned back toward Garner.

"Why are you so interested in my building security? Why, for that matter, are you even here? When we last met on the subway, I got the clear impression that we wouldn't be seeing each other again except for a very urgent reason…." Her voice trailed off as she became aware of her words.

"I hadn't planned on it," he said after taking a swallow of coffee, "but I had a meeting with the Chairman yesterday. He is very anxious about your mission. Thirteen days have passed and you have only located one person for the list. Four more individuals are needed and you only have... uh, we only have eight days left."

"Only eight days? You didn't tell me about a deadline."

"When we started out, there wasn't one. But I always knew it was inevitable. The Chairman is patient but his endurance is limited. If I didn't mention that there would eventually be a time limit, I apologize. That was my omission."

"You mean you're not perfect?" There was more than a hint of sarcasm in her voice that Eli seemed to miss entirely.

"I never claimed to be," he answered. She noticed a sense of genuine puzzlement in his response. "The Chairman has given me until the next Management Team meeting to solve the inventory problem. If the count is still short, he will advise the Management Team that we are... are going to withdraw from the project." A real, perceptible physical chill ran through Suzanne's blood as Garner spoke the words.

"And... and under what name would I know 'the project'? Would that be one of my clients?" she asked, still hoping that this whole thing may still turn out to be just some weird, eccentric business deal after all.

"I'm not at liberty to release that information. Consider this answer sufficient. You have a major vested interest in our continuing to participate in this project." Now his voice was quite stern and the temperature in her veins dropped a bit more.

"And why are you so interested in the security of my building?" Suzanne continued. Though compelled to ask the question, she was sure she truly didn't want to hear the answer.

"Because Elizabeth Luckholt has just as strong an investment in seeing our role dissolved. You refused her offer of money. Her normal next step will be to attempt to entice you to her side with power. Failing that, she may try to frighten you. Either she or one of her lackeys could actually try to visit you in your home. I would like the front door to offer them more resistance than it offered me."

The thought of receiving a visitor with a personality anything like the Minnesota State Trooper horrified Suzanne more than she wanted to admit. She wrapped her arms around herself to keep from visibly shivering.

"How... how did you know she offered me money?"

"The Chairman told me."

"How did he know? That happened way out in Minnesota."

"There is a phrase around headquarters," Garner said, a portion of his old smile returning, "It takes the form of question that says, is the Chairman chairman because he knows everything, or does he know everything because he's Chairman? We don't have the answer. He simply always knows all that he needs. But the Boss does keep a close eye on Luckholt. In this case, she probably drew a cashier's check and somebody in the accounting department tipped off the man. Just how doesn't matter. Take my word for it. You need to be more careful."

"I'm always careful," she said, knowing that he knew she was lying. "Though from now on, I'll be extra cautious."

That seemed to satisfy Eli. He let loose a long breath and appeared to relax, just a little.

"I might be able to provide a bit of additional security," he said. "I'll work on it, but you have to work on filling out the rest of the list. That's very important."

"Obviously you consider it so." She sat down at the table across from him. "To tell you the truth, though, I have a problem."

"Only one?" he asked, the sparkle restored to his dark eyes.

"No, two... two big ones. First, I have great difficulty continuing to believe in this project. Sometimes I'm fine, even for days. The quest seems to be the most important thing in the world. Then, I just lose it. When I run the situation through my head, the whole escapade sounds so ridiculous. If I'm going to continue, I've got to 'keep the faith' so to speak. Tell me how to do that when you refuse to provide me with any information?"

"And the other problem," he said growing very serious.

"What about the first one?"

"Tell me about the second, please." Despite the courteous phrasing, his tone was very demanding. Suzanne decided to comply with the request even though she knew that failing to solve problem one would make problem two completely irrelevant.

"How do I tell an ordinary decent human being from a righteous person? I met some good people, but they didn't qualify. Yet Monty did. How do I know who knows the divine will, if there is a divine will?"

"Your two problems are intertwined," he said, with the softness of a priest in the confessional, "like a braided rope. Solve one and you solve both. The order doesn't matter. Separate them and all you've got is pile of string."

"Wonderful, talk in riddles. That's a lot of help."

"Don't despair, Suzanne," he said, placing both of his large dark hands over hers as she rested them on the table. "Think back to when you first took on this quest. You had a reason, something that provided you with enough faith, despite limited information, to get in your car and drive all the way to South Dakota. Revisit that reason."

"It was a person, a special gentle old man who convinced me that even though this was probably a farce, even though you, Mr. Elias Garner, are probably a phony, the risk of not doing what you asked was just too great. I didn't really have a reason. I had Professor Abromowitz."

"Then revisit Professor Abromowitz," he said very tenderly as he squeezed the tension from her tightly clasped hands.

CHAPTER FIFTEEN

Suzanne felt like not one single moment in time had passed since her last visit to the office of Professor Abromowitz. Not the slightest thing had changed to indicate that nearly two weeks had irrecoverably disappeared into history since her previous entry to this room.

The same books with the same titles were still piled on the same chair that he still had to clear in order for her to sit. The untidy mounds of papers continued to overflow from the baskets. The possibility existed that the book open in the center of his desk might have been different, or maybe just turned to another page. But even if this was a completely unique volume, it was still the same kind of book, one with a single paragraph of large Hebrew letters in the center of the page surrounded by many paragraphs of tiny Hebrew text, as though the footnotes, having a life of their own, were multiplying and taking over. The identical smell of fresh coffee filled the corners. She expected to still find her empty mug in the exact location she'd left it.

No, nothing had changed since Suzanne's first visit, and as she waited for the professor to pour the coffee, she wondered what had made her expect any change. The lawyer was now convinced that if she returned in two years or twenty, given the professor's continued good health, all these things would still be as they were now.

The thought occurred to Suzanne, as she accepted the steaming cup from the professor's outstretched hand, that simply because so much had happened to *her* in the past thirteen days, she assumed the rest of the world had progressed proportionately.

"Now Suzanne," Abromowitz said as he reached under his desk, "I am so pleased you returned for another visit. I wasn't sure you would. I thought you might decide that I was just a foolish old man, locked in an academic fortress and out of touch with the reality of the world, all of which may be true. But the important thing is that you're here, and you've chosen to return while my favorite bakery is in operation. Please accept a donut unlike any you've experienced."

He extended his arm again, but this time the wrinkled fingers were offering a white bag with an inscription printed in red letters, Amnon's Kosher Bakery. She had no desire for a sweet but knew a refusal would be insensitive.

The donut appeared to be common enough, though the aroma was very unusual. Even her tentative bite released the surprising flavor of exotic and unfamiliar spices. Abromowitz saw the startled look in her eyes.

"Israelis," he said by way of explanation. "The family that runs the bakery... they're Israelis… of Moroccan origin. Their background brings an Eastern flavor to their baking that reminds me of the Old City… of Jerusalem. Each time I bite into a donut, the taste carries me there for a moment, to my youth, when I studied in the Holy City and to the trips that I can now only afford to take every few years. But you've been traveling for real, not on a pastry fantasy, yes?"

"Yes, but how did you know?"

"I must admit," he said looking just a little bit like a child caught in a harmless yet still forbidden activity, "that I was curious about any result of our last conversation. I called your office and spoke to your secretary. I stretched the truth a bit and told her that I was, well, your rabbi. She sounded surprised to find out that you had any kind of spiritual connection much less a rabbi, and was very reluctant to give out any information. Eventually, I got her to admit that you were on a little vacation in South Dakota. So, I knew you were traveling. I still didn't know if your trip was motivated by our conversation or if you simply went to ride horses on a dude ranch." He pronounced the horse farm "dud ranch" and Suzanne almost laughed out loud.

"No, no Professor, I didn't go to ride horses. I might have been better off if I had. The truth is, and you are the only one in New York who knows this, I accepted the challenge and went in search of these righteous people."

"And you had to go so far?" he asked, only half in jest. "There aren't righteous people in... in Queens?"

"That thought occurred to me as well and that's one of the reasons I came to see you. I have some questions that I hope you can answer."

The professor's face grew serious and he leaned back in his chair, his body posture a firm confirmation of his undivided attention. He set down his half-eaten pastry on a piece of waxed paper placed, specifically for that purpose, near, but not too close, to the open volume of Talmudic Law that rested on his desk.

Suzanne told Professor Abromowitz, in detail, the saga of her trip west. She started with the subway ride right after she last left his office and included every item she could remember. Even the little blonde girl at the rest area was mentioned and, of course, her disappointment with the Nobel Prize winner, her fear of the State Trooper, her affection for Monty, the confusing encounter with Red Cloud, the confrontation in the parking lot with Luckholt and finally Elias Garner's visit and warning just a few hours earlier.

"You have been through a considerable experience Suzanne," he said sounding quite concerned. "But what can I do to help?"

"Professor, I have two questions. First and foremost, how do I keep my faith in this project? One minute I truly believe that if I do not find the Righteous Ones…" Suzanne hesitated, as though she had a hard time accepting her own words, or that the words were just too terrifying to articulate, or both. "The... the world will end in eight days. Then the next minute I am convinced that I'm the pawn of a group of clever people whose real agenda is being hidden by an elaborate charade. And then a minute later I'm convinced that either I'm surrounded by insanity or a victim of mental illness myself. How can I persevere if I can't even continue to believe?"

"Did you say eight days? I wasn't aware there was such a deadline. And what makes you expect that the result of your failure will be the end of the world?" His voice was troubled.

"Nor did I know of a deadline until Garner told me just this morning. He said his Chairman just set one yesterday. And the world ending, well, you said something during our first meeting that you believed God would end the world if there were not enough Righteous Ones. Then Garner said that his company would 'withdraw from the project' and I assumed...." Her voice trailed off.

"Well, I guess you have to trust your sources," the professor said simply, "And your other question?"

"It has no meaning unless we can answer the first one."

"Indulge me, ask the second question anyway."

"OK... if you insist," Suzanne responded, stunned that Professor Abromowitz seemed to be following the same path of reasoning taken by Eli in her own kitchen earlier that same morning. "How do I know the difference between a righteous person, in the sense I am seeking them, and just a plain, ordinary, decent human being. You, for example, are you one of the Righteous Ones? And if not, why not? You are easily the kindest person I've known... since my father died."

The professor blushed briefly at the compliment but did not permit his embarrassment to deflect his direction.

"Suzanne, understand that I can answer both of your questions and still not know if my answers are anywhere near correct. At this point you may have more experience with the issue of the Lamed Vav Zaddikim than any living human being. And yet, you lack the perspective that history provides. That's where I hope I can help you.

"Forgive me if a ramble a bit, but this is important. The Jewish scholar lives with constant conflict. Our belief in that one, singular, all-powerful God is old, older than that of any other Western religion. We have devoted much of our history to trying to understand and carry out His will. As a result, we *should* be a very spiritual people. But we're not.

"Because we've spent so many centuries wandering the earth... oppressed, expelled and often murdered, we've had to develop a code of law that tells us how to live, day-by-day, year-in and year-out." He tapped the open volume in front of him.

"This is a book of the Talmud," he continued. "It contains a few words of written law and many, many words of commentary written over centuries of study. These tiny letters, printed in the margins, are the thoughts of great scholars and are supposed to help us understand this law. Sometimes we're more confused than enlightened. Yet this is our challenge, to study and try to understand what the ancient rabbis thought to be the will of the Almighty, in a spiritual sense, while still living every day in the real world. Few of us can attain both of those requirements.

"Your Indian craftsman and I have something in common, something beyond the fact that we are both, I hope, decent human beings. We live in our own worlds, choosing not to walk among our fellows and share whatever we have to share. He is isolated, bounded by the stones of his quarry and I by the high walls of this institution. Neither of us reaches out beyond our carefully constructed borders. This is where we seek spiritual enlightenment. Yet, how could we ever know the Divine Will when we live in such a narrow place?

"Your truck driver is different. He is truly out there among God's creatures, living every day with knowledge of the Divine Will, even though unconscious of his special gift. In my opinion, that is the answer to your second question. As one who still fears venturing from behind my walls into the rest of the world, and envies those who can, I believe

I'm right."

Suzanne was silent for a moment, absorbing the professor's words, examining, in her own mind, the impact of his criteria on the people she'd met.

"I think I understand, Professor," she finally said. "Now what about my first question."

"Suzanne, Suzanne," he said, a huge fatherly grin crossing his face, "you've already answered it. That's why you are here."

She looked at him with incomprehension.

"You didn't come here so I could tell you that these people you've met are crazy," he continued. "You didn't expect me to advise you that perhaps you need psychiatric help yourself. If you had desired that particular answer, you would have talked to someone whose view of the world is more... well, rational than mine, someone like one of your law partners. You came to me because I am the only person you know in all of New York who would support your involvement in this strange quest. Mind you, I give that support with the full knowledge that you, or the others, or all of you, might well be a collection of mental cases. I think that's possible, but I don't believe it's the reality. Certainly if what you fear about the future is true, then these people you've met represent some truly powerful forces. They certainly do not fit the image I would have imagined them to take. But what do I know? The important thing is that you, Suzanne Rosewell, already know how I feel on this issue and you came here anyway."

"But I'm always doubting."

"Of course you are. We all doubt the things we believe in the most because they are the things most important to us. We doubt the fidelity of our marital partners even though we haven't a shred of evidence because loyalty is critical to the well being of the relationship. We doubt that God watches over us. We especially waver every time something happens that shouldn't happen, and even times in between.

"I can't take away your uncertainty. I can only tell you that your reservations are no different than mine. We are frail beasts, we human beings. We rest our stability on a whole set of beliefs and then we question those beliefs over and over again. I like to compare our fears to those of the engineer who constantly checks the structure of a bridge that he already built and uses every day. Most of him believes in the bridge's ability to stand, but part of him is worried a support will collapse. You would consider this engineer a reasonable person, yes?"

Suzanne nodded her assent.

"Then do not consider yourself unreasonable when you begin to inspect the beams that are holding up the bridge of your life at this particular moment in time. After all, you didn't even put them there. You have a right to scrutinize them carefully. Worry only when the fear prevents you from crossing the span."

Suzanne felt like a stranger on the subway, a frequent tourist whose New York skills were advanced enough to know which train to ride but whose experience was still too limited to provide even the beginnings of comfort. She felt an extra unease that she couldn't identify, beyond the one New Yorkers always feel when locked underground in their dark, hot, dirty transit system, sealed in a train with dozens, often hundreds of additional citizens along with the probability that at least one was a dangerous sociopath and a number of others were on the border of psychosis.

She looked around carefully, the added edginess causing her to shift in her seat and pay more attention to her fellow passengers than was either normal or prudent.

At one end of the car, a young woman and two children, their dark skin, eyes and facial structures indicating origins in the Indian subcontinent, their designer clothing and a portable stereo in the ear of each of the little ones projecting their assimilation to American culture.

The scene was tranquil and watching them helped Suzanne to relax until the mother noticed her attention. She returned Suzanne's smile nervously, as though afraid not to respond to unwanted attention. Suzanne averted her eyes, flustered at the discomfort she caused. She turned away and looked to the other end of the car.

It occurred to her that she was riding in the same type of car, on the same line, where she'd encountered both Elias Garner and Luckholt. In Suzanne's mind, this wasn't a similar car, it was exactly the same one in which the terrifying rendezvous took place. Attempting to remain calm, she admitted to herself that all subway cars look alike.

"Although," she thought, "I seem to remember those two duplicate advertisements, both for the same dermatologist, side by side near the door."

Below the sign was an all too familiar New York scene, a homeless man, curled up in a tight little ball on a tiny two-seat section, trying to sleep, and seeming to succeed. Suzanne saw mostly the bottom of his worn shoes and the back of his shirt as he locked out light and noise by pressing his face into the curve of the metal seat. She tried to imagine what sleeping on the subway would be like… no king-size bed or designer sheets, without six pillows and the security of her apartment. The thought brought a shudder and she wondered how the man could feel protected enough to sleep with his back to the rest of the world. She thought about the stories she heard of the violence in New York's "living-on-the-street" culture, of murder for a few pennies or piece of crack cocaine and she shivered even harder.

Suzanne had been staring at the man for several long moments, again violating the New York rule of looking past or even through strangers, when he began to stir. He moved as though her stare had become a gentle prod, a shaking awake of the slumbering figure. She was immediately conscious of his motion and considered the possibility that maybe her intense gaze was, in fact, responsible. Still, she could not bring herself to look away. There was something about him that held her attention as he squirmed, shifted, turned and sat upright, his eyes still closed and his head shaking slowly like any man awakened prematurely from a deep sleep. He was a most unusual figure.

The vagabond's long dark hair was tied into a dozen tight dreadlocks in the style of the Jamaican Rastafarians. His hair was filthy and unkempt as though the dreads were tied months ago and ignored ever since. But by itself, the hair was not so unusual. What made the vision so strange was that this mass of dirty hair was perched upon the head of a white man. At least that's how he looked. His skin was light and his features quite Aryan, even Nordic. He appeared to be a northern European wearing a black person's wig, one that he found in the trash.

Suzanne was considering the possibility of a hairpiece when the man, as though answering her unasked question, began to pull and scratch at his head in a manner that automatically dispelled the theory, unless the thing was nailed or sewn to his scalp. The rest of him fit the expected image of the homeless person perfectly. Only his face seemed superimposed on the unwashed, rag clad body. The scene was downright bizarre.

Suzanne quickly glanced around the car, focusing on the faces of the other passengers to see if they too were puzzled by the strange sight near the door. None had seemed to notice, the mother still intent on her children, the others reading magazines and newspapers or following city convention and staring at some preselected spot on the ceiling. She looked back, half expecting the strange apparition to disappear. He was still there, his eyes wide open, a broad grin displaying broken and dirty teeth, and his eyes locked directly on Suzanne.

The glare wasn't unusual. This sort of thing happened to her all the time, to all reasonably attractive women, she imagined, on a regular basis, especially in the subway. And the leer didn't always come from a down-and-out street bum either. Just as often, the man wearing the offensive expression was also wearing an expensive suit and carrying a tanned leather briefcase.

Suzanne had learned how to immunize herself to this kind of attention, but the strange looking homeless man stared and grinned through her defenses with an expression so powerful that all her internal warning lights went off at the same time. Suzanne was frightened, again... just as she had been two weeks earlier when Luckholt entered the car.

The vagabond's eyes are still locked on her as the train jolts to a stop and the car doors hiss open. Suzanne tenses her muscles and the homeless man does the same. She waits a long moment, listens as the conductor speaks through the barely audible public address system... "this is Canal Street, City Hall Station is next, stand clear of the closing doors." With the first tiny mechanical motion, she leaps through the doors with less than an inch to spare, just as they slam behind her, exactly as she'd planned.

The strange man also moves, but not nearly as quickly, and when she turns to face the train, there he is, almost nose-to-nose with her, only the safe barrier of steel and glass partition separating them. The smile is still on his face. His eyes lock on Suzanne even as he steps backward to reclaim his seat. For one terrifying instant, the doors open again.

This is a regular happening on the New York City subways ... the trainman, opening and closing the doors for a second to clear somebody blocking them or a briefcase that got caught. But for some reason, Suzanne had not considered the possibility. Her moment of safe relaxation turns to panic.

The man suddenly lurches forward. Suzanne leaps in reverse, her motion accented by a short, sharp scream that ends abruptly when she crashes into a woman hurriedly moving across the platform. The energy expended by each of them, Suzanne in retreat, the woman rushing to catch the train, merge in their collision, creating enough force to send them both sprawling on to the platform's filthy floor.

Suzanne never averts her eyes from the bizarre man, even as she falls. She watches as the subway doors close on his hand and stares when his mouth twists into an unheard raging howl. Strangely enough, the other passengers seem to take no notice, though the man charged into the closing doors with enough force to shake the entire train. Suzanne is the only person who behaves as if she were aware of his presence, the only one who can see him. But though she sits on the platform, arms and legs entangled with a complete stranger, her dress soiled by the subway dirt, she still feels a great sense of relief as the car disappears into the darkness of the tunnel.

The relief isn't destined to last very long. Concentrated entirely in her left ear, Suzanne hears what has to be described as the snarl of an angry animal. She turns, tracing the sound and finds that the beast-like noise comes from the throat of her collision companion who is lying flat on her back on the platform floor. The woman, elegantly dressed and wearing far too much jewelry for the New York City subway, appears to be somewhere around fifty with streaks of gray in a mostly black head of hair. She's very tall and very thin, with arms like an athlete and a face that, though human, belongs more on a bird, in particular a hawk. Her pale skin is coated with a thick covering of makeup. And the sound that still comes from her throat is so unhuman that it pierces Suzanne's stomach and leaves her feeling terribly cold.

Her first concern is for this person's health. Had she been injured in the fall? Is that why she's making such a weird noise? Suzanne tries to unwrap herself from the tangle of limbs so she can assist the older woman.

Even as she pulls her arms and legs free, Suzanne looks around, expecting, hoping, someone will stop to offer assistance. No luck. The people on the platform are busy fulfilling their New York stereotype and walking around the two fallen women as though they didn't exist.

Finally, and completely on her own, Suzanne manages to stand. She reaches out her arm to the older woman who responds with a black-gloved hand. At least the growling has ceased.

"I am terribly sorry," Suzanne says as she takes the woman's outstretched hand to help her to her feet. "I didn't see you and I was trying to get away from…."

Her apology freezes in midsentence. The growling noise is back, but more intense, like a prelude to an attack. The woman, now halfway up, is wearing a most unusual expression, her mouth twisted into a wide, sadistic grin. This is not a smile of pleasure but a sneer of triumph. Her eyes are wide and reflecting light so strangely that her pupils appear to glow red in their sockets. Surrounded by that animal-like growl, Suzanne thinks, for a brief moment, that she is hand-in-hand with a demon.

She lets go, simply relaxes her grip, expecting the woman to go tumbling back to the concrete. But that doesn't happen. The red-eyed lady's grasp on the young attorney's arm tightens with strength seemingly impossible for a human hand. She continues to rise up from the floor under her own power, her fingernails digging deep into Suzanne's arm even though she wears gloves, the red eyes brightening and the horrible sound rising like a savage's victory cry. The more Suzanne struggles, the tighter the woman's grip becomes.

"Help me, please," Suzanne cries out but no one responds.

The black clothed body of the growling woman

continues to rise off the platform. Now the fingers of her free hand twist into what looks like a claw and she is drawing her arm back as though she is planning to strike at Suzanne's face. The war cry is very loud now, echoing off the concrete ceiling, ringing with twice the real volume in Suzanne's ear.

Everything around her moves in slow motion, everything except Suzanne's terror, which is growing geometrically. She is approaching hysteria and knows that if she doesn't act quickly she'll soon lose the ability to make a rational choice. A moment before the panic takes hold, Suzanne lifts her left foot and drives the point of her high-heel into the growling woman's instep. The snarl turns to a scream of pain. The woman releases her grip and tumbles back onto the concrete.

Suzanne does not waste a second. She turns and runs up the nearest staircase.

"Stop that woman," she heard shouted behind her as she fled. "She assaulted me. She knocked me to the platform and then she stepped on me."

The voice did not sound like one that belonged to a demon. This voice, complete with a thick New York accent, sounded as though the owner was a frightened, middle-aged matron. Suzanne had already decided not to stop and find out. If she were wrong about the danger, if the terror had not been rational, she would apologize later. Her first priority remained putting distance between her and the jeweled lady. Despite the cries for help, none of the other subway patrons exhibited any interest in getting involved.

"A cop... I'll find a cop," she thought, muttering out loud as her eyes searched the upper level of the station. The familiar blue uniform was spotted near the token booth, a tall, broad shouldered policeman, twirling a nightstick and standing with his back toward Suzanne. She ran to him, forcing herself to maintain a minimum level of reason by not screaming out across the platform, demanding protection.

"Excuse me, officer," she said, tapping him on the shoulder. The man turned and Suzanne gasped. Smiling at her was the Minnesota State Trooper, Luckholt's friend, dressed in a New York Transit Police uniform, or, at least someone who looked enough like him to be the Trooper's twin brother.

> *"Can I help you, ma'am?" he says politely. Is this her imagination or do his eyes seem to glow with the same red as the woman on the platform? No, that isn't possible. She backs away and he steps toward her, closing the distance between them.*
>
> *"Is there anything wrong?" he says as he advances. "Is there something I can do for you?"*
>
> *"No, no, never mind," she blurts out. "I made a mistake. Everything's fine." She takes another step backwards.*
>
> *"I don't think so," he says, the courtesy draining from his voice. "You're not being truthful. I heard that lady scream before. Maybe you and I should go to the station and talk this over." He moves still closer.*
>
> *"No," she almost screams, "You can't take me anywhere. I didn't do anything and you don't have probable cause to detain me. I'm a lawyer... I know...."*
>
> *"Oh, a lawyer," the cop says, as he continues to advance. "That didn't mean anything before. Why should I care now?" He reaches out his hand to take her arm when Suzanne turns and flees toward the exit.*
>
> *"Wait," he shouts, "stop right there!" She ignores him and continues to run, reaching the staircase in a few seconds and mounting the flight of concrete steps just as quickly. Behind her, she can hear the sound of the cop's leather soles pounding the floor. And his shoes are not the only ones in pursuit. Suzanne is convinced she can also hear another set of feet keeping time with the policeman, feet in high-heeled shoes. The*

woman in black? Are both of them chasing her?

Suzanne bursts from the dark to the bright sunlight of the street. She's on the edge of Chinatown, just a few blocks away from City Hall. The streets are mercifully crowded, jammed with late morning New York commerce. The mass of people is a security blanket. She feels safe enough to slow from a run to a fast walk, but still looks over her shoulder every few moments to see if she can spot her pursuers. They're not to be found. Gradually she reduces her speed until she's walking only a little faster than those around her. She allows herself a moment to inhale – one long, deep breath. Maybe the time of terror has ended. She feels safe on the street, just part of the crowd, and on the street she'll stay, above ground, walking the rest of the way to her Wall Street office.

From the danger of the subway to the sanctuary of her office is at least fifteen blocks, and the shoes she's wearing aren't made for walking. But that doesn't matter. Suzanne isn't willing to go back into the subway.

The traffic on Canal Street, as usual, is completely snarled. A taxi would be a serious waste of time. So she continues to walk, ignoring the discomfort in her feet. The distraction of the pain actually makes her less tense with each passing block, until she hears the footsteps.

Two pair, oddly clear and explicit over the street noises... the wide, flat leather of a man's shoe and the distinctive click of a woman's high heels, the same sounds Suzanne heard behind her in the subway. But now, somehow, impossibly, the steps are separate from the sounds of hundreds of others, as though artificially amplified.

She stops and turns and scans the crowd for the hawk-faced woman and the cop, half convinced that her own imagination has produced the sounds. Not surprisingly, their forms are not to be found and the footsteps in Suzanne ears fall silent. She turns back to continue the journey toward her office, but the moment she starts forward, the footsteps begin once more. This is impossible!

Three times, in the next two blocks, Suzanne stops and turns abruptly, examining the people behind her. Three times the sounds disappear and no evidence of her being pursued presents itself. Her overworked nervous system can no longer stand the strain. Without planning or thought, she turns and walks through the door of the very next business establishment she reaches.

Suzanne's eyes don't have to adjust to the dark room for her to know that she's probably made an error. The assaulting smell furnished the clear message that she'd entered a tavern, and not the kind of establishment that a respectable young woman normally walks into at eleven o'clock in the morning. The aroma was that of the subway, enhanced by years of stale beer and tobacco. The six pairs of eyes that turned toward her and stared suspiciously bore right into her body. She turned to walk out, but then remembered the footsteps.

"Frying pan or fire?" she muttered, smiling at the thought of talking to herself out loud. She took a stool at the bar far enough away from the window to be protected from the street and not particularly near the knot of men who gathered at the darkest end of the ancient mahogany bar.

"Can I help you, miss?" The bartender was well beyond middle age, still in good physical condition, with the distinctive red-face that advertised too much alcohol over too many years. He was polite, but spoke with a note of caution in his voice, probably suspecting that she represented the Alcohol Beverage Commission and would either present him with a summons or conduct a surprise inspection.

"I'd like a club soda please, or maybe a cup of coffee?"

"Which one?" Voiced with a certain amount of impatience, but no real hostility.

"Coffee, please."

He left, disappeared into the darkness and returned quickly with a battered heavy, white cup resting on a chipped saucer and filled with lukewarm black liquid. He set the coffee in front of her, picked up the dollar that she'd placed on the bar and returned to the knot of men in the corner without saying a word.

Suzanne could hear the whispers from the dark but couldn't make out any specific words. Several of the men laughed and the particular sound of their mirth left no doubt that the nature of the conversation was sexual. Her discomfort increased and then increased again when one of the men left his stool and started to shuffle toward her. She glanced at him only for a brief moment. He was illuminated by a stream of stray sunlight that poked through the otherwise darkened front windows.

The man had to be at least seventy. He swayed as he walked, likely from equal parts of age and alcohol. He didn't seem particularly threatening but Suzanne was hardly in the mood to deal with even the most minor annoyance. A rescue came in the form of a voice from the dark.

"Hank, don't you bother the lady!" the bartender shouted unexpectedly.

"Oh, I wasn't gonna' bother her, Bill," the old man whined as he turned around and stumbled back to his stool.

Suzanne was deeply relieved and grateful. She took a sip of coffee, finding the fluid tasted just as bad as it smelled, and pushed the cup away. The gesture brought the bartender back into the half-light.

"Is there something wrong with the coffee, miss?" His tone indicated genuine concern and Suzanne decided to take a risk.

"No, not the coffee. There's something wrong with me. I came in here because I think I'm being followed. Do you mind if I just sit for a few minutes?"

"No problem," he responded. "Stay as long as you like."

The bartender retreated to the shadows and the whispering resumed, this time with a different tone. A few moments later he again appeared to Suzanne.

"Would you like me to call the cops?"

"No," she said, thinking about the transit policeman from Minnesota, "I don't think that's necessary. The whole thing was probably just my imagination anyway."

"Well, you can't be too careful in this city," the bartender said. "One of the boys... Joshua... has offered to go with you to wherever you're going. Would that help?"

He saw the hesitation, the near fright, in her face.

"He's alright, believe me miss. Joshua works the midnight shift at one of the garment factories. Works from twelve at night to ten in the morning. Comes in for a couple of beers before he goes to bed. No different than most folks do after work, only his day is a little weird because of his strange hours. Never drinks more than two beers. Hard working boy. I'd trust him to do this if you were my daughter. Take him up on the offer. You'll feel better."

The bartender's tone was so sincere that Suzanne could not resist the opportunity.

"OK," she said, "thank you. I'd like having some company. I'm only going to Wall Street."

The bartender smiled and waved toward the darkness. A young man emerged from the corner and stood for a moment in the single beam of sunlight as though he was displaying himself to Suzanne.

He was in his late-twenties, Asian, dark hair cut close, soiled blue jeans and an equally messy denim work shirt. In contrast to his dirty clothes, he was wearing the most gentle, pleasant smile Suzanne had seen since leaving the professor's office.

"I'm Joshua," he said, his thick accent obvious even in those few words. "I'll walk with you. Where do we go?"

"Thank you Joshua. I'm Suzanne. We're going to Wall Street."

"Oh, Wall Street. Good. One day, I will work on Wall Street. One day soon." He turned to the bartender and waved. "Goodbye, see you tomorrow."

Joshua held the door open for Suzanne and together they stepped into the hot sunlight of the street. For a moment, she hesitated, looking right and left for familiar and unwanted faces.

"Do not worry, Miss. I am very tough. No one will bother you."

She wanted to laugh at his old-fashioned posture of chivalry, but the truth was that she felt safer than she had all day. Joshua did look tough. He was a small man with broad shoulders, his arms and back decorated by rows of work-hardened muscles. He walked tall, projecting an air of protection as he accompanied Suzanne.

"Thank you Joshua," she said, not knowing what else to say. "I appreciate your taking the time."

"No problem, Miss. I like helping people."

As she was thinking about what to say to start a conversation, Joshua launched an autobiographical monologue.

"My name was not always Joshua. I used to have a Chinese name but changed when I came to America. I'm called Joshua Wilson now. Very American, yes?" He didn't give her a chance to respond. "Yes, American," he continued. "Came from China, People's Republic. I was in the People's Army but ran away. Got in a boat with other people, lots of people, and went to Hong Kong. Most got sent back 'cause the government say they were...," he hesitated as he searched for the words in English. "Economic refugees... yes. I stay. They said I was political refugee because I ran away from People's Army. Man say if they send me back, I get shot. Not true. People's Army would put me in jail, but not shoot me. But I did not argue. Man think I will get shot, I stay in

America. Not think I will get shot, I go back to China. Not argue. I am in America now six months. Work in factory. Want to work on Wall Street... be," he hesitated again, but this time because he wanted to see the impact of the words he stored in his head. He spoke very slowly. "Be a stockbroker." Joshua paused again to see how she'd react, whether she'd laugh at him. When she didn't laugh, he continued. "Are a you stockbroker, Miss?"

"No Joshua, I'm a lawyer. But I think your dream to be a stockbroker is wonderful. You will have to study very hard."

"Oh, yes, I study every afternoon. Maybe soon I will find a job during the day. Study in the evenings and sleep at night, like regular people. Men back at the bar make fun when I say I can be a stockbroker."

"You can be whatever you want to be," she answered. "Don't listen to them. They're just jealous of your ambition."

"Yes, yes… that is what I say. They are jealous. You are a smart lady, Miss Suzanne."

"Thank you, Joshua, but right now I don't feel very smart."

He sensed that she was feeling pain and fell silent. They walked for blocks that way, the tall, well-dressed woman in high heels, the small, soiled Asian man striding confidently alongside her. Suzanne was completely at ease. Her fear of the street had disappeared in Joshua's company. She permitted her mind to explore where she'd gone.

Suzanne wondered if the homeless man, the hawk-lady and the policeman were somehow connected. Were they all Luckholt's agents or just the product of Suzanne's overactive imagination? Elias Garner had told her on the subway car before she went to South Dakota that she had nothing to fear as long as she kept her faith. Did that mean these people couldn't hurt her even if they did work for Luckholt? But to believe that she could be protected from harm by some shield of faith would be to accept that the quest truly belonged in the world of the supernatural. Could she go that far? Could her rational, legal mind make that huge leap of faith? Maybe. She'd taken a small jump in the bar, trusted someone in a circumstance that should not have, logically, generated trust. But so far the results were turning out just fine. Joshua seemed like a nice guy and he'd made her feel safe. The footsteps had not returned and now they were only a block from her office building. Maybe she should continue taking leaps. Maybe that would provide the protection she needed from them, whoever they were, and from herself.

Suzanne felt elated. She stopped and turned toward her Asian companion.

"Joshua, can you read English?"

"Yes, Miss," he said proudly. "I studied very hard, studied in China too. I can read well."

"He can also use more proper verbs and nouns than most immigrants," she said silently inside her head. "More than most of us that were born here!" she smiled.

"Then you come with me." She said out loud as they approached the entrance to her building. "I might help you find a day job."

Joshua followed without expressing the questions that were written all over his face.

Suzanne led the young man up the elevator and down the long corridor to her office. Inside the plush offices, Joshua seemed to lose some of his confidence. He appeared very small as he walked down the carpeted hallways.

"Ms. Rosewell," Margaret said the moment she saw Suzanne, "I've been worried about you all morning. You have a pile of messages and Mr. Johnston has been demanding to see you."

"Thank you Margaret. Forgive me for not calling. I'll get to the messages in a moment and the Managing Partner can wait just a few more minutes. I have something I must do first."

She motioned Joshua to a seat inside her office, picked up her phone and dialed an internal extension.

"Hello, Sam," the lawyer said in her sweetest, professional voice, "this is Suzanne Rosewell. Are you still looking for a new man in the mailroom? Good. I think I have a candidate for you and I think he'll last more than the usual couple of months. Fine, I'll send him over. His name is Joshua Wilson, but don't be too surprised when you see him. And Sam, he works a factory job at night, so he's not dressed very well right now. I'd like you to look beyond that. OK, just so you understand, and Sam, this is a favor to me. If you can help out my friend Joshua, I'll owe you one. Yes, of course, the investment portfolio. I'd be happy to review your account with you, any time. Can I send Joshua right down? Good. Thanks Sam." She hung up the phone and turned toward the man in the chair.

"I might work here?" Joshua asked with a smile larger than life.

"You might. The money won't be great, but you will probably make more than you are earning now. And you'll have medical insurance and the firm will help you pay for school. Are you interested?"

"Yes, yes, thank you. I want to work on Wall Street."

"You won't work as a stockbroker Joshua."

"Not today, but some other day," he responded with a knowing grin.

Suzanne instructed Margaret to guide Joshua to the mailroom and when the pair had gone she picked up the phone to call the Managing Partner.

"Maybe this day didn't start out so well," she thought, as she waited for Mr. Johnston's secretary to complete the connection, "but it sure is getting better."

CHAPTER SIXTEEN

Donald "John Brown" Rothman mounted the subway stairs at City Hall Station, one stop past Canal Street, the point where Suzanne had escaped the transit system. Without displaying any of the tension and frustration that had earlier left him banging his head against the car door and bellowing, he quietly shuffled across the platform. He ignored those who watched him with curiosity, passed by those who stared at him with disdain, and snarled at those who looked right through him as though he wasn't there. The last group, the ones with the blank stares, they were the people that used to bother him.

"I'm still human," he once thought, "Why do you look past me as if I'm not even a person?" But that was back in the early days of his transition from Donald K. Rothman to John Brown. Now he didn't care.

Truthfully, even in the time before the metamorphosis had been completed, thoughts that centered on the issue of "personal dignity" didn't come very often. And when they did, they didn't last very long. The distorted electrical impulses in Don Rothman's brain left him little room for concern about other people's opinions.

Don's passage had started about six years earlier. The promising young engineer who traversed these same streets around City Hall and who was then called Donald K. Rothman, started to fade and John Brown began to emerge. "John" didn't care if people treated him as something other than human because that's just what he was… something other than human.

John Brown knew himself to be an entity composed of hundreds of souls, all of whom had died more than a century ago. His dominant being was the radical nineteenth century abolitionist whose name he preferred to use. Included inside him were also the souls of John Brown's son and of all the black men who were killed or executed in Brown's failed slave revolt. As a result of this joining of spirits, Donald "John Brown" Rothman considered himself both black and white – not a man of mixed race, but... he was very careful when explaining this point... someone both African and Anglo-Saxon at the very same time.

Of course, the narrow, stupid doctors at the psychiatric hospital where Sarah and Henry Rothman, Donald's parents, tried to have John confined, did not believe in the complex history of his entity. They called John's explanations "delusional behavior," and said the obsession with race was probably a result of Sarah and Henry having their child along with them during the struggles of the Civil Rights era when the Rothman's were registering voters in Mississippi. In those days, with the exception of his parents, Donald's role models were all brave, battling black people. The bedtime stories told to the children were often about white oppression and slave resistance, including tales about Nat Turner and John Brown.

Sarah Rothman considered the form of her son's illness to be the cruelest twist of fate. The part of Sarah and Henry's life together of which they were most proud had become the manifestation of their only child's delusions. The doctors kept reassuring the elder Rothmans that the fantasies would have come anyway, though maybe in a different form, even if child Donald hadn't spent three years in Mississippi. But the information did little to ease their sense of guilt.

Bit by bit, Donald K. Rothman disappeared, conceding his physical being to the one known as John Brown. Unlike Donald, who was willing to do anything to rid himself of the torment in his brain, John objected strongly to being confined in a hospital. He knew that he was destined to do important work, but out in the world. That's why all of these souls had been raised from the dead and placed inside him, to do something really consequential, though he had to admit, even to the doctors, that he had no idea what his destiny might encompass.

John might have been crazy, but he wasn't stupid. He knew that if he pretended to be Donald, made the doctors believe that he accepted the lies they told him, they'd eventually let him out. They had no choice. He also knew that he couldn't be held against his will unless he was a danger to himself or someone else. Though unaware of the source of this knowledge, he knew the revelation to be true, and he was right.

And that's what the hospital administrator told Sarah and Henry the day he was forced to release Donald "John Brown" Rothman to the streets. The chief psychiatrist did manage to delay the release long enough to phone Donald's parents who responded immediately. They came in the hope that they could convince their son to come home with them to Scarsdale. Donald was already gone when they arrived. Carrying a small suitcase, he disappeared into New York City. Three years had passed since Sarah and Henry had heard anything from or about their child, despite the efforts of the best private detective they could engage.

During those thirty-six long months, the transmutation had become complete. John Brown no longer even remembered that his body once belonged to Donald Rothman. Though that name was familiar, and it crossed his mind every once in a while, he remembered Donald as someone he once knew, but not very well.

There were more important things on John's mind than old acquaintances. First he had to develop a physical presentation of his multi-souled self so other like entities would recognize him as one of their own. He accomplished this first step by allowing his curly hair to grow long. Then he dyed the brown mop black and dressed his head with dreadlocks in the manner of the Jamaican men he met in the shelters. John was certain that at least one of his souls was a Jamaican slave brought to America only to eventually die in the revolt. That made the hairstyle very appropriate even as his face continued to reflect the influence, and skin color, of the old abolitionist himself. The final effect was of a white man wearing a black man's wig. The look attracted lots of stares, which was precisely what John was seeking.

Once the desired appearance had been accomplished, John Brown set out to find his purpose on earth. This task was much more difficult. He had no idea where to start. So for months John wandered around the city, revealing his secret only to other street people, carefully avoiding the police, mental health people, social workers and every other representative of established authority. John was sure of little, but he was certain that those who represented the government, just like those in power when the soul of the original John Brown was still in his own body, were his mortal enemies. Still, he was unable to find his task, his reason for being on the planet.

One fine spring day, a full two years into his wanderings, John found himself sleeping in an abandoned storefront not far from City Hall. There he met two men who roamed the streets together. They called themselves Larry and Sam and said that they were brothers. John knew the designation was probably one of convenience and racial solidarity, rather than genetics. They claimed to be combat veterans of the war in Viet Nam. John remembered hearing about the war, recalled that the Viet Nam conflict was an evil escapade and that the soldiers, especially black soldiers, were as much victims as the people who lived in that battered nation. Therefore, he concluded, Larry and Sam were kindred spirits with the entity that occupied his body. So when they offered to share the smoke from their glass pipe, John did not hesitate to accept.

The crack cocaine carried him a major step closer to his goal. John Brown discovered that when he was high he almost understood his hidden earthly purpose. He always felt within an inch of grasping his reason for being. That's when the drug would begin to wear off and the resolution would slip away. Logically, the only thing to do was continue to smoke the stuff until he could stay high long enough to achieve his goal.

For the next year, John Brown and Larry and Sam became a team whose sole reason for being was to purchase and consume crack-cocaine. John would panhandle or steal, or, very occasionally, work a menial job to bring in the money that the two vets would use to buy drugs. Every night they'd get high together and every night John felt he got a little closer to his answer. The thought never occurred to him that his priorities had changed. That now, obtaining and smoking crack cocaine had become the prime directive of his life.

There he was, in his usual place on the Lexington Avenue Subway, sleeping off the effects of another night of searching, when he first became conscious of her.

John felt her stare penetrate his backbone even as he slept. There was an actual physical pressure that woke him, much like the familiar prod of the policeman's nightstick. The sensation brought him fully aware. His eyes opened wide and he studied the back of the gray metal seat, considering the imperfections and the scratches in the paint. Then, as if from a projector behind his eyes, a clear, sharp picture of a woman appeared in front of him.

John had encountered visions before, lots of them, but this was a completely new experience. In the images of his prior revelations, figures were always somewhat vague and unclear, difficult to recognize. This picture was sharp and focused, coming from a tiny television in his brain. He knew, without even turning around, that he was watching a woman who was, at that very moment, watching him. John decided that this experience was an important one. He tried to sit up, to center his attention and understand what was happening.

The act of changing from the prone position was not easy. For the past few months he and the veteran brothers had added large quantities of cheap wine to their nightly ventures into cocaine's world. The wine helped to even out the intensity of the high and make the drug induced tension easier to control. But the raw, cheap alcohol gifted John with a terrible hangover to add to the dry, drained feeling that was the usual morning-after legacy of the tiny crystals in the glass pipe. Still, he felt the image of this lovely young woman was somehow important, so he forced his body to respond.

And, as he expected, there she was, the very woman of his vision, sitting directly across the aisle. He smiled at her and she seemed almost to smile back just before she averted her eyes. That's when John knew he'd finally taken a step forward in the long hunt to find his purpose on earth. This woman was at the center. He didn't know the role she'd play in his destiny, but he knew, with absolute certainty, that she was closely tied to him and would be a significant force in his future.

The obvious thing, John decided, was to talk to her. Maybe she too was an entity like him. Maybe she was even made up of the very female souls who were mates to the men he carried inside. The two of them could join forces to fulfill their joint destiny, whatever that might be. They should sit down over a bottle of wine and share their secrets. Yes, he concluded, he would talk to her and right now.

The train reached Canal Street. The doors opened and the passengers who needed to board, boarded. Those leaving, left. In a moment the car would seal again and John would move across the narrow open space and sit with the lovely young woman to offer her an alliance. He was just about to start his motion when the woman leapt from her seat and fled the car. The doors closed directly behind her.

John didn't understand. Her actions confused him.

"Why is she running away?" he thought. "We're supposed to be together."

The doors reopened for an instant and John hurried to jump through them. His body simply could not respond fast enough. The sliding panels closed on his hand. With a subway rider's instinctual reaction, he pulled his arm back, allowing the doors to complete their closure, and signaling the trainman that conditions were safe to move forward.

John howled in frustration and rage, pounding his head against the secured subway doors. He glared as his vision leapt backwards and collided with another woman on the platform. He watched as the pair fell into a tangle of arms and legs and he stared at them as the train pulled away into the dark tunnel.

Then his anger faded. By her actions, the woman had at least provided part of the answer. She was not, after all, to be his ally, this person who fled his most gentle advance. Therefore, she must be his enemy and somewhere, through their conflict to come, John Brown would still find the answer he was seeking.

By the time the train arrived at City Hall Station, by the Brooklyn Bridge, John was perfectly at ease. This was his regular stop, closest to the vacant storefront he shared with Larry and Sam. John Brown stepped onto the platform, watching people purposefully move aside so they wouldn't accidentally brush against him. He sat down on a bench to watch the trains roll by and to think. He remained there for about twenty minutes, contemplating his experience, examining his purpose, and then finally, climbed the stairs to the street.

Across the line of traffic, silently shimmering in the summer sun, rested the century-old span known as the Brooklyn Bridge. As always, the cars crawled across the steel connection between Manhattan and Brooklyn, each on the bumper of the one before, substituting their horns for the acceleration that the condensed mass of machines would simply not permit. The sound of car horns and the roar of engines blurred together into an audio salad. The mixture was dressed by a distant siren altogether creating that distinctive sound universally associated with New York. John guzzled the stimulus through his eyes and his ears and for a brief moment the fog over his brain lifted. He was, once again,

Donald K. Rothman, engineer.

But the lucidity fled in a few seconds and Donald returned to being John Brown, a crack-addicted street person who carried no money, had no job and no address, a man who slept on the subway and in an abandoned store, panhandled on the corners near City Hall but who'd finally begun to understand his purpose on the globe.

And the proof of his destiny was across the street, coming up the hill from Chinatown, the very woman of his vision. She appeared just as he'd seen her on the subway, still dressed the same, still carrying the same handbag. But she was no longer alone. Now she was in the company of another man, shorter, young, walking with a strong and confident stride. Maybe this person was her boyfriend. If so, then he too had to be John's enemy. But this was a man who also looked dangerous. John decided to follow the couple at a safe distance.

For the second time in only a few days, Elias Garner was furiously pacing the full length of his luxurious office, walking back and forth with such intensity as if speed and motion were the only things able to defuse his anxiety. Up and down he tramped, across the same path on the plush carpet, his hands moving in jerky motions from his pockets to his belt to his face to his hair and back to his pockets again. The light on his speakerphone glowed and Eli nearly shouted his message to the unseen person at the other end of the line.

"That's not good enough," he said angrily. "I am absolutely certain that Luckholt is not just sitting back and waiting. That's not the way she works… never! Something is going on. Something is going on right now, as we speak, and you have find out what."

"I'm sorry sir," the male voice responded from out of the box. "We're doing everything we know how, but there appears to be no activity in her section at all. Everything *appears* to be utterly normal. But we're still checking. I've got people out everywhere... everywhere."

"Not good enough," Garner repeated. "I need information. I need information now. Right now! Put everyone on the job. This is a priority one operation. I can not leave Suzanne Rosewell undefended and I can not protect her unless I know what Luckholt has planned. Pull out all the stops. I want to know what stunt she's pulling and I want to know yesterday. Do you understand? Be in my office first thing in the morning and make sure you have a full report."

"Yes, sir," the voice said sadly. "I'll put every available operative on the job right away."

"Not every *available* operative!" Garner shouted. "*Every* operative!"

"Yes sir!" There was soft electronic click and the red light went dark. Elias Garner ceased his pacing and fell into the tall chair behind his desk. He opened the top drawer and reached to the spot where he once kept cigarettes. Only then did he recall that he'd given up smoking years ago.

"It's enough to make a person resume bad habits," he mumbled out loud to the empty room.

Suzanne Rosewell returned to her office and reached for her own cigarettes. The meeting with the Managing Partner had been difficult, but the rebuke was not unexpected. First, he'd complimented her on the fine work she'd done up until a few weeks ago. That's when she knew she wasn't getting fired. But then he complained about her recent lack of attention to clients. His voice was firm and bit threatening, but not deadly. And after he'd made his point, he softened his tone, sounding more like a favored uncle offering assistance than an angry boss chastising a subordinate. Suzanne could understand how this man had earned his reputation as a master at manipulating juries.

She apologized, considered sharing the entire story with him but rejected the thought. Then she promised to apply herself so well that no one, not even the Managing Partner, would remember her brief lapse of discipline. Mr. Johnston seemed satisfied and dismissed her with only a mild warning.

Suzanne wondered, as she removed the cigarette from the fresh pack, if she'd be able to keep her promise. She studied the thin, white tube, picked up her lighter and placed the gold-plated device back on the desk again. The clean paper wrapped around fresh tobacco somehow failed to offer the familiar promise of escape and relaxation. In a sudden gesture of defiance, she crushed the unlit cigarette, crumpled the entire pack and, along with the lighter and her ashtray, threw them all into the wastebasket. Then Suzanne left her office and walked down to the mailroom to learn the results of Joshua's interview.

Elizabeth Luckholt sat quietly behind her big desk, her eyes intently focused on the darkest corner of the room.

In size and shape, her office was a duplicate of Garner's but that's where the similarity ended. Elias Garner's huge windows were always uncovered, allowing the sunshine to reach every square inch of the room. Luckholt kept her blinds shut tight. Where Eli's furniture was light, both in design and color, Luckholt's was heavy and dark. She decorated her office like she dressed. The atmosphere of the place made strangers very uncomfortable and that was exactly her intent. Seated in a chair, half-hidden in the dark, was the Minnesota State Trooper, the man with no name. Now his outfit consisted of a business suit covering a black turtleneck.

"Tell me again," she said to him. "I want to make sure we haven't missed anything."

"OK," he responded in a half-whisper. "Eli's people are running around like beheaded chickens." He seemed to like the image and smiled as he spoke. "They're watching all of our regular agents, everyone within a hundred miles of the City. The surveillance is keeping his entire team occupied twenty-four hours a day and still they provide him with no information. The man is furious." His smile broadened.

"And?" Luckholt asked.

"And we've activated... I mean, *I've* activated... because I'm the only one who knows about them, just in case of leaks... two guys that we've had in deep cover for several years. To the outside world they appear to be street people, drug-addicted, homeless men. But they're two of the best-trained operatives we've ever put out. They, in turn, have recruited someone else. A genuine wacko and crack user, a guy who talks to ghosts, the whole bit. The men are convinced they can easily direct him to our target and without him having the slightest idea of our real agenda. When the guy succeeds, there will be three layers of protection between you and the action. Even the Chairman won't be able to prove that you had anything to do with it."

"Don't count on it," she responded turning her eyes toward him. He seemed to wilt a little in his chair. "Don't ever underestimate the Chairman. But the plan is good. There's not much time left, so see that everything moves quickly. When the deed is done, let the wacko fall into the hands of the police. I don't want this to be another unsolved crime. Some dedicated cop may look too closely. Then get our people out of the city immediately. Put them in charge of a branch office as far away from headquarters as possible but see that they're rewarded well... very well. Those who serve me with loyalty should always know that they'll be taken care of properly."

"I'll see that everything is done," he said simply.

John Brown found a large abandoned box in an alley across from the office building. He crawled in between the folds, determining that the cardboard made a perfect place to wait until the woman came out again. Then he would follow her and he'd know where she lived.

CHAPTER SEVENTEEN

"On the Upper East Side, Eighty-fifth and Madison, in a big steel building with a doorman." John Brown's hand shook as he held the disposable lighter under the glass bowl until the small, white rock crystal began to glow. Then he drew both lungs full with gray smoke and held the vapor as long as he could. The pipe was passed to Larry.

"Doorman shouldn't be a problem, not for you John," Larry said as he reheated the instrument. "You've been able to get into those kinda buildings all the time. Remember how you stole the vases from the hallway of that rich joint on Park Avenue? Boy, we got a lot of crystal for those babies. You just wait till the doorman has to take a crap or something. Right?"

John was listening, but he couldn't answer. His brain was too busy experiencing every millisecond of the intense, but terribly short cocaine high, inching toward the shuttered door of revelation that had moved just a bit closer when the pipe made the last trip through the trio of companions.

They'd started smoking just after midnight and the first pass of the glass tube had gifted John Brown with a major leap forward. But even in his condition, he knew the drug wasn't the only thing responsible for his progress. Most was because of the girl. He could see her face, still as clear, sharp, and bell-like as the moment he peaked. That insight advanced his consciousness toward the goal. This was the most exciting thing he'd experienced in months. With each pass of the pipe, he progressed further and the glass stem seemed to reach his hands often this particular evening.

While on the slope down from the peak and into the shadows, John reviewed his evening, trying to uncover additional clues that he might have overlooked. Like a detective on a TV mystery show (*Did he once, long ago, used to watch television?*), he reexamined the details to the extent his numbed brain would permit.

Following the woman uptown had been simple. She left the office building fairly late. John never wore a watch but since the streets were already dark, and this is, after all, summer, the clock must have passed eight.

"So," he concluded internally, "she has to be a seriously hard worker to stay in the office so late." John was very pleased with the quality of his deductive reasoning, though Don Rothman, who'd been a member of MENSA, probably would not have found Brown's mental powers very impressive.

"What did you say, John?" asked Sam, who had just finished reheating the pipe. He was ignored.

Following her on the street was also easy. At that time of night, the financial district is always empty and all the businesses closed. Without the crowds to interfere, he could watch her from a full block away, hiding in the shadows of the open doorways, keeping his form invisible on the narrow old-New York streets. The neighborhood was so quiet he could hear the click of her high-heeled shoes echo off the stone facades. Her pace and the sound of her step indicated a woman in good spirits. She even seemed to be singing out loud to herself, but of that John couldn't be sure, not from the distance he maintained.

"Hey, man! You want this again or should we skip you?"

Sam was prodding him with one hand and passing the pipe with the other. There was a fresh crystal in the bowl. Was this the third or the fourth rock? John couldn't remember.

"No, no," he said, "Don't pass me by. Just a second."

"I didn't think you wanted to be skipped," Sam said with a smile. He held the pipe while John took a long pull off the wine bottle that was resting at his side. They each had a bottle of their own this night and that was unusual. Normally the three of them would share a single jug. But John was in too good of a mood to question the fine fortune of abundance. He accepted the pipe and fired his lighter, drew a deep breath and focused on the closed door in his mind.

John watched his hand reach for the knob, his fingers only inches away. He stretched hard but the image faded as the peak passed him by once more without providing an answer. The pipe went to Larry.

The woman had gotten on the subway, the Lexington Line, number four train. He rode in the car behind her and worried a bit, since she'd seen him on the subway before and would likely recognize him. Even though people often appeared to look through him, John knew he wasn't one who could fade into a crowd. At each stop he stepped halfway out on the platform, using his body to block the closing door and the train's forward progress, until he was sure the woman was still traveling north.

City Hall Station, Union Square, Grand Central Terminal, Fifty-Ninth Street and still she continued. But at the Eighty-Sixth Street Station he saw her depart and literally bound up the stairs. Her pace was still light, unaware she was being followed.

He chose a different stairway and came up across 86th Street from where she was walking. John watched as the woman first paused to look in the window of a Chinese restaurant and finally went inside. He lurked in the doorway of a store, now closed and shuttered for the evening, until she came out again. He'd prayed that it wasn't her intention to eat inside and his silent request was granted. His quarry was carrying a small take-out bag. The aroma drifting from the exhaust fan over the door reminded John that he hadn't eaten all day (*Didn't I eat Chinese food once and even sit in the restaurant?*) and now he was hungry.

The woman's pace had increased. But she wasn't walking in the fast and furious manner that frightened people use when they want to get off the streets quickly. Her gait was one of someone going toward a special place, or person, and she just couldn't wait to arrive. Her buoyancy made following her all the more effortless. She never once looked over her shoulder.

Just a block from the Chinese restaurant, the woman suddenly turned, without warning, into the doorway of a new, modern apartment building. John was still following her, now from the other side of Madison Avenue. He'd chosen to watch from a distance, allowing himself a broader view just in case she made a sudden turn. John Brown complimented himself on his foresight as the doorman greeted his quarry. She was known in this building. This is where she lives, of that he was certain.

Some of John's confidence faded as he returned to the subway, jumped the turnstile while the token booth clerk was looking elsewhere, and boarded the first express train going downtown.

"Could be where her boyfriend lives," he thought, "and that's why the doorman knows her. "Or where her parents live *(parents?)* or a good friend. How am I supposed to know?" The doubt brought him full into a state of high anxiety by the time he'd reached the abandoned store.

Sam was waiting, and without Larry, which was the first out-of-the-ordinary event of the evening. But John had bigger things on his mind than the separation of his two companions. He started to blurt out the thoughts spinning through his brain.

"Sam, Sam," John muttered. "I am so glad you're here. I've made a great discovery but I have a problem, lots of problems. I don't know where to begin."

"Let me begin for you," Sam said in a calm voice. He put his hands on John shoulders and looked directly into his eyes. He thought he saw Sam's eyes glow red but decided his vision was playing tricks on him. The effect must have come from the flickering of the candles they used to light the empty store. For a brief moment John felt a unfamiliar chill in his blood. The feeling dissipated and John Brown was attentive as Sam spoke.

"You saw someone today and you know that person is part of your destiny. Am I right?"

"Yes, how did you know?"

"That person is…" Sam closed his eyes as he concentrated. "...a young woman and you followed her to where she works and then to where she lives... yes?"

"Well, yes, I followed her but I'm not sure she lives there."

"Where is the building?"

"Madison Avenue, in the eighties."

"That's where she lives."

"How do you know?" John was both excited and frightened at the same time.

"Because I'm your friend," Sam said softly. "The souls you carry around know that I am your friend and they send me messages all day long telling me what's going on inside of you… so I can help. While you were following the woman, I was investigating her. I have my sources, you know?"

"No, I didn't know. I had no idea at all." John sounded a bit suspicious.

"Let me prove it to you," Sam said. "I know that you were so busy following this woman that you didn't do any panhandling or stealing and now you've got no money to buy crack." This revelation revived John's fright.

"Oh dear, oh dear, oh God, oh God," he stammered. "You're right… and I need some tonight. I've got to find out what that woman means. And there are hardly any people on the street. I can't cop enough! Oh, this is bad. This is very bad."

"Calm down!" Sam said firmly. "Everything is under control. Larry is out getting the dope right now. We got lucky and picked up some money today. He'll be back any minute. Here, have a little wine while we wait." Sam passed a quart bottle of John's favorite, a sweet mixture labeled MD 20/20. The guys on the street called the stuff "Mad Dog," a reference John understood all too well. He took a long swallow and the thick burning liquid coated his empty stomach. For a moment he thought he might vomit, but before that happened, the alcohol took hold of his nervous system and he settled into that familiar first phase of getting stoned.

"Oh, I am very glad that Larry is getting the stuff," he said, as he slid into the pile of old blankets that substituted for a bed and covers. "I am so relieved."

Possibly, if John had not been quite so comforted, the thought might have occurred that this was the first time Larry and Sam had bought drugs without using John's money. But that particular concern never entered John's mind.

The pipe was being passed once more. Was this the fifth crystal? John was very, very stoned, higher than he'd ever been. Though the source of the drug's financing still did not enter his mind, the quantity available had made an impression.

"We've never had so much crack before at one time," he thought. "Larry and Sam must have gotten a lot of money today from somewhere." John allowed even that tiny sense of discomfort to flee as soon as the stem was again placed in his hand.

"On the Upper East Side, Eighty-fifth and Madison, in a big steel building with a doorman," he said.

"You can get in that building, right John?" Larry asked, returning to the theme. "You got into that one on Park Avenue where you stole the vases. Should be easier to get into her house than say, her office. Don't you think?"

Larry's questions seemed very pointed and persistent for someone who also should have been very wasted. Yet he and Sam seemed lucid.

John took brief note of their condition but dismissed them both, as he preferred to concentrate on his own situation. The difficulty of processing and responding to Larry's questions was increasing. Finally, with superhuman effort, John made his mouth work.

"Yes," he said, "easier to get into her house, not her office." He paused in thought. "But, who is she? Why is she important? What do I do with her when I get inside?"

"One problem at a time, my friend," Sam responded to him. "We'll talk about those tomorrow night."

Just as the rising sun stroked the twenty-two floors of steel and glass at Madison and Eighty-fifth, Suzanne Rosewell awoke. She felt refreshed, alert and remembering her dreams clearly… very clearly.

Tossing aside the single, lightweight, designer sheet that was her summer blanket, Suzanne almost bounced out of the bed and directly to the window. She opened the tiny fresh air vents and encouraged as much of the morning breeze as the small slots would permit. Enjoy the smell while she could, was what she thought. Enjoy, before the day got too hot and the air too heavy to breath. Now she was regretting that the windows were not designed to open, though, originally, that was one of the reasons she'd chosen this apartment. Most of the time one didn't want New York air to reach the interior without being conditioned and filtered. The small opening at the bottom of each window was a city dweller's compromise with nature. Suzanne took a moment to wonder if her fabulous mood was the result of her dream… or was this really as glorious a morning as she felt?

> *The answer is irrelevant, your honor, as is the question. All that matters is this sense of confidence and well being. We ask the court to accept that feeling as defense exhibit number one.*
>
> *Defense against what? The charge that the earth is*

lacking the appropriate number of Righteous People? Isn't that a bit ridiculous, your honor? How could the District Attorney have the nerve to bring such a case into court? Even if this fantasy were a reality, the defense maintains that the entire issue is irrelevant. For the sake of argument, let us say that humanity has had all these Righteous People around for years and years. What use did we make of them? None. Throughout recorded history, and probably before, one part of the human race was always doing unspeakably horrible things to other parts... despite the presence of the Righteous Ones. Therefore, why concern ourselves if we are a bit short on the inventory?

Now, your honor, consider the possibility that after thousands of years of ineffectual history, nobody wants to be a Righteous Person anymore. Who would take such a useless, unappreciated position? Yes, your honor, I understand that my function is not to debate the justice of the law. My role is confined to proving that there is, in fact, a sufficient inventory. Whether the population chooses to draw on that supply, is not my business. Well, I reluctantly accept that limitation, and hope the court will take note of my exception and place my concern in the record, just in case I have to appeal.

I wonder where one finds a higher court. Sorry your honor. No disrespect was intended. Yes, I wish to make a motion in support of the goal as defined by this court. I offer the name of Joshua Wilson. Yes, your honor, I saw him in my dreams.

Whenever Suzanne permitted her rational mind to take charge, the entire thought process, the search, even the concern over the quest appeared foolish, and, frankly, a little insane. (*Could one be only a little insane?*) To avoid rationality, she was tapping the portion of her mind that allowed fantasy to rule unchallenged. Besides, the rational process was incapable of explaining the extraordinary sense of well being that floated over her like a winter comforter on a January evening, and from the moment she opened her eyes, she just felt so good! And, of course, there was the dream.

The same nocturnal drama repeated three times, each precisely like the other two, as though the repetition was performed specifically for emphasis. She was walking on Canal Street, but watching herself like a theater patron at a stage play. Those same footsteps were behind her once again. The Suzanne character appeared frightened. But suddenly, from out of nowhere, Joshua appeared, center stage, at the side of the terrified young woman. The footsteps fled. She could hear them fleeing from her seat in the otherwise empty audience, as did the fear on the face of the stage Suzanne. The two players walked together and approached a building that was a duplicate of the one that housed her law firm, just as they'd done in the real world. But in this cosmos Joshua grew taller. With each passing block, he became a larger man. The Suzanne character did not notice the change until the pair had arrived in her office. She was telling Joshua about the job opportunity in the mailroom when the man stood up and the dream-image Suzanne became aware of his increased height. At the very moment of awareness, the young Asian transformed into Elias Garner who silently displayed that famous Garner smile. Then the house lights would dim, the images disappearing in the darkness. When the lights came back on, the Suzanne character was back on Canal Street with the footsteps behind her and the fear once more etched on her face.

She went through three performances and failed to understand the obvious message. The answer came only when Suzanne woke. Joshua Wilson was a Righteous Person. She'd found number two. Only three more to go. This was a fact, she was certain. Well, almost certain.

Suzanne would have been more comfortable if only she could've talked with Garner. But she had no phone number, nowhere to leave a message. Still, he always contacted her whenever she needed him. Any moment now the phone would ring, and she would hear his voice just as she had in her car after her meal with Monty. Or the doorbell would sound and Eli's cheery voice would offer his congratulations for her success.

The phone didn't ring, not as she made coffee and not through breakfast. Nor was there a sound while she was in the shower, though she cranked the electronic bell up to its highest setting and had the water running as gently as possible. The silence continued while she dressed and groomed herself. The phone still had not rung up to the very moment when she was ready to leave for the office. Suzanne began to doubt. Her sense of well being had dissipated.

Actually Suzanne was on Elias Garner's mind, right up front. The agenda of his morning meeting was directly connected to the young attorney. Still, the thought of calling her had not occurred to him. Garner sat behind his desk, wearing a studious expression, totally absorbed in the pages of a document. His two aides sat on the other side of the shined wooden expanse, anxiously awaiting the boss' judgement of their work. After a seemingly endless period of silence, Garner lifted his eyes and pointed them toward the young man and woman sitting with their hands in their laps.

"The report is interesting," he said, "but this contains more about what you tried and failed than about the successes of your operation. Review for me, out loud, just what progress we have made in this effort."

The pair looked at each other and exchanged expressions concluding that the young woman should be the one to speak first.

"All we're getting are rumors, sir. However, we are getting the same rumors, over and over, and from so many diverse sources, that we are convinced we're on the right track," she said.

"And we do have a few hard facts, sir" the young man added. His was the voice that had been coming over Eli's speakerphone the day before. The intrusion was greeted by harsh, angry frowns from both Garner and the young woman.

"I'm sorry," he said with his eyes down. "I shouldn't have interrupted. Please continue Rebecca."

"Terry is right, sir," she said, still glaring at her contrite companion. "We have a few hard facts. Ms. Luckholt's favorite agent, the macho man, the one with no name...."

"The fellow who played the cop in Minnesota?"

"Yes, him. He's been in and out of New York City, virtually on a daily basis. With Ms. Rosewell living in New York, that alone wouldn't be unusual. However, at the same time, there's strange financial activity."

"Really?" She had earned Garner's undivided attention.

"There have been no out-of-order voucher requests to accounting but there have been a considerable number of transactions in Ms. Luckholt's petty cash account, far beyond what would be called normal at this time of the year. The pattern indicates that someone is spending a lot of money and they don't want to be noticed."

"Maybe No-name is in New York on legitimate corporation business," Garner didn't believe that to be the case, but he wanted to know if his young assistants had considered the possibility. This time Terry was permitted to answer.

"That's their mistake," he said, delighted to be on center stage. "If No-name was on real company business, there would be expenses charged, vouchers drawn, something financial to indicate that he was working. He's being so careful not to draw attention to himself that the very lack of a paper trail makes him the central focus of our whole investigation. We're convinced that whatever Luckholt's doing, No Name is the guy personally carrying out the plan."

"Not exactly," Garner said, "though you've almost got the answer.

No name is directing the operation, not carrying out any particular plan himself. Ms. Rosewell knows him, so he can't get too close to her. Therefore, he's got to be recruiting helpers."

"We reached that same conclusion and that's where these rumors come in, Boss," Rebecca continued. "There are rumblings about two really bad guys who live on the streets. At first these individuals seemed unconnected to Ms. Rosewell. We knew about them, just a couple of bad apples who, every once in a while, came to our attention because they're an annoyance to some of our departments. What made us sit up and take notice is that, all of sudden, they had money. They've always been broke but now they're spending big time."

"And we don't think this is a coincidence," Terry concluded, "not with No-name in town and thousands disappearing from Ms. Luckholt's petty cash account."

"Put somebody on a search right now," Elias Garner ordered. "Find these guys and watch them closely. Learn who they're hanging with. We can't let anything distract Suzanne. She has just one week left and four more people to find."

Terry and Rebecca looked at each other, confused.

"What's the matter?" Elias Garner asked. "Did you miss something or did I?"

"Well, sir," Rebecca answered. "We understood that there were only three left to find. We checked the computer this morning before we came to your office.

Eli Garner scratched his head and moved directly to the terminal resting on the window behind his desk. He powered the unit up, watched the screen light, tapped a few keys, squinted his eyes as the words appeared and then broke into his broad smile.

"Who's Joshua Wilson? No matter. Thank you for telling me. I guess I'm not paying proper attention. What a great way to start a Friday. I'd better call Suzanne right now."

CHAPTER EIGHTEEN

Suzanne's arrival at the office long before anyone else was more in response to the concerns of the senior partner than her own rekindled job interest. The hour was familiar, even on a Friday morning, but in the two weeks that had passed since her career had last held her undivided attention, Suzanne no longer felt the same way about the office, especially just after the crack of dawn. This particular revelation made Markam, Wilber, Kent & Todd's youngest partner more than just vaguely uncomfortable. She searched for something to disperse the uneasiness, something to help her feel like she still belonged in these classically decorated rooms.

Burt, the night guard, was readying to leave. Suzanne watched from a small distance as the man packed books, pads and pencils into a canvas backpack. Except for the uniform, he appeared much like an over-age student who had just finished cramming for an exam. Suzanne knew that she was long overdue at paying some personal attention to the usually anonymous worker.

"Good morning, Burt," she said with as much cheer as the hour and her disquiet would permit. "How are you today?" She recognized an air of exhaustion that literally floated around the man.

"Just fine, Ms. Rosewell," he answered, pleased with her seemingly sincere though uncharacteristic attention. "It's been quiet, just like the night should be. Had a chance to get some studying done."

"Studying?"

"Yes, I'm taking a couple of college courses in literature."

"Oh, something to do with all those spare hours," she said sarcastically, regretting the tone of her voice the moment she used it.

"God wouldn't have given me a mind if he hadn't intended for me to learn," he said with just a hint of annoyance.

"I'm sorry, Burt. I didn't mean to sound so superior. I know how little time you have in your life and I'm surprised you found some for schooling. I think it's great!"

Burt didn't respond and she wondered if her apology sounded condescending. The only way out was to change the subject.

"Are you going uptown now?" she asked.

"Yes, Ms. Rosewell. If I hurry, I have just enough time for a quick change of clothes and a cup of coffee with the wife."

"Don't let me keep you then."

"Thank you, Ms. Rosewell." He moved toward the elevator.

"And Burt," she half-shouted as the big man walked away.

"Yes, ma'am?" He turned in anticipation.

"Please call me Suzanne."

"Oh, I don't know if I can do that," he said looking very ill at ease.

"Sure you can," she responded. "If you don't, then I will just have to call you by your last name."

"You don't know my last name," he said with a broad grin.

"I'll find out from personnel."

"OK then, Suzanne." The tired lines under his eyes faded just a bit as he held the smile. "I hope you have a prosperous day."

The elevator arrived and he stepped aboard. As the doors closed behind him, she pondered on his unusual parting statement.

"What events," she thought, "might constitute a prosperous day?" The image of Mr. Spock from Star Trek appeared in her mind, Leonard Nimoy facing the camera, hand in the air, fingers apart, reciting the traditional Vulcan phrase "Live long and prosper." She remembered reading somewhere that the hand sign had been adopted from Jewish ritual. The thought sent her mentally back to the quest.

"Mr. Spock," she mused as she navigated the empty corridors

leading to her office, "now there was one righteous man." She turned back, glancing briefly at the elevator door and her thoughts returned to Burt, who, by now, was on the street and nearing the subway.

The private line message light was blinking and the voice that came through the speaker both inspired and chilled her in the very same breath.

"Congratulations, Suzanne," Elias Garner's distinct articulation echoed through the quiet office. "Two down and three to go. I want you to enjoy your success but I also want you to be very careful. The closer you get, the more dangerous Luckholt becomes. Remember, she can't hurt you as long as you 'keep the faith.' But staying faithful to the cause may be the most demanding task you will face in the next few days. Besides, even if you are able to muster all the trust that's available in heaven and on earth, you must still be careful to avoid doing anything foolish. Watch what goes on behind you. I will call again soon."

Suzanne dropped into her chair and reached for the cigarette pack that was no longer there.

John Brown had spent the night without sleep. His biological machine, the body that he thought of as no more than a repository for all those souls, had been fueled for hours by a combination of cocaine, alcohol and adrenaline. The latter was produced by the strength of his conviction that he and the woman on the subway were destined to meet, and soon.

The events of the night had convinced him, at least for a while, that the two drugs he was ingesting were being drawn from an endless supply. There had never before been such a quantity of crack and wine in the abandoned store. But at dawn the bottles and the pipes were finally empty. His companions were unconscious, passed out maybe. John was wide awake, his nervous system electrified by the crack, his mind flying at such a heightened state that he found the state of sleep shared by both of his companions to be completely incredible.

John never considered that their cocaine intake had been minimal. In part because he couldn't conceive anyone ever finding a reason strong enough to pass by the pipe. He was also far too excited and too stoned to even notice. Instead he credited his upright posture to the exhilaration felt by all the souls. They gave him strength and they were more than ready for action.

John knew that he dare not disappoint his collective. Though he was aware of his human shell's need for food, he still spent his last few coins on several cups of black coffee at the corner luncheonette in an attempt to force his mind to focus. Then he set out for Eighty-fifth Street. Suzanne and John missed meeting each other in the Upper East Side subway station by something less than five minutes.

As the hour was still quite early, John wrongly assumed the woman of his obsession would not yet have left her apartment. She might even still be in bed. His twisted, distorted and drugged thought process could handle only one scenario at a time, so the probability that someone who labored late into the night, might also leave for the office early in the morning did not receive any attention. John stopped across from the building and sat in a doorway watching the residents leave for their daily labor.

The evidence playing out before his eyes told him that most of the building's occupants were employed during the day. Men and woman came down to the lobby together, both dressed in business suits. Often they would kiss and go in opposite directions. Sometimes they came down with children, but then, almost always in the company of some dark-skinned woman who would take charge of the little ones while the parents disappeared into commerce. John wondered if the women of color were slaves. Possibly he was here to repeat history and try to free them. The man sat for almost half an hour, staring at the Upper East Side play performed in the lobby across the street. He guessed at his purpose but had no thought as to what he should do next.

"Hey, fella', how are ya'?" The voice came from a very tall, exceptionally muscular policeman who stopped directly in front of him. The bulk of the man frightened John.

"I wasn't doing anything wrong, officer. Just sitting here."

"Did I say you were doing anything wrong?" the cop answered in a very unpolice-like voice. "I wanted to know if you needed some help."

"Help, what kind of help?" John was even more nervous. He had learned on the streets how to deal with official hostility, but he had no idea how to handle a lawman who sounded like a social worker.

"You look like you could use a meal, maybe a shower, even a fresh change of clothes. You're a good looking fellow. If you had all those things, except for your hair, a guy wouldn't even notice how out of place you are in this neighborhood." John had an ambiguous feeling that the policeman was offering more than friendly advice.

"Yeah… I could use some food… and a shower," John said, weighing his words carefully. He wished he could make his brain work faster.

"I thought so," the cop said. "Turn left at the next corner and go three blocks. You'll see a big church. In the back they have a soup kitchen and showers. You can eat and clean up. They have used clothing, too. Get rid of those rags and see if you can find a hat to cover your hair." The last sentence was spoken like an order.

John stood up. He didn't want to leave his observation post, but he was fearful of not obeying the patrolman's suggestions. If he were arrested, he'd never accomplish his mission, whatever it was. Besides, the man proposed a good plan. Why not try to blend in a little? And with the cocaine rapidly wearing off, some food in his stomach wouldn't hurt.

"Thanks, officer," he said, "I'll do that."

"Good, good," the cop responded. "Here, take this envelope. The people in the neighborhood took up a collection. You know, to help out folks like you, people with no home of their own. They asked me, and the other beat cops, to sort of administer the fund. I'll bet you could use a couple of bucks." He handed John a rather thick white envelope.

"Probably filled with literature from A.A. or some drug treatment place," he thought to himself. Out loud, though, he expressed only his thanks.

"Don't mention it," the cop returned to the center of the sidewalk and stood unmoving while he watched John walk to the corner and go left. Once safe from the officer's stare, John tore open the envelope. The package contained fifteen twenty-dollar bills.

"Son of a bitch," John Brown said, speaking to some of the other souls. "The guy screwed up and gave us too much money." He increased his pace, afraid the policeman might become aware of his error and chase after him. His concern was unnecessary. The cop was walking rapidly in the opposite direction. Also unaware that Suzanne had left long ago for the office, the officer was leaving the area simply because he didn't want to risk running into her. The woman might not recognize him in the uniform of New York's finest, but if she mentally superimposed the outfit of a Minnesota State Trooper, there was no doubt she'd recall their first encounter.

John located the church and the soup kitchen, but spent a while on the sidewalk as he contemplated passing the place by. After all, as soon as the cop discovered his mistake, he would probably go directly to the shelter. For the entire past three blocks, John had expected to feel a hand on his shoulder at any moment. The restraining touch never came. Besides, the idea of food, a shower, new clothes, especially a hat, sounded good. The money was not important. His real reason for being on the Upper East Side had nothing to do with the stroke of good luck that brought him the three hundred dollars. Even if he had to return part of the cash, he was still way ahead. So... he went inside.

Within an hour, John Brown was back on the street feeling and looking like a new man, or, at least, another man. The nice ladies inside fed him with oatmeal, toast and lots of coffee and still the policeman had not appeared. Nor had the law arrived while John showered, shaved and picked out clothing from the selection of used items donated by neighborhood people. He chose a business suit, slightly worn at the cuffs but still in good shape. The ladies helped him find a tie to match. The black oxfords needed new soles and heels, but they fit pretty well, and the white shirt had a tear in the back but it was well hidden by the suit jacket.

John left the church and rapidly put two blocks of distance between himself and the shelter. Comfortable with the margin of safety, he paused and studied his image in the plate glass of a store window. John stared hard at his appearance, focusing especially on the way he looked from the neck down. The picture seemed to raise a piece of an old memory, one that faded very quickly as he told himself that this was no time for extraneous thoughts. He had to find a hat and nothing in the pile of used clothing had been appropriate.

The very moment he stopped admiring himself he found the solution to his problem. John had been checking his reflection in the window of a western wear shop. Once he focused past his own image, he saw exactly what he needed. The newly dressed gentleman checked to see that the thick envelope was still in the breast pocket of his recently obtained suit jacket, then walked through the door as though doing so was the most natural of actions.

"Can I help you, sir?" a pretty young woman asked him immediately after he passed the entrance. If she considered his appearance strange, she gave no indication. John pointed to the broad-brimmed, Texas hat in the window.

"Yes, sir," she said and disappeared through a curtain behind the counter, emerging a few moments later burdened by three boxes. Each contained a hat in his exact size, all matching the one in the window except in a variety of colors.

"Which do you think goes best with my suit?" he managed to ask.

"The gray one," she responded, without hesitation as she handed the hat to him. He placed the molded felt garment on his head and looked in the mirror. Most of his dreads still stuck out from under the brim, but he appeared almost respectable, though, granted, a bit strange. Once more he glanced at his body below his neck and the old memory stirred again. This time he felt almost like he knew what he was trying to recall.

"I'll take this one," he said, leaving the hat on his head and reaching for his money.

"Cash or charge?" she asked.

"Uh, cash," he answered, passing her the entire envelope. This time she responded with a questioning look. The expression passed as she thumbed through the twenty-dollar bills.

"One hundred and twenty-eight seventy-five, with tax," the saleswoman said, making change from the register and putting the excess back into the envelope, accompanied by a receipt. She passed the package back to him across the counter. "Would you like me to put the hat in a box?"

"No, this is part of my outfit now," he declared and turned toward the exit.

"Excuse me, sir," she said. John Brown froze in his tracks, fearing that the woman was about to confront him with the information declaring she'd finally figured out that he didn't belong in this neighborhood. "Are you a musician by any chance?"

"Why do you ask?"

"You look familiar, like one of those new country rock performers that are so popular now. I mean, with your hair and all." John worked to force his brain into gear.

"Good guess," he said, trying hard to project a friendly smile. He must have succeeded because she grinned back, more a fawning fan than the efficient sales person she had been. He was sure she was going to ask another question, probably his name and then request his autograph. John stole her chance by leaving the store as quickly as he could.

"A country rock musician," he thought as he directed himself back toward the woman's building. "That's what I am, at least for now." Since many of his souls were from the South, he was sure he could draw on one of them for the accent needed to expand that particular charade.

He walked once past the building on the other side of the street. The doorman, standing outside and enjoying the morning sunshine, paid no more attention to him than to anyone else wandering Madison Avenue. A relatively well dressed white man, in a business suit and a cowboy hat, with a Rastafarian hairstyle just wasn't *that* unusual in New York. John decided to try a pass on the very sidewalk where the doorman stood.

The trip was uneventful. He nodded at the uniformed man and Carlos nodded back, but John's joy was short-lived. He was only inches past the door when he realized how strange his behavior would appear if he now tried to turn back and enter the building. Something had to be done to avoid suspicion.

John's action was completely unconscious. He always simply assumed that one of the souls inside him came to his rescue and took over his behavior. John's hand went into his jacket pocket and he withdrew the envelope. Staring at the white paper, as though he were reading written directions, John stopped, turned with a grand flourish and walked back to the front door of his quarry's home.

"I almost missed the place, wasn't watching the numbers," he said to Carlos, effecting a cowboy drawl.

"Yes, sir. Can I help you sir?"

"Oh yes, I have an appointment with the dentist. I've never seen him before. Dr...?"

"Dr. Richardson or Dr. Bernstein?"

"Damn, I don't remember. I'm from out of town and a friend of mine referred me." The DDS sign in the window of one of the ground floor apartments had been his inspiration, but now he was taking a risk. "All I know is that my friend said that the dentist had an interior entrance, that you had to go through the lobby."

"That's Dr. Bernstein," Carlos said without any distrust in his voice. "I'll ring the office. What is your name, sir?"

"Rothman. Donald Rothman," John answered after an imperceptible hesitation. *Where had he gotten that name?* Carlos pressed the intercom button.

"There is a Mr. Donald Rothman here for his appointment," the doorman said to the speaker right after the female voice responded.

"Donald Rothman?" she answered, the question mark flowing from the device.

"Yes, ma'am," John called out in near perfect Texas. "I spoke to your answering device last night about this toothache. Your patient, Mr. Schwartz, told me to call you." He figured they had to treat at least one person by that name.

"Yes, of course," she said, "but I am afraid that the answering service didn't pass on your message. Please come in and we'll try to help."

Carlos pressed the buzzer and the keeper of a hundred dead souls walked through the once secure portal.

"Down the hall to your left," the doorman said. "There's a sign on the wall." John waved in acknowledgment and moved as directed.

The medical authorities considered John Brown crazy, but no one ever thought him dumb. The native intelligence that came with the mind of Donald Rothman was enhanced by the street survival skills developed by John Brown and company. He knew that if he simply disappeared into the interior of the building, he would only have a few minutes before the dentist's receptionist called to check on his whereabouts. Then the doorman would look for him. He might even call the police. John's only option was to literally visit the dentist. He stepped into Dr. Bill Bernstein's office and was greeted by a pleasant, older woman, dressed in nurse's whites.

"Mr. Rothman," she said to him, "I am terribly sorry but the service does not seem to have your message. You know these night operators. You just can't get competent help in this city. Anyway, Dr. Bernstein is backed-up with regular patients trying to get their dental work completed before they go to the office. If you can wait, we can accommodate you in an hour."

"Oh, that'd be just fine. But I think I'll go get myself a cup of coffee and come back. Would that be alright?"

"Certainly, sir. I will put you down in the book."

She smiled and started to write. He smiled and backed out the door. Now he had at least an hour, probably more. He considered the possibility that his failure to return would not even be noticed. He was sure that lots of patients, especially brand new ones, broke their appointments. Chances were that Mr. Donald Rothman had as much time as he needed. *(Why did that name sound so familiar?)* But, what to do with that time?

The white envelope was still in his hand and as he stood in the hallway outside the dentist's office, he moved to return it to his pocket. That was when he noticed that there really was something written on the back. In pencil, just a few characters scrawled in the center of the flap, almost obliterated when he tore open the envelope, 22D. Was this an apartment number? And, if so, was the number connected to his woman of the subway? John accepted the information as a sign from the spirits and decided to find out where following this lead would take him.

To avoid passing through the doorman's field of vision and use the lobby elevators, John climbed the fire stairs to the second floor and called the elevator from there. The car arrived rapidly and just as rapidly carried him up to his destination.

Like the second floor, the hallway of 22 was empty. John imagined that all the hallways were empty, confirming what he thought he'd learned by watching so many folks go off to work earlier… that almost no one was home in the entire building. Number 22D was right in the center of the floor. The name on the bell read "Suzanne Rosewell."

Is that her name? Could this be the home of the woman from the subway, the one who works in the tall building downtown? How is he to know? Something inside him screams at his doubt, orders him to believe this is truly the right place. But a shadow of uncertainty still haunts him and, to make matters a bit worse, the brief period of clear, lucid thinking is fading away.

Cocaine and caffeine are both stimulants but neither is capable of providing a body with anything like true energy. When their effects wear off, a physical being, even one with a hundred souls, is forced to pay heavily for the privilege of having obtained temporary chemically created potency. Drug users refer to this sudden end of elation as "crashing." Anyone who has gone through the experience knows that the term is very accurate. The effects of the cocaine finally were depleted and John started to fall toward a very heavy crash. He was even beginning to forget the name he'd used in the lobby.

John's mental collapse could be favorably compared to the destruction of skyscrapers in an earthquake disaster movie. With the initial rumblings, the very tip, usually only the decorative stonework, tumbles to the street and shatters, a warning of what is still to come. The earth shake intensifies until the middle section of the building just disintegrates withdrawing support for the upper floors. They hang in the air for a second, as though flaunting gravity, only to then fall and merge into the growing pile of rubble.

Was this the right woman? And if she is so, what was he to do with her? What was to be their destiny together?

John didn't know what else to do. There was little time before all the support for his upper floors would be gone. He simply rang the doorbell. No response. He was about to try once more when the elevator doors opened.

Not knowing if he should run or hide and if to hide, where, John Brown did what most people do in a moment of indecision. He did nothing and simply stared as a middle-aged Latina stepped off the elevator. He continued to watch as she eyed him with suspicion but without fear even though he was a lone, strange man in an empty hallway. The woman walked boldly to the door of the apartment across from Suzanne's.

"Ms. Rosewell is not home. She works in the day," she said with firmness in her voice.

"Oh, thank you," John answered, trying to hold the middle of the building together. "I'm the new neighbor *(Why did he say that?)* and I wanted to borrow some floor wax."

"Floor wax?" she laughed, "Nobody in the building uses that stuff. All the apartments have no-wax floors. Did you just move into 21A?" She pointed with her chin toward the staircase as though to tell him that she knew his apartment was one flight below.

"Yes, that's right," John answered, obscurely aware that he might be stepping into a trap.

Apparently not.

"You men are all so helpless about cleaning, or at least you pretend to be. You should have a woman clean for you. I can give you names but you can't hire me. I'm doing too many apartments in this building already."

"Thank you," he answered. "Please leave the names with Ms.

Rosewell. She's a friend of mine and I'll get them from her."

The woman had the door of the apartment open and was moving her equipment inside. Had she not been so distracted by her work, she might have noticed that the man in the hallway was reading his "friend's" name directly off the plate over the doorbell. But her attention was elsewhere.

"Fine," she said, closing the door. John was glad to be rid of her. His limbs were growing weaker as the stimulant effect of the cocaine and the adrenaline of the adventure both rapidly dissipated. John's brain kept drifting toward the precipice of sleep. He discovered himself semi-consciously retreating to the staircase.

John Brown worked hard to develop a plan. Maybe that woman would enter Suzanne Rosewell's apartment next. She probably had her own key. That might create the opportunity for John to find a way to the other side of his quarry's steel door.

He sat down on the stairs, trying to focus one ear toward any sound that might come from the twenty-second floor. John planned to have the noises tell him when the woman finished her work in the first apartment and was about to enter another. The other ear was directed toward the staircase to detect anyone who might choose to approach him, on purpose or by accident, by that route. John focused, but his intense attention to the most minute of vibrations lasted less than a minute before he fell asleep.

The reason he woke about an hour later was unclear. All he knew for sure was that he was jolted out of a deep sleep. The image in his dreams of a tall, muscular man, standing in the hallway, trying to shake him to consciousness remained in his mind. But when he opened his eyes, John found himself alone in the staircase, except for his usual chorus of dead-soul companions.

There were soft but steady noises coming from the 22nd floor so he opened the fire door and peeked down the corridor. The woman was moving from 22H into the apartment occupied by Suzanne Rosewell. Both doors were wide open and she was in the process of shifting a mountain of cleaning equipment from one side to the other. Her movements were rapid, too fast for John to sneak in between trips. Still, he focused his attention and poised his body, ready for any opportunity that might arise. The phone rang in 22H and the cleaning woman crossed from Suzanne's apartment to respond.

John had simply not expected the maid to stop and pick up the telephone. He'd assumed that she'd let the always present answering machine take the call. A few seconds elapsed before he became aware of his good fortune. Dancing gently down the hall to the buzzing tune of the woman's barely audible telephone voice, prepared to run and hide if the music stopped, John's luck held. He slipped into Suzanne's open door and hid in her coat closet. As he closed the door behind him, he silently celebrated the circumstances provided to him by fate.

There was no reason the woman would have for entering this closet, he thought. But just in case, John curled up in a corner behind a collection of long, heavy winter coats. Someone opening the door would probably not even see him. His precaution was unnecessary. A few moments later, he heard the vacuum cleaner working on the rug in the bedroom and the steady sound of the electric motor lulled John back to sleep.

He didn't know how long he'd slept or how he was awakened. Maybe the maid slammed the outer door when she was leaving and jarred him into consciousness. He didn't know and he didn't care. He'd achieved his purpose and was alone in the home of the woman, he was now sure, that he'd followed downtown. John had no objective evidence to support this assumption, but every one of the souls inside howled that he was right. All he had to do was wait until she arrived. And hope the souls would tell him what he had to do then.

He searched the rooms carefully without any clear idea as to why and then slowly opened the outer door to double check that the hallway was still empty. At that moment, Suzanne's phone rang.

John slammed the door and stood like a statue just inside the threshold. He froze with the irrational fear that, at any moment, someone would come running from one of the empty rooms to answer the call. Suzanne's machine picked up on the fourth ring and John relaxed into the sound of her tape-recorded voice. The caller left no message and the apartment returned to silence. John moved away from the door without fully closing it and without resetting the deadbolt. As one who often slept in the open, without doors or locks to protect him, John Brown, New York City Street person, never gave the matter a second thought. He just walked away from the door and unknowingly left the apartment unlocked.

Still aware that his target worked late and realizing that the clock had not yet reached eleven a.m., John decided that he could now rest in safety. The man knew he had to sleep, to restore his body to some semblance of strength before she returned. Maybe too, in slumber, his souls would finally tell him what he had to do when he and the woman finally met face to face. Often they chose to tell him the most important things when he slept.

John stretched across Suzanne's bed, detecting a hint of her perfume on the pillows. He tried to imagine her surprise when she found him in her most private and intimate sanctuary.

In the moments before he dozed off, John saw the book on the nightstand by the answering machine. ***Jewish Legends and Folk Tales, a collection by Elias Abromowitz,*** the cover read. Again, a familiar feeling stirred as he read the title, just like the tingle he felt when he used that made-up name, what was that… Donald Rothman? Maybe one of his souls was Jewish. Maybe a dead slave of the Pharaoh slipped inside him. Anything was possible. John shrugged his shoulders as the fleeting familiarity disappeared and, absorbing the sense of Suzanne's body from the bed, he fell into a deep sleep.

At 2:30 in the afternoon, Dr. Bill Bernstein's receptionist finally found time to go out to lunch. As was her habit, she stopped to ask Carlos if he wanted anything from the deli.

"Oh, no thanks, Ruth," he answered. "I had them deliver something an hour ago."

"OK, then, but do me a favor. If that Mr. Rothman comes back, tell him he's too late. There's no time left in the doctor's schedule."

"Come back?" Carlos asked, "I don't think I ever saw him leave. I frankly forgot all about him."

"Well, maybe he went out one of the back doors."

"No, we put on those fire alarms, remember. The back doors are only for emergencies now. If someone uses one of them, an alarm goes off."

"No big deal," Ruth said, "the guy probably left while you were doing something else. But if he comes back, tell him to call for an appointment."

"How long was he in your office?"

"Oh, only about two minutes. Said he would go for coffee and come back in an hour." The receptionist stepped out on to the street.

Carlos was distressed. Despite Ruth's lack of concern, he was certain he hadn't left the front door, not for a single moment, during the entire hour after the man with the braids had arrived. He had no doubt that he'd not seen the strange fellow with the Texas accent leave.

Carlos knew he could call the new security agency contracted by the building's owners. They would help, but they would also be very critical since several hours had passed since the man had entered the building. It was part of Carlos' job to have noticed the man's failure to exit much sooner. Security was a big issue in this building.

On the other hand, he would be in real trouble if the guy did something, robbed an apartment, or God forbid, hurt someone and

Carlos had failed to report his suspicions.

There seemed to be no choice. Even if he was going to be criticized, he had to call the security people. Better late than never, Carlos hoped.

Ten armed and uniformed officers arrived within fifteen minutes. They were directed by a female supervisor and her young male assistant, both of whom were impeccably dressed in a manner more suited to fancy corporate executives than to security personnel.

"Floor to floor search," the supervisor said to her troops. "Carlos will give you the names and apartment numbers of the people who are normally home during the day. Be gentle but firm when working near those apartments. Check all the doors. Make sure they are double-locked. You can feel if the dead bolt's in place when you turn the handle. Then knock hard and listen carefully for noises. If anyone finds a sign of forced entry, call-in right away. Don't do anything stupid. Squad "A" goes to the penthouse floor and works their way down. The rest of you start on the second floor and work up. This level is all business and professional offices. Terry and I will handle them ourselves. Report in as you finish each floor. Go!" They went.

For private security guards, these men were well trained. The search proceeded quickly and efficiently, but not nearly as unobtrusively as Carlos had hoped. Though very few residents were at home, a number of live-in babysitters and other domestic helpers were present in the building. When these people noticed the halls filling with armed guards, they immediately called their employers who responded by making calls of their own.

Some dialed Carlos directly, tying up his lobby phone with one call after another. Still, he managed to convince these people that it was simply a safety precaution and everything was, probably, perfectly all right. Others spoke directly to building management and those calls would most likely get him in trouble with the bosses. Carlos had only one chance in three to come out on top.

If the guy had already committed a crime and fled, that was bad, the worst. The owners would really be mad at him for waiting so long to turn in the alarm. If the guards found no guy and no crime, his supervisor still might be all over his back for starting a panic, but that wouldn't be nearly as bad. However, if they caught the joker, in the act, or just hanging out, Carlos could be a hero. He didn't care for the odds, but there was no time to think and his lobby phone kept ringing.

The upper search team had quickly cleared the penthouse level as well as the two floors below. The lower team was already on the fourth floor and so far nothing seemed to be out of order. They had confronted a couple of residents but mostly they found maids and babysitters, all of whom quickly contacted their employers. Carlos was constantly on the phone as he listened with one ear to the reports that were being radioed down to the supervisors. The upper team was just beginning to examine the twenty-second floor. The two young people in the fancy outfits seemed to be especially concerned about this part of the search.

"Rebecca, should we put extra people on twenty-two?" Carlos listened as the one called Terry asked his boss.

"I don't think so," he heard her respond, "that would be a bit too obvious. I think the five guys that are up there should be enough." Then she radioed to the upper team and ordered them to report back on an apartment-by-apartment basis.

Unfortunately, private security guards, even those trained and licensed to carry firearms, are not really New York City policemen, even though they often wish they were. Sometimes they even harbor secret desires to be heroes and sometimes those urges affect their judgement. Once in a while, a security guard or two can be found who resent being supervised by a young woman. All of those "sometimes" factors were present, on that particular July day, in Mr. Carlan Willright, who, as luck would have it, was the one to detect the open apartment door belonging to Suzanne Rosewell.

Instead of reporting his discovery and waiting for instructions or alerting his comrades who were inspecting the other doors on the 22nd floor, Carlan drew his weapon and entered alone, against all orders but just as he'd seen other "heroes" do on television.

He thought he'd entered quietly. His thirty-eight police special led the way and when he found the interior in perfect order, with no visible evidence of a break-in, Carlan was surprised. A man with more training might have become extra cautious but Carlan relaxed, thinking he had only found a door accidentally left ajar.

John Brown heard the footsteps. Assuming that his quarry had arrived, the man of a hundred souls quietly left the woman's bed and hid behind her bedroom door. From his vantage point, John saw the tall, uniformed man slowing inspecting the kitchen, the pistol pointed forward.

John Brown was not afraid. In his previous life he'd led a slave revolt against the United States Army. He'd bravely faced the gallows and died with courage and honor. A single armed man did not disturb him in the slightest. When Carlan's back was toward the bedroom, John left his hiding place, picked up a vase from a table in the hallway and brought the heavy china piece down on the security guard's head. The vase shattered and the big man in the blue green uniform folded onto the floor. John retrieved Carlan's thirty-eight and headed for the hallway.

The sound of the breaking vase alerted the other four security guards to their comrade's disappearance. They gathered at Suzanne's apartment door to investigate. Since they'd heard no other strange noises, and since Carlan had not called in an alarm, none of them really thought anything was wrong. In their minds, they had no reason to draw their own weapons. Suddenly the door flew open and the four men found themselves facing the raw barrel of a thirty-eight.

"Don't move," John shouted, making full use of the booming preacher's voice for which he'd become famous in the days before he was hanged. "Hands up high and against the wall." The men obeyed.

On by one, he disarmed the security guards, piling their pistols and their portable radios on the floor.

"Get inside," he shouted, "and stay there. I'm going to stay in this hall and the first person to poke his head out will be wearing a bullet." The men rushed inside Suzanne's apartment and John closed the door behind them. Pausing only for a moment to collect one more pistol and to pick up a radio, he ran toward the stairs. Inside the apartment, one of the other disarmed guards was dialing 911.

After phoning for the police, the men in Suzanne's place tried to call Carlos but the doorman's constantly busy line made that impossible. After wasting precious minutes, one of them finally remembered the intercom system and shouted the events of the past few moments to the lobby. His voice was nearly drowned out by the sound of approaching sirens. As an ambulance and the first police car pulled up to the front door, the emergency alarm sounded. Someone had just passed through a fire exit.

The confusion in the lobby was so intense that a full thirty seconds elapsed before Carlos was able to accurately communicate the meaning of the alarm bell. New York's Finest moved immediately to the alley behind the building where they found no one. Five minutes later, after combining information gathered from the men on the 22nd floor with facts provided by Carlos, the NYPD broadcast a description of the intruder that included the warning, "known to be armed and assumed to be dangerous."

John Brown tucked the two thirty-eight caliber police specials invisibly under his jacket as he boarded the downtown express train at about the same time Carlos was trying to call Suzanne Rosewell's office.

CHAPTER NINETEEN

Suzanne's face went chalky. The client sitting across the desk watched the color fade from her complexion. Rosy changed to pale pink and pale pink to ivory and finally to bed sheet white as though there were no pigment at all remaining in her skin. Then her hands began to shake. Once more, she reached for the formerly ever-present package of cigarettes and finding the spot empty, considered sending Margaret out to buy a replacement. She probably would have done just that if only the police captain on the telephone had offered her a moment of silence. Though the information he was relating was very frightening, Suzanne still found herself strangely amused with the man's ability to convey data in one apparently endless sentence.

"The intruder seems to have entered the premises fairly early in the morning and without any forced entry, probably as a result of sneaking in during the time the maid was cleaning the apartment, as she reports having seen a man who fits the description in the hallway…." The voice withered from Suzanne's consciousness to become only an electronic drone buzzing in her ear. S*omeone inside her apartment … doors unlocked.* Her thoughts focused on Elias Garner's warning, *avoid doing anything foolish, watch what goes on behind you.* How could she have avoided this? What thing might she have done that could count as foolish?

"Ms. Rosewell, are you there?"

The voice brought her back to the office.

"Oh, I'm sorry Captain. This news is just so upsetting that I am finding it hard to concentrate. Please repeat that last part."

"I asked how long before you can get away and inspect the

apartment, to let us know if anything is missing?"

"I will come right now... uh... be there within half-an-hour."

Though her hands were still trembling and the desire for a cigarette had increased geometrically, Suzanne's mind was, oddly enough, able to clearly focus on what she had to do. The client was more than sympathetic.

"Terrible thing when your apartment is robbed. I've had the experience. You go right ahead, Suzanne. I've got other business in this part of town. I'll be back later this afternoon and I'll check in with your secretary, make an appointment for tomorrow... have a feeling you won't be back in the office today. When they broke into my place, the police kept me tied up forever with silly questions. Never found any of my stuff, either."

"Try to clear my calendar for the rest of the day," Suzanne instructed Margaret. "I'll get back as quickly as I can but I don't know how long this will take."

"You have a very heavy schedule today. I was trying to make up for the time you were away. Maybe, you'd better carry your mobile," Margaret said, clearly reluctant to make the suggestion. There was good reason.

"I hate that thing. You know I hate that thing." Suzanne's reaction was sudden and severe. "That device makes me feel like I'm on an electronic leash. Why do you really think I need to carry that stupid little box? I don't even use the one in my car."

"You know that I wouldn't make the suggestion unless I thought it was necessary. I may have to change some of your meetings from our office to the client's. I'll try not to have to call you and I promise, I won't tell anyone that you're wired to your desk."

"I'll know," the client said jokingly, but the expression on Suzanne's face made him wish he had not spoken at all. "Only kidding. I won't say a word. That thing really bothers you, huh?"

"I know I'm being silly, the new millennium and all," Suzanne responded, beginning to calm down, "but I've just got a hang-up about cell phones. The firm issues one to every partner and to each associate, even to some of the more important secretaries. We're supposed to carry the stupid thing with us all the time, even in the building. I'll admit that the thing makes locating people very easy. But it makes me feel like a dog on a leash. Still, I guess Margaret's right."

Suzanne reached into the lower drawer of her desk and withdrew a small black phone designed to clip onto a belt. She switched the device on, noted the positive response of the automatic battery tester, and put it in her purse. Margaret made sure the batteries were always well charged.

With one last apology to the client, Suzanne departed. Aside from the expected anxiety over the police at her apartment, she would not have described herself as exceptionally distressed when she headed up the hallway, down the elevator to the street and toward the subway. But when Suzanne reached the stairway that would take her below the sidewalk to the dark and dirty station, the young attorney paused.

Without doubt, the subway was the fastest means of transportation in New York City, and the only one usually immune to traffic jams, impromptu political demonstrations, street repairs and the other hazards that made moving around the island of Manhattan so difficult. That's why Suzanne, along with tens of thousands of others, used the ancient system every day, particularly when fast service was needed.

But at the top of the stairs, Suzanne's emotional state suddenly changed. A new sense of apprehension invaded her and she could not make her foot take the initial step down the staircase. Hers was a strange feeling, unfocused, far from specific. She was filled with a force that seemed to be projected into her body from outside. The sensation was similar to the one she experienced when first entering the Wooden Horn Case. Similar, but not the same.

At that time Suzanne had been nearly overwhelmed, terrified, unable to cope with an unfamiliar sensation. Now she was feeling something quite different, a gentle fear that evoked caution, not terror. This strange sensation found its origin in a friendly place before invading her mind. Emotionally she was "looking over her shoulder," though she couldn't quite bring herself to physically turn her head.

But neither could she bring herself to terms with being underground. Though her mind told her that giving in to the feeling was foolish and that the subway was her best transportation option, Suzanne Rosewell stopped, turned suddenly toward the street, and waved down a passing cab. She gave the driver her Upper East Side home address.

"Please hurry," she literally shouted through the plastic security shield, "This is an emergency."

"Yes, ma'am," the driver responded, knowing that emergency rides usually meant good tips.

As Suzanne paused, for that very brief moment, at the top of the subway stairs, John Brown stepped back into the shadows of the building.

"Go," he said to himself as though he were instructing her. "Go down the steps." He focused all the psychic power of all his souls on the command. The man was energized.

John's close-call escape from the apartment had not disturbed him at all, or deflected him the slightest from his cause. He was grateful for what had happened. The legions of his opposition *(whatever or whoever they were)* had come out in force and they would not have done so unless he were following the right track. And he defeated them, and came away, uncaptured, with two pistols and a portable radio. Now he knew that this was the right woman and the right house.

But more importantly, he came away with the knowledge that this person, this Suzanne Rosewell, had to die. That's why the spirits had given him the guns. In his life incarnation before becoming John Brown, he'd never even fired a pistol. But as the leader of the slave rebellion, he certainly knew how to shoot. Still, John would have to allow for the fact that the knowledge was more than a century old and had not been recently tested.

Once he escaped, rather easily, from the building, John knew he had to go immediately downtown, be there when Suzanne came out of the office, when she went for food, or for coffee or an appointment, and he could get close to her and use one of the thirty-eight police specials tucked into his belt, hidden under the suit jacket. He was prepared to wait all day, and her appearance on the street only moments after he got off the subway was a pleasant surprise. John followed Suzanne, less than half a block behind her.

The leader of the slave rebellion wanted desperately to shoot the woman, but he knew enough not to do the deed in the open, not on a crowded street. After all, her death was not the end of his destiny, just a key to the future. He couldn't allow himself to be locked away in prison and be unable to fulfill his true mission, whatever it was to become. But if he could get her in an isolated place, away from other people, he could escape capture. The subway would be the perfect place to carry out the act. Spirits be praised. That's just where she was heading.

He even knew the staircase she was using, long and narrow, with an often empty hallway at the base, seventy-five or a hundred feet of tunnel before reaching the token booth. The corridor was "protected" by a security camera connected, John presumed, to the Transit Police. That didn't matter. He would pull his hat down over his face, shoot the woman from behind and flee. Once back among those who lived in vacant stores and on the city streets, the police would never find him. He would shed the business suit and they'd never be able to identify him. John carefully tucked his dreads under the ten-gallon hat so even that part of his distinctive description would not show up on videotape.

Then the keeper of the souls moved forward to open the locked door of his destiny.

That was when the woman paused. There was a brief moment of electricity in the air as though another power, separate from either him or the woman, was trying to interfere. John could physically feel the presence. Some of his souls, the more sensitive ones, cried out in pain though by the time their cries reached John's throat the screams had been reduced to no more than a barely audible gasp. For a split second the whole street seemed to glow and John Brown and all his souls disappeared.

Standing in his place, confused and frightened, was Don Rothman. For that moment, Rothman was aware, conscious of his presence on the street and of his own hand inside his suit jacket grasping a gun. Then he dissolved into oblivion and John Brown returned to resume control of the body. The disappearance and resumption all happened in a flash of light so fast that John wasn't at all aware of the temporary transformation. The whole event was a lot like the brilliant flashes he'd see in the corners of his eyes when smoking crack. He'd long ago learned to ignore them. But in that place, within the void where Don Rothman's conscious mind rested, asleep, the memory was preserved like a vivid dream. The experience had been so paralyzing that Rothman knew he'd remember the feeling of terror, the knowledge that something else had taken over his body and was planning to use it for the purpose of murder, for the rest of his days, assuming he was able to experience another day of his own.

The woman was turning toward the cab and John Brown wanted to scream. He couldn't follow her. He had no idea where she was going and, despite what one saw in the movies, a person couldn't simply get into a taxi in New York City and tell the driver to "follow that car." Not if that person wanted to avoid a lot of attention, and especially if that person was someone who looked like John Brown.

If he'd had the time and the mental energy to think through his dilemma, John probably would've realized that Suzanne was on her way home, responding to the alarm that he'd caused. Had he the capacity to consider her destination, he would have also known that her building would be full of security guards and policemen, so going there would be dangerous for him. He didn't know any of these things, but he knew well the painful sense of frustration he felt.

As the cab carrying Suzanne Rosewell disappeared into traffic, John Brown sat down hard on the stone steps of a building whose protective shadow offered refuge. The man sat down and cried, and the button of his suit jacket opened while the handle of one of the thirty-eights appeared in plain sight for anyone who bothered to look.

And for the longest time no one did bother to look, as people intentionally avoided the sight of a decently dressed, strange-looking man, crying on the steps of a bank. One New Yorker after another averted their eyes and failed to see the danger. Everyone except Markam, Wilber, Kent & Todd's newest mail room messenger who was calmly walking down the street.

Joshua Wilson was on an important errand, carrying critical documents to another law office. The papers contained the written certification of a major deal between clients represented by the two firms and embodied transactions totaling tens of millions of dollars. His new boss had explained all this carefully to Joshua and he was fulfilling his mission with full knowledge of the grave responsibility he carried in the heavy envelope at his side.

Still, Joshua could not bring himself to ignore a man in tears sitting on a public street, and not because he was appalled by the way people walked by the distressed person. Judgement of others was not part of Joshua's nature. He'd seen too much of that in China. Instead, he simply tried to act as he instinctively believed he should.

"Do you need help, sir?" he asked gently.

John Brown raised his head and stared directly and hatefully into the eyes of the man who had disturbed his mourning.

"No, be gone with you... mind your own business," he shouted. Joshua leapt away backwards across the sidewalk. He was a compassionate man, maybe even a righteous person, but those qualities did not diminish his intelligence or his survival skills. This man sounded dangerous. He confirmed the judgement when he spotted the butt of the pistol hanging out of the man's belt, only partially hidden by the suit jacket. A knot formed in Joshua's stomach.

"Sorry, sir," he said and appeared to quickly resume his mission, protecting himself within the anonymity of the crowd. But Joshua fled only as far as the mounted policeman posted on the corner almost a full block away.

"Officer, please, that man over there, sitting on the steps, he has a gun in his belt." Joshua instantly earned the policeman's attention.

"Did he threaten someone with it?"

"I didn't see that. He was crying. I thought I could help, but he chased me away. I did see a gun in his belt. And he seemed very angry."

"Thank you," the policeman said to the messenger. "Now stay out of the way. Don't play hero. I'll handle this."

The cop took a portable radio off his belt and, keeping his eye on the man perched on the step, called for additional assistance. The radio crackled, the responding voice unclear. The officer automatically moved his head to improve the reception. When he turned back, the man was no longer on the step or anywhere else in sight. Quickly he transmitted the new information and received instructions to wait for assistance. In a few minutes, the street was filled with reinforcements.

The policeman had used those few minutes to obtain a description from Joshua and then permitted the messenger to resume his critical delivery but only after advising him to remain available in case the detectives wanted to see him. By the time Joshua left the corner, the street was covered with blue uniforms. The police searched the area for more than an hour but never again encountered the man with the strange dreadlocks and the gun in his belt.

A full day passed before a copy of the report of the break-in on the Upper East Side arrived at NYPD Computer Central. On the same day, a document outlining the "man with gun" on Wall Street also appeared. A second day disappeared before an experienced officer reviewed the files and came up with the conclusion that these two men were probably one and the same suspect. But another day disappeared before the overworked detective who was assigned the case, still considered a minor one in a city where twice-a-day murder was the norm, finally had time to really read the files. Only then did someone realize that the owner of the apartment where the break-in, assault and weapons theft took place worked only one block from where the man with the gun had been seen. The connection concerned the detective and he wasted no additional time in informing his superiors of his concerns. They thanked him for his diligence, but told him that he had made his discovery a little too late.

John Brown was angry, frustrated and distressed, but his years on the street had taught him to never let down his guard, never stop being observant. Even when he was high on crack, a part of him kept one eye on the activities of the street. He always assigned two or three souls to guard the perimeter. One of his sentries watched as the nosey messenger moved away, back into the crowd. The soul also noticed that the man went directly to the police. Seeing that the officer was interested, a warning was transmitted to John Brown and all the souls were suddenly alerted to the possible danger.

John looked up, cleared his eyes of tears and watched the policeman as he used his radio. When the man turned his head, John took advantage of the moment and dashed into the subway. A train was rolling into the station. Unconcerned about direction, John jumped aboard and was probably in his seat before the cop even noticed he had gone.

The police did search the subway station and asked the token clerk if he had seen someone who matched the description. But John Brown, now dressed in a business suit with most of his dreads tucked under a cowboy hat just did not, any more, look so unusual in New York.

John was aware that people no longer stared, or even especially avoided staring, at him. He was conscious of blending into the crowd just a little more and while he'd spent three years trying to stand out, he considered the current advantages of being somewhat nameless and faceless, and thought about it all the way to Eighty-sixth Street.

Suzanne's cabby had done a pretty fair job of avoiding traffic and keeping the ride as short as possible. Though his passenger had shown all the physical signs of impatience, shifting in her seat, glancing at her watch every few seconds, moaning aloud when a traffic light turned red, she must have been happy with his speed because the tip was more than generous. Still the driver noticed the three police cars and the two from the private security agency parked in front of the building where his impatient fare instructed him to stop. Based on her attitude, he was sure that these vehicles were part of the same "emergency." While he couldn't think of any recent illegal acts, the cabby couldn't wait to remove himself from the neighborhood. After all, why take chances?

Suzanne paid with a twenty-dollar bill and waved away the difference. She was aware that she'd left him with an unusually large tip, but at the moment she lacked the time and tolerance for change. Her only thought was to get to her apartment.

Carlos, in his doorman's uniform, the police captain in plain-clothes, two cops in NYPD blue, a security guard dressed in green and a young man and a young woman, both wearing corporate gray, were all waiting in the lobby for Suzanne. The moment Carlos expressed recognition, the captain and the young people stepped forward to greet her. The balance of the uniforms gathered around protectively.

"Ms. Rosewell," the plain-clothes man spoke first and with the most authority. His was the voice from the telephone. "I am very pleased you are here. Some of my men are on twenty-two, guarding the apartment. Please, let's go up and see if you can tell us what might be missing."

He took her gently by the arm and started to move toward the elevators. The uniforms preceded them while the two corporate types tagged along behind. They both cleared their throats several times to remind the policeman of their presence.

"Oh, yes," the captain continued, "these people are supervisors from the security company your building hired. What were your names again?"

"I'm Rebecca and this is Terry," the young woman said quickly. She spoke fast, as though expecting her ability to communicate would be cut-off by the captain. "We are supervisors at the security company and we report directly to a friend of yours, Elias Garner."

Suzanne stopped suddenly, turned slowly around and looked hard at the two well-dressed youngsters. They didn't appear to be any older than college students on a summer job, which was how she had dismissed them until they mentioned that name.

"Elias Garner works at a security company?" she asked suspiciously.

"No," Rebecca continued, as pleased with the impatient look on the captain's face as she was with Suzanne's attention. "We are Mr. Garner's personal assistants. Our corporation bought the security company when Mr. Garner became aware that they held the contract for your building. We were sent, yesterday, to supervise. We planned to add additional security to the building but this incident happened before we could implement our program."

"You must be a very important young lady," the police captain said to Suzanne while pushing her back in motion toward the elevator. "In addition to your friend *buying* a security company for your protection, somebody with real influence called the Mayor's office right after the break in was reported. You understand that normally a captain, like me, would not come out on what appears to be a rather routine incident. But I got a call from the Commissioner's office and they insisted I handle it personally."

The group entered the elevator. Suzanne and the Captain each stared at the closed metal door in front of them. Rebecca and Terry shared occasional glances with each other. Everyone in the elevator was aware that all the special attention paid to Suzanne had not set her at ease. Quite the contrary. Nor had it provided protection from the invasion of her home by an apparently dangerous stranger. Not a word was spoken until the car arrived at the twenty-second floor.

The door to her apartment was wide open and flanked by two more NYPD blue uniforms, one of them male and the other female. Leaning against the wall across from the entrance was another green-clad private guard. All three stiffened their posture as the group moved from the elevator toward them.

"No one has been inside your apartment since the actual incident ended and the injured man was removed," the Captain told her as they reached the doorway. "We're holding a scientific team waiting downstairs. They'll check for fingerprints and other physical evidence. But before we let them in, we wanted you to tell us what was missing."

Without responding, Suzanne walked across the portal of her own home, immediately feeling like an outsider entering an alien place. The rooms looked familiar but she sensed the apartment as more like a duplicate of where she lived than her own beloved abode. Following the captain's instructions, she touched nothing, moving from one room to the other. Except for the pieces of the broken vase, a small amount of blood on the carpet and a slightly messed up bed, nothing appeared disturbed.

"Everything except the vase and the bed looks the same as it was when I left this morning," she said to the Captain, the stress apparent in her voice. "But I do have a jewelry box in the top drawer of the dresser, nothing terribly valuable, but... well, I would have to open the drawer."

"Show me which drawer," the Captain said. Suzanne pointed. He pulled a pair of pliers from his coat and gently opened the drawer, trying to avoid smudging any fingerprints that might be present. With his hand wrapped in a plastic glove, he withdrew a box and set it on the nightstand. Then he lifted the lid, careful not to place his fingers on any of the usual spots that someone might touch when opening the box normally. He gestured to Suzanne, who stepped forward and stared into the open box for almost a full minute.

"No," she finally said, "nothing appears to be missing."

The Captain closed the lid.

"Well, there are two possibilities. The first one says the man came to steal, was interrupted and fled before he could take anything. The fact that he was apparently laying on the bed, maybe sleeping..."

"He slept on my bed?" Suzanne interrupted.

"Oh, yes. Didn't I mention that on the phone?" She didn't respond and after a polite moment of silence, he continued. "As I was saying, that theory doesn't fit with his taking a nap... though you can never tell these days... people do strange things, especially drug addicts. The other possibility was that he came specifically to wait for you. Do you know anyone who might have a reason to hurt you?" Suzanne hesitated a moment before she answered.

"No, I can't think of a soul." Her eyes were on Rebecca as she answered. The agreement not to speak of certain things was sealed between them with a look. The police Captain saw the exchange and knew Suzanne was lying. He decided not to confront her at that particular moment.

"Very well," he said, "I'll call up my people, but I'm not too confident they'll find much. Fingerprints are going to be a mess since the suspect confined a whole team of security people while he made his escape. They probably touched everything in the place. We'll order DNA tests, but it's probably not worth the time. Think about my question again, Ms. Rosewell. I must say that the fact that your friend bought a security company and planned to put on extra guards, does not fit with a woman who can't think of a single soul who might want to injure her. Maybe someone will come to mind and you'll be able to help us in our investigation." The policeman reached for his radio and called the waiting team into action.

At the very moment the group of specially trained evidence gatherers rose up to the twenty-second floor in the elevator, John Brown emerged from the subway. He knew his destination and had already outlined his plan. Without hesitation, he marched directly into a chain-store hair salon only a block from the subway exit. The two guns were tucked carefully and tightly into his belt, one on each side of his spine with the suit coat draping gently over them.

"How can I help you?" asked the just-barely-out-of-her-teens receptionist. Her hair and her makeup were far too extreme when contrasted with the young and innocent expression she projected. To John, she appeared to be a living advertisement for the services of the salon. If so, she was not a good one. This was distressing, but now was not the time to go searching for an alternative. He took off his ten-gallon hat and allowed the dreads to fall loosely around his face.

"My hair has been twisted, bleached, processed and damaged. I want major work. I want it restored to normal so that I look like a Wall

Street business executive. I have a job interview, you see."

"I understand," the young woman responded, the shock on her face more than evident, aware that this customer's needs were out of her league. "This is a big job. Let me call my manager."

The manager, in sharp contrast to her young subordinate, turned out to be a perfect representative. She was a middle-aged woman, neat and professional, and did not express any reaction at all to John's strange hairstyle. She examined his head carefully, made notes for her technicians on a yellow pad and added up the costs. John relaxed, checked his white envelope, determined that he still had more than enough cash, including a tip and still some left over, and instructed the woman to proceed. She then turned him over to two young men who sat John in a chair, surrounded him and went to work.

The operation took almost three hours but when John Brown emerged from the shop he looked more like a marine who had just returned to civilian life than a street person and the repository for century-old souls. For the first time in years, no one took any special notice of him. One hurrying gentleman who brushed by, nudging John's shoulder, bothered to excuse himself, a courtesy this homeless person hadn't experienced in so long he couldn't remember the last time it happened. The hair surgery had been a success. The patient was transfused and healthy. Now, to test the results. John Brown turned and walked directly toward Suzanne's building. The ten-gallon hat was left behind on the coat rack of the salon, intentionally.

Hoping that he looked like an entirely different person, John Brown boldly moved toward the busy lobby. He smiled as he excused himself, passing through the line of police pacing the sidewalk. He displayed what he hoped was the appropriate amount of curiosity at the crowd but, like any other New Yorker, proceeded directly about his business. He approached Carlos.

"I am looking for a Mr. Milton Williams. Is this his building? I am afraid I do not remember which block he was on."

"Just a moment," Carlos answered, seeming annoyed to be interrupted but without even a hint of recognition in his eyes. "I'll look on the list."

John watched as Carlos' eyes scanned the end of the alphabetical listing. Failing to find the name, the doorman double-checked the entire roster, running his index finger down the column as a way of focusing his concentration through the confusion and noise around him. John, on the other hand, had no problem centering on Carlos. The longer the doorman worked trying to find the mythical tenant, the more excited John became.

"I am sorry, sir," Carlos said. "I do not find the name anywhere."

"Oh, that's all right. I probably have the wrong block. I'll check further. Uh, what's going on?" The question, accompanied by a gesture indicating the official gathering in the lobby, seemed to generate nervousness in the doorman. Still, he showed no recognition. John decided to push the matter as far as he dare. The longer he stood there, the more confident he grew.

"Oh, nothing serious," Carlos said, obviously trying to protect the reputation of his building.

"Come on, that's a lot of cops for nothing serious."

"An unauthorized person got into the building and picked an important person's apartment to, uh... try and enter. That's why there are so many cops, but nothing got stolen."

Well, the man had not exactly lied.

"Oh? Whose apartment?"

"I am sorry, sir," Carlos responded, his posture straightening and his voice adopting a very official tone. "I can't give out that information. Our people like their privacy."

"I understand," John answered, deciding that here was the place to back down. "I was just being nosey. Sorry to have disturbed you."

"Yes, sir," Carlos responded automatically turning his attention back to the police activities. John Brown slowly, though not too slowly, walked out of the lobby, past the line of uniforms and across the street. Absolutely no one had paid the slightest attention to him.

The scientific team completed their sweep of Suzanne's apartment. They found a significant number of prints as well as some stray hairs on the pillow. Suzanne, the maid and all of the private security guards were fingerprinted on the spot so they could be eliminated from the collection. The police gathered up the pieces of broken crockery and the maid cleaned the blood from the carpet. Except for the empty spot where the vase-turned-weapon had stood, Suzanne's home was back to normal.

But the place certainly didn't feel normal. Suzanne felt she was sharing the apartment with a presence, something that had not been there before. She walked from one room to another feeling watched and unsafe.

In the analytical part of her mind, Suzanne Rosewell knew that such emotions were not unusual after a break-in, but knowledge of logic did not chase the demons. Instead, Suzanne decided to leave them behind and go out to find some dinner. The Chinese restaurant up the street would be just perfect. She picked up a legal journal from the nightstand beside her bed and headed out the door. A long and leisurely meal, accompanied by some heavy reading, that would be the ticket. The phone started to ring almost as soon as she was too far down the corridor to hear the sound.

John Brown, just a block away from Suzanne's apartment building, hung up the pay phone. He had no desire to leave a message on her machine. All he wanted was to speak directly to the woman. Now she wasn't home, or maybe she just wasn't answering. If she wasn't there, she might be out on the street. He might be able to find her alone and undefended. No, that wasn't likely. After what had happened earlier, she probably had police protection or at least some of the security guards hanging around. But maybe not. Maybe the spirits were providing him with the opportunity he needed.

John's mouth was dry. His nerves were beginning to mirror his addicted body's craving for more crack-cocaine. But instead of the yearning being an annoyance, something to distract him from his mission, John was enlightened by the reminder of his need for the drug. This was the stuff that continually brought him closer to finding the answers. This was just what he needed. He would locate some crack, get high and allow the souls to tell him what his next step should be.

John decided to wander east, across Lexington Avenue and toward Third. Then he'd turn and head uptown, toward a public housing project he knew, north of Ninety-sixth Street. He was sure that on such a fine summer's evening locating a dealer wouldn't be a problem. There was still a little cash left in the envelope and by the time he returned to Suzanne's neighborhood, he'd have the added advantage of the protection of darkness. John collected his quarter from the pay phone and started to saunter down the street. To everyone who noticed him, he looked just like another neighborhood resident out enjoying a warm New York evening.

"She's not home," Elias Garner nearly shouted at his two assistants as he slammed down the phone. He too had not left a message. "How can she go out after what just happened?"

Rebecca and Terry had hurried to Garner's office right after the police investigation was completed. They briefed him on the situation while watching the fury rise in his eyes. He went for the telephone just as soon as they'd finished and was angered by his inability to reach her.

"In all my years," Garner continued, trying to calm himself, "I've never known Luckholt to play quite this rough. This deal is apparently far more important to her than I had allowed. We have underestimated the seriousness of the situation and as a result, we are making mistakes. We can't afford to do that any more. Our next error, or Suzanne's, could have very serious consequences. Did you leave additional security behind?" Rebecca and Terry looked at each other.

"No..." Rebecca said with hesitation. "The building management was resistant and we assumed the police..."

"You assumed?" Eli was angry again. "Don't you realize why we took over the security company? Not to keep the building management happy, but to protect Suzanne Rosewell. Now don't assume anything and get a team over there right away." Terry was speaking into a cellular phone even before Garner had finished shouting his sentence.

The connection with a dealer required a little more persistence than John was used to, but he was finally able to locate someone in one of the hallways of the housing project. The locals were suspicious. His transformation had been too successful. John no longer looked like someone who might normally purchase drugs in their neighborhood. He now had more resemblance to those who usually arrested them for their preferred way of earning a living. Eventually John came across an overconfident teenager who not only took the risk but led his customer to an abandoned apartment used by the local crack-heads for getting high. A few sleeping bodies were hidden in the corners but there was no one conscious enough to see John or to try to pressure him into sharing his purchase.

In a few minutes the drugs were gone. John and all of his souls were, once more, reaching for that closed door. But this time, one of the hundred pairs of waving hands was able to separate from the crowd, grasp the handle, twist the knob and pull the gateway open. In his mind's eye, wasted on crack cocaine, John Brown saw everything he needed to see. His three-year search for the truth had reached an apex and his long hidden destiny was revealed. Without hesitation, without even waiting for the peak of his drug experience to diminish, John Brown left the empty apartment and headed downtown toward the building where Suzanne Rosewell lived.

Elizabeth Luckholt is too restless to deal with the mound of paperwork on her desk. She constantly picks up files, glances at them and puts them back down again. Periodically she rises from her chair and paces the room, glares at her Rolex, sits down again and tries to work, but work is impossible. Her patience is worn too thin. She looks at her watch again. He isn't even late, he's never late, but she can wait no longer. With all of the force of her intensely disciplined mind, she wills him to arrive quickly. A few moments later there is a knock at the door.

"Enter." He is here, walks in and drops down in one of the large chairs without saying a word. "Report," she says simply.

"We've lost him," he answers. "We know he was in her apartment. We know he stole two guns and a radio and we know that he was seen with one of those guns on Wall Street. The cops have not yet made the connection between the Wall Street incident and the apartment break-in, but they will. We know he went back uptown because he had his hair cut in her neighborhood. Then he disappeared. Our men downtown haven't seen him. Our people uptown haven't seen him."

"What can we do?" she asks.

"All we can do is wait and see where he shows up next."

"Not good enough. Figure something out."

He nods silently, gets up and leaves the room.

The egg foo young was perfect, though Suzanne knew the dish had more fat in it than should be eaten at one meal. But she wanted foo young from the moment she spied the item on the menu. The food reminded her of Chinese restaurants when she was a child. They were not nearly as numerous in those days and most of them had exactly the same menu. Her father loved egg foo young and was sure to order a plate every time. They'd get several different dishes, and share them, but the unspoken rule said daddy got the first and last portions of egg foo young, or rather, chicken egg foo young, that's what he'd always order. Suzanne preferred pork, but tonight memories had made her order chicken as well. In fact, she remembered that her father always seemed to avoid pork dishes at the Chinese restaurant, shellfish too.

Strange. She'd never thought about that before. Mother served shrimp, lobster, bacon, pork chops, just about anything at home, and he always ate. But in public he never consumed any of the foods that were forbidden by Kosher dietary laws. Probably just a coincidence. Suzanne couldn't imagine that her father chose his food that way intentionally. Her memory was probably fooling her. All this crazy stuff going on. A person can begin to think strange thoughts.

Still, the foo young was awfully good and the memories were warm. Suzanne lingered over her meal for a long time. The waiter came by often to refill the water glass and once to bring a fresh pot of tea, but she was so conspicuously enjoying herself, by herself, that he kept his service silent and undisturbing. The law book rested unopened on the table. Her memories were as much distraction as she needed.

Eventually she noticed that the restaurant was almost empty. Not wishing to be the last customer, Suzanne gathered her book, paid her bill, left a generous amount on the table and stepped back onto Madison Avenue. The evening was mild and the street strangely deserted for New York. For the first time in several hours, Suzanne was frightened again, this time by the emptiness. She focused her eyes on her building a few short blocks away and quickened her pace. The sooner she was off the street the safer she'd feel.

The second Terry put down the cellular phone, the thing chirped for attention. He glanced apologetically at Elias Garner, who was waiting for a report, and spoke into the instrument. The voice on the other end provided a few facts that Terry felt important enough to write down on a pad that he extracted from the inside pocket of his jacket. He concluded the call and raised his eyes back toward his boss.

"Well?" Elias Garner asked.

"An extra security team is on its way," he said. "They will be in position within ten minutes. But she's still not in the apartment, or at least not answering the phone. I've left several messages. If you like, I'll go personally to her door."

"Yes, both of you go. What was the other call?"

"Right, I almost forgot. The police have identified the man who was in Suzanne's apartment, or they think they have. Based on fingerprints, they have come up with the name Donald K. Rothman. He lives, or used to live in Westchester, an engineer. At one time he had a security clearance, which is why his prints were on file. The man had a mental breakdown a few years ago, walked out of a hospital and disappeared. No one has seen him since and his parents regularly inquire about an old but still active missing persons report. That's all we know."

"Find out more," Elias Garner instructed Terry. "Rebecca, you go directly to the building. Terry, call Mr. Rothman's parents and see what you can learn. Then you go to the building too. Someone will report to me every thirty minutes. EVERY THIRTY MINUTES, is that clear?"

"Yes, sir," they both said at precisely the same moment and left his office. Elias Garner picked up his telephone and dialed the Chairman's private extension.

CHAPTER TWENTY

The various cast members arrived at the theater within fifteen minutes of each other, but the order of their appearance became the critical factor in the drama. Had Suzanne not shown up first, she wouldn't have been in the apartment when John Brown came to call. Had the security team been ten minutes ahead, instead of ten minutes behind, they might have prevented the anguish that followed. And the play might have had a very different ending.

Madison Avenue was strangely empty. The lack of people out on the street made Suzanne more and more nervous as she walked.

"But then again," her mind tried to tell her, "no one on the street also meant no threat." And, as strange as the emptiness felt in the normally crowded New York borough, lots of people from her neighborhood take vacation in the middle of summer, which largely accounted for the vacant sidewalks.

But the explanation brought little comfort. Suzanne walked close to the curb so the entire width of the sidewalk separated her from the dark, shadowed doorways of the steel-shuttered stores.

She was forced to admit to herself that the man who'd entered her apartment was also her companion during each of those nighttime, New York blocks. The vague mental image was present, just over her right shoulder and just out of sight, unclear because Carlos' description had been so nebulous. Even the security officers locked in her apartment by the intruder had missed the subtleties of the man's physical portrait. Understandably, they'd been concentrating on the barrel of the thirty-eight. Some said his eyes were blue, while others described them as brown. They all found the hair sticking out from under his Texas-style cowboy hat the most distinctive of his physical traits. The unusual dreads reminded her of the homeless man on the subway. If her trespasser hadn't been described as nicely dressed and well-spoken, Suzanne might have assumed they were one in the same. But that was unlikely. This was probably just another damned coincidence.

The very word lowered the temperature of Suzanne's blood by several degrees. "Coincidences" had led her far down this strange path and still she hadn't learned one simple lesson, to pay special attention to even the slightest happenstance. Tomorrow she would call the police captain and report her remembrance of the similarity between description of the invader and the man she'd met on the subway. The information might prove useful. Suzanne's tension only began to dissipate as she safely entered the front door of her building.

"Ms. Rosewell," the regular night doorman greeted her with surprise. "I thought you were in your apartment. After what happened today, do you think you should be out alone?"

"Don't worry Henry," Suzanne said, succeeding in sounding as if she were truly unconcerned. "Things like that happen in New York. One can't stop living, right?"

"Yes, but Carlos had told me to call the security company if you decided to go out, so someone could go with you. He thought you'd stay upstairs."

"Well, you can tell Carlos that I left while he was still on duty. My protectors were all so busy with their investigative stuff, that they completely missed my departure. Now stop looking so concerned. I'm going right upstairs and will stay there all night, promise. Do you want me to call you on the intercom when I make it safely to the 22nd floor?"

"I would appreciate that Ms. Rosewell. Then we both can relax for the rest of the night."

"I was only kidding, but if that will make you happy...," she said with a smile as she walked through the double glass doors toward the elevator. Though Suzanne pretended that calling Henry was sort of a joke, the precaution did make her feel more secure. Maybe going out alone, without even telling anyone where she was headed, had been sort of foolish.

The elevator car was empty. So was the corridor on the 22nd floor. Her apartment door appeared as securely locked as when she'd left and a tense, but a thorough search of the interior, including the closets, revealed that Suzanne was the only occupant. After double checking the locks on the door, she pressed the intercom button to call Henry. By now, the doorman was probably getting nervous.

"May I help you?" Henry asked. The electronic box might have distorted his voice, but he did sound tense.

"This is Suzanne Rosewell," she responded, "safe and sound behind locked doors with no ghosts under the bed."

"Oh, Suzanne, good," Henry answered, "there's a man here from the security company who would like a moment of your time. Can I send him up, Suzanne?"

"Sure Henry, do that," and she took her finger off the switch.

The doorman had twice, in one brief conversation, called her by her first name, something he'd never done before. In the past she would not have permitted such familiarity. Well, maybe things really were different. She didn't find herself at all offended by his informal manner, but seemed instead to enjoy this new intimacy. Maybe her changed feelings were being subconsciously communicated to people like Henry and therefore she was, in fact, encouraging these new parameters of protocol.

Suzanne decided that Henry's use of her first name was not important, noted that not too long ago she would have made it an issue, and chalked up her slightly uncomfortable feeling to this eccentric change of attitude she was passing through. Suzanne managed to explain Henry's lapse in logical terms and ignored the soft but persistent alarm bell ringing in the back of her mind.

Henry had hoped that Ms. Rosewell had picked up his hidden distress call. Granted, this was not much of a warning, but it was the best he could do on short notice and with the working end of a thirty-eight pressed under his ear.

The visitor looked very respectable, not at all like the intruder described by Carlos. First the man offered a friendly greeting and then asked for someone, by name, who lived in the building. When Henry turned around to use the intercom, the stranger drew a gun from under his jacket and placed the barrel against the doorman's head.

"Not a word," the now armed man said. "Don't touch those buttons, don't do anything. Just listen and obey my instructions perfectly. You will call Suzanne Rosewell and tell her she has a visitor from the security company. If you do anything else, give her any warning at all, you will be dead, right now, right here. Do you understand?" He pressed the gun harder.

"Yes, sir... but... but, Ms. Rosewell will be calling me any moment." The intercom rang.

"Remember what I said," the man with the pistol hissed.

Henry remembered, but still had the courage to change his form of address hoping that Ms. Rosewell would notice the sudden casualness and conclude that something was wrong. He had no idea if his message had gotten through.

That was when Henry decided he was going to die. This man was going to turn him into another New York statistic, the second paragraph in a Daily News story. The least he could do was die a hero, look good in the newspapers for his family. One second before Henry made his move, the gunman spoke again.

"Where is the service closet? I need to put you someplace where you won't make any trouble."

Maybe Henry wasn't going to die. He led the intruder to the broom closet. The gunman, calm and wearing the strangest smile, locked the doorman in the dark.

"I am going to stand outside this door for a while," he said as he relieved Henry of his keys, "and if you make any noise, I'll shoot, right through the wall, and I'll kill you. So be quiet."

"Yes, sir," the prisoner muttered as the steel door closed. He was frightened, more frightened than ever before in his entire life, but he forced himself to listen, hoping to hear the man's footsteps as he walked away from the closet door. The carpeting in the hall prevented Henry's ears from recording the footsteps, but he was sure that the next sound he heard was the elevator door open and close. Still, a few minutes more were required to build up courage. Then he began to shout, kick and pound against the immobile door.

Unfortunately, all the space on the first floor was rented to commercial interests and no one was working late that night. To the tenants on the second floor, the muffled noises sounded much like a serious domestic dispute and the most they were willing to do was call the doorman's station and complain. Several people were annoyed when Henry didn't answer their page, but they assumed that he had also heard the racket and was on his way to solve the problem, or at least reduce the noise.

Suzanne, on the twenty-second floor, was too far above to hear the commotion. More than anything, she wanted to get ready for bed and was annoyed by the security official's late night visit. But, she assumed, he was in charge of her overnight protection and would probably be telling her where the guards were posted or how to handle a potential crisis. The information might make her feel less insecure, allow her to sleep better. The delay in her bedtime would be worth the wait, she hoped.

She heard the elevator door open, imagined the man walking down the carpeted corridor and correctly anticipated the moment he knocked on the door. Still she was cautious.

"Who's there?" she asked through the locked door, her hand ready on the bolt.

"My name is Brown, ma'am," he said politely, "I'm from the security company and would like a word with you. I won't take much of your time."

"No, not much," John Brown thought, "just all the time you have left in this life."

Suzanne peeked through the eye-port. The man looked respectable. He wore no hat and she could clearly see the close-cropped military style hair. She considered asking him for identification, but in his right hand he carried the ever-present radio, the unofficial badge of a security agent. If anyone had mentioned to her that the intruder had stolen a radio, it was not something she recalled.

Her fingers threw back the first bolt and quickly moved to the second. When the third and final lock cleared, John Brown grabbed the handle, twisted hard and burst through the door. In a second he was inside the apartment, relocking the door behind him. Suzanne was backing away, too frightened to scream.

"My name is John Brown," he said as Suzanne's spine dug into the opposite wall. She was using both her hands to cover her mouth. Her eyes were wider than humanly possible.

"The same John Brown," he continued, "who, in history, led the great slave rebellion, was captured by Robert E. Lee and hanged by the United States government. I have returned to your time, in this body to complete a great mission. And you Suzanne Rosewell are part of that mission."

John Brown reached into his coat and drew out one of the thirty-eight police specials taken from the security guards earlier in the day. Suzanne gasped at the sight of the gun and fought to keep her mind from falling into hysteria. She was rapidly losing the battle. He leveled the gun, pointing the barrel directly between Suzanne's eyes. The huge pistol was less than six inches from her head. She was frozen with fear and could not move.

"This is your fault," John Brown resumed speaking after a dramatic moment that allowed Suzanne to suffer a good long look at the weapon. "You and I met on the subway and you ran from me. I was going to sit with you, enlist you in my holy cause and you ran. That action identified you as an agent of evil and it is part of my mission to destroy evil on earth."

He held the gun steady while he spoke. Suzanne could hear him, but his words came to her as unconnected sounds beyond any human understanding. Her mind refused to focus on anything but the hollow steel tunnel pointed at her eyes. From deep inside she fought to regain control, knowing that if she was unable to act, she would soon be dead. Even this almost subconscious knowledge could not overcome the terror that completely immobilized her body. Behind her, in the bedroom, she could hear the phone ringing.

"You see," John Brown continued, "when I was first on this earth, before the Civil War, I tried to eradicate the evil of slavery. Yes, my tactics were savage. I killed people and they hanged me for doing so. But only a few years later, tens of thousands would die in a great war between the states that produced far more murder than I could have ever generated by myself. So you see, Suzanne, a little violence, used properly in the battle against evil, can prevent greater violence later. That's what made my actions, in Virginia, way back then, holy. And what I am about to do now, is also holy. You have been revealed to me as evil and I must remove you from this earth. This is my role and my destiny."

John Brown pulled back the hammer on the shining blue pistol. The metallic click sounded to Suzanne like a military firing squad drum role before an execution. The noise filled her ears and she felt as though she might finally be able to scream.

A scream did fill the apartment, but not from Suzanne and not one human. An electronic screeching noise was pouring from Suzanne's purse that was sitting on a table near the door. Downtown, Margaret, still working in the office, failing to reach Suzanne at her apartment, had activated the hated cellular device. The tiny machine was shouting for attention at a volume so loud that the noise unnerved John Brown. The man swiftly directed his pistol at the offending clamor and pulled the trigger, twice.

A policeman's pistol is intentionally designed to produce a thunderous noise. This feature helps scare criminals while attracting the attention of other officers. The gun that John Brown fired filled the apartment with a din that spilled out into the hallway and echoed throughout the entire building. Dozens of people became instantly aware that something serious had gone wrong somewhere.

The fast lead projectiles successfully silenced Suzanne's cell phone, tearing her purse apart in the process, and flinging the contents into the air. The bullets then buried themselves in the hardwood floor. The sound and the flying debris were more than Suzanne's overloaded circuits could handle. Her mind chose the most rapid defense that could be found and retreated toward a trauma-induced catatonic state. But in the moment before unconsciousness something deep inside Suzanne's brain reached out into that special place in the universe where unexplained communication takes place and dispatched a frightened message begging for help. Then Suzanne fell to the floor, completely unconscious but with her eyes wide open, staring at the ceiling in terror.

CHAPTER TWENTY-ONE

Monty's fancy silver rig was parked in a rest area on the westbound side of Interstate 90 in Wyoming. The trucker had been asleep in the "living space" behind his cab, catching an hour's nap because his highway vision was starting to blur from too much time on the road. A disturbance had awakened him and he couldn't identify its source, or shake the feeling of distress. Monty poured himself a cup of coffee from his thermos, but drank only half the cup before engaging his own cell phone and calling a dispatcher somewhere in Eastern Ohio.

"Yeah George, Montana Monty here," he said into the phone. "What's the deadline on getting that pickup back west? Well, I don't think I'll be able to handle that one. I'll find you a substitute and then I'm going to go to New York for a couple of days. Don't worry, I'll get someone. OK? Yeah, New York. I have to visit a sick friend."

Joshua Wilson was settling down for the evening in his tiny apartment. Life was so much nicer since he'd gotten his new job. He came home at a normal hour, just like his neighbors, and with clean clothes, his head filled with new experiences. Tonight, and every evening right until Monday, he could just relax. Next week his after-work college classes began, but now he could stay home, eat his dinner and watch the news, content with the world.

"...a disturbance at an Upper East Side luxury apartment that involved private security people as well as the New York City Police," the man with the perfect hairdo was saying to the camera. "No details have been released and the names of the parties are being kept confidential until family members have been notified. But building residents reported hearing the sound of gunshots and someone was taken to Lenox Hill Hospital in an Emergency Medical Services ambulance. In other local news...."

Joshua turned off the television set, left his apartment and knocked on the door of his neighbor, a postal worker. When the man answered, Joshua smiled.

"Excuse me," he said, "sorry to bother you, but tell me where I can find Lenox Hill Hospital."

Elias Garner's appearance at the main door of the Madison Avenue high-rise came at the same moment as the special security team's arrival. Garner had consumed precisely three minutes before deciding that waiting in his office, passively receiving half-hour progress reports was simply not acceptable. He instructed his secretary to advise Terry and Rebecca that he was on his way to Suzanne's and that they should join him there. From the first moment he surfaced on Madison Avenue, he knew they had big trouble.

There was no uniformed presence in the lobby, not police, not the doorman, nor a single security guard. Several residents were wandering around in confusion, unable to pass through the locked interior doors and gain access to their own homes. One very annoyed man was behind the counter trying to unwind the mysteries of the intercom while another simply pounded on the glass and cursed. Both stopped and stared at the arrival of the armed force led by a tall, distinguished black man.

"Break it down," Garner ordered, referring to the glass barrier. There was a moment of confusion as the lead man searched for a tool adequate to the job. That was the same moment that the sound of the two shots fired on floor twenty-two vibrated down the walls of the building. Eli seemed to be the only one to actually hear the gunfire. His ears separated these special sounds from the ambient New York noises that, for most people, merged everything together in one massive city din. The others only knew something was wrong by observing the expression of terror that became Garner's face.

"Break it down!" he shouted, his remaining patience dissolving, "Right now!"

One member of the team stepped forward to take charge, a large man, carrying the bulk of a professional football player, who moved the others out of his way. Using the handle of his pistol as a hammer, he shattered the glass and reached through to unbolt the door. Without success. Equipped with a security lock, a key was required to free the lock from the inside as well. Garner remembered his last visit to the building.

"There's an electric switch, hidden somewhere in the doorman's desk. Find it!"

While they searched, Eli took the portable radio from Terry's hand. He glanced at the device for a moment, turned up the volume, pressed the talk button and directed his performer's booming voice at the box.

"Donald Rothman," he said in clear, round tones, "can you hear me? I must speak with you right now."

Twenty-two stories above, John Brown was recovering from the shock of firing the revolver. The pistol had made a louder noise than he'd anticipated but he had succeeded in silencing the devil's scream that was coming from the woman's purse. And then the woman collapsed. He knew he had not shot at her, but she had fallen anyway, maybe hit by a piece of flying debris. He considered examining her for blood but decided that none of this mattered anyway. There were four bullets left in the gun and only one was needed to end her earthly life.

John was just beginning to direct the gun back toward Suzanne when the radio in his left hand spoke with an unearthly, deep tone. To John, the sound was like the cry of God coming from his hand. Every muscle in his body stiffened.

"Donald Rothman," the box said, "can you hear me? I must speak with you right now."

"Rothman? Who's Rothman?" John Brown thought. "He doesn't want to talk to me. The voice wants to talk to Rothman." Finally, through the crack cloud that fogged his brain, John Brown remembered that Rothman was the name he had used to enter the dentist's office. The voice really did want to speak with him. He was just using the wrong name. Well, now was obviously the time for John to reveal himself.

"This is John Brown," he said into the radio, "there is no Donald Rothman here. Rothman is a myth. I am reality. Who is this who speaks to me?"

Everyone in the lobby became mute. One of the men had found the release button but hesitated to engage the mechanism for fear that the sound would interfere with Eli's concentration. Even the two irate residents knew that something very important was happening. They moved out of the way, afraid even to whisper their concerns to each other.

"I am your friend Mr. Rothman," Garner said into the radio, still using his carefully measured tones and intentionally avoiding the mention of his own name. "I am here to help you, to release you from your prison." There was not another sound in the entire city beside Eli's voice. Even the traffic noises on the street appeared to be held in suspension.

"I told you," the man on the twenty-second floor replied, "There is no Rothman. I am John Brown, the same John Brown who led the great slave revolt. I invented Donald Rothman for my convenience. What do you want of me?"

"I want Donald Rothman," Eli responded, in slow but firm words. "You did not create Mr. Rothman. He created you. You, Mr. John

Brown, are not real. I must speak with someone authentic."

Silent anger gripped John Brown. How dare this voice tell him that he did not exist? He would prove his reality by finishing his task and destroying the evil woman. Again, he directed the weapon toward Suzanne but Brown's hand started to shake as the radio spoke once more.

"Mr. Rothman... Donald... speak with me. I need you... I need you right now!"

Deep inside the dementia, Donald Rothman heard his name being called, repeatedly called by a strong, confident voice, a sound that would not accept anything less than a response. Rothman awoke and took control of his own body. The engineer discovered himself, still half-stoned on cocaine, standing in the hallway of a strange apartment with a gun in one hand and a radio in another. For a moment he was terribly confused, but almost immediately became aware of what had happened. Donald found that he knew all the events, everything the usurper had done since taking over his being. But he knew them not from the perspective of one who had lived the occurrences, but rather, more as if a distant observer. Still, the knowledge was sufficient for him to react. He dropped the gun on the carpet and took the radio in both hands.

"This is Don Rothman," he said, "please help me."

In the lobby, Garner waved the team forward. The man standing at the button moved his finger and the doors opened. Everyone dashed toward the elevators. Eli remained behind, alone with his radio in the lobby.

"Mr. Rothman," he said quietly, "I am Elias Garner and help is on the way. Is Ms. Rosewell all right?"

"I don't know," Rothman responded, clearly on the edge of tears. "He wanted to kill her. He would have shot her in another minute. But she's lying on the floor. Maybe fainted. Maybe hurt. Please send help right away. I don't know how long I can keep him away."

"They will be there in minutes, Mr. Rothman," Eli continued. "Will you unlock the apartment door now please?"

"Certainly," came the immediate answer. Don Rothman went to the entrance, turned the three bolts and left the door open wide. His body shivered as he fought to retain control.

"I think I am losing myself to him again," he said into the radio.

"Not yet," came Garner's reply, firm and commanding. "First you have to protect Suzanne. Put the gun under water, in the toilet, so if Brown comes back he can't use it."

"Yes, of course." Don Rothman stumbled into the bathroom, battling the strengthening attempt on the part of Brown to return. The engineer could not submerge the entire gun. The toilet bowl was too small, but enough was immersed, he hoped, to render the weapon useless. As he turned toward the front door, Don Rothman could feel the bulge of the second pistol cutting into the small of his back. Continuing his losing battle against John Brown, Don Rothman drew the gun from his belt, held the steel in his right hand, and tried to decide what to do. The toilet would not hold another, so Rothman plugged the sink and started to fill the basin with hot water. Just as his hand came off the faucet, he lost control of the body and John Brown returned.

"Sorry Rothman," John Brown said out loud. "I'm back." The keeper of the souls dashed the radio to the tiles of the bathroom floor and crushed the receiver under his heel.

"No more voices," he said just as he heard the elevator door open. Brown knew that a group of people was rushing in his direction. John smiled as he stepped into the hallway and leveled the gun directly at the open door.

"The first one through is dead," he said, still speaking as though he had an audience. "Then we take care of the lady and then anyone else we can get before they get us. I'll make them kill us. After that, we can return in some other body." His finger tightened on the trigger.

"Oh, no you won't!" Donald Rothman shouted. Using every bit of strength he could muster, he snatched back his body. "I will not let you hurt anyone."

Donald threw the gun on the floor and fell immediately to his knees. The weapon slid across the carpet and was retrieved by Rebecca, the first of the team through the open portal. The two men behind her jumped on the kneeling figure and handcuffed him.

"Thank you, thank you, thank you," Don Rothman said. The guards took the placid prisoner toward the elevator.

"Be careful," he instructed his keepers, "I don't know who I'm going to be from minute to minute. The other one won't be so easy to handle." They had no idea what he was talking about, but caution was good advice. Their grip on his arms tightened as they took him into the elevator.

"Good, that's good," Rothman said with a smile of relief. "Keep him tight, under *your* control."

Rebecca's attention centered on Suzanne. She examined the lawyer for blood or bruises and, finding none, moved the unresisting body into a sitting position. All Suzanne offered was a blank stare.

"Ms. Rosewell. Can you hear me? You're with friends now. Everything is all right." There was no response. Rebecca pulled her cell phone from her waist and dialed 911.

Terry and the others had entered the elevator with a peaceful Donald Rothman but twenty-two floors later, they departed the car with John Brown in custody. The hefty security guards had John under physical control, but the keeper of the souls was well beyond simple anger.

"How dare you," he snapped at Elias Garner in the lobby. "How dare you interfere with my work? I am on the earth to eliminate evil and you have intervened. For this you will be punished."

Eli placed his hand on John Brown's shoulder and looked deeply into his eyes. The anger seemed to drain from the old revolutionary, his strength for resistance disintegrating. His body slumped and had to be supported by the two men who held on to him.

"You are wrong, John Brown," Garner said gently. "You have been an unknowing tool of evil and you almost succeeded in carrying out one of their most important missions. But thanks to Mr. Rothman, that did not happen. It is now time for you to give Donald back his life and for you and the other souls to return to your resting places. Do you understand?"

"Oh God, Oh God... forgive me," was his only response.

"Have him transported directly to the hospital in Westchester," Garner said to Terry. "And then call his parents. I will handle the police when they arrive."

Terry acknowledged his instructions with a nod and led Rothman-Brown to the nearest security car. A few moments later the ambulance arrived and Eli personally took the emergency crew to the twenty-second floor.

In the ER at Lenox Hill Hospital, the attending physician offered her initial opinion.

"She appears to have lapsed into a catatonic state induced by trauma," she said, shining a flashlight into Suzanne's only mildly responsive eyes. "The human mind uses such devices to escape terrifying situations. This condition could last anywhere from a few hours to the rest of her life. I don't know what to tell you. Physically she's in perfect shape." Elias Garner leaned against the wall, buried his face in his hands and began to cry.

Across town Elizabeth Luckholt listened to the report from her unnamed agent.

"...and now she's at Lenox Hill Hospital under guard but still in that trance-like thing. I am afraid I can't get near her. And if that wasn't enough, John Brown keeps fading and Rothman keeps emerging. Rothman has all of Brown's memories, so if he stays in charge of the body, he'll eventually expose Sam and Larry. That might lead to me and if that happens, well... I got Sam and Larry out of town. It appears that all we can do is wait."

"Waiting doesn't make me happy," Luckholt said, wearing her unfriendly smile, "but we're better off than Eli. He's invested everything in that woman and if she stays in that silly coma for just a week, all his investment goes down the drain. So we'll wait, that's just what we'll do."

CHAPTER TWENTY-TWO

Monty used three days driving to New York. The man was energized, initially by his repetitive dreams that created an almost irresistible compulsion to see Suzanne, and later by a strange sensation that time was growing short. Why the clock *(Or was it the calendar?)* seemed so important was beyond his understanding, but with each mile east, his anxiety grew. To make matters worse, the information, or more accurately, the lack of information from his in-route phone calls raised his adrenaline.

At first he was unable to reach anyone. Suzanne's tape-recorded voice was the only response to his repeated calls to her office. This alone should not have disturbed him. He was calling over the weekend, but still, his sense of unease grew. The discomfort was fed by the failure of a live human voice to answer the phone at Suzanne's home. And while the possibility existed that the New York lawyer was just away for summer vacation, Monty was still worried. Finally, early Monday morning, still a day's drive from New York City, a living person answered Suzanne's work line. The truck driver and the secretary were in direct communication.

When the conversation first began, Margaret was reluctant to give Monty any information at all. She softened after hearing about the two western highway encounters with Suzanne, his role in helping locate Professor Fields and the timely intervention during a confrontation with a mysterious Minnesota State Trooper. When the truck driver finally told Margaret about his dreams, adding the important fact that he possessed Suzanne's home number, the secretary broke down. Anyone with access to her boss's carefully guarded private, personal line, must be considered a friend, even if he had strange dreams. She told Monty about Friday's near tragedy and of Suzanne's confinement to Lenox Hill Hospital, now entering the third day of her coma. The Montanan decided that once-in-a-while substantially exceeding the speed limit was justified.

Montana Monty was most puzzled, and more than a little frightened, by how close his dreams, most of them experienced in the back of an overheated cab during short naps at asphalt covered rest stops, had matched the reality of Margaret's tale. No, the dream had not been perfect. The story related in the sleeping illusions bore little incidental resemblance to the secretary's description of recent events. But the emotions were the same, exactly the same. When Margaret finally told him the story, Monty was nearly overcome by the same fervent waves produced by the nightmares, as if the feelings had been stored inside him, to be released only when strengthened by the conviction of reality.

Suzanne was in trouble, in danger. She needed help from understanding friends. Not anyone would do, only certain people, individuals specially selected by the victim herself. The dreams had told him so. And as much as he had wanted to reject their message, to dismiss them as the result of sleeping in a truck far too hot for comfort, he could not do so. Instead, he drove harder, stopping only when necessary, and arrived at the midtown hospital early Tuesday morning. Monty took the time to wonder why anyone would want to live, much less drive, in such a crowded, compact space as New York City.

In a sudden change of sensations, he found himself wanting desperately to leave, head immediately back to the open highways on the other side of the Mississippi River. The tough Montana truck driver was actually frightened by New York... or... was it by something in New York, something he only began to perceive when inside the city? He didn't know, so he forced his body to continue, reminding himself that he had both a friend who needed him and the Western teamster's bold reputation to maintain. Still, the fear was strangely stubborn.

He overcame his discomfort by immersing all his senses in the search for a place to rest the big silver cab. The multiple restriction signs strapped to every steel pole confused him. Monty had no idea of what "alternate side of the street parking" even meant. After the third pass around the block, the driver guided his rig into an open place along the curb decorated by at least five different "no parking" signs. The action attracted the attention of a young New York City policeman walking along the sidewalk.

"Excuse me officer," Monty said from the height of his cab, speaking first, before the cop had a chance to say a word, "where can I park this thing?"

The policeman more than simply looked at the truck. His eyes absorbed the vehicle. He started with the tip of the chrome grill and carefully scanned every foot of steel, right back to the edge of the huge, rear tires. This member of New York's finest was a truck enthusiast, a young man who roamed the streets of the Big Apple, protecting and serving his fellow citizens while dreaming about driving a big rig on the open highways of east Texas. He had even planned to take a vacation out west, one day, just to watch trucks. The sight of a real-life, super fancy truck, entranced the man in blue. Monty's was the kind of machine he'd only seen in magazines, movies and country western music videos. The cop's personal interest in the vehicle outweighed any concern he might have had with the posted restriction signs.

"From the size of her," the officer said to Monty, "I would think you can park her wherever you please, maybe on top of that Mercedes over there."

"Right," Monty responded with a friendly smile, "but this sign says that you guys are going to tow illegal vehicles and I really can't afford to lose this one."

"First, I doubt if we have a tow big enough to haul your rig away, but..." and the policeman thought for a moment, "this *is* a delivery zone for the hospital and I assume that's what you are here for, delivering something to the hospital, right?"

"Well, I was headed for Lenox Hill Hospital."

"Good, then you just leave the truck right there. I'll keep an eye on her. Just don't be gone too long."

"Thank you," Monty called out as he started to climb down from the cab. "If you're going to be here, I'll leave the door unlocked. Maybe you want to check out the interior. Just lock up if you have to leave." The policeman's child-like expression of pleasure was enough of a response.

Monty was delighted. He knew that this cop didn't really think he was delivering to the hospital. The kid just liked trucks and had found an excuse to indulge his fantasy. The Montanan silently praised his good luck. He could easily have wasted hours more finding a place to park.

"Time?" Monty thought to himself, "why am I still so concerned about time?" A few moments later, he was strolling down the hallway toward Suzanne's room, trying to keep himself from breaking into a dead run.

Suzanne Rosewell was housed in a semi-private room, but the other bed was unoccupied. An older woman, her eyes red from crying, was unsuccessfully trying to rest on the tightly tucked fresh sheets. In a chair beside the patient's bed sat a young Asian man who displayed the countenance of a statue. Between the two strangers was the woman he'd come to see, dressed in a hospital gown, the covers pulled up to her waist, the adjustable bed holding her body in a half-sitting posture. Her hair was brushed carefully around her face and intentionally draped to hide the wires that were attached to the monitor displaying the measurable impulses of her life. An illuminated reading lamp above her head cast a glow that projected a halo of light around her quiet face.

Suzanne did not appear to be even asleep, much less in a coma. She seemed so restful that he expected her to momentarily open her eyes, smile and project that same happy, friendly expression he'd last seen through the window of her car as they parted company in Pipestone, Minnesota. But she didn't move. Instead, the other two faces turned toward the visitor in the denim shirt and the cowboy boots.

"Hello," the older woman said wearily, "I'm Evelyn Rosewell, Suzanne's mother." She sat up on the bed and extended her hand. Monty walked around and took the long, delicate fingers into his large, rough palm.

"My name is Monty. I'm a friend of your daughter's and I came to see if I could help." Evelyn smiled her gratitude but said nothing further and Monty turned toward the sitting man.

"I am Joshua Wilson," the young man said, carefully fighting both his emotions and his accent. "I am Suzanne's friend also. I know you, but I do not know why I know you."

"Yes," Monty said. "I know who you are as well. Not your name or even your face. I just know who you are, but I think I do know why. And it's a crazy story."

"What are you men talking about?" Mrs. Rosewell said, confused by the cryptic conversation.

"The truth is, Mrs. Rosewell," Monty said in an attempt to explain. "I'm not sure I know how to answer your question. I'm talking about a whole set of feelings, mixed together with a series of dreams and centering on a conversation your daughter and I had over coffee in a small town in western Minnesota. Let me start there."

Monty began to speak and though he was supposedly answering the question posed by Suzanne's mother, the conversation was directed entirely at Joshua. He told about his encounters with Suzanne and repeated the strange tale she had related to him over lunch, a meal that must have taken place a hundred years earlier.

Joshua nodded comfortably throughout the story, appearing to have almost anticipated the entire scenario. Nothing Monty said seemed to make the young man uncomfortable. When the truck driver finished the factual part of his monologue, he paused and took a deep breath.

"So I believe that Suzanne thinks that I am one of these Righteous People," he said, visibly uncomfortable with his own conclusion. "Somehow she has, in this troubled moment, sent out a message to me, some sort of mental thing, that I saw as a dream. I think she believes that you too, Joshua, are also one of these special people."

Joshua only nodded, as though the information, while interesting, was unimportant. He told Monty his own story, beginning with how he first met Suzanne and concluding with the police account of the assault resulting in her current condition. Each was exceptionally patient as the other shared his experience. The same could not be said for Suzanne's mother.

The more they spoke, the more distressed Evelyn Rosewell became. Finally, she could not contain herself any longer.

"This is just like the book," she said. "Has everybody gone crazy?"

"What book?" Monty asked, spitting out the words a moment before Joshua was about to ask the same question.

"A book I gave to Suzanne," Evelyn answered with hesitation, "Jewish legends. There was a section about these righteous people... but... but that's just stories, folk tales. You men don't actually believe you are some of those... people, do you?"

"I think Suzanne believes we are," Monty answered. "And right now, that's what's important."

"But it was probably just part of the stress, you know, the tension she was under that finally resulted in this... coma, or whatever you call it. I gave her the book and she wove that story into her fantasy. My daughter was having a nervous breakdown, a simple nervous breakdown. Don't... you... agree?" Evelyn's voice faded away as though she were challenging her own statement. But just in case she wasn't, Monty decided that he would.

"No, I don't think so, Mrs. Rosewell. When Suzanne spoke to me about the Righteous Ones, I found the story very strange but I listened closely because this was a lucid, serious young woman speaking to me. Even though she expressed her own doubts, she gave the myth credibility. I refuse to believe that the smart, sincere person I had lunch with in Minnesota was in the middle of a nervous breakdown."

"Maybe the book would help us," Joshua said, impatient with the banter that he saw as only a diversion from the main task, helping Suzanne to get well. "If you have a copy Missus. We could read and see if it gives us information."

"No I don't," Mrs. Rosewell responded, so surprised by the complete rejection of her theory that she lost the will to resist. "I gave my copy to Suzanne. The book must be in her apartment. I could go to a store and get another."

"That won't be necessary," said a deep voice from the doorway, "I have a copy."

They all turned toward the sound, except, of course, for Suzanne, whose eyes were closed and whose expression remained serene. Standing in the doorway was a tall, black man in a finely pressed, fashionable business suit. He carried a book in his right hand.

"I know who you are," Monty said immediately. "Suzanne told me about you. You're the musician."

"I am Elias Garner," the man said, "the person who, I am afraid, is responsible for Suzanne's condition. I got her into this in the first place."

"Mr. Garner, please tell me the truth. Is it real? Are there really Righteous People that need to be found?" Monty asked.

"Suzanne believes so," Eli answered.

"And if she doesn't find them, what will happen? Suzanne was afraid, as silly as this sounds, that the world might end. Is that what's going to happen?" Monty continued his inquiry, ignoring the gasp his words evoked from Evelyn.

"Suzanne believes so," Eli answered again.

"You're a lot of help," the truck driver shot back, agitated by the cryptic responses. "Maybe you can at least tell me why I feel pressured, like there is so little time left."

"Possibly because there are only four days remaining until the deadline expires and still three people missing from the list."

"Suzanne never told me about a deadline," Monty responded, testing Eli's answers.

"When she last saw you, she didn't know that there was a deadline. That too is my fault. I thought the knowledge would put too much pressure on her. I only told her about it recently."

"Oh, come on," Monty interrupted. "The truth now. This is just some sort of game gone wrong. Not at all real, is it?" But he continued talking, without allowing Elias Garner to respond. "Yes, yes, I know. Suzanne believes. Just give me the book. Maybe that will tell me more."

"Yes, of course," Eli answered passing the volume to Monty. "But the book will not be of much use. You'll have to look elsewhere for answers. I wish I could give them to you, but that's not permitted."

"If you won't give me the answers," Monty said thumbing through the pages and pausing at the author's biography, "and the book doesn't have them, maybe the guy who wrote the book can help. Tell me, where do I find this Jewish Theological Seminary?"

CHAPTER TWENTY-THREE

Monty had never seen a complex of buildings quite like the Gothic structures that composed the Jewish Theological Seminary. The design seemed misplaced surrounded by the other buildings of upper Manhattan. Monty thought that the whole business should have been set out in the middle of a great, wide, open field so people could see the entire architectural panorama as they approached. Maybe the Seminary had originally been constructed in such a setting and the city simply grew around it. The main buildings reminded Monty of churches, but Jews don't go to churches, do they?

Never in his life had he seen so many Jewish people at one time. Not that he hadn't met Jews before, but not more than one or two together, even in the army. Here, they seemed to be everywhere. And they didn't quite fit his image of a twentieth-century Child of Israel either. Well, some did. Some were dressed in dark clothes and wore long side-curls, but the others, except for their skull caps, Monty would never have known were Jewish. They dressed normally, like Suzanne Rosewell.

He stopped the truck at a curb near the main door, a spot completely empty of vehicles and heavily ornamented with parking restriction signs. Monty was mindful that his arrival caused people to pause in the middle of their conversations. He guessed that he was just as curious to them as they were to him. Still, his first task had to be to find a place for the truck, the activity that was becoming his regular New York pastime. He was reading and trying to understand the collection of signs when a stocky black man in a guard's uniform exited the school's security booth and walked directly toward him. The man looked strangely familiar, though Monty was fairly sure they'd never met before.

"You can't park there," the man said to him with a friendly grin to offset the unpleasant information. He really did look familiar. Monty wondered again when they might have ever met.

"I assumed as much," Monty answered. "Everyplace in New York seems be a 'no parking' zone. Do you have any idea where I *can* put the truck?"

"No, I don't, not something that big. Are you trying to go into the school?"

"I've come to see Professor Elias Ab… rom… ow… itz," Monty announced phonetically, waving the book as though the volume were a passport that identified his mission. The expression on the black man's face immediately changed, becoming very grave.

"You're here about Suzanne Rosewell," he said without asking.

"I am," Monty answered, only a little surprised by the comment. "How did you know?"

"I'm not sure. I just sort of guessed. My name is Burt and I work another job at night, at Ms. Rosewell's office. You looked very familiar. I thought maybe I met you at the law firm."

"No, I've never been to Suzanne's office. If we've met, I can't remember. My name is Monty."

"No, I don't think we have met, but any friend of Ms. Rosewell is welcome. I've heard about her trouble."

The two stood silently for a long moment until Monty finally extended his hand. Burt grasped it and the two greeted each other like old friends after a long separation.

"I tell you what," the security guard said, "you leave the truck here and I'll watch out for it. If some cop gets too upset, I'll call you in the professor's office. In the meantime, do whatever you can to help Ms. Rosewell."

"Thanks, Burt," Monty said, still wondering about the strange feeling of familiarity. Burt provided directions and the Montanan headed for the elevator. A few minutes later Professor Elias Abromowitz was pouring coffee.

"Burt told me about Suzanne's terrible experience," the professor said, holding his mug with both hands. "I feel responsible. I don't think she would have undertaken her search without my encouragement. You do know about that?"

"I do. I think Suzanne believes I am one of the people she was seeking." The professor's expression grew brilliant as though someone had switched on a spotlight.

"Oh, you're the one. She told me about you," he said. "This is an honor, sir."

"Well, I don't know about that, but do you think the attack on Suzanne resulted from this quest, as she called it?"

"I don't know... I just don't know. There *are* forces of good and of evil in this world. I believe that the legions of evil become frightened when we human beings actively search out the light of good. Maybe they chose to strike back because Suzanne was getting close to success."

"That thought, Professor, is a little scary. If they went after her, they can go after any of us who try to help her. But, I've come this far, so I might as well continue. What can we do to help?"

"This is a tough question. In reality, I am no more an expert than you. In fact, if you are who Suzanne thinks you are, you may be the real expert on this topic."

"I don't get it," Monty said, genuinely confused.

"Please understand," the professor said, leaning forward over his desk in the traditional teacher's posture. "To me this is just a legend. Yes, I believe the story. I always have, but I also know that over centuries of retelling, a tale changes. I don't know if the version I've put on paper has anything more than the slightest resemblance to the original... or, for that matter, to the truth. But you, if you are truly one of the Righteous Ones, then, by definition, you know the Divine Will. You live that way every day, doing what God wants you to do. Don't get me wrong. I don't think you talk to the Almighty. You just *know* what he wants of humans on his earth. And, probably, this knowledge is not even on a conscious level, so you may have to work very hard to become fully cognizant of the awareness inside you."

"But something happened to me years ago, in the war, something terrible," Monty said with the pain in the front of his eyes. "Certainly that couldn't have been God's will."

"God is not a magician, my friend. I know your story. Suzanne told me. Even a Righteous Person gets caught in circumstances beyond his control or, God forbid, makes an error in judgement. That does not make a person less righteous. Or maybe you became one of the Righteous Ones afterwards, or even as a result of your tragedy. Who knows why God chooses particular people at particular times for particular tasks?"

"What do you mean about becoming a righteous person? I thought one had to be born that way. Isn't that what the story says?"

"No, the legend doesn't say anything except that these Zaddikim simply exist. Who says that God has to grant divine knowledge at birth? None of us has the slightest idea as to what might be in the mind of God," the professor said with conviction.

"OK, OK," Monty replied, "this all makes my head spin. For the sake of argument, let's assume I'm one of those people. How do we help Suzanne? Can we find the missing Righteous Ones for her?"

"Who do you mean when you say *we*?"

"There is another that Suzanne found. A Chinese guy. He's in her hospital room right now, waiting for me to return. What if the two of us continue the search on her behalf, while Suzanne gets well?"

"I don't know," the professor pondered, leaning back in his chair, "it's possible. Unless I miss my guess, you and this Chinese man should be able to recognize the other Zaddikim... uh... Righteous People. There should be some sense, some connection between you. But without Suzanne, I wonder if that will do any good?"

"What do you mean?"

"This Elias fellow. There must be some reason why he chose only one person, one young woman to do the entire search. Wouldn't the quest have been more efficient if he chose, say, five people to seek the missing five Zaddikim? But no, he only picked Suzanne. I feel that she is more than just an instrument that can be replaced when not functioning correctly. My fear is that unless she awakens in time, Mr. Elias Garner's goal will not be fulfilled. I could be wrong, though. So, it's at least worth trying."

Monty was far from elated as he dragged himself down to the elevator and back out on the street. He'd come to see the professor seeking answers and all he came away with were more questions. He tried, as had Suzanne, to convince himself that the whole project was probably some sort of fraud. But he couldn't shake the feeling that the risk of such an assumption was too great.

Burt was seated in a chair that he'd moved outside the security booth to provide himself a clear view of the truck. The black man stood as Monty approached.

"Well, that didn't take long," he said.

"Bad news doesn't usually take very much time."

"The news was that bad?"

"Well, really just not good enough," Monty related. "The professor told me... he said.... Well, he told me a lot of things. It's a very confusing story. Excuse me, I just can't seem to think straight."

For a moment, Monty's eyes glaze over. In the back of his mind, in the depth of his semi-consciousness, he senses a feeling, one that he needs to heed. Something... no, someone telling him something, but he can't figure out quite what. His heart races, his mind reaches out. His whole body feels, for a brief moment, just as it had when he first had the premonition that Suzanne was in trouble. During that brief moment, Monty feels as though Suzanne is reaching out to him from the depths of her coma, from way downtown in the hospital room and telling him to... to what? To look straight ahead? Is that what this feeling is asking him? What does that mean?

Monty did what he thought the feeling was telling him. He focused his gaze and looked straight ahead, directly into the concerned face of Burt.

"God, I must be stupid! Here I thought I was listening to the professor, but I wasn't. If I had been, I would have known..."

"I'm sorry," Burt said. "I'm confused."

"No, no, don't be sorry. I'm the one who's confused. You remember that feeling we both had... the one that said we knew each other? Well I think I know why. My friend, get ready to hear a story that you will not want to believe. I'm not sure I believe it. But first, read this chapter in Professor Abromowitz's book."

They retreated to the shade of the guard station and Burt read carefully while Monty waited with diminishing patience. When the guard was finally finished the truck driver began to speak, sharing as much of the story as he could remember. He told Burt about his adventures with Suzanne in Minnesota and his own experiences in Viet Nam. He repeated each and every word he could recall of his conversation with Professor Elias Abromowitz.

"Do you mean that I..." Burt said, refusing to finish the sentence.

"I think so."

"No, not possible. Not me."

"That's how I feel about myself, but the professor says that Suzanne could very well be right, and if me, why not you? That would be one way to explain why we feel we know each other. Let's test the theory. Come to Suzanne's hospital and meet Joshua. If the two of you relate to each other any way near the way you and I have, then, well..."

"I don't know," Burt answered hesitantly.

"What have you got to lose?" Monty replied. "Besides, this might just be the way to help Suzanne."

"Alright, you've convinced me," Burt said with a smile. "I don't know any other way to help her and I have been praying that I'd find a path. I'll try anything, even something this nuts."

They agreed to meet at the close of the guard's shift, before he had to report to the law firm for his night job. Now Monty was elated. He was finally making headway.

His elation was hit hard when he returned to the hospital. Everyone was just as he'd left them, Suzanne still in the seemingly peaceful coma, her mother stretched out on the other bed and Joshua just keeping watch. Somehow, after what he interpreted as the victory with Burt, he had expected something here to change for the better.

Monty wanted desperately to share all his experiences but he knew that he dare not explain any of the events that took place at the Seminary to Joshua. If he did, the information might predispose the intense young man to react positively toward Burt, subconsciously of course, just the way Monty hoped he would. Burt was already mentally tainted and to add Joshua would destroy any proof their meeting might provide. Monty simply told Joshua that the professor had been kind and gracious but of little assistance. He felt physical pain telling even such a small lie to his new friend. Now, all Monty could do was to sit down and join the vigil.

During the next three hours, Suzanne did not move. They knew because they watched her. Only her steady breathing and the lines on the green screens of the monitoring machines gave any indication of life.

The trio continued to quietly observe as a different nurse entered every hour. Each one of the women in white copied data from the electronic devices and wrote the information on a chart attached to the clipboard hanging at the foot of the bed. The first two came and went in silence, ignoring the visitors as though they were not in the room. The third was far more vocal.

"Just watching this lady isn't going to make her wake up," she snapped at the surprised gathering. "Talk to her. Touch her. Tell her who's here. Try and reach her. She was frightened into this condition. She has to be convinced that it's safe to come back."

This woman was older than the others, older even than Suzanne's mother. The nurse's hair was gray, tight and curly. Her skin was dark as though she were either very tanned or from a mixed racial background. Her body was thin and hard, like an athlete who refused to age. Her voice, reflecting a very slight, and indeterminate accent, was strong and commanding. She was someone who had been in charge so long that no one questioned her authority.

"I'm sorry," Suzanne's mother said, speaking for the group. "Nobody told us."

"Hasn't the doctor been in?" the nurse asked.

"No," came the answer.

"Figures," she said with annoyance. "Well, I'll look into that. In the meantime, offer this woman some stimulation or get out of the way. We don't need you just sitting around and neither does she!" The nurse stormed out of the room and ran directly into Burt who was just arriving.

"Excuse me," Burt apologized.

"Oh, another one. You're just what we don't need. Well, they have their instructions. The same goes for you." The nurse disappeared down the hall.

"What was that all about?" Burt asked of Monty.

"I'll explain in a moment," he answered, "but first I would like you to meet Mrs. Rosewell, Suzanne's mother, and my friend Joshua."

Burt nodded politely at Evelyn and turned his attention to the small man in the chair. The moment their eyes met, both started to speak at the same time. Joshua got his sentence out first.

"Have we not met?" he asked.

"I can't think when, but I'm sure I know you. I work at Ms. Rosewell's law firm, the night guard."

"I work there also… as a messenger," Joshua answered, "but just for the last few days. I haven't worked late enough to meet a night guard."

"But isn't it possible that's where we met?"

"No, not possible," Joshua retorted and turned toward Monty. "He is also one, yes?"

"Yes, I think so," the truck driver said.

"Well, I'm impressed but not convinced," Burt interrupted. "Joshua and I could have met before. I still think it's possible."

"Does that really matter?" Monty asked.

"No, I guess not. I will do what I can to help. Actually, I'm ready right now. I called my company after you left the Seminary, put in for some vacation and someone else is already set to cover my shift on Wall Street. If there are only a few days left, I want to be part of it."

Monty grinned at Burt who returned the smile with a slightly embarrassed grimace. All three of the men knew that Burt, by making those arrangements, had admitted that he was willing to, at least, accept some of the absurd story even before the test meeting with Joshua.

"What are you men going to do now?" Suzanne's mother asked.

"Good question," Monty said, "what *do* we do now?"

"If there are two more Righteous People to be found," Burt said, "and if we are able to recognize these folks, then we should split up and tour the city, find two more and bring them back here."

"That is good, but not right," said Joshua. "Each of us by our self will not have confidence. We will think we have found them but will not be sure. But if we are together, then we will all know and be sure. Besides, together we can be stronger against, well... whatever hurt Miss Suzanne."

The other two agreed and all of them turned and moved as a group toward the rapidly darkening city streets. Evelyn Rosewell shifted to her daughter's side and began speaking softly, praying to the God she'd ignored most of her life.

In the hospital lobby, the man with no name turned his back, pretending to use the pay phone. To say that No Name was surprised to see the truck driver in New York would have been a profound understatement. He was shocked, so much so that he almost forgot to face away and avoid recognition.

He had no idea why the man from Montana was in the city, or who his two friends might be, but he was sure of one thing. When he found the answer, he wouldn't like what he'd learned. Elizabeth Luckholt was going to like it even less.

CHAPTER TWENTY-FOUR

Elizabeth Luckholt was livid. Her pale face transformed bright red while the veins in her forehead throbbed with an intensity that made them appear ready to rupture. Yet, at the same time, the tone of her voice remained perfectly tranquil. If No Name had been speaking to her on the phone, he wouldn't have known she was angry. Unfortunately for him, she had demanded his report be delivered in person.

He stood in front of her desk, watching the physical manifestations of her anger while hearing her calm, collected tone and wishing that she'd at least shout. The pretense of composure was almost more than he could handle. He kept expecting the pressure in her temples to grow beyond their capacity. The stress she generated was so great that he began to empathize with her emotions and lost his ability to concentrate.

"You'll have to handle this yourself," she said, "and very, very soon."

"I beg your pardon," No Name replied, not sure he'd heard the instruction correctly.

"Do you have a hearing problem? Which part didn't you understand?" she retorted, her voice cooling several more degrees. No Name shuddered. "There's no time to seek out and train operatives. Four days remain until the next meeting of the Management Committee. I want to be absolutely sure that Suzanne Rosewell is incapable of any action that will disrupt that meeting."

"But she's still in a coma."

"Then be certain that she never gets out of the coma, and make sure her friends can't do anything to help her."

"If I handle this personally, you might be implicated."

"I'm willing to take that risk and so are you." This was not a request. "And I don't care how you do your job. Just get it done. Now get out of here."

Despite having received an unpleasant set of marching orders, No Name was relieved to have been dismissed.

"And then the man with no name visited with Luckholt for a few minutes and was spotted leaving headquarters in a big hurry," Rebecca reported to Elias Garner. "Shall we do something special to protect Ms. Rosewell?"

"There is nothing more for us to do," Eli replied with just a touch of sadness in his tone.

"I don't understand."

"Orders, straight from the Chairman. She has three Righteous Ones in her company. Their task will be to protect her. This is no longer our responsibility."

"But these men are rank amateurs, boss. They're not even confident in their status. No Name... he's a cold, calculating, experienced professional. What could the Chairman be thinking?"

"Who knows what's in the mind of the Chairman?" Eli responded to the young woman's concerns. The two of them sat silently for more than a minute. When Eli began to speak again, Rebecca wasn't, at first, sure if his statement was connected to the conversation or an entirely new topic.

"There are those who believe," he said, "that the world was created only to be a battleground between good and evil." He paused again, this time for almost two minutes before joining his thoughts together.

"Maybe the Chairman thinks the contest should now take its own natural course. And our orders are clear. We may observe, but we may not interfere any longer."

The three men wandered the streets of New York with purpose but without a plan. They hadn't the vaguest idea where to begin and for their initial two hours the stops were totally random. Burt found a church and they went inside. A few scattered worshipers spotted the otherwise empty pews and the searchers moved among them, offering gentle greetings and trying to find the sought-after vibrations in their responses. Nothing positive came through. In fact, the sight of a black man, a white man and an Asian traveling together, breaking New York rules by greeting complete strangers, made the pastor suspicious. He called the police but the trio had harmlessly departed before the squad car arrived.

Next, thanks primarily to Joshua's somewhat strange early immigration experiences, they tried a run-down bar. This time they only stayed a few moments. One didn't need to be especially empathic to read the suspicion generated by the appearance of a racially mixed group of men traveling together at so late an hour.

Monty suggested they establish some sort of pattern and after a few minutes of discussion, the group decided to tour hospital emergency rooms, shelters for the poor and abused, and any other social service agency they could find operating in the middle of the night. They were in and out of the subways, wandering dark, empty streets and finding every conceivable haven used by those without money or friends. They learned more about New York City at night than they had either expected or desired to know. Revealing the actual extent of human suffering that was available for observation shocked native New Yorker Burt as much as the Montana truck driver and the Chinese immigrant.

As Righteous People, the anguish of the despairing touched them just a little more than the same pain might have affected others making a similar tour. Though their souls ached, their resolve remained firm and they continued from one storefront to another as the night grew longer and the streets more and more empty. Still, not a hint of the feelings that they shared for each other was detected among the dozens of strangers they encountered on their odyssey. They were beginning to get discouraged.

"I don't think this is working," Monty said, as the hour neared three a.m. "I can't believe that none of these people we met qualify. We're just not *that* unique."

"Agreed," said Burt as they walked toward another church-operated alcohol detoxification center, "but we have to admit, nothing is happening. Maybe the professor was wrong. Maybe we can't just tell."

"But what about the sensations we get from each other?" Monty replied. "That strong sense that we'd all met before. I can still feel it."

"Maybe we did," Joshua said, sounding very thoughtful, "maybe we did meet before but not in the usual way." Monty and Burt listened carefully as Joshua slowly thought out the new line of reasoning.

"We have to examine what we have in common, what is the same about all three of us," Joshua continued. "Me and Burt, we both work at law firm, but not Monty. We are of different races, different ages, have different family backgrounds, different cultures, not even the same religions. We are all different faiths from the Jewish religion where Miss Suzanne found the legend...." Joshua paused holding the revelation. The other two also stopped. All three knew the answer at the same time.

"Ms. Rosewell herself, right?" asked Burt. "She's our only common factor. She knows us all, maybe even considers us all to be her friends."

"Who knows what else, but she's definitely the key," Monty joined in. "We related to each other because we'd all met Suzanne. Which means, if we're going to find two more Righteous People, they have to be among those who Suzanne has already met or will meet real soon."

"Yeah. So, what do we do now?" Burt asked.

"I don't know," Monty responded.

"We go back to the hospital," Joshua commanded, now sure of his direction. "Check on Miss Suzanne. Then we find places where she knows people, the law office, her family, even restaurants where she likes to eat. We ask her mother to tell us things. Then we search."

The trio was relieved to have a direction as well as an excuse to discontinue wandering the city's centers of human misery. Even Righteous Men have a limit.

No Name watched them move from the illumination of the street light back into the shadows of the old buildings. He recognized that there was a new purpose in their stride and wondered where they might be heading. He'd been following them all evening, though considerable time, and several stops, had passed before he realized just what they were doing.

When their purpose finally became clear, he used all his mental powers to try and block any feelings transmitted by the people they met. Maybe, just maybe, he could camouflage any other Righteous One they might encounter. No Name had no idea if his plan would work or if he even had the power to accomplish such a major blockage.

Luckholt would know. She could tell him just what to do but he was afraid to call her. He knew that she'd order him to directly confront the three men and frighten them away from their task. And if they weren't frightened, well, he'd have to do more, whatever was necessary. For some reason, the man with no name was almost as reluctant to face these three as he was to see Elizabeth Luckholt again. And since they seemed not to be accomplishing anything, he decided simply to continue following. But he did wish that he could have overheard the conversation that took place beneath the street lamp.

"We're being followed," Monty said in a whisper as they entered the subway once more. "I don't want to sound paranoid, but I am convinced that I'm right."

"I agree," added Burt. "I have felt that way for quite some time, but I thought the sensation came just from being on these streets at night. I haven't seen anybody, but I know he's out there, one man."

"Right," confirmed Joshua, "I feel him too. I feel like I know him."

"I do know him," Monty said, completing the circle. "We met in Minnesota. Suzanne went up against him twice. He works for that Luckholt woman and he's following us. That's good news."

"Oh?" asked Burt, trying to smile, "doesn't sound like good news."

"No seriously," Monty answered, grinning back. By this point they were boarding the train. "If he's following us, then he's concerned. If he's concerned, we must be on the right track."

"These people did a very bad thing to Miss Suzanne," Joshua interjected. "Maybe they want to do things to us."

"I was thinking about that too," Monty answered. "When he was hassling Suzanne in Minnesota, I arrived, she said, just in time. But he backed down awful fast. I've been wondering if this Righteous Person thing might have something to do with his retreat. If he's afraid of one middle-aged, slightly overweight, bearded truck driver just because he might be some sort of righteous being, then how would he handle confronting all three of us?"

The other two nodded in agreement. The thought gave them courage and slowly the fear they were feeling began to disperse. Two cars back, the man with no name began to shiver. Unfamiliar with the emotion of raw terror, he didn't recognize it when the feeling settled in his gut.

CHAPTER TWENTY-FIVE

The three Righteous Men returned without pause or incident to Lenox Hill Hospital where they were prepared to gather information from Evelyn Rosewell and then, with the new data in hand, return directly to the streets. The more they discussed their revised plan of action, the more they became convinced that this was the track to the solution. Not one of them wanted to express the worry that each, as an individual, was feeling, and that each suspected the others were sharing.... What do we do if this idea doesn't work?

When the sun rose, there would remain only three full days. At dawn of the fourth day... maybe there wouldn't be a dawn on the fourth day. That day could represent the final mark on the calendar, and this last night that might come without a dawn was fittingly a Saturday. Monty thought to himself that if the world really ended, that'd literally be one hell of a way to mess up a weekend. They were all so absorbed in their own individual deliberations, that the challenge from the security guard at the hospital front desk came as a shock. The clock was showing four in the morning and they were a strange looking bunch, tired and drawn from the night of walking with no rest. The uniformed man would not have been doing his job if he let them just pass by.

"Excuse me gentlemen," he said from behind the desk as they attempted a confident walk through the lobby. "May I ask your business here?"

"We are friends of Ms. Suzanne Rosewell in room 807," Monty answered, having, throughout the night, evolved into the regular spokesman for the group. "We were told that she has special 24-hour visiting privileges." The guard held up his hand to halt their progress while punching a few keys on his computer terminal.

"That's true," he responded, "but only for immediate family. Everyone else is supposed to visit during regular hours. Mrs. Rosewell, the patient's mother, is up there now."

"Yes," Monty continued, "we know. But there are important issues that we must discuss with Mrs. Rosewell and we need to check on Suzanne as well."

"Sorry guys. I'm afraid your issues will have to wait until eight o'clock. Rules are rules and…."

"Excuse me," Burt interrupted, "but I know you." Joshua and Monty exchanged a hopeful glance at the mention of recognition but, this time, they did not share Burt's sensation.

"You're George, aren't you?" Burt said. "We work for the same security company." The guard stared at him for a moment before the light appeared on his face. "Right, you're Burt, night shift on Wall Street, right?"

"Yeah, that's me, and if you ring the room, Mrs. Rosewell will vouch for us. George, it's important that we go upstairs." The hospital guard paused only a moment before answering.

"Your word's good enough for me, Burt. Go on ahead and don't tell anyone I'm so easy."

"Thanks, George," Burt responded, urging the others forward with a gesture.

"Now that was a fortunate coincidence," Monty said as they entered the elevator.

"Yes, a very fortunate coincidence," Burt replied.

Neither the trio nor George had noticed the tall, broad-shouldered man who slipped past them while they were absorbed in conversation. The man with no name hid in a phone booth until Monty, Burt and Joshua had gone upstairs. Then he reluctantly dialed a special private line at headquarters.

The three nurses at the medical station on the eighth floor ignored the men passing from the elevator into the empty corridor that led to Suzanne's room. They assumed that anyone who got past security had a right to be there.

In the quiet of the hallway, the sound of their shoes on the tile floor echoed loudly against the bare walls. The men slowed their pace, in part to reduce the noise but more to delay their entrance. When they finally arrived, the trio found their fears realized. Nothing had changed. Suzanne was still in the coma and her mother had fallen asleep in the empty bed. Monty gently woke Mrs. Rosewell.

"Oh, hello," she said as soon as enough sleep had passed from her eyes to realize who was standing over her. "Did you have any luck?"

"No, I'm afraid not," Monty responded in a half-whisper. "But we think we know why and we need some information that only…."

"What you need to do," a booming voice from the doorway nearly shouted, "is to go back from where you came and do so before you are unable to go anywhere at all." Everyone turned toward and focused on the man with no name who was standing just inside the entrance.

No Name was breathing hard as though he had just completed a tough run. The motion of his huge chest helped to emphasize the developed muscles in his neck and shoulders. His presence filled the room. To further demonstrate his strength, he flexed the tendons in his bare arms so that their hardness was accentuated. His eyes appeared to glow an impossible shade of red as though his eyelids were a window looking in on a coal furnace that burned inside the man's skull. The impression of fire was so strong that the temperature in the room seemed to rise the moment he entered. Initially, the very tight hand of terror gripped them all.

"This is your last warning," No Name bellowed. "Go home. Go anywhere you please. But go away. This is not your business and if you try to interfere, you will have to deal with forces beyond any you have ever imagined." Monty was the first to find his voice.

"I know you," he said. "You pretended to be a state trooper in Minnesota. I wasn't afraid of you then and I'm not afraid of you now." But the man knew Monty was lying.

"If that's true," he said, "then you were a fool in Minnesota and you are a bigger fool here, and I don't believe you to be such a fool. I think you're afraid… all of you, and well you should be. But I'll give you a chance to leave the fear behind as you depart, without harm, from this place. And, as a gesture of good will, I promise that I'll do nothing to hurt Ms. Rosewell." The big man cleared the doorway by stepping further into the room and made a grand gesture with his arms indicating the path for retreat. No one, except Joshua, moved a muscle.

The little fellow stepped forward and, at first, No Name thought that Joshua was accepting his invitation. A smile of victory started to cross his face but disappeared quickly when the young Asian, the shortest person in the room, stretched his body in a vain attempt to stand nose-to-nose with the monster.

"You will be the one to leave," Joshua said defiantly, "or you will be the one who suffers. I fear you not. I met generals in the People's Army of China tougher than you and I did not fear them either. They are still there, and I am here in a free country. You are not welcome in this room. Leave or I and my friends will put you out. My friends are very..." he searched for the right term and when he found the word, he smiled. "Powerful, very powerful."

Joshua's courage inspired the others. Not that they were no longer afraid, but now they had confidence in their ability to manage the fear. Burt and Monty moved forward, standing directly at Joshua's back. Even Suzanne's mother sat up on the bed in a posture of defiance. The man with no name involuntarily took a tiny step backward and hoped the others had not noticed. They had.

"That's not enough," Burt said with power in his voice. "Take bigger steps and leave, right now. I have this strange feeling that all I have to do is place my hands on you and your strength will be drawn away, you'll be mush between my fingers." Burt reached forward and the big man retreated yet another step.

"Yes," Monty added, "I have the same feeling. What do you think if we both take hold of him?"

"Or all three," Joshua joined in as they simultaneously reached for the man with no name. Their hands remained empty. The man turned, and with amazing speed for one so large, fled in terror down the corridor. The elevator opened just as he reached the door and he almost knocked over the white-haired supervising nurse as he leapt inside. The nurse glared at him with disgust and then turned her back and walked away. When the elevator door closed, the three men knew that they'd never encounter the man with no name again.

"Joshua," Monty asked, "did you really think that if we touched him, he'd melt, like the witch in the Wizard of Oz?"

"No, I was scared to death," Joshua answered with a smile, "but I tried a poker bluff. Was it good, yes?"

"Oh, yes," Burt joined in, "and I thought I was the only one bluffing!" They'd won the first round, but they were still no closer to accomplishing the goal.

"Forgive me, Mrs. Rosewell," Monty said to Suzanne's mother. "I'm sorry for the interruption."

"Who was that?" she asked. The woman was still frightened but defiant.

"To tell you the truth," Monty answered, "I don't really know. He works for the same corporation as that Garner fellow, but for someone on the opposite side. If I were a religious man, I might say he represented the army of evil, but I'm not a religious man."

Still, it was a thought that left them all drained and speechless as though the enormity of the event had finally started to penetrate. The room was cold. Each of the three men assumed, separately, that the change in temperature was something they alone were experiencing as their emotional strength drained. Mrs. Rosewell got up off the bed and maternally pulled Suzanne's covers tight around her neck. The three men looked at each other and allowed themselves to shiver.

"Monty," Evelyn said, " you were going to ask me something before that man came in and behaved so boorishly."

"Yes, Mrs. Rosewell," Monty said with a grin.

"Evelyn, please."

"Certainly, Evelyn. We've decided that your daughter is the critical factor in identifying the two missing righteous people. She's the only common factor between all three of us, so we think the way to proceed is to go around to Suzanne's friends and contacts. Go where Suzanne used to go and see if we can find the missing ones among these people. Can you help us? Tell us about her friends, where she likes to hang out, anything."

"Oh dear," Evelyn answered. "I'm afraid that my daughter and I aren't very close. I don't know if I can be of much assistance. I can't think of a thing to help you. I don't know why, but I just can't."

"You can't, because for years I've kept my personal life a secret from you and from everyone else. But that's going to change, starting now."

The voice was from the other bed. Sitting up, sharp eyed, smiling, and looking completely rested, Suzanne Rosewell was wide-awake.

CHAPTER TWENTY-SIX

Joyful pandemonium erupted. Suzanne was instantly surrounded by the three men, all inquiring at the same time as to her physical condition and the state of her memory. But Suzanne Rosewell's focus was solely on her mother. The two shared a long, tight embrace while the men fell respectfully silent. The embrace lasted so long, that the male trio drifted into discomfort as each of them started to sense that they were in the presence of a special private moment. A second before they all decided to leave, Suzanne turned her attention back to the assembly.

"What happened?" she asked the group at large. "Where am I?" And to Monty, "How did you get here? I *am* happy to see you, but why are you in New York?"

"What do you last remember?" Monty asked.

"Mother's voice," she answered without hesitation while looking toward Evelyn, "cutting through the darkness, blocking the bad dreams and telling me that I was safe. I followed her voice, it seemed to take forever, and then I woke up. And I remember that terrible man with the huge gun who came into my apartment. He fired, and... and that's all I can recall."

Talking in turn, as though they had rehearsed from a script, the three searchers recounted the events of the past few days, each telling their own specific part of the continuing tale.

Suzanne was both horrified and fascinated. She found the four days missing from her life to be especially frightening. But Monty's dream, the source of the inspiration that generated his compulsion to drive to New York and the emotional connection that the three men had immediately felt for each other, captivated her imagination. She shivered a bit when they described the minutes-old confrontation with No Name, but the presence of her new friends furnished her with what she needed to disperse the last remnant of her dread.

"Am I safe now?" she asked, almost childlike.

"I wish I knew for sure," Monty answered. "I think so. But I just can't be certain. The big man is gone, but there is always his boss. If she is who I think she is, then we are likely to see her hand again."

"Who is she, really?" Suzanne asked.

"The professor spoke about battles between good and evil. I think we all know on which side of the line she stands."

Suzanne realized that for the first time since the quest began, no one in the room challenged the assumption of the existence of forces beyond reason. There were no protestations about not believing in the supernatural, no excuses made for the mystical references. Not even her own legally trained mind touched on the theory, often used as her intellectual retreat, that the entire story was someone's elaborate fabrication. With only a few days left, they'd finally all become true believers.

"I'd like to go home," was all she said out loud, her eyes moistening. "Can I get dressed and leave now?" Wednesday morning's sun was beginning to lighten the New York skyline.

"I'll go find out," Evelyn said, and with purpose in her step left the room, heading toward the nurses' station.

"How much time remains?" she asked of Monty, hoping her own mental calculations were in error.

"As best we can figure, three full days," he answered. "Elias Garner said that the meeting would be held at dawn on Saturday. Today is Wednesday."

"Then I must leave," she said. "I can't just sit here. There are two more to be found." She started to lift herself out of the bed.

"And where do you think you are going, young lady?" said the supervising nurse who had just arrived towed by Suzanne's mother.

"Home," Suzanne said while a strange smile that had to be described as mirroring contentment decorated her face. Monty noticed the change in Suzanne's appearance. He had expected her to be either firm and angry or painful and pleading as part of her attempt to leave the confines Lenox Hill. What he saw did not match the circumstances and he turned his puzzled eyes toward the nurse. Then he understood and matched his smile to Suzanne's.

"You are not going anywhere until the doctor has an opportunity to check you out," the nurse said, glancing quizzically from Suzanne's face to Monty's. "I'm delighted you are awake and alert, but I'm not letting you out of here until we're sure you are totally recovered. You've been through a major trauma... and what are you two grinning about?"

Joshua and Burt saw the interplay and also turned their attentions on the nurse. After a moment, their smiles duplicated Monty and Suzanne's. The woman was becoming very confused and feeling a little threatened.

"All of you with that silly smirk," she said, with a hint of anger. But then she paused contemplatively. "But did we all meet somewhere, sometime in the past? Is that why you're grinning? We know each other but I can't remember when we met, so you're making fun of me?"

"No, ma'am," Suzanne responded, "no one is making fun of you." And to the others. "Please, take Mother and go get some breakfast. I'd like to be alone with this lady for a few minutes, although after I tell her the story, she may never let me out of the hospital."

The trio followed Suzanne's instructions and moved out the door. They could still hear Suzanne as they walked down the hall.

"I know you won't believe this story," her voice carried into the corridor, "but please listen with an open mind and...."

An hour-and-a-half later they returned. The nurse was sitting in the room, her face pale and her expression very puzzled. They didn't know if she'd been there all the time or if she'd gone and returned and they weren't going to ask.

"My friends," Suzanne said, "I would like you all to meet Margo Garcia, the supervising nurse in charge of this floor. Margo has worked here for thirty years. She was the first native Spanish speaking nurse ever to reach management in this hospital. She has four grown children, all of whom are college graduates and she has cared for more patients than we can imagine. And…."

"And," Mrs. Garcia interrupted, "I don't believe this story for a minute. I think you all may be crazy."

"We don't believe it either," Burt responded, "at least not in our heads. But here..." he pounded his chest, "I feel something I can't ignore. So, well, that's why I joined the loony brigade."

"I understand what you're saying," Margo said. "But I can't go with you. Even if I did believe, my responsibilities here are just too great. But I did find a doctor who'll check Ms. Rosewell and, if everything is in order, he'll sign the release papers."

"Thank you," Suzanne said.

"I'm required to call the police when you wake up. They want a statement about what happened in the apartment. Should I call?"

"Can you make a mistake?" Suzanne asked, "Like forgetting the call until I've left. I'd rather speak to them from home."

"I can do that. I'll apologize. My other patients kept me too busy."

"Thank you again."

"I really do have other duties to attend," Margo Garcia rose to leave but paused at the door and turned toward Suzanne. "God go with you, young lady," she said and disappeared.

"I hope so," Suzanne responded in half a voice to the empty doorway. "I really hope so."

Within an hour, a young resident appeared with the assigned task of checking Suzanne's vital signs. Another hour passed before he declared her to be in "the best of health." He was uncomfortable with the crowd in the room and when he asked them to leave, Suzanne requested that they remain. The doctor was too young and inexperienced to defy the determination of the group. Maybe they thought that if he found something wrong, they could make it right. And maybe they could.

By eight a.m. Suzanne had been discharged. Monty was leading the group to the parking lot where, at insane expense to a man from Montana, he'd finally found someone to care for his truck.

"No taxicabs, no more subways," Monty said. "I am taking everyone home in my rig. You won't ever get a ride like this in New York again."

Suzanne was first. She accepted the honor only when the men promised they'd get some rest. The night without sleep was written in the circles under their eyes. Burt invited Monty to his house, offering him a place to park, a troupe of friends to watch the truck and the use of his son's bedroom. The deal was too good to refuse. They agreed to gather again at two in the afternoon at Suzanne's Wall Street office. The lawyer, having awakened from a multi-day sleep, was rested and decided she ought to return to work. The others objected, but their exhaustion left them with far less strength than their opponent and they surrendered quickly to Suzanne's posture.

Within moments, she was on the phone to the office, reaching Margaret just as the secretary arrived for work.

"Oh, Ms. Rosewell," Margaret said, "I'm so glad that you're well again. We were all so worried. But don't you think you should take a couple of days off?"

"No Margaret, I'm fine," she answered, "And didn't I tell you to call me by my first name?"

"Did you? I don't remember you doing that."

"Well, if I didn't, I should have, long ago. So please do so." Her voice was gentle, almost apologetic. Margaret did not utter even the mildest of protests.

"Very well, Suzanne," she said, seeming only barely comfortable with the change. "I look forward to seeing you."

"And... that will be in just a few minutes. Please call Mr. Johnston, the Managing Partner, and see if I can get a few moments of time. I have some issues to discuss."

"Yes, boss," Margaret responded, her pleasure evident even through the telephone lines.

As Suzanne fell easily into her usual morning routine of coffee, a light breakfast and a shower, little things kept reminding her of the reason for her days-long absence from the rooms she called home. When she passed the intercom she could almost hear the voice of the doorman intentionally using her first name, twice, apparently as a warning, and one that she failed to understand. She thought about his small act of great courage, imagined him performing with grace while facing the wrong end of a pistol. She made a mental note to thank him for his efforts when he came on duty that evening.

The bolt on the front door was the catalyst that recalled the terror of John Brown's forced entrance. And off in a corner, where the cleaning woman had missed, were tiny remnants of the leather purse destroyed in the gunfire blast that marked her last conscious memory.

But fear did not return with the remembering. Suzanne Rosewell was much like old man Scrooge on Christmas morning, touring his barren flat and pointing out to his confused housekeeper where the various visiting spirits had rested. Like Scrooge, Suzanne did not relive the terror of the visitation but reveled in the clear sense of purpose she had seemed to achieve from it.

"Just one more to go," she said out-loud to the mirror as she applied the last touches of makeup. "That nurse, Mrs. Garcia, was right there, right under our noses. There must be a hundred more like her around the city. All we need is one. Luckholt, your luck has run out."

The post-rush-hour subway ride was uncrowded and equally uneventful. Suzanne's stride reflected her still growing comfort as she entered the building and took the elevator to the main reception floor for the law firm of Markam, Wilber, Kent & Todd.

"Good morning, Ms. Rosewell," said the receptionist just as Suzanne stepped off the elevator. "I'm so glad to see you back at work. That was a terrible thing that happened to you."

"Thank you Shirley," Suzanne answered as she started to walk by. Suddenly she caught a thought and returned to lean on the edge of the traditional high law office reception desk.

"Shirley," Suzanne continued, "did I ever tell you to call me by my first name?"

"No, of course not, Ms. Rosewell," the woman was in a near panic thinking she had unconsciously made a terrible error. "and... and... I don't think I ever have."

"No, you never have and if you don't start immediately then I'll have to call you...," Suzanne looked at the name plate posted prominently on the desk, "Ms. Jorney, from now on."

"I don't understand," came the reply.

"I'm sorry. It's very simple. I would like you to call me Suzanne. I have discovered that I am much more comfortable if people use my first name, OK?"

"OK, Suzanne. But don't get mad at me if I forget. Old habits are hard to break."

"They certainly are," the young lawyer grinned back, "and I am trying to break a few myself." She proceeded down the corridor toward her own office.

Margaret's first sight of her boss carried her from behind her fortress desk and into an instant embrace. Without thought, Suzanne returned the affection by throwing her arms around the older woman and squeezing her with all her strength. Neither of them was aware of how improper they would have both considered this simple gesture only a few shorts weeks ago.

Those occupying the neighboring offices recognized the uncharacteristic manner that Suzanne and her secretary were displaying. The scene left them unsure how to express their own welcomes to their returning colleague.

After all, Suzanne had not been the most popular of coworkers. Her stern manner of dealing with her secretary was well known and all the others expected Margaret's greeting to be brief and certainly formal. The hug upset their equilibrium. As tears came to the eyes of the two embracing women, emotion began to spread throughout the floor.

Within a few minutes, Suzanne's terrifying experience and her miraculous recovery was transformed from something that had simply happened to a disliked coworker into an incident that had effected a colleague, a member of their own professional family. If this thing could have happened to her, they all were thinking, something similar could happen to any of us. Soon they were standing in line to hug Suzanne and while waiting, found themselves touching and hugging each other. When the greetings were finally completed, Markam, Wilber, Kent & Todd's youngest female partner, her eye makeup smeared by tears, settled behind her desk with her secretary seated in front of her.

"There are very few messages," Margaret said, "except those expressing personal concern. I've already started returning those calls to tell people that you are recovered and back at work."

"Thank you, Margaret. What about clients?" she asked.

"Mr. Johnston came by the day after you were taken to the hospital. He said that you were in a coma and no one knew for how long, so he had to reassign your clients to other lawyers until you were better."

"Good move. Do I get to see him today?"

"He said for you to come to his office the moment you were available, that he would make time," Margaret stated, closing her notepad in her usual manner that said all significant information had now been communicated.

"Then I'll go right now," Suzanne said. "Maybe I can get him to leave my clients reassigned until the end of the week. I do have something very important to attend."

Once, in the time before, Suzanne had loved taking the private elevator to the corporate penthouse, the rooftop floor where the senior partners maintained their office suites. Each trip was an excuse to focus on a fantasy that centered on being the first female partner to have a penthouse office. In the dream part of her mind, she'd even picked out the suite, the one facing the Hudson River and currently occupied by old Mr. Wilber himself, a member of the firm's founding family. Wilber was in his eighties, still practicing and in good health. If he continued that way for another eight or ten years, Suzanne's fantasy said, she would be just ready to move up.

But on this trip, the fiction wouldn't play. She couldn't get the mental movie to start and felt as if she were trying to make an old, worn video work on a machine badly in need of repair.

"There's just too much on my mind," she thought as the elevator reached the penthouse floor. "No time for fantasies."

True to his word, Johnston saw her immediately. She hadn't even had time to settle into one of the comfortable leather chairs in the waiting room before the door guardian came to lead her into the dark pine-paneled office.

"A real man's office," she found herself thinking, and without the slightest touch of envy.

"Suzanne," he said, wearing his best courtroom smirk, "I'm so glad you are well. Please sit." An atmospheric disturbance in the room made her uncomfortable. Something unexpected was about to happen. "How do you feel?" he continued.

"I'm at one hundred and five percent, Mr. Johnston. Strong, well, and ready to take back my clients." Her instincts told her what was going to happen next. If they were correct, she might as well provide him with the appropriate opening line and let him get right to the point. He accepted.

"Suzanne," Johnston said, trying to affect the demeanor of a wise old uncle. The posture came very hard to Arthur Edmond Johnston, Esquire. She thought about how easily it came to Professor Abromowitz. "The other partners and I have been talking and I am afraid that we have to admit that we made a mistake. To be perfectly frank, we've decided that we should not have offered you partnership status."

"Oh," Suzanne was surprisingly unsurprised. Still, she was curious about what was to come next. "Are you taking the partnership away?"

"I'm afraid so," he answered. "You know that we have the right to do that, to any partner, under the terms of the agreement."

"Yes, Arthur," she said, intentionally using his first name for the first time ever, "providing you appropriately compensate that partner for her share of the firm."

"True, and a compensation check for more than an appropriate amount has been drawn. I think you will find the settlement generous."

"Am I to be returned to the status of an associate?" she asked, pretty sure that she already knew the answer.

"Oh, Suzanne, we thought that would be too great an embarrassment for you. After all this, we knew you'd want to leave the firm, so we are prepared to make public announcements that this departure is your choosing. That *is* what you prefer, I assume?"

"Please, do not assume," she snapped back. "I find your conclusion outrageous. You're firing me because I was the victim of a crime."

"I'd hoped we wouldn't have to get into this, but since you brought it up..." the friendly demeanor had disappeared. "We've discovered that the attack upon you was not random. That the madman tried to kill you because you are involved in some sort of spiritual quest thing, the same adventure that carried you to South Dakota when you should have been working here. We don't know the details, but we know enough to know that you are not the kind of person who should be associated with our firm."

"Who told you these things?"

"We have a private source. Do you deny them?"

"Would that make a difference?"

"No, not really."

"Then I think this conversation is over, don't you?"

"Yes, Suzanne, I think it is." He handed her an envelope. "You'll find your partnership settlement, salary, vacation pay and a little extra. The firm will continue to pay your health insurance for one year. You probably don't believe me, but I wish you luck and I'll be more than happy to provide you with a personal reference."

Suzanne opened the envelope and looked at the check. The amount was truly substantial.

"Well Arthur," she said, finding herself not only lacking anger, but feeling a certain sense of relief, "this is very generous, not what I would have made as a partner, but very generous anyway." She paused for a moment and took a deep breath. "I would like to clean out my desk and leave at the end of business today, have Margaret handle whatever calls come for me over the next few weeks and refer the personal ones to my apartment. And let me tell everyone myself why I'm leaving.

"Alright, Suzanne, I don't have a problem with that. What are you going to tell people? So we can support your story."

"Oh, that'll be easy. I'm going to tell the truth," Suzanne rose and started to leave. “That you SOBs on the top floor fired me because you don’t approve of my private life....” He started to protest. “Or its impact on my clients. Yes, I know Arthur. But I’ll bet the clients didn’t complain one bit, and some of them will be mine again. All in good time, you’ll see. I don’t know the real reason you’re doing this and I guess I never will, but I hope you can live with yourself Arthur. Goodbye.”

“Goodbye Suzanne and good luck. You’ll do fine, probably better on your own than you ever would with us,” he said, but she was already gone and didn’t hear him.

Arthur Edmond Johnston walked over to his desk and picked up a thin file, opened the cover, glanced at the first page and dialed a number. The phone rang several times before a machine voice answered.

“A message for Ms. Elizabeth Luckholt from Mr. Johnston at Markam, Wilber, Kent & Todd,” he said simply. “Ms. Rosewell no longer works for this firm as of the close of business today. We are prepared to begin handling your corporation’s affairs immediately. And I await your call. Thank you.”

As he spoke, and even after hanging up the phone, his finger kept stroking a second sheet of paper in the file, a copy of a bank deposit receipt for a retainer check in the amount of $750,000.

CHAPTER TWENTY-SEVEN

Margaret took the news badly. Suzanne told her at once, right after returning from the penthouse. She spoke directly and plainly about having been fired from the firm of Markam, Wilber, Kent & Todd, but avoided all mention of her strange quest. She finished by saying that she would be leaving, forever, at the end of the day.

"Frankly," Suzanne said to Margaret, "I'd be happy to go right now except that I've arranged to meet some friends here at two."

"But how could they do this?" Margaret choked through the tears, "You've worked so hard for them, helped make them so much money."

"That's true, and I've even gotten to keep some of that money myself. Don't worry Margaret, in a few months, I'll set up my own practice and maybe you'll come to work for me."

"In a minute," she answered firmly.

"Well, not this minute, anyway. You stay here and continue to draw your salary and benefits. When I'm ready, I'll call. I promise. First I'm going to take a couple of months off."

"Can you afford to do that?"

"Thanks to the firm's unique method of dealing with their own guilt," she waved the envelope, "I can afford that and more. Which reminds me, maybe you should take this check down to my bank before they change their minds. They are, after all, lawyers."

Suzanne was smiling as she passed the check across her desk, almost laughing. Margaret wondered if her soon-to-be ex-boss was really as happy as she seemed or just effectively covering the pain. If the secretary could have squeezed inside Suzanne's skin, she would have been very surprised at the lawyer's response to this life crisis, almost as astonished as Suzanne herself.

After the initial wave of indignation over the injustice had passed, Suzanne Rosewell was not at all distressed. She was relieved. Immediately, she found herself projecting new fantasies to replace the recently shattered daydreams, the illusions she prophetically failed to conjure in her elevator ride to the professional execution.

These replacement scripts included starting her own firm that eventually outgrew Markam, Wilber, Kent & Todd, setting up a practice to service poor people or even going to work for The Legal Aid Society.

Something about the lawyer had changed. She felt different. Suzanne was suddenly no longer comfortable in these modern, plush offices. And she realized that this discomfort had been there before her firing, even before the incident with John Brown. She'd simply failed to recognize what her insides had been trying to tell her. That is, until after Johnston announced the partners' decision.

Suzanne was sorry that Margaret was so pained over the dismissal, but she was grateful for the new sense of freedom she felt. Finally, she could direct her entire attention to the search for the remaining righteous person without the distraction of her job. Margaret would recover, Suzanne thought, as she watched her loyal secretary head for the elevator, the firm's generous severance check gripped in her right hand.

The balance of the morning dragged. Since Suzanne Rosewell, super-lawyer, had a very limited life outside of her office, there were few truly personal possessions to be packed. Most of her time was spent organizing the remaining client files still in her care, cases that were awaiting action in court or by outside parties before being resolved.

She felt an obligation to keep a frame of professionalism around her departure and gave herself the excuse that she could never steal these clients unless they knew she had continued to protect their interests even after she and the firm were traveling in different directions. But somewhere inside, Suzanne knew that she was unlikely to pursue these accounts. She'd be practicing a different kind of law and her only true reason for updating the files was simply because it was the right thing to do.

Though Suzanne told no one other than Margaret, the word of her departure spread through the hallways like fire in dry underbrush. Maybe Margaret had found a need to share her distress. Maybe Johnston had started his own rumor so that Suzanne would not be the one to take the initiative in the battle of the office gossip mill. None of this seemed to matter. While Suzanne wasn't in a hurry to tell her story, she had no objection to people dropping in to say goodbye and learning the first-hand truth.

At first only a few came. When they left, and reported to their colleagues that their parting conversation with Suzanne had been pleasant, more found the courage to call. Some who heard the news chose intentionally not to go, out of fear of being seen with one who had fallen from favor. Others, who didn't like Suzanne from the beginning were pleased to hear she'd no longer be among them.

The news reached Arthur Blake while he was buried in the far corner of the main law library, deep in research.

"Your girlfriend, or your former girlfriend anyway, just got canned," the messenger said, taking some delight in the news.

"What are you talking about?" Blake responded, unable to correlate the information he was hearing with his own sense of reality.

"Rosewell, Suzanne Rosewell. Word is… she's outta here. You did go out with her, right?"

"For a little while. But she's a partner."

"Was a partner. After today, she's just unemployed."

Arthur Blake rose quickly from his chair. Leaving behind his research and the open law books on the table, he went directly to Suzanne's office where he found her sitting behind a completely clean desk, hands folded in front of her, staring straight ahead like an obedient grade-schooler awaiting the start of lessons.

"Are you all right?" he asked, confused.

"I am Arthur. I am perfectly all right. In fact, I think I'm better than I've been for weeks, maybe years. This whole partnership thing, even working in this firm, it was a mistake… for me," she said with more calm than he ever remembered her possessing.

"You worked hard for that partnership, sacrificed most of your personal life. You were singularly focused for years on that one goal. Now you tell me it was a mistake?

"That's right. I guess a person can get so lost in the actual process of traveling that you forget to question the direction," she said, her eyes focused directly on him. "In the process, I treated a lot of nice people… not very nicely, including you. I'd like to make it up to you, if you'll permit me."

"I think that can be arranged," he answered with a sly smile. "How about dinner tonight?"

"Not tonight. I'm already committed. Let's go out on Saturday night, providing we're all still here."

"I'm sorry?"

"Oh, just a figure of speech. After all, the world might end Saturday morning." The words were presented as a joke, but the expression on her face disturbed him. He chose to ignore it, at least for now.

"OK, assuming the world does not end and barring nuclear war, tornado, earthquake or an elephant stampede in Central Park, I'll pick you up at your apartment at seven. Deal?"

"Deal," she responded.

"You're sure you're all right?"

"Yes, I'm sure. Go back to work. If they fire you too, who's going to pay for dinner?" She chased him out of her office with a gesture, and he left with mixed feelings. He was concerned about her mental state, but they could discuss it over dinner on Saturday, if the world didn't end first. Arthur Blake wondered why such a strange thought rested in his brain and refused to depart.

The entire trio of Righteous Men was upset about Suzanne's change in professional standing. They arrived, together, a few moments before two o'clock. Joshua was furious and threatened to quit his new job in protest before Suzanne convinced him that the gesture was futile. Burt expressed his regret at not seeing her anymore in the office but recognized the new calm in her personality. Monty suggested she now could leave New York and move somewhere civilized. Each hour that passed provided him with less understanding as to why anyone would ever choose to live on this particular island.

"The important thing," Suzanne said, "is to focus on the balance of the search. I have a map of New York and I've made some notes."

She spread the map on her clean desk, pointing out the places she had marked. Like the late night wanderers who crossed the city while she lay in the coma, Suzanne had also focused on institutions where people are at least supposed to be helping other people. As a lawyer, her direction was a little different and offices of the NAACP Legal Defense Fund, The Legal Aid Society and the American Civil Liberties Union were listed along with other advocate groups for everything from abused children to neglected pets. Monty was skeptical.

"Suzanne," he said, trying not to sound too negative, "this is basically what we've already done, and without success. But take a look at us. I'm a truck driver. Burt's a security guard and Joshua's a messenger, a factory worker before you met him. If we all qualify, why are we looking among the city's do-gooders? Why don't we go to a truck terminal or the mail room?"

"You're right Monty," she answered, "but I don't know what else to do. We found Margo in a hospital, so I thought maybe some of the other places where people are helping people."

"My head says that this is as good a plan as any," Monty continued, "but my heart says we should just go out on the streets and start talking to people."

"I feel this way also," Joshua added.

"Include my vote," Burt said.

"OK, feels right to me too," Suzanne concluded. "Have you guys had lunch?" They all shook their heads. "Then let's start our search with the hot dog man on the corner outside. Maybe we'll get lucky and finish our day's work early."

They all rose to leave when their progress was halted by the entrance of Margaret, her face pale and her hands on the edge of shaking. She was carrying a business card.

"Excuse me, Ms. Rosewell... uh, Suzanne," she stammered. "There is someone here to see you, a potential client, she says."

"I guess she hasn't heard the news, whoever she is," Suzanne laughed in return.

"I told her," Margaret continued, "and she claimed to know, but said that it was in your interest to see her anyway. And she gave me her card. The paper, the type, reminded me of the business card that Mr. Garner carried. I thought I'd better check with you before I sent her away."

"Let me see." Suzanne held out her hand and Margaret passed the small piece of paper.

ELIZABETH LUCKHOLT

Suzanne realized that now her hands were shaking but she took courage from her companions and passed the card around. Each of them read silently and made no comment.

"Tell Ms. Luckholt," Suzanne said, gathering her fortitude, "that I'm meeting with friends but she is welcome to join us."

"That's the strangest part," Margaret answered. "She knew you were with people, described them as a cowboy, a black and an Asian, and said she would only meet with you if they were not present."

"Then to hell with her," Suzanne remarked.

"That may be a fitting response, but be careful," Burt warned. "If she is truly our enemy, then wouldn't we be better off knowing what she has in mind? We can wait outside." Suzanne hesitated for a long moment and then nodded in agreement.

"Show these gentlemen to a conference room. See that they get coffee or something and then, only after my friends are good and comfortable, not before, show in Ms. Luckholt." Margaret gave a smile of understanding and led the trio from Suzanne's office. Almost ten full minutes passed before the blond woman, dressed in black, was permitted to appear in Suzanne's doorway.

"Good afternoon, Ms. Rosewell. It has been a long time, has it not?"

"Yes," Suzanne responded, "a long time and lots of miles but I would not have minded if both time and distance had been allowed to grow larger. Please get down to business. I have things to do." Luckholt sat in a visitor's chair while Suzanne wondered why the temperature in her office seemed to be rising.

"Very well, I have no problem with being direct," Luckholt said quickly. "I know your situation. You are without employment and though you have some money, that won't last long with your high-priced apartment and your car payments. But despite your difficulties, you are continuing to persist in the unprofitable venture forced upon you by Elias Garner."

"I was hardly forced."

"Whatever, that's not important," Luckholt continued. "I am prepared to engage you on a retainer to handle some of the legal work for my company. You would share that responsibility with the firm of

Markam, Wilber, Kent & Todd who we've also just hired." This was Luckholt's way of telling Suzanne the real reason behind her dismissal.

"Please continue," Suzanne said coldly.

"I have here a cashier's check for one hundred thousand dollars made out to you personally. You will represent us in matters to be determined later and only those with which you are personally comfortable. But, as a precondition, you must agree to give up Garner's assignment."

"Ms. Luckholt," Suzanne said in measured, calm tones, "you made your first mistake in Minnesota. You offered me money to give up the search right at the moment I had already decided to do so. Your offer actually made me reconsider. I simply don't like you and if my stopping is that important to you, I guess I'm going to continue. I don't feel like selling my soul to the devil."

"Oh, stop being so dramatic," Luckholt countered. "You and I are both businesswomen. We can make a good profit together, but I'd never be able to convince my people to use your services while you're still involved in that silly search. I hope you'll reconsider."

"I won't."

"Well, in case you do," Luckholt was rising to leave, "there is a phone number on the back of my card. This offer remains valid until dawn on Saturday morning. Call that number anytime, day or night, before then and we have a deal. Once dawn arrives on Saturday, all bets are off. Goodbye Ms. Rosewell."

Suzanne said nothing as the blond woman in black departed. She turned over the business card and there was, in fact, a telephone number hand-written on the back. Suzanne could have sworn that the back of the card was blank when Margaret handed it to her, but she wasn't absolutely certain.

"No matter," she said out loud to herself and dropped the business card into a wastebasket already filled with the unneeded papers she'd removed from her files. Suzanne paused for a moment and reached down to retrieve the card. She tore the paper in half, twice, and returned the remains to the trash.

The heat in Suzanne's office seemed to recede. At the same moment as Suzanne tore up the card, Elizabeth Luckholt was alone in the elevator, heading for the street. In an instant, the climate in the elevator increased by twenty degrees. Had someone else been in the car they probably would have thought the woman in black was about to have a heart attack as her expression appropriately matched her increase in temperature. But Luckholt was alone and able to use the rest of the ride down, and a little more, to regain her composure.

"She tried to buy me off with a lot of money," Suzanne explained to the trio when she found them in a conference room, "but I turned her down. To my own surprise, I wasn't the slightest bit tempted."

"Good for you," said Monty. "What we're trying to do must be of great concern to her if she still expects to turn you around. And her involvement may also mean that we still have a shot at success."

The search did not end at the hot dog stand. Nor did it conclude with the next ten people, or the next hundred, touched by the explorers.

They wandered, seemingly without aim, from place to place. Nowhere did they sense even a tiny projection of the feelings they felt for each other. Had they not had the experience with Margo at the hospital where they were all sure they sensed her aura, they certainly would have come to doubt their ability to detect the special vibrations of a Righteous Person.

The quartet examined a trucking company and the Fulton Fish Market, numerous hospitals and several churches. They eventually returned to the idea of public service law offices from Suzanne's original list. Not a hint of success.

The evening meal was also taken from a street vendor but without the joy and optimism of lunch. They trudged on, past the setting sun and long into a black New York night, slowly navigating the heavy, humid streets. Finally, a sudden summer thunderstorm, catching them in the open and unprotected, put an end to Wednesday's wanderings. Feeling a little less than hopeful, but not ready to surrender, they went home to rest, agreeing to meet at Suzanne's apartment for breakfast.

Suzanne Rosewell was hardly ready for sleep. Once free of her soaked clothing and the recipient of a cleansing shower, she tried to settle in front of the television to watch the news expecting the distraction would clear her mind. The escape attempt failed.

Every piece on CNN reminded her of the search. The positive news of medical breakthroughs, peace talks, prize winners, and a county fair in rural North Dakota became the subjects of her own responsibility for personal preservation. These things must continue. Life must continue. The reports of crime, war, disease, starvation and poverty became representative of the challenges faced by the human race. To meet those challenges, that's right. Life must continue.

Her thoughts were getting so soppy that she decided *she* deserved inclusion among the do-gooders and bleeding hearts she had criticized without compassion all her adult life. That was too much even for a changed Suzanne Rosewell, so she shut off the television, poured a large glass of red wine and walked to the window.

"There," she thought to herself, "was where I saw, or thought I saw, the image of Elias Garner. That was eons ago, or just a few weeks." So much had happened.

Although the tension of the so-far failed crusade still invaded both her brain and the muscles of her body, Suzanne knew, that beyond the pressures of this obligation she was going to find her life very different and possibly a lot better. That is, if there was anything to experience, besides oblivion, after dawn on Saturday.

She gulped back the rest of the wine, using the liquid as an anesthetic to the thoughts that had come forward. That was when she saw the figures, two of them, walking in opposite directions on the street below, one, the male, with his back to the park, the other, the female, moving away from Madison Avenue. From this distance she should never have been able to identify them, but she knew who they were and stood frozen as Elias Garner and Elizabeth Luckholt walked toward each other on the damp, empty, half-lit sidewalk. A voice invaded her brain.

"Choose," the female voice said clearly from inside her head, "there is still time to choose."

"No," Suzanne screamed out loud, throwing the palms of her hands against her head to stifle the sound. "I won't listen!"

The wine glass fell to the floor and bounced harmlessly off the thick carpet. Suzanne looked back out on the street. The figures were gone. So was the voice in her head.

CHAPTER TWENTY-EIGHT

If the searchers had kept a chronicle with the thought of recording the final Thursday and Friday of the planet Earth, the book would have reflected an uninteresting and unproductive set of wanderings. Between the lines describing the repetitive meetings with dozens, and dozens, and dozens of New Yorkers would be the heart of the document, a sad record of sinking hope and rising fear among the four who traveled the city.

"Maybe between Burt, Joshua and Margo," Monty suggested, early Friday afternoon, "we've used up the entire Righteous Person population of New York."

The concept seemed ludicrous but they were desperate, so they boarded the PATH train to New Jersey and pursued coffee in a diner, visited museums, watched a concert in a park and went anywhere else they thought they might find a gathering.

New Jersey was proving less than productive, so they returned on the ferry to Manhattan and took another boat to Liberty Island to stand in the shadow of the great statue and hope patriotism might draw some Righteous Person from the tourist population to the famous shrine. While they watched thousands walk by, nothing but the expected noises and smells emanated from the crowd. Without bothering to climb Miss Liberty, they returned to the city just before dusk.

"I didn't think we were going to fail," Monty said, more than sad. "After all we'd been through, after all the victories, to come so close and not succeed."

"I know," Burt added, "and I expect that you guys might want to search until dawn. But I am going to have to stop. I'm trying real hard to believe that the world will not end just before dawn, but in case that's what happens, I've got to be with my family."

"I have friends I must say goodbye to," Joshua added, almost afraid to speak the words.

"And you Monty?" Suzanne asked turning to the truck driver. "Tell me what's on your mind. If this will help, I think I'm going to visit my mother. The search is over."

"Thank you Suzanne," Monty replied, without attempting to hide his tears. "I could never make it home by dawn, but I can get into open country. I'd rather not be here in this city when everything ends. I've been thinking about going for hours but I wasn't going to leave you alone."

"Go, my friend," she said, "get out on the open highway where we met and where you belong. The rest of you go, too. I think I believe that whether we are right or wrong about what is going to happen at the end of this night, we *will* meet again."

Standing in Battery Park, the setting sun casting long shadows over the water, the quartet of wanderers embraced and cried. Those walking by assumed that the four were tourists, maybe recent immigrants, moved by the majesty of the lady with the torch in New York Harbor. Some smiled, some ignored them, all passed with thoughts centered on their own plans for the weekend.

Suzanne remained and watched until the three men had moved out of her sight. She waited a little longer, until the orange ball disappeared behind the hills of New Jersey and then, guided by the remaining twilight, she went to find a subway.

The sound of chanting that drifted through the doorway to her left caught her attention. Suzanne slowed her forward motion, finally stopped and turned toward the ancient music. Above the double wooden doors, both of them in bad need of paint, she saw the faded Star of David etched in the glass. There was no need to search for a sign, Suzanne knew that she'd paused before a synagogue and without considering further, walked through the doors.

An ancient man greeted her with a slight bow of his head and a half-smile. She nodded in return and started toward the sanctuary, the source of the chanting she'd heard on the street. The old man blocked her way.

"I'm sorry," he said, the sound of Eastern Europe still in his voice, "you must go upstairs. This is an Orthodox shul."

"I don't understand."

"You are Jewish?" he asked.

"Yes, but I have very little education," she answered without being defensive. He nodded knowingly.

"In Orthodox custom," he responded in a whisper, "men and women may not pray together so neither are distracted while communing with God." Suzanne wanted to laugh until she realized that the man wasn't teasing her.

"You're serious?" she said.

"Oh, yes, young lady," he answered, "quite serious. Would you like to go upstairs to the women's gallery?"

"No thank you," she snapped. "If I can't be part of the main congregation, then I won't go in at all." Suzanne turned and stormed out onto the street before the old man started to argue her protest. But on the sidewalk, she stopped again and listened to the chanting.

"This is silly," she said to herself. "If the world is ending tomorrow, I guess I don't have to worry much about sex discrimination." Suzanne Rosewell swallowed her pride and went back through the doorway. "May I change my mind?" she asked of the guardian.

"Of course," he said, handing a prayer book and directing her to a narrow staircase half-hidden by a curtain. Suzanne climbed the stairs and arrived in a small balcony overlooking the main floor. She was alone, the only woman in the synagogue.

Below her stood nearly twenty men, all reading from a copy of the same book she held. They seemed to be chanting each at their own pace, unconcerned about unity. She confirmed her observation by noting that no two of them turned the pages of the prayer book at the same exact moment. Yet, every so often, they all seemed to come together, the faster ones stopping, waiting for the others to catch up so that certain songs could be sung in unison. Then they continued, each again operating his own individual service and seeming to ignore the man in front, whom she assumed was the rabbi. After only fifteen minutes, they came together for one last prayer and the service was finished. The men then turned, one to the other, and started to shake hands, sharing greetings for a good Sabbath.

Suddenly Suzanne felt a great desire to disappear. She did not wish to participate in conversation with these men who now seemed to constitute a group of very holy people. She tore down the stairs and ended up right in the middle of the departing crowd.

They hardly paid any attention to her. Those whose eyes she accidentally caught offered a smile and words like "Gut Shabbos," or "Shabbat Shalom." She acknowledged with a smile of her own and listened to their conversations as she elbowed her way through to the street.

They spoke of business and baseball, lawns and mortgages, children and grandchildren. Somehow she had expected they would be speaking of more spiritual matters. By the time she reached the street, Suzanne realized that these people were no more, or less, holy than everyone else, and that the issues they spoke of, were, to them, the matters most important to their spirits at that particular moment in time. She envied their ignorance and knew that many expected to arise in the morning and go to synagogue as they had most every Saturday for years. She desperately wished that she too could feel the same sense of tomorrow. She needed to go home.

Her arrival in her apartment was greeted by the blinking light on the message machine.

"Darling," said her mother's voice from the tape, "I know from what you and your friends were saying in the hospital that you think this is the last night before some terrible tragedy. But you know that's not true. I've gone to play bridge, like I do every Friday and you should go out to a night club or something. I'll talk to you tomorrow." Her mother hadn't even told her where she was playing cards.

Suzanne judged the maternal advice worthy, left her apartment and traveled back downtown to hear some folk music. For weeks she'd heard people in the office rave about the "sixties" atmosphere of a new place in Greenwich Village, and now, before it was too late, she wanted to experience it.

The West Broadway café was almost empty and the waiter explained that the usual crowd came rather late. Live music would not begin until around ten. So with an hour to kill, Suzanne went walking and quickly found herself following the same route she'd traveled with her friends the night before. The wave of loneliness sent her back to the café where she chose to pass time drinking espresso and staring at the wall. The waiter respected her solitude.

The first performer finally came out at ten-thirty, a young woman with a guitar who looked as though she'd just escaped from the Woodstock movie. But she had a strong alto voice, good musical technique and a large, varied repertoire of Sixties protest songs by the likes of Bob Dylan, Phil Ochs and Tom Paxton. The music captured Suzanne and by the time the set was over, the café had become, without her noticing, completely full.

"May I join you?" the voice said, bringing her back to earth. Rising above her was the young woman who had just been on the stage.

"Please," Suzanne responded, "I enjoyed your performance very much."

"I couldn't help but notice how intent you were," the folk singer said as she sat down. "That's why I wanted to meet you. So many people come here only to be seen and see others that sometimes I feel like part of the background. I just wanted to thank you for paying attention."

"My pleasure. You really are very good."

"Thank you again and... Oh, excuse me," she said, standing suddenly. "My boyfriend just arrived. Missed my set. I have to go and scold him." She spoke with mischief in her eye. Suzanne knew the young woman could not be more than twenty and she watched with slight envy as the singer pushed her way through the crowd and embraced a longhaired, thin man who was still standing by the front door.

"Why couldn't she be the one?" Suzanne thought as she watched them, "or him? They seem like nice enough people. Why does this all have to end in a few hours?" Moisture in her eyes forced her to change her focus and she scanned the room.

At a table in the corner, in the darkest part of the café, Suzanne's somewhat blurry gaze rested on a couple, a black man and a blond woman. The sight brought her suddenly to her feet and she plunged through the crowd intent on confronting both Elias Garner and Elizabeth Luckholt and demand a reprieve. But when she arrived at the table, she found it occupied by two strangers.

"I'm sorry," she said as the couple looked up, a bit threatened by her charge toward them, "I thought you were someone I knew. Forgive me." She returned to her table to find still another couple standing alongside.

"Are you leaving?" the female asked. "We were waiting for a table and thought you might be going."

"I am," said Suzanne, as she tossed down more than enough money to cover her bill. Moments later she was walking the sidewalks again.

Suzanne Rosewell concluded that on the last night of the planet Earth she had no reason to be anxious about crime, exhaustion, worn-out shoes or other mundane concerns. She decided to walk all the way home from the Village. So what if it took all night? Where was she going in the morning?

Two hours before the end of the last night of the last day of the planet Earth, Suzanne Rosewell, former super-attorney, found a bench at the edge of Central Park, not far from the spot designated as Strawberry Fields in honor of Beatle John Lennon, murdered just across the street from where she sat. She remembered the childhood joy she took from the music of the group known as the "Fab Four," and determined that this was the appropriate place to wait.

Maybe they avoided her because she wore a look of calm confidence on her face. Maybe the atmospheric pressure was wrong for mugging, or maybe some guardian angel watched over Suzanne. For whatever reason, the night people left her alone and she was free to stare at the black, cloud-covered sky without threat or even interruption.

She was concentrating on the sky when the thunder erupted, just as the eastern horizon started to grow light. For the first time all evening, Suzanne became frightened. After only a few flashes of heat lighting, the noise stopped and the clouds broke away, fleeing the power of a rising sun.

Early morning weekend workers' cars started to fill Central Park West. Joggers appeared. Then mothers with baby carriages and some other fitness types walking briskly. The sky was blue, the morning bright and crisp. The air was even strangely clean, like October not July, but still warm enough for an unemployed lawyer to sit on a bench and watch the urban parade.

Suzanne was terribly confused. Then, slowly, she became angry as the thought invaded her consciousness that the entire thing, her weeks-long obsession, the sacrifice of her career, had been for nothing more than one big fraud. Deep in her mind she battled the nagging doubt, wanting desperately not to fall back to her old cynicism, to find another answer for this beautiful, uneventful morning. Still, the skepticism became strong. A little less than sixty seconds before her mind was about to finally reject the validity of the quest itself, Elias Garner appeared on the asphalt path.

He was dressed in casual clothes, designer jeans, a golf shirt with a little alligator over the pocket, new running shoes and he walked as though he had no idea that Suzanne Rosewell was watching him. When he reached her bench, he sat down beside her.

"The world didn't end," she said simply.

"No it didn't," he answered just as simply.

"Why not?"

"Why should it?"

"Because there are only thirty-five Righteous Ones listed on the inventory," she said.

"Really?" he said, "That's strange. I have a list in my pocket with thirty-six names. I've had this list for several days. Would you like to read?"

She put her hand out and he reached into the pocket under the alligator and extracted a folded sheet of white paper. Suzanne opened the paper and scanned the names, passing rapidly over the first thirty-one. She'd seen them before and didn't know who they were anyway. At the bottom she found Monty, Joshua, Burt, Margo and, in the last line, Suzanne Rosewell.

"Me..." she almost shouted, "all along, I was one?"

"No," Garner replied, "not all along. Sometime earlier this week, the Chairman added your name. Remember, when you awoke from the coma, you were the one who recognized that Margo was one of the Righteous Ones. You could recognize others because you were on the list. I thought you would figure it out yourself, but I was wrong."

"Then why didn't you call, like you did with Monty, and tell me my task was completed? Why did you let us all suffer and worry?"

"The list could have changed. Right up until dawn. You might have accepted Luckholt's offer and then the Chairman would have removed your name. Besides, I was under direct orders not to interfere. Congratulations, Suzanne."

"I don't feel any different. I don't feel like I know anything new."

"Neither do your friends. In fact, right now they're all feeling a bit stupid… and embarrassed. Now that the world hasn't ended, they think that they might have been used, for some unknown evil purpose… by some clever con man. Soon, not wishing to continue to feel foolish, they'll try to forget they were ever designated as 'Righteous Ones.' And that's good."

"Why?"

"Because… just to know the Divine Will is an awesome responsibility. Imagine the weight they'd have to carry if they truly know that inside them is the knowledge of God's desires for the human race."

"You mean people have never known?"

"Some have, but it's better if they don't. If humanity ever decides there is a need to consult the Righteous Ones, they'll find them. After all, I have a list." With an almost laugh, he snatched the paper from Suzanne's hand. "I'm afraid I can't let you keep this." Garner started to stand.

"Wait," Suzanne said, "I know the truth. What if I call the others and tell them?"

"You won't do that, Suzanne," Elias Garner said while he finished rising from the bench. "You are a logical person with a legally trained mind. In time, you too will doubt the reality of the entire story. A small doubt lives in your brain already. Next week, next month, maybe next year, you'll decide that you're not one of the chosen ones after all. That there probably are no chosen ones. Maybe there's no one to even do the choosing, just some wacky CEO of an unnamed corporation who keeps silly lists in his spare time. Another successful executive with a God complex. Goodbye Suzanne, and thank you for your help."

"Do you have to leave? I... I don't know what I'm doing next, with my life, or even with the rest of the day."

"Suzanne Rosewell," he said as he started back down the path, "I have complete faith that you, of all people, will figure out what to do with the rest of the day, and with the rest of your life." Elias Garner turned behind a bush and when Suzanne managed to finally get up and chase him, he was nowhere in sight.

"I wonder what I'll do with the rest of today," she thought to herself. "I need some sleep. Can't have bags under my eyes when Arthur comes to pick me up for dinner. But first maybe I can find a synagogue, one that lets men and women sit together, and go there, just for a little while."

ABOUT THE AUTHOR

After appearing on the pilot episode of Prime Time Live, Diane Sawyer called Marty Gallanter's writing "compelling." And we at Dead End Street certainly agree. His articles have graced the pages of the *New York Times*, the *Chicago Tribune*, the *Baltimore Sun*, *Parade* and *TV Guide*. He's appeared on Saturday Night with Connie Chung, and he's written for more than one hundred Jewish-American publications. Gallanter regularly appears on radio and television, and lectures at universities throughout the country.

Gallanter has been a publicist, writer and fundraiser for more than twenty years, including stints as Director of Development at the Washington Pavilion of the Arts and Science and the Director of Fundraising for the Legal Aid Society of New York and the United Jewish Appeal.

If you liked this book, we recommend...

Fifty-year-old Bill Harness is on a strange but seemingly benign journey, rambling across the country in an old Pontiac and anonymously leaving large checks with promising young opera singers. His fuel, however, is sorrow, and it isn't until he arrives on a small island outside of Seattle and befriends Gabriella Compton, a phenomenally talented soprano, that he is able to address the three great tragedies of his vocally gifted family.

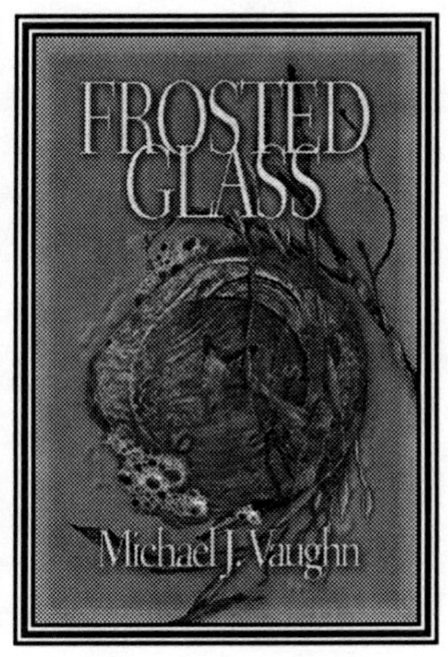

A painful break-up/breakdown chases 39-year-old Sandy Lowitry from her Silicon Valley home to the Oregon coast in search of answers. Instead, she finds Frosted Glass Man, a fellow tech refugee who left behind a computer-programming job to spend his days harvesting sea glass along Knickerbocker Beach. The strange man's enchanting stories wrap her in a blanket of comfort and wonder, but the whispers of ambition persist and quietly chastise her for settling.

Available everywhere books are sold.

ANOTHER FINE OFFERING FROM

DEAD END STREET®

Printed in the United States
89793LV00003B/1-48/A

9 781929 429516